COOKIE JOHNSON

Tank Gunner

Tank Gunner
HPB
Garland
11/21/20

Tank Gunner is the pen name for a retired combat cavalry trooper, decorated with a Silver Star, three Bronze Stars, one for Valor, and a Purple Heart. He served his nation with pride and honor for more than a quarter century as an enlisted soldier and officer. *Cookie Johnson* is his third book following *Prompts a collection of stories* and *Prompts Too another collection of stories*. He and his wife live in Texas with Toby.

Third Printing • December 2018
ISBN: 978-1-54391-179-4

OTHER WORKS

PROMPTS
a collection of stories
(fiction)

PROMPTS TOO
another collection of stories
(fiction)

WAR STORIES OF AN ARMED SAVAGE
(nonfiction)

ANY NAME BUT SMITH!
(play)

DIRECT HIT
(newspaper column)

For Sylviane, Rob, Rich,

and

for Terry, Chloe, Zak, and Toby

ACKNOWLEDGMENT

This is my special salute to Capn Lee Sneath, who was a corporate communications executive, public affairs spokesperson, and managing editor, and is an instructor, word coach, editor, and patient friend.

and

Another grateful nod to Wayne Peterson, author of *Canopy of Hope* and *Canopy of Mystery*, a talented storyteller, and friend who shared his passion of the craft and provided ears, eyes, and reactions during the development of *Cookie Johnson*.

COOKIE'S COVER

Idea	Capn Lee Sneath
Illustration	Victor Hernandez
Format and Color	Wayne Peterson
Text	Tank Gunner

This book is a work of fiction. Some scenes are based on places where the author served and events in which he participated in the United States, France, Germany, or Vietnam. Other than reference to historical persons, names and characters come from the author's imagination.

PLAYERS

"J J/Cookie" – Private James Jerome Johnson
Rifleman, 3rd Platoon Infantry Squad

"Katie" – First Lieutenant Kathleen Tatum Patton
Shift Nurse, Sixty-Second Field Hospital

"Holt" – Staff Sergeant Henry Holt
Army Recruiter, Ferdinand Avenue Office

Nguyen Mai Li
Laundry Lady, Fire Support Base Linebacker

Nguyen Kim
Daughter of Mai Li

"Jinks" – Private Holly Jenkins
Rifleman, 3rd Platoon Infantry Squad

"Bo" – Private Bonino Vitali
Rifleman, 3rd Platoon Infantry Squad

"Nelly" – Private Francesco Cicchinello
Rifleman, 3rd Platoon Infantry Squad

"Deak" – Staff Sergeant Burl Deakins
Infantry Squad Leader

"Boss" – Sergeant First Class Boswell Tweed
Platoon Sergeant, 3rd Platoon, Delta Troop

"Lucky" – PFC Leroy Jerrigan
Machine Gunner, Bravo Team, Infantry Squad

"Red" – Sergeant Raleigh Hawk
Alpha Team Leader, 3rd Platoon Infantry Squad

"Dimples" – Staff Sergeant Darby Dutchman
Squad Leader, 3rd Platoon Infantry Squad

PLAYERS

"Doc" – Sergeant Merlin Swanson
Senior Medic, Delta Troop

"Jerry" – Captain Gerald Thompson
Commanding Officer, Delta Troop

"Top" – First Sergeant Marion Morris
First Sergeant, Delta Troop

"Alex" – First Lieutenant Alex Versailles
Platoon Leader, 3rd Platoon, Delta Troop

"Lonzo" – Staff Sergeant Alonzo Medina
Mortar Squad Leader, 3rd Platoon, Delta Troop

"Mickey" – PFC Michael Fowler
Machine Gunner, Alpha Team, Infantry Squad

"Jordy" – Sergeant Jordon Mosley
Bravo Team Leader, 3rd Platoon Infantry Squad

"Billy" – PFC William A. Butler
Grenadier, 3rd Platoon Infantry Squad

"Sally" – Lieutenant Sallsetta Malmarie Norman
Ward Nurse, Sixty-Second Field Hospital

"Tex" – PFC Glenn Pollard
Rifleman, Bravo Fire Team, Infantry Squad

"Cotton" – PFC Oliver Obadiah Lindseed
Supply Clerk, Delta Troop

"Vannoy" – Specialist Fourth Class Vance Vannoy
Troop Clerk, Delta Troop

Colonel Dermott Dickerson
Commanding Officer, Sixty-Second Field Hospital

PLAYERS

Colonel Eli Carson
Brigade Commander

Lieutenant Colonel Tracy Tolon
Infantry Battalion Commander

Colonel Phan Van Minh
Chief, Phuoc Long Province, Republic of Vietnam

Sandra
Personnel Clerk, Long Bien Replacement Center

Sergeant Kane
Supervisor, Personnel Section, Long Bien

Kip Johnson
Younger brother to J J

Jodie Johnson
Younger sister to J J

Imogene Sandlin
Manager on Duty, Sugar Babe's Cafe and Grill

"Vern" – Vernon
Server, Sugar Babe's Cafe and Grill

Elmer
Day Shift Fry Cook, Sugar Babe's Cafe and Grill

"Benny" – Captain Benjamin Ballesteros
Assistant S-4, Article 32 Investigating Officer

"Danny" – Captain Daniel DeSoto
Brigade Adjutant

"You Number One"
Septuagenarian, Pedicab Driver

ENLISTMENT

James Jerome was hard to say – especially to say three times, fast, after a few beers. That is why he preferred J J. He also reckoned J J would be easier to remember, in case anybody wanted to.

On Thursday, the third day in the rotating day shift, still wearing his white tee shirt, white trousers, and white apron, James Jerome walked away from his civilian job. He marched the four long blocks up Ferdinand Avenue to the Army recruiting office and volunteered for military service.

Later, on reflection, James Jerome wondered if it would have been better to keep his job cooking eggs and frying bacon at Mr. Albert Dickerson's Sugar Babe's Cafe and Grill. J J liked preparing meals. He took pride in serving a dish in a unique way, instead of just plopping down eggs, bacon, hash browns, and grits on a plate. He also took pleasure in keeping his hands clean and his kitchen and utensils sparkling.

Unlike Freeman, who worked evenings, and fat Oradondo on the graveyard shift, J J was meticulous about cleanliness. When off duty, he made special trips to the cafe to inspect, fuss at, and chastise

Freeman and Oradondo. He didn't like either of them.

Often, he nagged Lillie Mae, the manager, about their carelessness, sloppiness, and filth. This particular day was the same. He was in Lillie Mae's face about it.

"They don't even clean under their fingernails. They gonna poison somebody and you and Mr. Dickerson is gonna have a lawsuit, Lillie Mae."

"They ain't gonna be no goddamn lawsuit, J J. And you mind your own P's and Q's on your own shift. Freeman and Oradondo have grumbled about you. They're fed up. So you leave them alone and keep your nose outta their business. I'm the manager here. I got my finger on the goings-on. You hear?"

"You got your finger stuck up your fat ass, Lillie Mae. You don't manage shit. All you do is sit around, smoke your stinking French cigarettes, and take in the money. We do all the work round here. If you don't make things right, the code boys will shut the place down. And we'll all be fired."

"You go to hell, J J. I've a mind to fire you right now."

And that's when he walked out the door, with two servings of eggs, bacon, and hash browns on the grill.

"You're the fry cook at Sugar Babe's," the recruiter said. "Down the street. I recognize you."

"Was a cook. Yeah, I was there damn near a year. In all that time, I never got a pay raise. I'm tired of the boss. She don't do things right and lets staff slide on their duty. Customers whine all the time, even when I make their plate special. I quit. I just walked off the job to come down here to your recruiting office to join the Army."

"That sounds to me like you're a man who takes responsibility. You got leadership potential. My Army needs a man like you."

"Yeah, I'm interested."

The recruiter was short and chubby. The color of what little hair he had on the sides of his head, matched the black-framed glasses perched on his nose. Staff Sergeant stripes adorned both shirtsleeves. White capital letters engraved into the shiny, black, plastic, rectangular-shaped nameplate, pinned and aligned with the top seam of the right pocket, spelled HOLT. A single-line ribbon frame over his left shirt pocket held the green and white Army Commendation Ribbon, the red-and-white Good Conduct Ribbon, and the red-and-yellow National Defense Service Ribbon. Pinned below the ribbons, centered on the left pocket of his starched khaki shirt, was a recruiter's badge. His bright, gleaming, collar brass sported a U.S. on the right and the Administration emblem on the left.

"Well, Son, you've come to the right place. What do you want to do in my Army?"

"What'cha got?"

"I got a lot of good job openings in all of our fighting units. You'd have a lot of fun and adventure in armor, artillery, cavalry, or infantry. Any one of these branches would be exciting. There are vacancies all over the world for a combat arm soldier."

"What's a combat arm soldier? What do they do?"

"That's an Army expression for the combat branch of service. Combat arms is armor, artillery, cavalry, and infantry. They're the fighting units and soldiers."

The Sergeant shook a Pall Mall cigarette from the red pack. When his walk-in prospect declined and waved off the offered butt, the soldier pulled it, stuck it in his mouth, lit it with a Zippo lighter, and leaned back in his chair. He exhaled blue-gray smoke. "I might even can put chu in Combat Engineers. Ah, tell me again what's chur name?" The recruiter practiced slang to relate to young potentials when they came in.

"James Jerome Johnson. J J."

"Okay, J J. I can put you down as a volunteer for an overseas assignment at the same time you sign the paper. After eight weeks of basic training and eight weeks of infantry training, you'll ship over to where Uncle Sam needs you the most."

"Where's that?"

"To *Vee-it-nam*, J J. You have heard about *Vee-it-nam*?"

"Of course. I watch the news on TV and read the paper ever morning at the cafe."

"Then you know we got boys over there fighting the *Vee-it-Congs*."

"I don't know about any fighting. I hadn't thought about being in the infantry."

"How about jumping outta airplanes."

"You mean like sky-divers?"

"Sort of. How tall are you?"

"I dunno. Six feet?"

"Yeah, that looks about right. How much you weigh?"

"Hunnert 'n forty or so."

"You got any medical problems? Diabetes, weak heart, high blood pressure, the clap, mental issues, or anything like that?"

"Not that I know of."

"Okay, then airborne infantry would be the way to go for you, J J. You're just the right size and weight to be an airborne infantryman."

"Don't you have nothing else?"

"As an airborne infantryman I can fix it so you get paid extra money every month. On top of your base pay of $78 a month, you get another $55 each month for doing parachute jumps. That's $133 a month. Big money. And, it'd be a lot of fun to be a paratrooper. All the horny girls would be all over you. When they see those silver jump wings pinned on your chest they know you got what they want."

"I've never been in a airplane, let alone to jump outta one."

The recruiter paused. Using sex, big money, and being a paratrooper as a sales tactic didn't persuade his customer. He needed to close this deal to meet his monthly quota. Last quarter, the Captain increased the number of enlistments recruiters had to make to receive their semi-annual bonus. Thirty dollars of good money was at stake.

"Okay, J J. We'll come back to jump school. You got a college degree?"

"No."

"If you had a college degree I could make you an officer."

"You mean like a general?"

"Yeah. But you got no college degree, you see. How about junior college? Do you have two years of good credits, with at least a C average? You have an Associate Degree? If you got an Associate Degree I could sign you up for O-C-S."

"What's OCS?"

"Officer Candidate School. They make Second Lieutenants."

"No. No, Associate Degree neither."

"Damn, J J. Did you finish high school?"

"No. I had to quit. Halfway through my senior year. I had to help my mama support Kip, my younger brother, and little sister, Jodie. My mama's a temporary aide. She's on contract. Works the night shift out there at the VA hospital. She cleans toilets, mops floors, and empties bedpans. She ain't a government employee and don't belong to the VA union, so she don't make enough money to pay bus fare, buy groceries to feed her family, and pay rent. That's when I went out and got the job at Sugar Babe's."

"What about your old man?"

"I ain't seen or heard from that no-good deadbeat in four years. He got up from the TV one night to go down to the 7-11 to buy cigarettes and beer. He never came back. It was good riddance, too. He is a sorry-ass son-of-a-bitch. Beat on my mama and me ever day. The day he pulled his belt from his droopy-ass pants to hit my little sister, I told him if he hit her I'd kill him."

"Did he?" The recruiter leaned forward and braced his arms on the desk. He flicked the end of his cigarette and a long ash crashed and crumbled into flakes in a round, amber ashtray.

"Did he what?"

"Hit your sister? With the belt?"

"No."

"Then you didn't kill him."

"No, but I've wanted to for a long time. If he'd a kept on, I would've stuck a knife in his gut and twisted it."

The recruiter paused, evaluating this proclamation, gauging whether danger lurked in front of his desk.

"Did you hit him?"

"No. Why do you ask?"

"Police reports. Assault. Domestic disturbance. Charges. Convictions."

"No. I ain't never been in no trouble."

"Never been in jail?"

"If I ain't never been in no trouble, then I ain't never been in no jail."

"Okay, I understand. Don't get pissed at me, J J. It's part of my job. It's my responsibility to pertect the Army, you see. I got to ask these questions."

"Well, you made it sound like I did something wrong."

"Well, that you didn't do nothing wrong is good, J J. Now, here's the facts. Since you didn't graduate high school or college, you ain't gonna be no general or lieutenant – at least, not right away. So your choices for an Army job are limited."

"Lemonned?"

"Limited. That means there are only a few jobs I can offer you."

"Like what?"

"How old are you, J J?"

"Twenty-one."

"That's the perfect age to be a paratrooper in the Infantry."

"Seems like you're dead set on this jumping and infantry business."

"I know you'd fit right in, J J. You'd be just like John Wayne, Van Johnson, and Audie Murphy – throwin hangernades, handlin a flame-thrower, mowin down the *Vee-it-Congs* with a machine gun, or pokin one of them little grinnin bastards with your bayonet. In *Nam*, you won't have to march. You'll either fly around in a C-130 and jump into the fight, or you'll be ridin high in helicopters. Just like a taxi. Everywhere you need to go, you'll go in style. You know paratroopers can blouse their jump boots."

"I'm a cook. I know how to cook, prepare food. I feed people. Why can't I be a cook in the Army?"

The Sergeant snuffed out his cigarette in the glass ashtray. He rubbed his thumb, forefinger, and middle finger together and raised them to his nose to sniff. He leaned away and looked around James Jerome Johnson, toward the door.

"How much money you got on you, J J?"

"Sixteen dollars."

The recruiter straightened up and nodded. "Okay. I can make you a deal. While you here, in my place of business. Just for today, J J. If you walk away, if you walk outta my office, the deal is off. Understood?"

"What's the deal?"

"Here's what I'll do for you, J J. For ten dollars, I'll

sign you up as a cook."

"Why do I got to pay you to join the Army?"

"Let's say it's for a little persuasion. I'm the one does the forms, fills in the blanks. I can say what jobs people get. For ten dollars, J J, I say you can be a cook."

"I can be a cook?" J J smiled; he was pleased.

The recruiter shrugged and nodded. "But you still have to go through eight weeks of basic training and eight weeks of infantry training at Fort Benning, Georgia before you can be a cook. After all that, once you're in a Army mess hall everybody will be calling you Cookie."

"Okay, let's do the paperwork."

"What about jump school? An extra $55 a month. Good spendin money."

"Okay. Add that in too."

After eight days of processing, paperwork, haircut, and receiving his military clothing and footgear at the reception station, two months of basic, two months of infantry training, and four weeks of jump school in the Peach State, the installation's Adjutant General issued orders directing J J to report to the Commanding Officer, USARV Replacement Center, Vietnam. His assignment in-country was as an 11-Bravo. 11-B was the military occupational specialty for Infantry.

J J came to realize the ten dollars he turned over to Sergeant Holt was a waste of money. The four times he was on the working-side in a mess hall, during his entire period of training, was to pull KP. He was a conscientious expert at washing the huge pots and pans in hot soapy water and became a dependable fixture over the steamy aluminum sinks in the back corner of the kitchen.

Following his training, on the first afternoon during his ten-day furlough at home to arrange affairs and say goodbye to his mother and siblings, he went to the cafe to display his transition from a civilian to a paratrooper.

Private James Jerome Johnson was no longer a cafe fry cook in whites. He was a combat arms soldier with a new persona and uniform.

In bloused, spit-shined Corcoran jump boots and starched khakis with the Infantry Blue Cord, a fourragere, draped under his right shoulder and under the right epaulette, he proudly walked through the cafe door.

Instead of Lillie Mae, Freeman, and Oradondo, three colleagues he knew from Mr. Dickerson's cafe over on Bird Parkway greeted J J.

"They all been fired. About two weeks after you quit. Mr. Dickerson let the hammer down," Imogene said. "I'm the new manager and cashier."

"All of them was sacked on the spot," Elmer said. "I'm the new day shift fry cook. You remember Franklin, he's evenings, and Scotty is graveyard. Vernon, here, is new server."

"Hey, Vern."

"Yeah, how you doin, J J."

"I'm alright, Vern. How's Eloise and nem?"

"They all fine. Little sister got a basketball scholarship way over there at LSU."

"That's great, Vern. So, they was all fired. I told Lillie Mae it would happen."

"Well, Lillie Mae and Oradondo was, J J. Freeman was out sick, and when he learned they'd been fired he decided not to come back, cause he knew damn well he didn't have no job no more," Elmer said.

"The day Mr. Dickerson came down to swing the axe, he brought us along in his van. We just acted like it was a ever day thing to change over mid-stream like that. The six or eight customers in here never looked up, never paid attention," Imogene said.

"Man, you look sharp as a tack," Vernon said. "You are a new man, J J. Short haircut, clean shaved, Army khakis, blue rope on your shoulder. That's infantry, ain't it?"

"Yes. Yes, it is. I'm airborne infantry. I made five parachute jumps out of a C-130 Hercules."

"What's a C-130 Herpulese?"

"It's an airplane, Vern. A big ass, four-engine propeller job."

"You jumped out of a perfectly good airplane?"

"Yeah. And I get paid extra money each month for doin it, too. I'd never been in a airplane before, but I liked it. And I liked jumpin out of it too. It was a lotta fun."

"My, my, look at that shiny brass belt buckle. You musta worked all day shining that up," Imogene said.

"And look at those boots. I can see my reflection in those boots, they so shiny," Vernon said.

Paratrooper James Jerome Johnson grinned.

Imogene laughed. "You sure are sweet looking, soldier boy. I'm thinkin bout gettin me a taste of that sweetness."

Paratrooper James Jerome Johnson's grin widened, his eyes brightened with gleaming pride.

"We ain't got no business over there in *Nom*. It's a piss-ant country. Just a bunch of chop-stick ricers," Elmer charged. "And you gonna go over there and shoot people who never done you no harm, Boy."

"Leave the boy alone, Elmer," Imogene chimed in. "He joined up to defend our country."

"Bull Shiiiiiiit," Elmer countered. "This boy ain't defended *our* country atall, he's going over there to defend somebody else's interest. Probably France."

Vernon spoke up, siding with Elmer. "Vietnam was a colony of France. The Viet-Minh kicked ass at Dien Bien Phu. I read about it. That guy Ho, he made France pack up and go home. France was pissed, too. They had to leave their rubber plantations and mineral mines. It's all about somebody's money, believe you me. It's always about money if you ask me."

The three continued jawing about the state of foreign affairs, ignoring J J.

"He's gonna git hisself kilt cause LBJ ain't got the guts to cut his losses and leave out," Elmer said. "It ain't gonna end good, I tell you. A lotta our boys are gonna die over there for no goddamn good reason, I tell you. Defending our country, my ass, Imogene. That's a bunch of bullshit, I tell you."

Imogene, Vernon, and Elmer, together, looked at J J and paused. They waited for his rebuttal.

Baffled, J J shook his head. He said nothing, not even a goodbye. And as he had done almost a half-year earlier, walked out the door of Sugar Babe's.

J J had listened to it all, there in the cafe. But now he was a soldier. If nothing else, there was a reputation and legacy to maintain and defend, he thought, just because he wore a uniform. But Elmer's assertions and Vernon's argument disturbed him.

What was in Vietnam that caused the President of the United States to declare war on a tiny nation?

Did the French president have LBJ by the balls because Michelin was squeezing ole Charlo's nuts?

And there was Imogene. She was the boss. She was friendly enough, on his side, but her defense for him seemed weak, half-hearted. All of it bothered him as he marched down the street.

J J maneuvered through pedestrians and gawkers for the four blocks to the recruiting office. He was going to seek out the recruiter. He wanted to speak with Staff Sergeant Holt about ten dollars.

"He ain't here no more," the new recruiter said. "I'm the new recruiter. My name's Urban."

"Where's he at?"

"Vietnam. He shipped out seven, eight weeks ago."

"That's where I'm going."

"Well, maybe you'll run into Sergeant Holt over there," Staff Sergeant Urban said. "You a friend of his?"

"Sort of."

"I got a letter a month ago. He was at Long Bien, the replacement center near Saigon. He expected assignment to a Division up north, in the Central part of the country."

"Yeah, okay. Thanks. My name is Johnson. Holt signed me up."

"Johnson. Yeah. I remember. Holt told me about you. He signed you up for airborne infantry. Said you wanted to be a Army cook."

JOURNEY

Twenty-one-year-old Private James Jerome Johnson, United States Army, began his journey on a Trailways coach when the packed passenger liner pulled away from the 4th Street bus station, headed to the overseas replacement center at Fort Lewis, Washington. His odyssey would take him along paths few have travelled to a place in life he never imagined, expected, or predicted.

J J matched the bus driver's nod and smile. After J J helped her slide the bulky duffel bag in the undercarriage bin, she took his ticket and invited him to board first. He moved down the aisle to the middle of the carrier. After stowing his AWOL bag in the overhead, he sat on the left side in a window seat.

An elderly man, his chiseled face full of gray whiskers, approached.

"You saving this seat, Soldier?"

"No, Sir."

The man lifted a small, hard-sided, tan Samsonite suitcase onto the bin and placed his gray fedora on top of it. He sat in the aisle seat.

"My name is Lee Slocomb." He shoved an open

hand with extended fingers across his chest. His smile was inviting, friendly.

"J J." He grasped Lee's hand and shook it three times.

"Where you headed, J J?"

"Fort Lewis, Washington. To the overseas replacement center."

"I know it. Been through there myself, sixteen years ago. I was in Korea, in the Chosin fight."

"Chosen?"

"Yeah. I was an infantry soldier, like you. I was in the 31st Regimental Combat Team, 7th Infantry Division."

"You was in combat?"

"My company fought two Chinese Divisions for five nights and four days, so Marines could withdraw to the sea. Hell of a battle. In daylight, I know I shot two of the gooks myself. I may have killed more of the little bastards in the night fights we had. Goddamn, it was cold in Korea. I damn near froze to death." Lee paused. "Some of our guys did." He looked at J J. "They were like concrete."

Through speakers, the bus driver announced their departure.

"On behalf of American Traveler Trailways, welcome aboard folks. My name is Carol Sparks. For the next six hours, I'll be your chauffeur and do what's necessary to insure you are comfortable and safe. Our route today is about 250 miles up through beautiful Pacific Northwest country, with brief stops in Portland, Saint Helens, Longview, Centralia, Olympia, Tanglewilde, Fort Lewis, Tacoma, and Seattle. For those going farther, you'll change buses in Seattle. Now, lean back, relax, take in the view, and enjoy the ride. Thank you for choosing American Traveler Trailways."

"So, J J, you're going overseas?"

"Yeah, to Vietnam."

"It's a son-of-a-bitch that we are still fightin gooks sixteen years later. Truman shoulda let MacArthur have his head when he had them slant-eyed bastards on the run. Both my sons are in Vietnam. Maybe you'll run into them. Wayne and Gil."

Lee got off the bus at Saint Helens. He told J J he was visiting a friend incarcerated in the state prison there. After a couple of nights, he would return to Salem and his job of mixing paint for Montgomery Ward. No one sat in the seat he vacated.

J J pondered some of the several things they covered in a mostly one-sided conversation. If J J revealed a piece of himself, his life, Lee seemed to have a bigger tale and broader experience, and went on and on about it. It seemed, on reflection, Lee was a talker and not a listener. When J J told about his trip to the zoo and watching the alligators at feeding time, Lee topped it.

Even though he didn't know much about it, J J was pretty sure Lee was mistaken about crocodiles in Korea. Recalling Mr. Denham's geography class and the world maps J J looked at in eighth grade, he concluded Lee's story about receiving the coveted Soldier's Medal for pulling a soldier from the jaws of a crock was, well, a crock. He also was convinced Lee never captured the crocodile, skinned it, and ate crock meat for supper.

I bet the old fart was never in Korea, J J thought, and he probably don't have no sons named Wayne and Gil, neither. And the story about chasing twelve Chinese soldiers up the Yalu River with only his bayonet was hard to swallow. It sounded to J J like those G I Joe stories in Action Comics he used to buy in Klines' drugstore, next door to Sugar Babe's.

He thought he had overcome homesickness during basic and infantry training, but the thought of Klines and Sugar Babe's refreshed his pain of leaving a secure existence. J J looked at his reflection in the window, at the sadness shaping his features. Tears welled. He wiped despair from both eyes and rubbed his face with vigor.

At Longview, a thin, small woman sat next to him. A tiny girl sat in the aisle seat across from the woman.

To J J, his new seatmate's features were Asian. She had short black hair, black eyes, and smooth, olive shaded skin. Her short fingers and little hands were not much larger than the girl's. He did not have the experience to be able to determine if the woman was Taiwanese, Chinese, Korean, or Japanese. With the current situation on his mind, he thought she might even be Vietnamese. He refrained from asking the discourteous question – *Where you from*? He knew it was none of his business.

"Okay, Nancy, you wait until on highway. Stay right here with me, Baby."

"I can't see anything sitting here, Momma." The girl's enunciation was pure American.

"Excuse me, Mam. My name is J J. I can change

seats with your little girl. She can sit here by the window so she can see out."

"No, that's kind, Sir. When bus moves, she be alright, go up front, stand by driver, and look. My name is Lin."

"My little sister is about the size of your little girl. My sister's name is Jodie. She's got short black hair cut in bangs, like your little girl."

"Nancy is six. Her Daddy beat her with a belt last night. He hit me with belt, too. I was afraid he would kill us. We run away, hide at bus station. We have no clothes. Nothing. I beg for dollars at station to have enough money to buy bus ticket to take us to Tanglewilde, to my girlfriend. I so ashamed ask strangers for money."

He gave the three one-dollar bills in his pocket to Nancy's mother when they stood to leave the bus at the Tanglewilde station. That gesture made Lin weep; she covered her face in embarrassment.

"You so kind, Sir. God bless you."

J J now had seventy-eight cents in his pocket, but Lin's story about the beatings made his heart pound. He could not shake the image of his drunken old man yelling and waving his leather belt. He felt blood flush his face as anger rose from a place he thought suppressed and secure. His mother, Kip, and Jodie filled his thoughts from Tanglewilde to Olympia. Once settled in Vietnam, he would need to start an allotment to send most of his $78 base pay and $55 jump pay home. During training, he managed to buy a money order each payday to send money to his mother to continue to help with family expenses.

A soldier in uniform boarded at the Olympia stop. After stowing his AWOL bag in the overhead, he stuck out his hand to J J.

"My name's Burl Deakins. Friends call me Deak. You going to Fort Lewis?"

J J grasped Burl's firm hand.

Burl was short and thin. He sported a neat, well trimmed, pencil mustache. His friendly smile brightened his face and black eyes.

J J liked Burl straight away.

"Yes, to the replacement center."

"Me, too." Burl sat next to J J. "Been home on emergency leave. My mother had breast cancer. When she died, Pop asked the Red Cross to help me come home for the funeral. Now I'm on my way back to my unit."

"I see your infantry division shoulder patch. What do you do, Deak?"

"I'm an infantry squad leader. Third squad, First Platoon, Hotel Company. I see you're airborne infantry."

"Completed jump school last month. Only the basic five jumps."

"Are you on your way to *Nam*?"

"Yeah. My orders are to report to the replacement center at Fort Lewis for processing and shipment. I don't know what will happen next."

"Well, we'll be at Fort Lewis a couple of days and nights, take a bus to Sea-Tac in Seattle, board a 707, and crammed like sardines fly for eighteen hours."

"That's a long time."

"Yeah. It is a long ass flight, J J. After we land at

Tan Son Nhut, we'll ride an Air Force bus to the Long Bien replacement station, about eight miles northeast of Saigon. There is where you'll get assigned to a unit. I'll spend a day or so at Long Bien, too, before catching a bird up to Linebacker."

"What's Linebacker?"

"Fire Support Base Linebacker is a big-ass place in the smack-dab middle of Vietnam. It has an infantry battalion, two artillery batteries, a helicopter battalion – they got Hueys, Loaches, and Cobras – a support battalion, a company of engineers, a bunch of other little outfits, and a ground cavalry troop."

"Maybe I could go with you, Deak?" He wanted to be Burl's friend, but J J wished he had not blurted that hope. It came out because he felt a comradeship with Burl. It was an immediate realization that when his words spilled out, it was the same as toothpaste oozing out of the tube. He couldn't put the toothpaste back in the tube or the words back in his mouth.

"Okay. If that's what you want to do, I'll speak up for you. We'll tell the clerk we're cousins and want to be together. It'll be okay cause we're not brothers."

"Being brothers makes a difference?"

"The Sullivan Act passed by Congress."

Burl looked at J J's questioning stare.

"Five Sullivan brothers were sailors serving on the same ship in World War Two. Two torpedoes hit their ship. The first caused some damage. The second torpedo hit the ship when it was on its way to a port for repairs. It sank and all five brothers perished. So if we say we're brothers they won't let us go to the same unit. That's why we'll be cousins."

It rained the next two days and nights. Fortunately, processing was indoors.

J J spent the daytime hours shifting from one line to the next. Typewriters clicked and clacked. Army clerks acted like robots. They received papers, typed in the blank spaces, stamped papers with a round rubber stamp, handed papers back, and pointed to the next line. The last clerk pointed at the shot line.

"Go over there next. You gotta get vaccinized."

J J balked. "I gotta get what?"

"*Vaccinized*. Your shots. Over there. *Next man*."

J J lost count after twelve immunizations. He had no idea what the injected substances were. Medics on either side pushed their automatic vaccination gun against his shoulders, simultaneously, and squeezed their triggers. A doctor, without gloves, poked his fingers in J J's mouth and butt, peered in his ears, nose, and throat, and held J J's balls when he ask J J to cough. It was a line to remember.

During nights, J J watched groups play poker, bridge, pinochle, Whist, Spades, Canasta, or shoot dice. He, along with dozens of soldiers, watched the evening news broadcasts, firefights, and interviews with commanders and soldiers, sailors, airmen, or Marines. Once he saw a snippet of an interview with a nurse, and once with a Red Cross volunteer. The guys sitting in the dayroom hooted and hollered at the volunteer and called her *Doughnut Dolly*.

Food in the center's mess hall was below J J's standard, but he ate it anyway.

Sometimes he talked with Burl.

"Was you in combat? I mean, in a fight? Shooting people?"

"Yeah, but a lot of times in jungle thickets we never see who we're shooting at. The point man on a patrol gets it first with AK-47s, and the next three or four in the column get it too. The others spread out and return fire."

"Being point-man is dangerous."

Deakins looked at J J.

"It's all dangerous, J J. Never take chances, even when it looks innocent enough. There are booby-traps, tripwires, buried bombs, or grenades, you name it. Kids with their hand out for a cigarette, chewing gum, money, or a C-ration might have a grenade in the other."

"Kids have hangernades?"

"They're part of the VC, or the VC hold their parents or grandma and pa hostage. Force em to frag American soldiers. But, going down in a tunnel is worse. Scary as hell. When you're underground, there's no place to go but straight ahead or backwards. All you got is a pistol and flashlight. You never know what you're gonna run into or what's gonna jump on you."

"I guess guys get mad when they can't see what they're shooting at."

"Mad as hell, J J. That's when we burn the hamlet."

"What do you mean?"

"We take our Zippos and ignite the straw roofs. They use dried bamboo and dried rice stalks to build houses so, in seconds, the whole damn hamlet is on fire. Flames engulf the house, it burns to the ground."

"You burn people's houses?"

"Yep. If we get fired on from a hamlet, we set fire to every last one of them. If the VC runs into the hamlet, then we know there are sympathizers, and we burn it."

"Geez. You burn people's houses?" J J struggled to accept Burl's admission.

"Well, it ain't like Uncle Jim's and Aunt Sara's house down the street, J J."

"Yeah, I know. But it's *their* house you're burnin. Where they gonna live after that?"

"We don't give a shit, J J. They helped the Viet Congs, they knew the consequences."

"I don't know what I would do if somebody burned down my house."

"You'd know what to do if they killed your buddy. You'd do what we do."

The third day they boarded the bus for the ride to Seattle. The Boeing 707 was waiting and ready.

It was still raining when the bus stopped at the stairs to go up into the plane. Burl and J J made seven running strides off the bus, twenty-seven steps up the stairs, and fifty-two steps down the aisle to their seats. J J got a window seat; Burl sat in the middle. An Airman First Class sat next to Burl. The original design was for 189 passengers. Military charters to Vietnam needed more seats per flight. The plane they were in had three seats abreast on each side of the aisle. The aircraft was full, all 219 seats taken. Cabin attendants swapped turns sitting on flip-down boards.

There was little talk and a lot of sleeping. And after ten hours in flight, the cabin smelled of stale smoke and perspiration. They lost a day crossing the International Dateline. The next morning the plane touched down at Tan Son Nhut International Airport, Republic of Vietnam. All noses were stuck to windows.

Handlers hurried to unload the plane and tossed mailbags, boxes, crates, baggage, and duffel bags into the back of deuce-and-a-half trucks. In short order, the heavy trucks sped away.

It had rained moments before they deplaned and steam rose from the tarmac. The smell of Vietnam was different. For J J, the stench of stewed cabbage came to mind. As they walked with ease in single file from the aircraft toward the terminal building, four mortar shells thumped two hundred meters to their north, near the airfield perimeter. At that moment, the rookies did not "hit the dirt". Instead, their lax stroll turned into a free-for-all sprint to the doorways.

Inside, they stood in line while Military Police tried to gain control and arrange the arrivals by busloads for the trip to Long Bien. Extensive exclamations of excitement to be in a mortar attack drowned out orders and commands from the MPs.

Quickly, J J surmised the exploding ordnance was not blasts seen at the movies, on television, or in a training exercise. He had experienced the real thing. In an instant, he made the transition from stateside service to serving in a war zone in style, welcomed by an enemy mortar attack.

He had arrived.

Next morning at Long Bien, processing and the issuance of jungle boots and clothing was the order of the day.

Burl handed his orders to the clerk. He jerked a thumb over his shoulder at J J.

"We're cousins. I'm returning from emergency leave and my cousin here would like to be assigned to my company."

The clerk did not look up. She scribbled on a form, stamped it, and handed the paper to him.

"Okay, Sergeant Deakins. This is authorization for you to catch a ride up to your firebase. Be at the bus stop in front of this building at 1500 hours. A bus marked *Upcountry Departures* will bring you to the chopper pad. The chopper is a Chinook. Its markings are CG 40884. It has a skull and crossbones painted on both doors. This is your taxi to Linebacker."

"Thanks, what about my cousin?"

"Give me your folder," the clerk said. She held her hand out for J J's personnel record.

"You're 11-Bravo, airborne infantry, unassigned," she said. "I'll send you to Linebacker, but you'll be going to the Cavalry Troop there. The Troop is under strength, they need infantrymen."

"Could you assign me to Linebacker as a cook?"

She looked at Burl and then at J J.

"A *cook*." She pronounced it as if it was a mystery word. "A *cook*?"

"You're infantry, J J," Burl said. "Why do you want to be a cook?"

"That's what I do, Deak. I was a cook before I

joined the Army. I paid a recruiter to sign me up as a cook."

Burl and the clerk blurted the same words.

"YOU WHAT?"

The personnel sergeant, the clerk's supervisor, was standing nearby and reacted to their exclamations.

"What's going on, Sandra?" the sergeant asked.

"Private Johnson paid a recruiter to sign up to be a cook, Sergeant Kane."

The supervisor looked at J J. "No shit. How much did you pay?"

"Ten dollars."

"What's his MOS, Sandra?"

"Eleven Bravo, Sergeant Kane. Airborne infantry."

"If you paid money to be a cook, Johnson, how come you ended up infantry?" Sergeant Kane asked.

"Sergeant Holt, the recruiter, said I had to go through basic and infantry training first. I could be a cook after training."

"You been screwed with, J J," Deakins said. "You been ripped off, man, by this Sergeant Holt."

"Yeah, I know. I realized that later. He's over here someplace. I'll find him and settle the score."

The three grinned at J J and shook their heads.

"You're gonna find a Sergeant Holt, here, in Vietnam? There must be a hundred guys, maybe two hundred, with the name of Holt in-country," Kane said.

"Well, I'm supposed to be a cook."

"What about it, Sandra, where could we send this young man to be a cook?"

"There are no requisitions in the file for cooks, Sergeant Kane. I was going to send Private Johnson to the cavalry troop at Linebacker. They're under strength and need infantry."

"Okay. Private Johnson, when you get to your unit, you'll have to talk to the First Sergeant about transferring from 11-Bravo to 92-Golf."

"What's a 92-Golf, Sir?"

"It's the MOS for a food service specialist," Sergeant Kane explained. "A mess hall cook."

"I'm infantry, but I'm supposed to be a 92-Golf."

"Well, you were supposed to go to cook school at Fort Lee, Virginia for culinary training and award of the 92-Golf MOS first, Johnson. Instead, you went to Fort Benning, Georgia and became an airborne infantryman. Cut the orders for the cavalry troop at Linebacker, Sandra."

In rapid succession, Sandra pounded typewriter keys with two fingers, and then slipped his personnel record into a manila envelope, scribbled on the paper she typed, signed and stamped it, and handed the paper and envelope to J J.

"You're assigned to the Cavalry Troop as infantry. When you get to Linebacker, you'll have to see your First Sergeant about a different job," Kane said.

Sandra smiled at Private James Jerome Johnson. "Good luck, Cookie."

"Cookie," Deak said. "I like that name. Cookie."

ARRIVAL

When the truck pulled up with its load of replacements and their gear, it was 1536 hours. The CH-47 helicopter, with the markings Sandra mentioned, stood quiet at the north end of an asphalt runway. The behemoth, with its heavy blades drooping under the hot, afternoon sun, waited. Revetments lined the sides of the airstrip. Most of the cubicles were empty; a few housed a Huey, Loach, or Cobra gunship. Army Birddogs filled two slots. In another pod, a bareheaded Air Force Forward Air Controller, in his silver jumpsuit, was inspecting an OV-10, a spotter plane used by FAC pilots. The airfield was eerily silent.

When the truck stopped behind the Chinook's ramp, J J, Deak, and a dozen other soldiers jumped off. Four soldiers handed down equipment and baggage while the others, with military discipline, automatically formed a line from the truck into the cargo bay to pass along the gear and place it in the helicopter at the direction of the chopper's crew chief. Each of them had signed for a rifle at the center, but no one received bullets because they were still in a "safe" zone. They would collect combat gear, grenades, and ammunition at their destination.

It took another seventeen minutes for the crew chief to check off names against his manifest, secure their gear with straps and cords, inspect the outside frame, struts, and blades of the helicopter, and stand ready with a fire extinguisher as the aircraft commander started engines.

Half of the contingent sat on the starboard row of canvas seats; the others sat on the port. The center of the floor had a gun jeep loaded with two dozen boxes of sleeping bags stacked around the empty pedestal on the driver, passenger, and back seats. Three rolls of concertina wire lay on top of these boxes, secured by aircraft cargo nets. Forward of the jeep was one pallet of 1-5-5mm artillery shells, one pallet of 1-0-5mm artillery shells, and ten barrels of MOGAS. Immediately behind the jeep was one pallet of 1-0-6mm recoilless rifle shells, two pallets brimming with cases of rifle ammunition, and two pallets of M60 machine gun ammunition. Aft, were one pallet of various colors of smoke grenades and one pallet of fragmentation grenades. On top of the pallet of frags was a pallet of one-hundred cases of C-Rations secured by four, two-inch, yellow Ratchet straps. Sitting on top of the smoke grenades, secured by cargo netting, was a 1950s, red Coca-Cola cooler.

While engines revved, the crew chief ran up the ramp and closed it, sat on a canvas seat near the rear switches and communication box, and fastened his seat belt. In less than twenty seconds, they were airborne, and he gave a thumbs-up to his passengers.

They loosened their seat belts and turned to peer at the beautiful terrain of South Vietnam through the small windows. From the air, from their perch, it did not look like a country involved in a war, where, in the final analysis a decade later, an American service member died every fifteen minutes.

The ninety-kilometer flight took less than forty minutes. As they neared their destination, the pilot changed course to begin approach into Fire Support Base Linebacker. The altered flight pattern provided a view and opportunity for Sergeant Deakins to point out landmarks.

"See the mountain?" Deak shouted so Private Johnson could hear above the roar of the two engines.

J J nodded. "Yeah, I see it, Deak. It's a tall mountain."

"That's Nui Ba Ra. It's over two-thousand feet high. It's a volcano. Probably been dead a million years. Look, you can see the communications bunkers and antennae on top of the mountain. And you can see some of the guys on security shift walking around. There's a Huey there, with its blades turning."

"Have you ever been on top?"

"Yeah, my platoon goes up there sometimes too."

"Maybe I'll get to go up for a visit."

"Maybe so. You can see the firebase north of the mountain. That east-west road between the mountain and the firebase is 3-10. To the left, to the west, you can see the village of Phuoc Binh. To the right, on this side of the river, are the towns Phuoc Long and Sông Bé."

"Why are all those big tents by the road, along the

stream?"

"That's the laundry and shower points along Dak Toll creek. All the tents belong to the quartermaster company. They hire Vietnamese to pick up our clothes and bring them to the laundry point to wash in the creek. If we're lucky, we can come down here every two weeks to take a shower. There's also some women who work here who'll trim your sail for a fee."

J J looked at Deak. Both grinned.

"Trim your sail," J J said. "I like the sound of that. I might have to go get my sail trimmed."

"Look, there. You can see the small airstrip outside the Province Chief's palace. That son-of-a-bitch is corrupt as hell. Now from his house, look east. That's the Sông Bé River. Okay, now look at the north-south road on the left side of the mountain. That's 3-11. It runs from Saigon to Cambodia. 3-11 intersects with 3-10 in Phuoc Binh."

"Look, Deak. There's a bunch of jeeps and buses and trucks stopped on the road. There's a lot of people, too."

"Yeah, that's part of your troop. They probably helping the police check traffic."

Lined up on both sides of the checkpoint were buses, pedicabs, trucks, and cars. The vehicles and passengers waited their turn to pass through the police inspection. Above and below the police congregation, spread out along the road, were cavalry scout gun jeeps.

"The cavalry troop does a lot of checkpoints with the police on both 3-10 and 3-11."

Fire Support Base Linebacker was a large,

permanent, military camp enclosed and surrounded by three barriers of concertina wire. Linebacker was designed and constructed to accommodate a combat brigade headquarters, an infantry battalion headquarters, an infantry company, one battery of six 1-5-5mm cannons, one battery of six 1-0-5mm howitzers, and a cavalry troop. There was an asphalt airstrip, landing pads and revetments for helicopters, as well as helicopter and vehicle refueling points. Dug-in, sandbagged fixed fighting positions dotted the perimeter, and dug-in, sandbagged bunkers with sandbagged overhead cover lay behind a trail or road that ran around the firebase.

The Chinook leaned and circled on final approach.

To J J, the firebase appeared to be a large rectangle-shaped clearing. He guessed the internal road was a quarter mile on the long sides, somewhat less than a quarter mile on the short sides. J J saw guard towers interspersed with the fortified, sandbagged bunkers and fixed fighting positions around the perimeter and outhouses. The three strands of wire encircling Linebacker sparkled in the sinking sun.

"That is a big ass place, Deak."

"Yeah, J J. It's a big ass target, too."

Around the outskirts of the firebase and villages was thick jungle. Outside the wire, for a hundred meters on all sides of the firebase, was cultivated clearing. This area was full of anti-personnel mines.

The heavy-laden workhorse hovered for a moment before its wheels bounced twice and settled on the tarmac.

On the ground, Linebacker was a busy city. Trucks and jeeps moved about. Soldiers toted materiel; a saw buzzed. Vietnamese civilians swept out bunkers, dumped trash barrels, and collected clothes. Soldiers stood alert behind machineguns in the observation towers, which now seemed larger, taller to J J.

Three of the 1-0-5 howitzers fired to the north. Smoke from these guns floated away with a westerly breeze. The smell of burnt powder and cordite drifted south.

Two 81mm mortars, with their distinctive thump and pop signature, fired toward the northeast, north of Sông Bé.

Twelve soldiers – bare-chested, dressed in jungle fatigue trousers and jungle boots – played volleyball.

Five soldiers worked behind one of the outhouses, burning excrement in the latrine barrels. The black smoke drifted their way as they deplaned – the stench of burning shit memorable and pungent.

A team of quartermaster soldiers stood waiting for the crew chief and the passengers with their baggage to descend the Chinook's ramp. These quartermasters, a front loader, four Army M-274s (otherwise known as mules), and six two-and-a-half ton trucks waited to handle the jeep and the pallets of cargo and ammunition.

One in the greeting-party spoke up. "Okay, you guys, listen up. Welcome to Linebacker. Bring all your gear and move to the first deuce-and-a-half. I'm your taxi driver to bring you home. I'll stop in front of each unit's headquarters."

Once everyone was loaded, the truck pulled away.

"We got here when the guns were firing," one of the passengers said.

"Yeah, I wonder what they were shooting at?" another asked.

"They shootin at the fucking enemy, Cherry," another said.

"Hey, asshole, I ain't no fucking Cherry. I'm coming back from R & R. I been in-country six months. I got my CIB and a Purple Heart." The soldier grabbed his crotch. "And I got your fucking supper right here in my hand, you fucking asshole."

"Well, you act like a fucking Cherry," the accuser accused.

"What's a Cherry, Deak?"

"A new recruit, J J. You're a Cherry. F-N-G."

"What's F-N-G?"

Deak's huge grin was contagious. "Fresh New Guy or Fucking New Grunt."

J J grinned and nodded. "That I am. That I am."

The deuce-and-a-half, the firebase taxi of sorts, hauled the soldiers from the chopper pad to their respective unit's HQ. At each stop, a soldier, or soldiers, with baggage, jumped off the truck.

When the transport stopped at Hotel Company, Deak rose from the wooden bench seat, picked his gear, and tossed it overboard. He paused and looked at J J before reaching out with both arms for a hug.

J J stood, and they embraced warmly as close brothers would at a family gathering after a long absence. They patted each other on the back, separated, and peered into each other's soul.

"It's hard for me to make friends. I've never been

very good at it, J J. I'm usually distant with people. But I feel a kindred kinship with you. You're like a brother, a younger brother. You're gonna be a good soldier. And before you know it, you gonna be a Sergeant. You are my good friend."

"Hey, buddy, you gettin off here, or what?" the driver yelled from the cab of the truck.

"Yeah, hold on a minute. I'm saying goodbye to my cousin."

"Well, hurry it up. It's gettin close to quittin time and chow."

"Thank you for being my friend, Deak. I think of you as my brother, too. And my cousin."

"Okay, Cuz. You listen to me now. You take care of yourself. This ain't no movie or TV show out here. It's the real thing. Shit happens. One minute it's hunky-dory, the next bad shit happens. So, you take care. My platoon is three weeks in the bush and a week here on the firebase. I'll come see you, or you come lookin for me. Sometimes I'll catch the duty up on the mountaintop. And when I come off, I'll be on the camp for a day before I go back in the field. You stay in touch. Let me know how you doin."

"I will, Deak. And thank you for bringing me along with you to Linebacker."

They embraced again. Deak jumped off the truck and banged the tailgate twice. "Okay, Driver, all clear."

As the truck pulled away, Deak saluted and yelled. "Take care, Cookie."

On a mast stuck in the ground on the right side of the opening of the sandbagged bunker, a red-and-white cavalry guidon wavered in the slight, intermittent breeze. Sewn onto the red top of the guidon was the white letter **D**, the designation for Troop D. On the left side of the entrance was a small, white, rectangular sign with black stenciled lettering that read ***DELTA'S DEVILS***.

Inside the HQ, J J reported to the First Sergeant.

"I'm the new arrival, First Sergeant. Private James Jerome Johnson, I go by J J."

"Welcome to Delta Troop, Johnson. I'm Marion Morris."

J J handed over the envelope Sandra had prepared, containing his orders and personnel record. First Sergeant Morris opened the envelope, removed, and scanned the documents.

A mortar began firing again, with a three-second pause between each round. As if reading from J J's papers, Morris addressed the popping.

"That is a sweet sound to me, the business end of a mortar tube. That crew is getting some good practice. I do miss being in a fight and taking care of cavalry business."

J J did not speak; he knew his First Sergeant was not talking to him.

"I see you're an 11-Bravo, airborne infantry. We're short-handed so you'll fit right in, Johnson. In this cavalry troop of a hundred and sixty-five, there are thirty-three positions for infantrymen."

"I'm not supposed to be, First Sergeant."

"Not supposed to be what?"

"Infantry."

"What do you mean you're not supposed to be an infantryman?" First Sergeant Morris asked. "I'm lookin at your orders, Son. You're an 11-Bravo, airborne infantry."

"I've been trying to get this straightened out, First Sergeant. The recruiting sergeant said . . ."

"Ah, the recruiting sergeant," Morris interrupted. "The recruiting sergeant. It's always – *The recruiting sergeant said*."

"Yes, Sir."

First Sergeant Marion Morris' fleshy, black face widen into a gigantic, mischievous grin. A large man – six-five, 270 pounds – Morris towered over his new soldier.

"And what did the asshole promise you, Mr. Johnson?"

"I could be a cook."

"A *cook*? A cook, you say. The recruiting sergeant promised you would be a cook in this man's Army."

"Yes, Sir. I paid him ten dollars to sign up as a cook."

"You what? YOU DID WHAT?" Morris bellowed. "You trusted a recruiter?"

"Yes, Sir."

"You were gullible, young man."

The troop clerk looked up from his Remington – typewriter, that is – and laughed. "Son-of-a-bitch, they oughta cut his balls off. Recruiters got a plush job in a air-conditioned office, drivin around in a air-conditioned sedan, goin to air-conditioned schools, eatin *Whataburgers*, and still rippin us off. *Son-of-a-*

bitch."

"He didn't take your money, Vannoy, so you stay outta this. Now, Johnson, I don't know what happened, what that recruiter said, or what he promised, but you are an infantryman. And we need infantrymen to bring our three squads up to full strength. So, you're gonna be in the infantry. Understand?"

"Yes, Sir, First Sergeant, I understand. But I'd rather be a cook."

"You know how to cook? You got any experience as a cook? Do you know how to prepare food for a lot of people?"

"Yes, Sir. I worked a year on the day shift at Sugar Babe's, a cafe in my hometown. We were stiff competitors of the local Waffle House and Denny's. I know all about food handling, preparation, and sanitation. I keep a clean kitchen and my food is wholesome, and it tastes good."

"I always liked to eat at Waffle House," Vannoy ventured. "My favorite was the *Toddle House Breakfast Special*."

J J grinned and nodded at Vannoy. "I made dozens of those kinds of specials ever day. We called then *Babe's Best Breakfast Special*. But I made better specials than the Waffle House Toddle stuff."

"Well, Johnson, first things first. I want you to earn your Combat Infantry Badge. That means 30 days in the field and exchanging gunfire with the enemy. Understand?"

"Yes, Sir."

"After that, if a vacancy opens up in the mess hall

I'll consider your druthers and make a recommendation to Sergeant Hale, the Mess Sergeant. I make no promises. Understand?"

"Yes, Sir, First Sergeant. I understand. Thank you."

Morris jabbed a thumb toward the soldier sitting behind the typewriter. "This here is Specialist Fourth Class Vannoy, Troop Clerk."

He handed envelope and papers toward Vannoy.

"Vannoy will send your pay record over to Finance and handle all your in-processing. Later on, he'll take you over to the supply tent so you can draw your bedding and combat gear."

Specialist Vannoy stood up behind the field desk, took the envelope from Morris, and shoved his hand forward to J J. "Welcome to the real cavalry, J J. My first name is Vance but friends just call me Vannoy. Be my friend, J J."

J J grasped Vannoy's extended hand and shook it in immediate friendship. "Thank you, Vannoy."

"I'm assigning you to Third Platoon, Johnson."

"Okay, First Sergeant."

"Vannoy, go get the Third Platoon Sergeant. Tell Boss Tweed I have a rifleman for his infantry squad."

"On the way, Top."

"Sit there, J J. We use the water can as a chair. Your Platoon Sergeant will be along in a minute."

"It seems kinda strange," J J said. He sat on the hard, uneven handles of the metal can.

"What's strange?"

"That infantry is in a cavalry troop, First Sergeant."

"A-TEN-SHUT!" First Sergeant Morris ordered.

In a trained and instinctive movement, Private Johnson jumped to his feet and braced, staring straight ahead.

"At ease," a soft voice said.

"Sir, this is the new infantryman we been expecting. Private Johnson, this is your Troop Commander, Captain Thompson."

The Private faced the Captain and saluted.

Captain Thompson smiled and returned the salute. "Stand at ease, Private Johnson. Welcome to Delta Troop. What's your first name?"

"It's James, Sir."

"James. James Johnson."

"Actually, it's James Jerome Johnson, Sir. But I just go by J J, Sir."

"Ah, okay, I understand. J J it is, then. Relax, have a seat, J J."

Even though he felt uneasy, unsure, J J liked Captain Thompson right off. He sat back down on the water can but remained alert, observant. He was prepared to jump to his feet again in the presence of his commanding officer.

"I've assigned Johnson to Lieutenant Versailles' platoon, Captain. I've sent Vannoy for Platoon Sergeant Tweed. He should be here any minute."

"What's your M-O-S, J J?"

"11-Bravo, Sir. Infantry." Private Johnson could not restrain himself. "But I'm supposed to be a cook."

"Cooks are 92-Golfs, Captain," Morris said.

Captain Thompson stared at the Private, looked at Morris, and turned back to Johnson.

J J felt compelled to continue. "I signed up to be a

cook, Sir. But the recruiter said I had to go through infantry training before I could be a cook."

Captain Thompson could not hold his official commander's face; a smile crept in. He looked at First Sergeant Morris, again.

"Hell of a story, Sir." Morris grinned and shook his head. "Johnson paid a recruiter to sign up as a cook."

With raised eyebrows, the Troop Commander's eyes fixed on the new soldier. "You paid a recruiter to join the Army?"

"Yes, Sir. I mean no, Sir, not to join the Army. I paid him ten dollars because he said I could be a cook after my infantry training. I been ripped off, Sir. I realize that now." J J looked at Morris. "I was gullible, Sir. I was too trusting."

Thompson once more turned to Morris. Both leaders could not hold a straight face. Their broad grins created deep creases in their sun-dried skin.

Morris managed to speak without laughing. "I told Johnson I'd consider his preference after he did some time in the field, exchanged gunfire with the enemy, and earned his CIB, Captain."

Captain Thompson was amused this new infantryman wanted to be a cook, but managed to maintain military decorum. He did not want to embarrass himself, his First Sergeant, or his soldier.

"We are short-handed," Thompson said. "We needed six infantry soldiers to come up to full strength in our squads, J J. With you, now we need five more."

The words spilled out of his mouth before J J realized he was making a suggestion and recommendation to his Troop Commander. He wanted right away to be a helpful soldier. But more than that, he saw an opportunity to be with his new friend.

"I know an infantryman who might be interested in coming here, Sir."

"Really?"

"Yes, Sir. He's Sergeant Burl Deakins, Squad Leader of Third Squad, First Platoon, Hotel Company, here on the camp."

"I see. Thank you for the recommendation. We'll look into it. Now, First Sergeant said he'd consider your preference to be a cook after you've served in the field and been in a fight with enemy forces, after you've been in combat. But, understand, there are no promises. The needs of the Troop come first. Is that a fair deal, J J?"

"Yes, Sir. Like you, Sir, the First Sergeant was straight up with me about it. I'll do my best, Sir."

"Good. Then that's settled. Again, welcome to Delta Troop. We're glad to have you with us. Be safe. Take care of yourself and your buddies."

Private Johnson snapped to attention and saluted.

"Carry on, J J." The Troop Commander returned the salute and went through an opening, a doorway, inside the command bunker.

Vannoy and Platoon Sergeant Tweed entered.

"This is your new infantryman, Sergeant Tweed," First Sergeant Morris said. "Private Johnson, this is your Platoon Sergeant."

HOME

"Okay, Johnson. Put your gear over there, in that corner."

Private James Jerome Johnson held onto the rifle sling with his left hand. With his right hand, he grasped the wide shoulder strap, bent over at his waist, and slung the stuffed duffle bag off his back. The Army-canvas container dropped in place on the metal PSP flooring, without rolling, next to an empty, wood-framed, canvas cot. Inside the bag was his rubber air mattress, folded and tucked into his green, nylon, camouflaged military blanket. He slipped the M16 rifle off his left shoulder and faced Platoon Sergeant Boswell Tweed. He scanned the square-shaped abode.

"This is home, Platoon Sergeant?"

"Yep. This is your new home. This bunker is where you're gonna sleep, Johnson. Your fighting bunker is on the firebase perimeter, right outside the doorway, across the road. I'll show you where it is after chow."

"I see more gear. It looks like this is home to other renters. Where are the guys?"

"Mickey Fowler and Billy Butler are on the perimeter, manning the fighting bunker. Sergeant Hawk, your Fire Team Leader, and Jinks Jenkins are with Lieutenant Versailles. They're working on a citation to present to Captain Thompson for Rosey."

"Rosey. What'd he do?"

"Private Shiloh Rose was killed last week. He'd been in-country eleven days, up here with us for three. Shot by a sniper, in a rubber plantation about three clicks east of the firebase."

"Yeah, but what'd he do? For the citation? For his decoration?"

"He died, Johnson. He deserves a medal just for being over here, for just being in Vietnam. They're working on a Bronze Star for him. And a Purple Heart. It's solace for his family."

Silence filled fleeting seconds. Sergeant Tweed peered into his new soldier's eyes before speaking.

"What's wrong?"

"A soldier is dead, and the consolation for his family is a ribbon?"

Sergeant Tweed gave a solemn nod of understanding. "It's all we got, Johnson, besides twenty-five thousand dollars Army insurance and a thank you for his service and sacrifice."

"It's J J, Platoon Sergeant."

"What's J J?"

"That's the name I prefer, Platoon Sergeant. Just J J. Just the last name Johnson seems stuck-up. James Jerome is too hard to say together. And I hate James, or Jim, or Jimmy. So, it's J J."

"Okay, J J. In an informal setting, everybody can

call me Boss – for Boswell. Let's go get some chow. After supper, I'll introduce you to Sergeant Hawk, Mickey, Billy, and Jinks. They're all 11-Bravos too. Sergeant Darby Dutchman is your squad leader. He's in Malaysia on R & R."

"I'm not supposed to be infantry, Boss. I'm supposed to be a cook."

"What kind of cook?"

"A cook. Army cook. To work in a real mess hall, preparing meals."

"Reel-lee." The way Tweed pronounced the word was impressive. "You're supposed to be a cook?"

"Yeah, I paid the recruiting sergeant ten dollars to sign up as a cook when I joined up."

"No shit, Sherlock. You paid a recruiter ten dollars to be a cook in this man's Army?"

"Yeah. He gave me the song and dance about how I had to go through infantry training first before I could be a cook."

"He gypped you outta ten smack-a-roos for assignment as a cook, did he?"

"Yeah. His name is Holt. He's a Staff Sergeant."

"Holt? What's his first name?"

"I don't know his first name. He's short and kinda tubby. He's bald in the middle of his head, from the front over the top. Black hair just on the sides. Wears black-rimmed glasses. About 30, I'd guess. He owes me ten bucks."

"Tubby. Bald in the middle top of his head. Black hair. Black military glasses."

"Yeah. And I aim to collect it if I ever find his fat ass."

"Goddamn, it is a small world, J J. There's a million guys over here and you're looking for one staff sergeant in the Republic of South Vietnam."

"Yeah. Holt."

Boss Tweed grinned and nodded. His boisterous laughter filled the sandbagged bunker. He slapped Private James Jerome Johnson's shoulder and patted the new infantryman on the back.

"I'll reintroduce you to Sergeant Henry Holt tomorrow, J J. Let's go to chow."

"He's here? On the firebase?"

"He's not only on the firebase, J J. He's in the troop. Been here a month or so. He's our new supply sergeant. Christ-all-mighty, what a coincidence. I got to see the look on his chubby face when he sees you, J J. That has got to be a *Candid Camera* moment."

Shouts of *INCOMING! INCOMING!* from a half-dozen soldiers filled the firebase at the moment three, 82-millimeter mortar shells exploded in thumped succession in the dirt outside Cookie's new home.

The cacophony of chattering machine guns, grenade blasts, and cracks from rifle fire merged with screams, yells, and shouts by soldiers.

"*IN THE WIRE! IN THE WIRE! THEY'RE IN THE WIRE! THEY'RE COMING IN!*"

"That's Mickey yelling. Grab your weapon and follow me, J J."

"I don't have bullets, Boss."

Tweed pulled his bayonet from its scabbard and handed it over. "Then use my bayonet! Come on!"

J J grasped the grip and followed his Platoon Sergeant. Together, they rushed through the doorway of the bunker, onto the road. J J paused and by instinct and training, in fluid motion, snapped the oiled steel in place on his M16 rifle.

Three enemy soldiers were standing between the first and second strand of wire, firing their automatic weapons at Mickey and Billy. With their rifles on automatic, the two riflemen returned heavy fire, cutting the VC to pieces.

Clad in black pajamas, four enemy soldiers stood on the other side of the road in assault firing positions. They squeezed off a short burst of rounds from their AK-47s. In a hail of bullets, green tracers streamed like a wavy line. Focused downrange, they did not see the two Americans come out of the bunker.

With his rifle switched to automatic fire, Boss Tweed cut down the two on his left.

In stunned surprise, the one to J J's immediate front stopped firing and gawked. J J raised his weapon and charged, striking the attacker square in his opened mouth with the M16 rifle's butt. Teeth cracked, and the nose burst. Blood splattered on J J's cheek, lips, and chin. The enemy soldier fell on his back, screaming in pain.

J J wheeled to confront the fourth and with a forceful parry, knocked the barrel of the AK-47 away. Three green tracers zipped past Boss Tweed's head. Before the enemy soldier could swing his weapon around and pull the trigger again, J J thrust his spear into the center of the VC's abdomen, just below the sternum, driving him to ground.

With a full force jab and push, the bayonet went through the thin body, and J J pinned him with the spike. He jammed his left jungle boot heel on the VC's throat. Standing over the dying enemy, J J saw his old man's face and screamed.

"Die, you fuckin motherfucker, you goddamn son-of-a-bitch!"

He held the bayonet steady and exerted forced pressure down on the throat as death throes gripped the attacker.

"Watch your six," Sergeant Tweed yelled.

Startled, J J jerked his head around.

The one with the smashed face had risen to a sitting position and was struggling to lift the AK-47 up to fire on J J.

Sergeant Tweed placed the muzzle of his rifle against the right temple of the injured combatant and pulled the trigger. Then, he moved to J J.

"Withdraw your bayonet," Boss said.

J J pulled the steel away but kept his boot in position.

Sergeant Tweed set his rifle's muzzle between the eyes of the dying cadre and pulled the trigger. The VC's body jerked and flopped; a foot twitched in death.

It had started quick and ended quick. The fight and gunfire were over in seconds.

Breathless, with elbows touching, Sergeant Tweed and Private Johnson stood their ground with the four bloody bodies at their feet.

The Platoon Sergeant turned and grinned at his new warrior. "You did good, J J. I am impressed. You're a natural born killer. Let's pick up these AKs."

"I don't know what came over me, Boss. I was scared."

"Yeah. I know. Most of us were our first time."

"I've never been in a fight like this."

"You were brave, J J. You handled yourself with honor in combat."

As he helped retrieve the enemy weapons, J J did not know he was rambling. He did not realize he was in shock.

"My last fist fight was ninth grade. My heart is still racing. I can feel the veins in my neck pound. They feel like they're gonna explode. Geez, I feel lightheaded."

"You did good." Platoon Sergeant Tweed paused and waited. "Can you hear me, J J?"

"But I liked it. I liked the taste of battle. I liked thrusting the bayonet into him. The blade just sunk in, smooth as a straw in a milkshake. Sticking him, pinning him to the ground, Jesus, that felt good. What a rush."

"Well, you've already earned your CIB without firing a shot."

"I didn't have no bullets, but I just killed a man. And I liked it. I liked killing my old man."

Boss Tweed stared at his new infantryman. He watched J J, knew the young soldier was stunned, still dazed.

"J J." Tweed paused. "J J." The Platoon Sergeant's voice was soft, calming. "Hey, J J. Are you with me, J J?"

Private Johnson looked at Tweed. "I just killed my old man, and it felt good."

"J J. Are you with me, boy?"

"Yes, Sir." J J nodded. He blinked his eyes and

matched his Platoon Sergeant's smile.

"Okay, lower your rifle. The fight is over. Take a deep breath, J J."

He responded and took in three huge gulps of air. After each deep breath, J J pursed his lips and exhaled.

"Damn, I thought I was going mean-crazy. I can breathe again. My ears have stopped ringing. My heart's stopped pounding. I can see you now, Boss. I can hear you."

"I'm going to put you in for a Bronze Star, J J. For Valor. You did a great job. You are a fighter. You are a baptized infantryman. Well done, Soldier."

J J's proud grin was short-lived.

A succession of moans snatched their attention. They stepped over the dead VC and moved toward the side of the bunker. Around the corner, a soldier lay face down in the dirt.

"I'm hit. I'm hit," the soldier complained. "Somebody help me. Get a medic."

Sergeant Tweed laid the enemy weapons on the ground and knelt beside the wounded warrior. "Where are you hit?"

"In the back. My right leg. In the back of my right leg. Oh, God, it hurts. I might bleed to death."

The soldier's jungle fatigue trouser leg had a small tear, exposing a faint dab of blood on the lower part of his right buttock.

"Give me the bayonet, J J," Sergeant Tweed said.

J J released it from the catch and handed it over. Tweed inserted the knife's point and slit the fabric. The tip of the bayonet flicked an AK-47 round that pressed an indentation into the bottom meaty part of the soldier's butt cheek. Now exposed, the wound was nothing more than an abrasion – like a nick from a razor. The wound, as it were, was from a spent ricochet, which had no substantial force of impact.

"Okay, I've removed the bullet. You're going to be okay. Can you roll over and sit up?"

Other soldiers up the road, and from the firebase proper, came out from behind protective cover. Some joined Mickey and Billy at the fighting position while others knelt on the road in a defensive posture, oriented toward the wire. Reinforcements arrived on a mule.

"We can load the bodies on my carrier," the mule driver suggested.

"Yes, do that," Sergeant Tweed answered. "Bring the bodies on the little four-wheeler to the main gate and dump them there. We'll notify Brigade, who'll contact the Provincial police to come get them for disposal."

Three soldiers joined Tweed and Johnson and stared at their wounded comrade.

"Is he dead?" one of them asked.

"He don't even look hurt," another said.

"Can you roll over and sit up?" Boss Tweed asked again.

The soldier groaned. "I'm hurt bad. I think I lost a lot of blood. Is my leg going to be amputated?"

"No, I doubt it," Tweed said. "You're gonna be alright. It's like a scratch, barely a flesh wound. An easy Purple Heart. Let's get you over to Merlin to have a look. With a little iodine and a band-aid, you'll be ready for duty in an hour."

"See, I told you he didn't look hurt," the soldier said.

With an assist from Tweed and J J, the warrior rolled over and sat up.

"Is that all it is, a flesh wound?"

"It's just barely that, Henry."

"Why does it hurt so bad?"

"YOU!" J J was surprised at his outburst. "YOU SON-OF-A-BITCH!" His exclamations drew the attention of all the onlookers, who recoiled when he shouted.

The wounded soldier looked up at J J, then at Sergeant Tweed.

"It is a small world, ain't it, Henry," Sergeant Tweed laughed. "Sergeant Henry Holt, may I reintroduce you to one of your former enlistees, Private James Jerome Johnson, United States Army, Infantry, who joined the Army to be a cook."

"You owe me ten dollars, asshole."

As a group, they marched to the aid station where the senior troop medic, Sergeant Merlin "Doc" Swanson, doctored Sergeant Holt's combat wound. Actually, Holt had not marched but hobbled, holding onto Tweed's arm.

Before Holt lay face down on a stretcher, the medic told him to lower his trousers.

They watched the medic pull a small bottle of mercurochrome from his medical bag and lift a roll of tape and several gauze pads from a tin with a red cross of its lid.

The trio followed the movements of Doc's hands as

he tipped the bottle over and doused a pad, then wiped away the smidgen of blood on Sergeant Holt's butt cheek before placing and taping in place a clean pad over the nick.

"Now, I've cleaned your battle wound with an antiseptic. If the scratch becomes painful, if it festers, or if it seems to be infected, you need to come to the aid station right away." Doc grinned. "If it gets to that point, Henry, we may have to perform an amputation."

"You mean cut off my leg?"

"No. To cut off your dick, Dumbass. You ain't bad hurt. It's barely a scratch."

Then, Doc withdrew a syringe and a vial of amber liquid from another bag.

"What's that? What are you gonna do with that, Doc?"

"I'll give you a tetanus shot, just to be safe."

"Oh, no. Not a needle, Doc. Give me a pill. I don't like needles."

"Sergeant Holt, a bullet just stuck you, a little pinhead needle is nothing."

"It is for me, Doc. I might faint."

The medic paused and looked at Sergeant Tweed and Private Johnson. All three grinned.

"Well, if you do faint, you're in the right place for medical attention and resuscitation. If I don't give you this vaccine, you might get an infection that'll soon be followed by lockjaw and then death."

"Okay, but be gentle. It's gonna hurt, Doc."

As Doc touched an area with alcohol, Sergeant Henry Holt flinched as if shocked by a jolt of electricity.

But he did not faint or cry out as the needle immediately followed and punctured his buttock.

"You did good, Sergeant Holt. Not a whimper. Usually I give the tetanus shot in the shoulder, but since your ass was stickin in my face, it was the logical recipient of the Diphtheria and Pertussis ingredients."

"Now, you be sure to record this in the medical book, Doc," Sergeant Holt said. "I want the award of my Purple Heart to be documented."

"I'll take care of it, Sergeant Holt. No whiskey for twenty-four hours. You have a nice day, now."

The trio marched in single file from the aid station to the mess hall for chow. The three-course meal of boiled frankfurters, sauerkraut, and fried potatoes was unimpressive. After eating supper, Holt, Tweed, and Johnson tarried over hot coffee before returning to the business of soldiering.

Reinforced with the presence of his Platoon Sergeant, Private Johnson again confronted the NCO.

"You ripped me off, Sergeant Holt. I trusted you. You owe me ten dollars. I want my money."

"Henry, I'm surprised you would ask for money to make an enlistment."

"I thought Johnson would walk away, Boss. Hell, I never expected to see him again. Anyway, it was never about his money. I had to make my infantry quota for the month so I could receive the quarterly bonus. Johnson was the ticket I needed. I wanted him to sign the paper right then. I couldn't let him walk out the door. He was my guarantee of bonus money, Boss. Hell, he was gullible. He wanted to join the Army anyway, to get away from being a fry-cook at that cafe – Babe's something."

"Okay, I'm right here. You don't have to talk like I ain't sittin here. It's Sugar Babe's. Where's my ten dollars?"

"Okay, okay, look, I'm sorry. I'm not trying to ignore you, Johnson. I hope you can understand why I did it. My bonus was thirty dollars. I needed it to pay bills, to buy groceries to feed my family, and medicine for my sick wife and three kids."

That plea for sympathy played a chord with J J, particularly the need for Holt to feed the family and buy medicine. Private Johnson could relate to that.

It was obvious to Sergeant Tweed that Sergeant Henry Holt could sell a blue suit to a customer shopping for a red one. With his practiced speech, Tweed thought, he could have been a successful used car salesman – he knew the tune to play for a parrot to sing to.

"You never said you was married and had kids, Holt." Tweed's voice projected his suspicion.

Holt ignored Tweed, skirting the probe. "Anyway, Johnson, I don't have ten dollars on me right now. Wait till payday, eight days. I'll give it to you then. Okay?"

"Okay. What can I say? I got to trust you again. I'll be first in your line for payback."

"And, I'll be second in your line, Henry, if you don't pay this boy his money."

"Can I join you boys' knitting circle?"

"Hey, Red. Come on, have a seat," Sergeant Tweed said.

"I see you got their AKs."

"Yeah, Holt is going to put them away in his supply room. We may be able to arrange to take home a war trophy."

"We can take automatic rifles home, Sergeant Tweed?" J J asked.

"We can try. Lot of paperwork, but I think it can be done."

"You know, some guys do it piece by piece," Sergeant Holt said.

"Yeah, I've heard of that," Sergeant Hawk said. "A guy will tear it down, disassemble all the big parts and ship them home through the mail. All the pieces will fit in a C-Ration meal box or the big C-Ration case."

"How do you know all that, Red?" Platoon Sergeant Tweed asked.

"It's just gossip I heard around the campfire, Boss. Anyway, word came to us in the Captain's CP that you guys had a little action on the perimeter."

"Yeah, we did, Red. There were seven. Mickey and Billy got three and me and J J got four. Sergeant Raleigh Hawk, this is your new rifleman, Private James Jerome Johnson. J J, Sergeant Hawk is your Fire Team Leader and acting squad leader until Sergeant Dutchman returns from Malaysia."

Sergeant Hawk stuck out his hand. "Welcome to Vietnam, Private Johnson. Call me Red."

J J took the firm, confident grasp. "How you do, Red. They call me J J."

"Hey, Henry. How's it hangin?"

"I got shot, Red. In the butt."

"No, shit?"

"No, shit, Red," Platoon Sergeant Tweed laughed.

"Doc threw a needle in the cheek of his ass, too."

"He gave me a tetanus shot. It hurt worse than the bullet did."

"Henry was J J's recruiter, Red. Signed him up for infantry," Tweed said. "Made the boy pay ten dollars. Promised him the moon."

"Oh, Henry, you sneaky bastard. Did you do that to this young man?"

Sergeant Holt smiled. "I never thought I'd see him again. His ten dollars was not important. I needed to fill my infantry quota for my quarterly bonus. Anyway, I thought Johnson would be able to get the job in the Army he wanted to do."

"And what job did you pay this crook ten dollars for, J J? What do you want to do in this man's Army?" Sergeant Hawk asked.

"I want to be a cook, Sergeant Hawk. And he owes me ten bucks."

"In this fight we just had," Platoon Sergeant Tweed said, "J J is an infantryman, a natural born killer. He might change his mind and shed the white apron for a machine gun."

Red Hawk laughed. "Well, Boss, either way, we can still call him Cookie."

RECRUITER

When Sergeant Raleigh Hawk asked J J why he paid the "crook" ten dollars, there was a deeper reason he used that noun. Some on the firebase knew the tag was accurate. But Hawk applied "crook" as a mild accusation, said among soldiers over a cup of joe.

Henry Holt was a recruiter long before he performed recruiting duties for the United States Army.

Beginning in eighth grade, at age fourteen, Henry Holt played angles and planned schemes. He was a talented, suave, and practiced liar who easily talked his way into deals and out of dangerous dilemmas. As the go-to shark on the high school campus, he loaned small amounts of money at exorbitant payback rates to classmates, and even sometimes to their parents, as well as to teachers, and an assistant principal. He stole school equipment and athletic gear and sold the items at knock-down prices out of the trunk of his red-and-white, two-door, 1956 Chevrolet Impala. He began selling a few joints of weed brought in from California but later graduated to pushing heroin, angel dust, and a variety of exotic pills, including LSD. He was a polished cheater at poker and managed to persuade high rollers to use his set of bones in floating dice games. He acquired four girls from the senior class to provide services for members of the school's varsity football, basketball, baseball, and volleyball teams (or for anyone else who had cash or goods to barter), and later expanded his stable to seven to accommodate clients throughout the county.

He was adept at ducking responsibility, but the last straw forced the judge to confront his own private dealer. To avoid prosecution for the charge of running a prostitution ring in high school, the juvenile adjudicator offered Holt two options – go to jail for three years or join a military service. Henry selected the Army.

Because he was able to manipulate the system and corrupt his supervisors, he received choice assignments and quick promotions. It was a fact that Sergeant Henry Holt volunteered for combat duty to avoid a court-martial for blackmail and extortion.

While in transit to Vietnam, Holt altered documents in his personnel folder and added Unit Supply Specialist, a 92-Y MOS, to his job experience. At Long Bien, Sandra and Sergeant Kane focused on the 92-Y. To clear a longstanding requisition, they cut orders for Sergeant Holt to report to Troop D as Supply Sergeant.

Drawn in and impressed during their interviews with him, First Sergeant Morris, Lieutenant Webb, the Executive Officer, and the Troop Commander, Captain Thompson, added to his portfolio. They gave Holt the responsibility to oversee and supervise Vietnamese laborers and laundresses who worked in the troop area. They created a kingdom for a monster to rule.

From his castle – the supply bunker – Sergeant Henry Holt wielded great authority, including the power of life and death. Unknowingly, the troop leadership reached a decision that would turn out to be a deadly mistake.

It was not his desire or intention to reimburse the ten dollars J J gave him. On that day, in his office on Ferdinand Avenue, he determined J J was a gullible simpleton and swindling him out of ten dollars was a deserved gesture – a lesson in life.

By late evening, word had spread on Linebacker that Holt had seven AK-47s – three with the swing bayonet still attached, five VC bandoliers with more than 300 rounds of 7.62x39 ammunition, ten AK magazines, and 15 Chicom grenades in his supply room. Souvenir hunters put out feelers and intermediaries floated by to see how Sergeant Holt was holding up from his battle wound.

"Yeah, they came through the wire like shit through a goose. I just happened to be on the road at the right time. I was the only one there to help because the guys on the fighting bunker only got the three outside the wire. Otherwise, they woulda had the whole firebase and could of killed a lot of my boys. It was fierce fighting, I tell you. I killed two of the little bastards with my bare hands."

"But I heard you got shot in the butt, Henry. If you was fightin all them bastards face on, how did you get hit in the butt?" the visitor prompted.

"Well, they shot at me with their AKs and missed. One of the bullets went past me, hit the tongue of the water trailer, and ricocheted back. They talked about the possibility of amputatin my leg, but I wouldn't let em. I told em I was tough enough to stand the pain, for them to go ahead and dig the bullet out. It was pretty deep. And I had lost a lot of blood. But I refused a transfusion, so they gave me a .45 caliber cartridge to bite down on and scraped the bullet out with a bayonet. After Doc stuck a band-aid on, I jumped right up, took an aspirin, and returned to duty. Captain wanted to put me in for a decoration, a Silver Star or a Distinguished Service Cross."

"Wow, a DSC. That's right behind the Medal of Honor."

"Yeah, well, I deserve it. I probably saved a hundred lives here on Linebacker. If I hadn't killed them all, no telling what woulda happened. But you know what?"

"No, what?"

"I turned him down. I said to the Captain, Capn, I was just being a combat soljer, just doin the job the Army pays me for. I don't need or want a medal."

"Well, that's a hell of a war story," the visitor said. "You are a hero, a brave hero, Sergeant Holt."

There was a pause before the visitor continued. Now, the primary purpose of the visit was about to be revealed.

"Word is, Henry, you killed all of them VC and captured seven AK-47s."

Holt's antenna raised, he knew business was at hand.

"Yeah, I got them in the back, in storage, locked up for safe keeping in one of my Conex containers. You know, they'd make great souvenirs if anyone was interested in that kind of thing."

"Well, just so happens I know a couple of friends who might be interested in acquiring a war trophy."

"I see. Just how interested are these friends of yours?"

"They're interested enough to send me over here to talk about the possibility of making a deal, to come to an understanding if you know what I mean, Henry."

"I see. Yes, I understand. I know what you mean. You do know these are AK-47s, they're automatic rifles. They're not squirrel huntin .22s. I risked my life to capture these rare weapons. You can't just walk into a gun store in Jackson and get one of these. They're pretty valuable."

"How valuable, do you think?"

"Gotta be seven thousand dollars for the bundle. For all seven and the accessories."

"I don't think my friends are interested in the bundle. What would be the breakdown?"

"It depends on whether we're talking about one item or several?"

"My friends are thinking in terms of two AKs with the swing bayonets attached, two bandoliers, and four magazines full of ammo."

"Well, you know, a AK magazine holds thirty cartridges, so that'd be a hunnert and twenty rounds."

"Yeah, that's what my friends figured."

"Well, I think a nice round figure would be two thousand dollars for that bundle."

"Hum, I think my friends were leaning more toward a figure of seven hundred, like three-fifty a piece."

"Well, your friends got to understand I risked my life and spilt blood for these valuable items. Seven hundred is not even in the ballpark."

"How about a thousand?"

"More like seventeen-fifty."

"Fifteen hundred?"

"I think you can tell your friends they've just captured the perfect war trophies."

"They'll probably ask me to return tomorrow about 1500 hours to thank you."

"I'll be here tomorrow at three, waiting for you. I'll have the items laid out on a blanket so anybody can come by to see what they look like and how they operate."

At 0900 hours, First Sergeant Morris formed the troop on the road in front of the Command Post, the HQ bunker.

"Private James Jerome Johnson, front and center," Top ordered.

Johnson stepped back out of ranks, did a left face, and double-timed to a position in front of his First Sergeant.

Top performed an about face, saluted the troop commander and reported.

"Private Johnson is present as ordered, Sir."

Thompson returned the salute. "Take you post, First Sergeant."

Morris took four steps and stood on Captain Thompson's left. Specialist Vannoy moved into position next to Morris.

With Top repositioned, Private Johnson now stood at stiff attention before his Troop Commander.

Among more than a hundred troopers in formation, gathered for the ceremony, were Lieutenant Versailles, Johnson's platoon leader, Platoon Sergeant Tweed, and Fire Team Leader Sergeant Raleigh Hawk.

"I think you set a record, Private Johnson," Captain Thompson announced. "After being in the troop for less than four hours, you earned your Combat Infantry Badge for participating in a hostile action with the enemy. It is my honor and privilege to pin this award on your chest."

Vannoy handed a small award case to Morris who opened it for the Troop Commander.

Thompson lifted the blue badge out of the case, removed the two clasps from the pins, stuck the CIB in place on the left pocket flap of Johnson's jungle fatigue shirt, and attached the catches to the pin tips. He stepped back and saluted.

"Congratulations, J J, you are a combat infantryman."

Johnson returned his Troop Commander's salute and took his Captain's hand in a congratulatory handshake. "Thank you, Sir."

"Next, we all want to recognize your bravery in battle."

Vannoy handed an opened award case and held it for Thompson who lifted out the Bronze Star Medal with a "V" device attached and paused.

Top read the six sentences in the citation citing J J's valorous actions.

The CO removed the clasps and pinned the decoration on Johnson's shirt pocket flap, placing it below the CIB.

Thompson stepped back and saluted again.

Johnson returned the salutation and shook his Captain's hand again.

"Okay, there's one more," Captain Thompson announced.

Top moved to stand on Johnson's left, and the Troop Commander positioned himself on the soldier's right.

Vannoy stepped in front of Johnson and handed stripes and safety pins to the First Sergeant and to the Captain.

As they attached the chevrons to his sleeves Thompson proclaimed, "It is my privilege to present this impact promotion to Corporal, thirteen months early and a jump of two pay grades. Congratulations, Corporal Johnson."

"Thank you, Sir," Johnson responded.

"First Sergeant, have the Troop carry on," the Commanding Officer ordered.

A few days later, Mai Li came to the opening of the supply room bunker but did not enter. Nguyen Mai Li was Eurasian, but her features and manners were Vietnamese. Her father was a French soldier; her mother Vietnamese. Abandoned when the French government withdrew its forces from Vietnam, Mai Li and her mother took refuge in the Sông Bé orphanage run by nuns. Her mother worked for Mother Clarice, and it was there Mai Li learned to read, write, and speak French and English.

Holt stood behind a makeshift counter filling in a

requisition form to order four dozen Claymore mines. When he looked up, Mai Li bowed.

"What do you want, Mai Li?" Holt demanded. His voice was stern, threatening.

She bowed again before she spoke. After all, Sergeant Holt was her supervisor. "Have you seen my little Kim? She is missing."

"She is here, with me. You should not leave her alone on the firebase. Terrible things could happen to such a sweet, pretty, little girl. Shame on you, Mai Li. You did not pay attention to your child. I found her in the storage bin out back."

"I am sorry, Sergeant Holt. Thank you for helping and protecting my Kim. Please let her come with me?"

This was not a new occurrence for Holt. He often picked up children who wandered while their father or mother worked on the firebase. Holt found the children useful as a bargaining chip to extort favors. He had held children hostage before, to persuade mothers to accept his requests – a form of human trafficking, prostitution. This was the first time Mai Li and Kim experienced his tactic, although he had approached Mai Li before.

Twice, Holt had used children to entice fathers to accommodate a couple of soldiers who paid good money for homosexual encounters, but the usual transaction was for young women.

Permitted access to the firebase, single women and men, as well as children's mothers and fathers, earned money working as laborers, tailors, and laundresses. That was Mai Li's job in the Troop area. It was her responsibility to enter sleeping bunkers and collect laundry bags left by soldiers. She walked to the laundry point with the bags of dirty clothes piled on a two-wheeled cart. With soap furnished by Sergeant Holt, she washed soldiers' fatigues, socks, and underwear in water that caused the clothing to smell like dead fish. She stitched torn clothing and sewed on nametags and stripes.

Men hauled trash to the burn pile, erected or broke down tents, filled sandbags, toted supplies and materiel for soldiers, worked with mechanics as tool, oil, and lubrication handlers or assistants, and worked in mess halls. The men could not handle food or water in kitchens. In supply rooms, weapons and ammunition were off limits.

Children, aged four to twelve, could accompany and assist parents. Babies and toddlers aged three and under, could not come on the firebase.

Little Kim appeared at the edge of the counter. Fear was in her black, wide eyes and round face. She had been crying. A rope was around her small neck, the other end wound around Holt's wrist.

"Please do not hurt my little girl, Sergeant Holt."

"Your baby is not hurt yet, Mai Li. But before I let her go, I want you to make a promise."

"Mama, Mama," Kim cried. She took two steps toward Mai Li.

Holt jerked the rope and Kim fell back against the front base of the counter. When the child stood up, Holt pulled on the rope until Kim's back was pinned against the counter wall. He kept pulling until the little girl was on tiptoes. She gasped for air.

"Please. Please, Sergeant Holt," Mai Li pleaded.

"Let her go."

Holt released tension on the rope. "All I want you to do, Mai Li, is make a promise."

Mai Li knew what Holt wanted her to promise. He had asked three times before, and she had refused. He never proposed they have sex; instead, he wanted her to have sex with a sergeant in the quartermaster company at the other end of the firebase.

Mai Li would do anything to protect her child. This time, with a rope around Kim's neck, Mai Li knew she had no choice but to do Sergeant Holt's bidding.

"What must I promise?"

"Come here at four tomorrow." Holt held up four fingers. "You will meet a man who wants to give you a necklace. You will go with him back there." Holt jerked a thumb toward the back part of the bunker. "While this man gives you the necklace, I will keep Kim in here. Do you understand?"

Mai Li hesitated. How could she refuse and be sure Kim would be safe. She knew there was no necklace. It was all about sex. She was certain the man paid Holt to procure her for sex.

"I do not want a necklace."

Holt jerked the rope and Kim screamed as she fell backward and slammed against the counter wall again.

"Mama! Mama!" Kim cried out and shook her head. The taut rope made her gag.

Holt twisted his hand and wrapped the rope around his wrist and forearm. He gripped the rope between his fingers and pulled Kim up. Her feet were off the floor of the bunker.

"STOP! STOP!" Mai Li cried. "Do not hurt my

baby."

Holt released tension on the rope and Kim dropped. She lay in a fetal position, coughing, gasping for air.

"All I asked you to do, Mai Li, is make a promise to come here tomorrow. A man wants to give you a necklace."

"My husband is fighting the VC with the Americans. He thinks I am safe, working on a camp with Americans. How can you treat us this way?"

"That's not a promise, Mai Li." Holt wrapped the rope with another twist of his wrist.

"STOP! Please stop," Mai Li cried. "I promise. I promise. Give me my baby."

Holt unwound the rope from his arm and tossed his end toward Mai Li.

She rushed to Kim, removed the rope and hugged her daughter.

"Tomorrow at four. Bring Kim with you."

Mai Li stared at Holt, the desire for brutal revenge burned in her heart. "You hurt my baby, Sergeant Holt."

"She'll live, Mai Li. Both of you will live." Holt leaned on the counter and smiled. "But if you do not come with Kim tomorrow, Mai Li, I will kill you both."

Sergeant Hawk, Mickey, Billy, Jinks, and J J were the Alpha Fire Team for the third platoon infantry squad. All five lived in the sleeping bunker. J J had met his roomies the night after the fight. Boss Tweed gave a thorough orientation, and J J had already pulled a day and night shift with Mickey in the fighting bunker. There was no jealousy toward J J's spot promotion to Corporal. His actions in battle spoke volumes to the hardened veterans. If anything, they admired his guts and grit. J J was the youngster in Alpha team.

They had been busy and had yet to sit and talk about how they came to be in the Army. Now, while there was no actual campfire, they sat around, talking, and smoking.

Lieutenant Versailles and Platoon Sergeant Tweed entered the bunker and interrupted the beginning of an old-fashioned bull-shit session.

"Uh-oh," Jenkins said. "Here comes trouble."

"Naw, no trouble Jinks," Lieutenant Versailles said. "I bring good news."

"We got a night mission for your team, Red. An ambush," Boss Tweed said.

"Boss likes to call it an ambush, Red, but it's really an LP. At the footbridge across the creek on the northeast side of the mountain," Lieutenant Versailles said.

"Yes, Sir, I know where it is. We were out there eighteen days ago. We killed three."

"Well, Brigade S-2 asked Captain Thompson if he would take a look again. The intelligence gathered leans toward enemy movement across the bridge at night. Informants tell Brigade that sapper teams might be using the footbridge to bring explosives over to stockpile for an attack on the Province Chief's headquarters in Sông Bé," Lieutenant Versailles explained. "Captain Thompson accepted the mission from Brigade and asked me to pick a small team to take care of business. We need to do a recon, to know what's going on. So, Red, how about it, do you want to take your team out for an overnight excursion?"

"Yes, Sir," Red said. "My team would be happy to take this mission, Lieutenant. Like Paladin, the soldier of fortune, we've got the guns and we will travel."

PATHS

Sprawled over eight acres of red dirt, in the center of the Republic of Vietnam, sat Fire Support Base Linebacker. Its purpose was to house the headquarters of cavalry, artillery, and infantry units whose combat mission was to find, fix, and destroy regional Viet Cong cadres and regiments of North Vietnam Army forces flowing out of Cambodia.

Infantry companies worked in jungles, conducting search and destroy missions. Gallant infantry soldiers – members of the Queen of Battle – were not interested in winning the hearts and minds of Vietnamese.

Two artillery batteries provided fire support from Linebacker with six 1-0-5mm howitzers and six 1-5-5mm cannons. These dauntless long-range shooters – members of the King of Battle – were adroit at planting pinpoint pain into plain pajama pockets.

Delta's Devils sometimes provided security and protection for the National and Provincial police who set up checkpoints to search for deserters, bandits, bad-guys, and contraband. But the Troop's real work was on the trails, roads, highways, bridges, and waterways in Phuoc Long Province. NVA and VC forces traveled toward Saigon using these various paths.

East-west road 3-10 – from Tuy Hoa, the South China Sea coastal city – ran west 400 kilometers across the Sông Bé River through the village of Sông Bé, intersected north-south road 3-11 in Phuoc Binh, and ended at the Cambodian border west of Tay Ninh. This asphalt thoroughfare was 200 meters south of Linebacker and lay between the military camp and the ancient volcano, Nui Ba Ra.

North-south road 3-11 ran from Phuoc Binh north for 40 kilometers to the Cambodian border and south for 40 kilometers to the national highway QL-14. 3-11 and QL-14 were vulnerable high-speed military avenues of approach into the capital city of South Vietnam.

Linebacker lay between Phuoc Binh and Sông Bé. Phuoc Binh was four kilometers west of the main gate, Sông Bé six kilometers east. Phuoc Binh and Sông Bé were equal in size and population – two thousand souls called each village home.

One kilometer farther east of Sông Bé, was the north-south Sông Bé River. A tall, 90-meter long vehicular bridge crossed over the river east of the village. In their movement south, NVA and VC units commandeered Sampans and smaller fishing vessels to cruise along the Sông Bé River to skirt American infantry companies or the cavalry troop.

Dak Toll was a deep, wide creek that carried runoff from Nui Ba Ra east into the river. Villagers, local merchants, farmers, and peasants used the 60-meter long footbridge that crossed Dak Toll. VC used it too, to bring supplies and food to NVA forces hiding in the thick jungle foliage at the base of the mountain in their pause while moving south.

Often, infantry squads or fire teams set up day and night ambushes at the footbridge to interdict enemy traffic. Now, intelligence revealed VC was using that path to bring ammunition and explosives across the footbridge to stockpile in Sông Bé for an attack on the Phuoc Long Province Chief's headquarters.

Sergeant Hawk's fire team sat on the floor of the bunker huddled around the map sheet. Except for Corporal Johnson, Hawk's tactical briefing covered details they'd all heard and practiced. One point concerned Johnson, but he kept quiet about it. After all, he reasoned, the team had conducted operations, even ambushes, at the footbridge before. Sergeant Hawk had said so. But still, to divide a small combat force of five into two groups and place only two guys at one end of the footbridge didn't seem like a sound tactical plan.

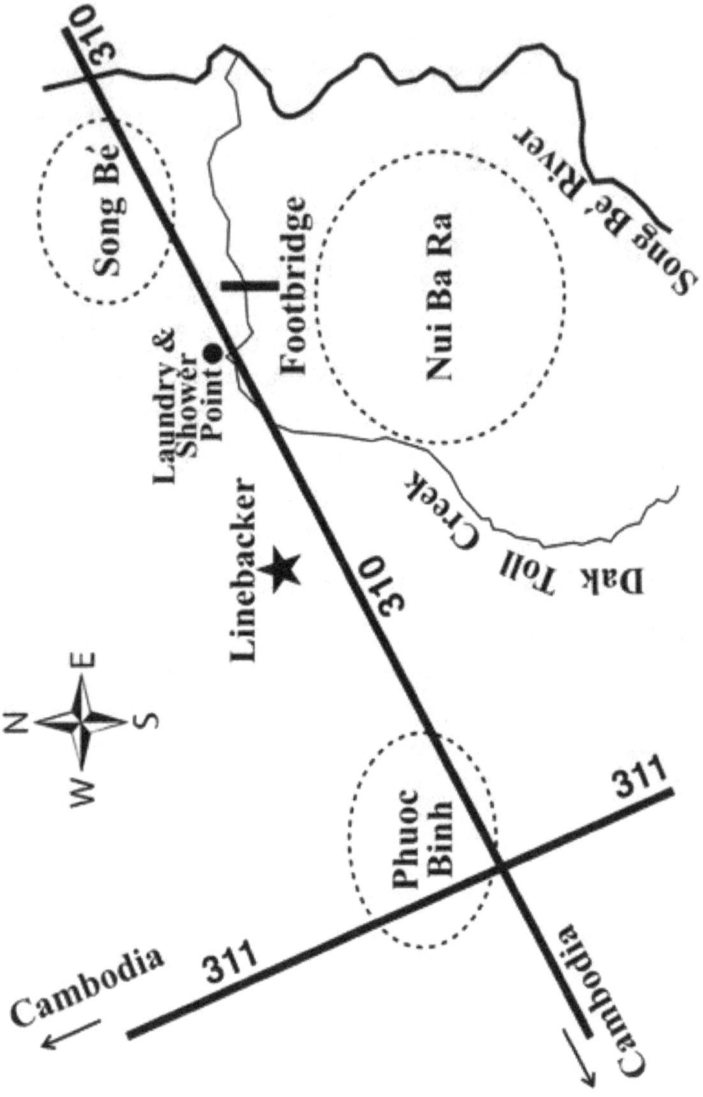
310
Song Bé River
Song Bé
Footbridge
Nui Ba Ra
Laundry & Shower Point
Linebacker
Dak Toll Creek
310
E
N
S
W
Phuoc Binh
311
311
Cambodia
Cambodia

"What are your concerns?" Sergeant Hawk asked.

Nobody spoke. Johnson held his apprehension.

"Okay, it's 1800. At 1845, we'll mount the scout jeeps for the ride to the shower point. We'll get off there, slip away, and follow the creek to the footbridge. So, do one last check of equipment and relax for the next few minutes. Any questions?"

The leader looked at his team's faces. There was a long pause. It was a silent space for anyone to fill.

In response to Hawk's invitation, PFC Fowler posed his question. "Where you from, J J?"

"Lake Oswego."

"Where's that?" Billy asked.

"Oregon. About ten miles southeast of Portland."

"I been to the Pacific Northwest," Fowler said. "Rained a lot."

Johnson laughed. "It still does. In season. But when the sun is shining and you see stark-white snow on Mount Hood, Saint Helens, Adams, and Mount Jefferson you can't remember when it rained last. I love Oregon. It's beautiful country."

"We gonna get wet tonight, Boys," Hawk laughed. "If we didn't have light from Sông Bé off the clouds, it'd be darker than tar out there."

"In the rain? We got to do this job in the rain?" Billy complained.

"Since when are you bothered by a little moisture, Billy," Jinks laughed. "You the one who had the bright idea to wash our truck while it was pouring. Naked."

"I've even seen Billy eatin his C-Ration just sittin in the rain. Didn't even put a poncho over his head to keep water outta his Ham and Lima Beans," Red laughed.

"What'd you do before you joined the Army, J J?" Jinks asked.

"I was a cook at Sugar Babe's. Mr. Dickerson, he's the owner, has three Sugar Babe's. I was at the one on Ferdinand Avenue."

"J J paid Holt ten dollars to enlist as a cook," Red Hawk revealed.

"No shit?" Mickey's emphasis was pointed.

"No shit, Sherlock," Hawk nodded.

"Our Holt? Sergeant Holt, the new supply sergeant?" Fowler asked.

"One and the same," Red said.

There was a pause. The four of them looked at Johnson. They waited.

J J shrugged. "What?"

"You paid that sneaky bastard ten dollars to join the Army?" Jinks asked.

"No, Jinks. I paid him to be a cook in the Army. Hey, look, this mule has been beat enough, okay? I didn't know better, I thought he would do the right thing for me. I trusted him. I want to be a cook."

"But you infantry, J J. You've already killed a gook, at close range, with a bayonet, for Chrissakes. The Captain pinned on your CIB three days ago and you ain't even fired a shot in anger," Billy said. "You're a fighter like us, you ain't no Cookie."

"J J, Holt ain't done the right thing since he's been here, and probably ain't never done the right thing for nobody except hisself," Fowler said.

"Scuttlebutt is he's got a couple of women workin in the back of his supply room providing services to payin customers," Jinks said. "When I was down at the shower point a couple of days ago, one of the quartermaster guys told me one of our sergeants had a couple of laundry women working as whores there too. He recognized the shoulder patch."

"Well, that's gotta be Holt," Red said. "I'm surprised Top or Lieutenant Webb don't know about the goings-on."

"Maybe they don't," J J offered.

They looked at him as if he had come from another planet. Surely, each of them reasoned, the Troop leadership knew about Henry Holt's activities.

"Okay," Sergeant Hawk broke the silence. "It's show time. Let's go play soldier. Time to get our guns and travel."

"What was that guy's name who played Paddlin on TV?" Fowler asked.

"It was Paladin, Mickey. Jack Paladin. Not Paddlin. His name is Richard Boone," J J said.

"What was that chess piece on his calling card?" Fowler asked.

"It was a horse," Billy answered.

"The chess piece was a Knight, Billy. Palaldin was a 'knight without armor'," Sergeant Hawk clarified. "I loved that show and Boone. He played in a lot of westerns, was always the bad-guy. Now, let's go take care of Army business, let's go look for some of our bad-guys."

It was twilight when the four gun jeeps from the third platoon cavalry scout squad brought the five-member infantry fire team to the shower and laundry point at the 3-10 bridge over Dak Toll creek. The surreptitious move would play out with the appearance of soldiers coming to clean their vehicles. When the jeeps stopped at the wash point, at the creek's edge, everyone dismounted. Few onlookers paid attention, but some thought it unusual the contingent came at the late hour to wash jeeps. More strange was small amounts of water lifted with cupped hands and splashed on the front wheels of the jeeps. Washed in less than fifteen minutes, but with five fewer soldiers on board, the jeeps were back on 3-10 headed to Linebacker. The scouts would return at 0800 the next morning for their infantry brothers and pick up Sergeant Hawk's fire team.

The team slipped away from the shower point one-by-one and regrouped as planned a hundred meters down the creek. There, they waited for nightfall.

At 2200 hours, they formed up in tactical order and marched to the bridge. Billy led, armed with his M-79 Grenade Launcher and a .45 caliber pistol, followed by Sergeant Hawk with a rifle and a PRC-25 radio in a harness on his back. Jinks and J J with their rifles, and Mickey with his M60 machine gun and a pistol, trailed their leader. Each of them had four grenades, two hand flares, a flashlight with a red lens filter, and their bayonet.

The drizzle started as they reached the north end of the footbridge. With town lights reflecting off low clouds, J J could see the bridge and looked down its length. Even in this setting, he thought, it is a picturesque structure. While the path and passageway were not wide enough for cars and trucks, they easily could accommodate motorbikes, scooters, and bicycles. A pedicab was possible but would be a tight fit. The surface, the platform, was wooden. Its waist-high walls were bamboo stalks. Bamboo string secured the stalks on both sides to a two-inch nautical rope that served as a handrail. J J could not see or imagine the type of stanchion support, but as he stepped on behind Jinks to cross the bridge, it was solid.

Red, Billy, and Mickey set up on the north side with Jinks and J J on the south. They did not bother to dig holes since their mission was to gather intelligence, information, not an ambush. They were prepared but did not expect a fight. They were there to watch, listen, and assess the situation. Within seconds of the fire team's settling, in a prone position two meters off the path, clouds opened and sprinkle turned into a downpour. J J shivered, chilled by the sudden coolness.

Their legs, hips, arms, elbows, and shoulders touched.

"You okay?" Jinks whispered.

"Yeah, just felt a chill is all. I'm okay," J J whispered.

Whispering was not entirely safe lying alongside a well-trodden trail, but soldiers who are foxhole buddies have difficulty keeping quiet. Whispering was the next best thing to talking – given their circumstances.

"Yeah, I felt you shakin," Jinks whispered.

"How long before they come by, you think?" J J whispered.

"Last I looked, it was almost eleven-thirty. There probably won't be any activity for another three hours.

Three or four in the morning."

"How do you know that?"

"I been on a couple of night ambushes. That's just the way it is. I guess Charlie thinks nobody'll be on the paths that late – or that early of a morning."

There was a long pause before J J broke the silence.

"I heard you was helping write a citation for a guy named Rose?"

"He was my buddy. Shiloh Rose. Everybody called him Rosey. A great guy. Sniper hit him in the chest. We was over there in the rubber plantation. He died in my arms."

"He was new over here?"

"We came over together. We'd been in the Mojave Desert and when we got back to Fort Campbell we both had orders to ship out. We pleaded the buddy-system at Long Bien."

"That's what Deak did for me when we were at Long Bien."

"Who's Deak?"

"Sergeant Burl Deakins. He's a squad leader in Hotel Company there at Linebacker. He told the clerks we was cousins and wanted to be together."

"But he's in the infantry company and you're in the cavalry."

"Yeah, but we're both on Linebacker. And who knows, maybe we'll end up in the same outfit."

"Yeah. I think having a buddy is important."

"You was in the Mojave, in California?"

"Yeah, that's the one. After the training exercise, we went into Las Vegas on pass. Had a ball. Won a ton of money, shootin dice. Rosey was hotter than a three-dollar pistol. But we lost it all, gave it all back to the casino. When we got back to Nellis, Sergeant Tyson, our squad leader, put us on KP."

Jinks paused.

"How come you wanna be a cook, J J?"

"I like preparing food for people. When they eat what I fix and it makes them happy, it makes me feel good. I don't know, I think it gives me satisfaction to know I did something somebody appreciated. Oh, shit. MOVEMENT."

A snake slithered along, in the center of the path, toward them. Even in the downpour, J J saw it was a long, huge, fat bugger. In faint light, the glistening sheen on its blackness was mesmerizing. J J watched and stiffened as it came closer. He realized his shoulders were aching.

"Oh, shit. Be still, J J."

"I don't like snakes."

"Neither do I, J J. I think that's a fucking cobra."

"Will he attack us?"

"Try to be still, maybe he'll just go on by."

But Mr. Snake didn't. Sensing quarry, the cobra paused – squarely in front of this concerned duo. A skinny tongue darted from its flat mouth, searching, detecting the warmth from their hunkered and scrunched bodies.

The cobra twisted, turned, and slid around to face its prey. Two meters off the path was not a lot of distance. J J was not an expert in determining lengths of serpents, but he surmised this one could reach them with one thrusting leap.

Both held their breaths. Jinks, in an ever so slow movement, slid his bayonet out of its scabbard.

The cobra raised, coiled in anticipation, and spread the skin behind its head to form a hood.

Blood rushed with expectancy, and J J's heart pounded preparing his body to fight or flee. He gripped his rifle, fearing he would lose control and wave his hand at the reptile to shoo it away. Before striking, it swung its upper body and fanned head to the left, lowered to the path, turned, and slithered off, away from J J and Jinks. The cobra had felt or heard the approaching cadre before its quarry did.

There were four, ten meters away, scurrying along the path toward Jinks and J J. In ten seconds, they came abreast. J J saw each had a bamboo pole across a shoulder. Two large baskets hung from both ends of the carry rod. Their bodies were unyielding with the weight, the baskets did not bounce as their legs whisked past in a fast pace. The two riflemen watched the VC enter the bridge and in unison turned to look down the trail to see if others followed.

Mickey's machine gun roared.

"He's coming your way, Jinks!" Red shouted. "He's coming your way!"

The enemy soldier, no longer toting baskets, came running down the bridge toward them. Jinks got up and raised his rifle. He snapped off four quick shots and the cadre dropped at the exit of the footbridge.

Rifle at the ready, J J knelt beside Jinks. But the action was over.

"You stay here, J J. Watch down the trail. If you see movement, anything, shoot it down. I'm gonna go up the bridge to help Red hustle up the bad-guys Mickey cut down."

"You gonna leave me here?"

"I'm not gonna leave you. I'll be on the bridge. You're our rear-guard, rear security. You'll be okay. Shoot anything that moves. As soon as we take care of these guys, I'll call you. With all this gunfire there's no sense being quiet now. Be cool."

"HE'S DOWN," Red screamed. "BILLY"S DOWN. HE'S BEEN HIT."

"YOU SHOT BILLY," Mickey Fowler hollered.

"Oh, my God," Jinks exhaled in a loud whisper.

He jabbed the muzzle of his rifle toward their yelling and looked down at J J.

"I killed Billy."

INVESTIGATION

As abrupt as turning off a faucet, the rain stopped. Even with red lenses on their flashlights, it was easy for the four of them to see where the bullet struck Billy's throat.

He lay on his back, gasping. Pooling blood behind his neck streamed away in thin rivulets with rainwater, toward the edge of the path. Billy's eyes were open, darting, pleading, searching, begging for their, and God's, help. When he tried to speak, blood mist spouted and sprinkled on his wet face.

Jinks could not stop crying. He knelt beside Billy.

"My, God, oh sweet Jesus, my God, what have I done to you, Billy. Please forgive me, oh sweet Jesus." Jinks rocked back and forth. He put his arm under Billy's head to raise it and J J thought Jinks kissed Billy's forehead.

Mickey Fowler opened the bandage pouch attached to Billy's web belt. He withdrew and ripped open the plastic packet, unraveled the bandage, and placed it under Billy's neck over the gaping hole of the bullet exit wound.

"Momma," Billy managed to whisper. "Ma . . .

Momma. Tell . . . tell . . . tell my Momma."

Red knelt at Billy's head. "I called Dustoff, Billy. Hang in there, Billy. The chopper'll be here in a minute. It's on the way. We gonna take you out. You gonna be okay, Billy."

Trapped, J J stood immobile, in place, like a granite monolith. He felt helpless. In the aftermath of cool rain, the warmth of deep anguish flushed his neck and cheeks. He wanted to reach out, take Billy in his arms, and make it all better. It was like a slow motion replay for him. Nothing seemed in rhythm, not his heartbeats, breathing, swallowing, or eye blinks. The ringing in his ears would not cease. All he could do was stare at Billy's eyes and the mortal wound. His mind raced. He knew he was looking at dying and could not look away.

Mickey pulled his own aid bandage and placed it over the bullet entrance hole in Billy's throat.

In the distance, the wop-wop-wop-wop-wop was heavy in humid air.

As he walked down the path, Red unscrewed the face of his flashlight, placed the red lens in his pocket, replaced the head, aimed it toward the chopper noise, and turned the white light on. The moment he did that, the Huey Med-Evac pilot turned on the bird's landing lights and illuminated Red in glaring whiteness. There was not enough clearance on the path for the chopper, so the pilot held the aircraft in a steady hover as the crew chief lowered the metal basket for Billy.

Red gave a thumbs up and turned away to help lift and carry Billy to the patient litter.

All the while, J J held his light on Billy's chin.

"He's dead," J J said. "Billy is dead."

"You son-of-a-bitch." Mickey's voice was flat, with deep emotion. "Jinks, you son-of-a-bitch, you killed Billy."

"No, no, no, no, no," Jinks whispered. "Oh, please God, please don't take Billy. I didn't mean to. I swear I didn't mean to."

"I know you didn't mean to, Jinks," Red said. "But it's done. There ain't nothing we can do about what's done. Let's get Billy on the bird so they can take him home to his Momma."

Even while they struggled to move down the path with Billy's body, all J J could think of was what Billy's family, his mother, would experience in a few hours.

Basket hoisted, with Billy aboard, the pilot switched the spotlight off and revved the turbines. With its green and red lights winking, the helicopter lifted, nosed over, and slipped toward Saigon, headed for the Sixty-Second Field Hospital and Graves Registration, forty minutes away.

Mickey picked up Billy's grenade launcher and J J retrieved Billy's blood splattered helmet.

"Okay, when I called for the Dustoff I reported our contact," Red said. "So, let's see what we can find on these guys and then dump them in the creek. After that we'll head to the house."

They did not find documents on the four bodies. They did not find weapons lying on the footbridge. They did not find grenades, explosives, or satchel charges. They did not find anything to indicate the four were an enemy, VC cadre.

They did find two baskets full of freshly picked

cucumbers, two baskets of fresh broccoli, two baskets of small, green, bitter melons, and two baskets of spinach.

"Jesus Christ, Red, we killed four innocent farmers bringing wares to market in Sông Bé," Jinks said.

Red ignored Jinks' assessment. "Okay, we gotta dump all this."

"These guys are farmers, Red," Jinks said. "We killed innocent people."

"Fuck em," Mickey spat. "They probably VC sympathizers, anyway."

"We can't just throw them in the creek, Red," Jinks said. "That's not right. We got to do the right thing and report this."

"Well, smart ass, what do you suggest? That we call another helicopter and bring them home in style?"

"I didn't think of that, but that might be the right thing to do."

"I reported the contact so as far as headquarters is concerned, we killed bad guys."

"I've killed two innocent people, Red. I killed a farmer and I killed Billy. We got to make another report," Jinks lamented.

"We ain't gonna do no such thing. You hear me. Do all of you hear me?" Red's anger was sharp and dangerous. "Answer me, all of you. We ain't gonna report this. What we are gonna report is we was in a firefight with four VC and Billy was killed in action. We killed the gooks and dumped them in the creek."

"I think Jinks is right, Red," J J said. "What about weapons, ammunition, documents, explosives?"

"What about it?" Red demanded. His voice was

threatening.

"If we killed enemy soldiers why didn't we bring their weapons and stuff back with us?"

"I'll handle that if it comes up, don't you worry about it." Red paused. "Do you hear me, Cookie?"

"Yes, Sir. I hear you," J J answered.

The bodies and veggies went over the side of the footbridge and splashed into Dak Toll creek.

The cavalry troop infantry fire team, minus Private First Class William A. Butler, marched toward the laundry and shower point to rendezvous with the scout jeeps for a return ride to Linebacker.

As Captain Thompson entered the Brigade Headquarters bunker, he acknowledged Lieutenant Colonel Tracy Tolon, the infantry battalion commander, and noted a short, fat Vietnamese officer who boasted three dozen ribbons on his khaki shirt. The Troop Commander saluted and reported to Colonel Eli Carson, the Brigade Commander.

Colonel Carson smartly returned the salute. He was a gaunt, tall man with prematurely white hair. His white eyebrows accented dark, sunken eyes which peered through wire-framed, rimless glasses. His lit Chesterfield cigarette was stuck in a silver holder which he clamped between his yellow teeth.

With his cigarette holder, the image of Colonel Carson reminded Thompson of movies and photographs he'd seen of President Roosevelt.

Colonel Tolon's skin was dark brown from all the time he spent under the sun leading his battalion. He was husky and stout; it was easy to conjure an icon of a pro-football middle linebacker. He was an affable personality, and all spoke of him with endearment. He was a soldier's soldier, and his soldiers loved him. Colonel Tolon was a mentor to Captain Thompson.

Colonel Carson made the official overture. "Captain Thompson, I'd like to introduce Colonel Phan Van Minh, the Phuoc Long Province Chief. Colonel Phan, Captain Thompson is Cavalry Troop Commander."

The Troop Commander mentally registered Colonel Carson's unusual introduction etiquette.

Captain Thompson stuck out his hand, and Colonel Phan shook it.

"Please have a seat, be at ease," Colonel Carson said. "Jerry, I've asked you to this meeting because Colonel Phan brings disturbing information that may involve some of your soldiers."

Without speaking further the Brigade Commander nodded at the Province Chief.

"Captain Thompson, yesterday one of my police patrols found the bodies of four farmers in the creek at the footbridge. Three had been shot by many bullets, like a machine gun. The fourth had one bullet through his left eye."

Colonel Phan spoke with the slightest accent, not Vietnamese but midwestern.

"Scattered in the creek and along the bank under the footbridge were their baskets and the vegetables they were bringing to the open market in Sông Bé. My police superintendent does not believe these four were killed by Viet Cong."

"Jerry, we believe the VC would have gathered up all the food," Colonel Tolon interjected.

"The Viet Cong also would have taken the wedding rings and watches these men were wearing," Colonel Phan continued. "Two of the farmers wore cheap watches, the VC would have taken them to use for trading or to sell."

Colonel Phan paused.

"You had an operation out that way the other night, Jerry," Colonel Carson said.

"Yes, Sir. A five-man team. Colonel Tolon passed the mission down to me to take a look because of reports VC were bringing explosives across the footbridge at night to prepare for an attack on Colonel Phan's headquarters."

"Jerry had a man killed in action out there," Colonel Tolon said.

"Yes, Sir. Private Butler. His team leader reported the contact and requested a medevac for Butler. My soldier died before the chopper could get him out. Shot through the throat. He bled to death at the footbridge, Sir."

"Would it be possible, Jerry, that your team may have ambused the farmers thinking they were VC?" Colonel Carson asked.

"Beg pardon, Sir?" Captain Thompson's question was intended to give a few seconds to think how he should answer the Brigade Commander's seemingly innocent query.

"Could it be possible that your boys killed the farmers, Jerry?"

"You know, Sir, anything is possible during night

operations. Especially over here in Vietnam." Thompson looked at the Province Chief. "We never know who our enemy is or where they come from."

"Okay, Jerry, okay." Colonel Carson's nudge was a warning to tread lightly.

"My team was not at the footbridge to conduct an ambush. They were there to observe if VC was using the footbridge to bring explosives across. My team reported enemy contact, they exchanged gunfire, and that's how Private Butler was mortally wounded."

"The four farmers were bringing vegetables to market, so I don't think they killed your soldier," the Province Chief said.

Captain Thompson looked at Colonel Phan.

"How about the enemy contact, Jerry. How many enemy soldiers were in the fight?" Colonel Carson asked.

The connection now was apparent to the Troop Commander. His infantry team may have slain four innocent people.

"It was reported as four, Sir."

The silent pause was telling. The Troop Commander could not deny the terrible possibility.

Captain Thompson shook his head, his voice was tentative. "If they were farmers, had no weapons, I don't understand how Private Butler suffered a mortal gunshot wound to his throat, Sir."

"That is a puzzle. Will you look into it for me, Jerry?" Colonel Carson's voice was soft. "We need to find out what went on out there, what happened. Like you, Jerry, now I also want to know how Butler was killed. I'd like for you to take charge and investigate this for Colonel Phan and me."

"I will look into it, Sir."

"If you need my help, Jerry, let me know," Colonel Tolon offered.

"Colonel Phan came to me for assistance, for answers. He did not go to his President. I don't want this to go to Westmoreland because he'll ask the commanding general to send down an investigating officer. I want our leadership to handle it here, on Linebacker, okay?"

"You dumped the four bodies in the creek?"

"Yes, Sir."

"How many weapons?"

"Four, Sir."

"What did you do with their weapons, Sergeant Hawk?"

"Geez, Sir. We forgot them. While we were waiting for our ride at the laundry tent, we laid all four guns at the entrance. We were all distraught over losing Billy, Sir. When the jeeps arrived, we just mounted up and drove off. We just forgot them, Lieutenant."

"You found no documents?" Lieutenant Versailles persisted.

"No, Sir." Sergeant Hawk held his ground.

"Captain Thompson asked me to conduct this inquiry into what happened at the footbridge, Sergeant Hawk. I'll be talking to all the team members."

"I understand, Lieutenant."

Questions for the four members of the team were

an exercise to determine the possibility if murders occurred. And if that were evident, the next step would be to determine the weak link that would lead to admissions and confessions.

"The Province Chief reported the deaths of four farmers at the footbridge to the Brigade Commander. Colonel Carson asked Captain Thompson to investigate because your team was at the footbridge, and the Captain gave the job to me."

"Yes, Sir. I understand, Lieutenant."

The interview took place in the Platoon Leader's sleeping bunker. Lieutenant Versailles sat on a small field stool. Sergeant Hawk sat on a water can.

"No ID cards? No personal papers?"

"No, Sir. Not even family pictures."

"No ammunition? No explosives?"

"No, Sir."

"You found nothing on them?"

"Not a thing, Sir. Each AK had a magazine. That was all, Sir."

"What about jewelry?"

"Jewelry, Sir?"

"Yeah, like rings, watches, those kinds of things."

"I didn't see any. Of course, Sir, I didn't look that close in the dark."

"Okay, Sergeant Hawk, tell me again about Butler."

"Yes, Sir. We was layin quiet, you know, just observing like we were supposed to do when they fired on us. Mickey stood up and began returning fire with his machine gun. In a moment, Billy stood up and that's when he was hit. An AK round hit Billy square in the throat, Sir. We cut em all down. I reported the contact and called a Dustoff. Billy died before the chopper got to us. He bled to death there at the footbridge before . . ." Red Hawk's voice trailed off.

"In a close range firefight, nobody else was hit?"

"Not a scratch, Sir. We were lucky."

"And when did you throw the bodies over the side of the footbridge?"

"After Billy was picked up, Sir. That's when we searched em, tossed em off the bridge, and picked up their weapons."

"How many weapons?"

Sergeant Hawk paused, wary of a question already answered with an explanation.

"Like I said before, Sir. There was four. All AKs."

"And you forgot them, left them at the laundry tent."

"Yes, Sir."

"Okay, Sergeant Hawk. If you have nothing else, send Fowler down. Then I'll talk to Jenkins and Johnson. Captain Thompson will want to talk with you and even the Brigade Commander, maybe. Can you think of anything else you'd like to tell me?"

"No, Sir."

The thirty-five-minute interview with PFC Michael Fowler was almost a repeat of Hawk's information. Fowler confirmed he had cut them down with his machine gun.

Private First Class Holly Jenkins came clean.

"I killed Billy, Sir. I didn't mean to. I was shooting a gook running off the bridge toward me. Red, Sergeant Hawk, yelled the gook was running my way.

So I stood up, snapped off four quick shots and dropped the gook at the edge of the footbridge. One of my bullets hit Billy in the throat. I lost Rosey to a sniper in the rubber plantation over there, and now I killed Billy. I think I'm going to crack up, Sir. I feel like eatin a grenade and ending it all. Am I gonna go to prison, Lieutenant?"

"How many weapons were picked up, Jinks?"

"Weapons, Lieutenant?"

"Yeah. How many weapons were picked up after you killed the VC?"

"We didn't kill no VC, Lieutenant. They were farmers. They had baskets full of fresh vegetables and melons. We threw all of that off the bridge."

"No AKs?"

"No, Sir."

Corporal Johnson confirmed Jinks' admission. It was all an accident.

"I was with Jinks at one end of the bridge. We watched the four farmers whisk past, carrying their baskets. We didn't know what was in the baskets, Lieutenant. They could've been carryin explosives, like we were looking for. The four got on the bridge, then we heard Mickey's machine gun. Then we heard Red shout one was runnin our way and that's when Jinks stood up and fired four quick shots. I guess cause Billy had stood up, one of Jinks' bullets hit Billy in the throat."

"You and Jinks were at one end of the footbridge and Sergeant Hawk, Fowler, and Butler at the other end? Hawk split his team up?"

"Yes, Sir. And the way it worked out is why Billy

was killed, Lieutenant."

"What do you mean, Johnson?"

"In a fight we could be shootin at each other, Sir."

"Yes, I see what you mean."

"And that's what happened. I shoulda spoke up when Sergeant Hawk briefed us about his tactical plan, but I didn't."

"Why not? Why didn't you voice concern, Johnson?"

"Cause Sergeant Hawk, all of them, had done this before and I was just the F-N-G, Sir."

"Your Sergeant murdered four farmers."

"Yes, Sir."

"What else, Jerry? I've seen that look on your face before. Something else is bothering you. What is it?"

"It's Private Butler, Sir. He was killed by friendly fire. A member of the team shot him. By accident."

Colonel Carson dropped into his chair. "Jesus. Oh, my God."

"It's a mess, Sir. I ask Lieutenant Versailles, the team's platoon leader, to begin the inquiry before I stepped in. Sergeant Hawk and his machine gunner maintain they killed four VC on the bridge. But two members of the team gave a clearer picture of the situation."

"Go on."

"Hawk split his force of five. Hawk, Private Fowler, his machine gunner, and Private Bulter remained on the north end of the footbridge. Hawk placed Private Jenkins and Corporal Johnson on the south end."

"My goodness. They could shoot into each other."

"Well, Sir, they were there to observe. It was not an ambush."

"So, what happened?"

"The farmers were in single file coming across the bridge. Fowler got antsy and opened up with his machine gun. He cut down the front three but the last man turned and ran. Hawk shouted one was running back and that's when Private Jenkins shot down the fourth man."

"And because he was firing toward the footbridge, to the north, one of his bullets struck Bulter."

"Yes, Sir, that's what happened."

"It is a goddamn mess, Jerry. What's your instinct? What do you think you should do about this, Captain?"

Thompson hesitated. The way Colonel Carson phrased it with the official title of Captain made the question a double-sided blade. An answer given might be the same as Thompson impaling himself on Carson's sword.

"It depends, Sir."

"Go on."

"When you report this to the Province Chief, Colonel Phan will demand reparations for the families."

"Yes, that he will, Jerry. Rightly, so. And he'll want a percentage for himself, no doubt."

"I don't think he would demand murder charges because he probably knows it wouldn't fly, Sir."

"Won't, in a combat zone. The lawyers would stand firm on that aspect, I suspect."

"Exactly, Sir. It was an authorized mission, at night, in the rain. A mistake was made. A terrible tragedy, a horrible mistake, a deadly error, but there was no malice or premeditation. So, official regrets and apologies to the families along with proper payments."

"And a cut for Colonel Phan."

"Yes, Sir, and a cut for Colonel Phan."

"What about discipline for Hawk and Fowler?"

"No courts-martial for them. Both are good men, good soldiers. Neither have ever been in trouble. But I will refer Sergeant Hawk to you for a field-grade Article 15 because he is a non-commissioned officer. You could reduce him to the rank of Private and assess a fine of four times the amount I could with a company grade Article 15, if you decide to assess your Article 15 and maximum fine, Sir."

"What's the charge?"

"False report of a combat action and lying to his superior officer in the conduct of an official inquiry."

"What about Fowler?"

"He's not a non-commissioned officer so I will deal with him. I think the non-judicial punishment will be sufficient. He also lied to Lieutenant Versailles about the action. It cannot be proved he knew they were farmers when he pulled the trigger."

Thompson became silent.

"There's more, Jerry?"

"Whatever we do or don't do, Sir, it won't bring back the lives of four innocent farmers. It won't mend the loss for their families or heal the heartbreak."

"Yes, you're right, Jerry. Even just for hurt feelings, saying you're sorry never repairs harm done."

Colonel Carson took in a deep breath.

"Okay, I like your instinct, Jerry. I will accept the referral, but I'll listen to Sergeant Hawk's side of the story and consider any mitigating circumstances he offers, like vision or determination of the level of threat in the rain."

"What about Butler, Sir."

"What do you mean?"

"How can we tell his family he was killed by a member of his team, by friendly fire?"

"We won't, Jerry. We'll tell a little white lie."

"What do you mean, Sir?"

"Private Butler was killed in action by a hostile force while on a combat mission. He defended members of his team in a firefight and gave his own life to save theirs. He'll be a decorated hero. We will honor his family the best way we can for his sacrifice."

"I see."

"And that's how you'll put it in your letter to his next of kin, Captain Thompson."

INVENTORY

Sergeant Holt stood behind the counter and stared through the doorway of his supply room. As seconds ticked, his impatience mounted, and irritation swelled. Only three minutes had passed since he last looked at his watch. Now, it was 1512 hours.

"She don't know who she's screwin around with here," he muttered. "She's been a no-show before and I don't like it."

"What'd you say?"

"I said don't worry, Horton, she'll be here. She probably got hung up, picking up somebody's laundry at one of the bunkers. She's got rounds to make here in the troop area. I told her about you, Horton, and she said she'd be here for you at 1500."

"Well, I hope she's all you say she is, Holt. Sixty-five dollars is a lot of money, you know. That's a goddamn month's pay."

"I know, Horton. I know it is. But Mai Li is worth it. You'll see. And you're going to be completely satisfied, I guarantee it."

"Well, I ain't got all day, Holt."

"I'll tell you this, after the first time with Mai Li

you'll be begging me to take your money for another round with her. She knows what a man wants. Believe me when I tell you, she sure knows how to make a man happy and fulfilled."

"One of the quartermaster boys here – they live down at the end of the camp by the trash dump you know – told me about your business enterprises at the shower point. I went down there looking for you and they steered me back up here. I didn't know you was in the cavalry troop. I thought you was a quartermaster."

"Naw, I'm a combat infantryman. I'm just waiting on my award of the CIB, my third Silver Star, and my third Purple Heart. I been in a lot of fights. You know I killed twelve guys on the perimeter quite awhile ago. Caught a bullet. Didn't even give me morphine, when Doc Swanson dug it out with a bayonet. I put a band-aid on and went back to duty. I'm just filling in here while the supply sergeant is on R & R. I'll probably be promoted two pay-grades to Master Sergeant and given command of a cavalry platoon."

"Yeah, I can see you're a busy man, Holt. Runnin a business here in the supply room and down at the creek."

"Yep, I got three regulars helping out at the laundry and shower point. Chi, Anh, and Tuyen. I think Anh is more popular. I had three up here too, but now I just got Mai Li."

"Well, I only saw two down there. I didn't get their names."

"What did you think about my stable of entertainers?"

"Those two I saw looked old and shriveled up. They looked more like Mama-Sans than girls."

"Well, Horton, it probably was real mama-sans you saw. They do the work in the creek, washing the clothes. My girls are young things, and they sure as hell ain't shriveled up. They ain't down there sloshing around in the creek water and they sure as hell ain't folding clothes. Cause you didn't see them, they was probably just taking care of business."

"Well, here I am. If we don't get this show on the road, Henry, you might as well give me my sixty-five dollars back."

"Now, there won't be any need for that. You won't regret coming to me. Mai Li is what you're looking for. I guarantee that, my friend."

"I can't wait much longer, Henry. My Lieutenant will be lookin for me."

"Okay, Horton. You wait right here. I'll go find Mai Li and tell her you're waiting."

Sergeant Holt was hot with anger when he walked out of his supply office. He hurried to the troop street, turned left and slowed his pace as he moved among the sleeping bunkers looking, searching.

Little Kim stood outside the third bunker. She saw Holt at the same time he saw her. She shrieked in fright and darted through the doorway.

Mai Li screamed in fear when she heard Kim squeal. She swept her little girl up and held Kim in a motherly embrace.

She spoke to her daughter with a soothing voice. "*Không sao, tình yêu của tôi, bạn đang an toàn với Mama*." [It's okay, my love, you're safe with Mama.]

Kim looked at Mai Li's eyes and smiled. She flung her small arms around Mai Li's neck and hugged her mother.

"Now ain't that sweet. Mama's little girl." Holt stood at the entrance of the bunker. "I hate to break up this Norman Rockwell picture, Mai Li, but you broke another promise. I don't like it that I had to come after you. That's not nice, and when you're not nice, I won't be nice."

Before Holt could rush Mai Li and Kim, Captain Thompson's voice jolted the supply sergeant as the Troop Commander, Lieutenant Versailles, and Platoon Sergeant Tweed approached from around the bunker's corner.

"I heard squealing, Sergeant Holt. What's going on?"

Sergeant Holt pointed through the doorway.

"I don't know, Sir, I heard the cry out too, and was just coming to check on it. Maybe the little girl hurt herself."

Holt glared at Mai Li and squinted. It was his signal that she should be careful with her explanation.

Mai Li detected Holt's chilling stare and understood the danger. Her fear was for Kim, not herself. When he had tied a rope around Kim's neck and pulled it taut, Mai Li knew she had to kill Holt. She carried a straight razor to snip threads from soldiers' clothing and that would suffice to render unto Holt his comeuppance and just reward.

The four soldiers entered the bunker. Rays from the sun slipped through the openings at the top of the sandbagged walls and doorway, and filled the inside with afternoon light.

Captain Thompson stepped close to Mai Li and Kim. "Do you speak American?"

"Yes. My name is Mai Li, Captain. I do household chores and pick up soldiers' laundry. This is Kim, my daughter. She is six years old."

Thompson was impressed with the clarity that Mai Li spoke. "I am Captain Thompson. I am the commanding officer of the cavalry troop here, where you work."

"I know. I have seen you here and was told you are in charge. My people say you are a fair and just man."

Thompson nodded. He reached out with a finger and touched Kim's arm. "You are a cutie-pie, little Kim. Were you hurt?"

Kim smiled and buried her face in Mai Li's neck.

Mai Li smiled too and shook her head. "She is alright, Captain Thompson. She was frightened by a snake."

"I see. Okay. Is your work here finished?"

"Yes, Captain. We were about to leave when the snake appeared." Mai Li glared at Holt.

"So, if you're done, we have business to take care of in this bunker. Thank you, Mai Li, for what you do for us. Goodbye, sweet Kim. You are a pretty little girl."

"Thank you, Captain. Please excuse us."

As Mai Li and Kim left the bunker, Thompson turned to Holt.

"Is she part of your laundry crew, Sergeant Holt?"

"Yes, Sir, she's a good worker. She is very

popular. I wanted to give her more responsibility but she refused. Her husband is a soldier. He's fighting Charlie down south, near Saigon. She hasn't seen him in a year. Mai Li lives with his folks in a hamlet near Phuoc Binh."

"We're here to take care of Private Butler's belongings. Sergeant Tweed went to your supply office looking for you. We need the proper forms to do the inventory."

Holt did not move, waiting for instructions.

The Captain walked to a ceiling support timber and pointed at the cluster of arsenals.

"I see frags, W-P, smoke, and incendiary grenades along with M-79 rounds and pouches of ammunition. It's a lot of loose ordnance," Thompson said. "I'm concerned about all the grenades hanging on harnesses and attached to web belts."

"The boys are careful with them, Sir," Lieutenant Versailles said. "We talk about it all the time. They need the grenades and ammo handy in case of a perimeter penetration."

"Don't forget we're dealing with people who are younger than we are, Alex." Thompson smiled and looked at the Lieutenant and Platoon Sergeant. "You do remember that horsing around and playing grab-ass are facts of a youthful life?"

Both nodded and grinned.

"I cover safety all the time with the non-coms and soldiers," Boss Tweed said. "They know how hazardous grenades are in an enclosed space, Captain. They know the danger, Sir. If a grenade explodes in a twelve by twelve bunker, the concussion is as bad as shrapnel. It would kill anyone in here."

"We just saw a child in here, Boss. We all know that shit happens. Play *what ifs*. What if little Kim or some other child was curious and pulled a grenade off a belt? What if Mai Li was a VC or sympathizer and stole grenades or ammunition? What about suicide?"

"That little girl could accidentally pull a pin on a grenade just by tugging on a web belt or harness, Captain," Holt said.

"I know. It bothers me."

"We live with that every hour, Captain. Even when we are out in our vehicles, a kid could come up with one hand out for candy or gum and have a grenade in the other to drop in a gun jeep," the lieutenant said.

"Well, tomorrow I want everybody to be reminded about the need for safety with weapons, ammunition, and grenades in sleeping bunkers."

"Yes, Sir, we'll handle third platoon tomorrow," Versailles said.

"Okay, Sergeant Holt, bring some inventory forms. We need to get on with this inventory. I have a letter to write to Butler's next of kin."

"I'll be right back with the forms, Capn," Holt said.

A thorough, detailed inventory was required of a soldier's belongings as soon as possible after his death when killed in action. Once completed, possessions were hand-carried to the rear area. Following processing, inspection, and another inventory there, Graves Registration would ship the soldier's property to his next of kin, most often to the wife or designated parent.

As Holt left, Sergeant Tweed moved to a corner of

the bunker where an air mattress, camouflaged nylon blanket, and a duffle bag with Butler's stenciled name on it lay. He lifted up and opened the bag. The Platoon Sergeant withdrew a pair of jungle fatigues, two pairs of tan woolen socks, four pairs of Army olive drab boxer shorts, two Army olive drab tee shirts, a toiletry bag, a pair of jungle boots, and a C-Ration meal box.

"Besides this box and the shaving kit, there's only military stuff in the duffle bag, Sir."

Tweed opened the meal box, peered in, and reached out with it to Thompson.

"This looks like the only personal item. This is all he had, Captain."

Thompson took the box and paused.

"This is the fourth inventory I've had to do in fifty days," the Captain said. "It is a sad chore. It is uncomfortable rummaging through someone's personal belongings, things they would certainly have wanted to remain undisclosed and kept secret from prying eyes."

"I remember Winchester and Rosey, Sir. Who was the fourth?" Lieutenant Versailles asked.

"Private Peter Wayne."

"Must have been before my time. What happened to him?"

"A cobra got him, Lieutenant," Boss said. "He was on an ambush with Sergeant Winkler and PFC Norton. They were in a hole beside the trail. It had rained on them all night, and early morning a cobra peeked in their hole. Wayne tried to be a snake tamer, like they do in India, wavin his finger in the snake's face. Well,

Mr. Snake latched onto Wayne's finger."

"And he died?"

"Sure did. He died before the Dustoff chopper arrived. Doc Swanson couldn't help Wayne. Nobody could."

"I'll probably write a similar letter to Butler's next of kin."

Because an inventory occurred so soon after the action, after the death, it proved to be doubly poignant and depressing. An officer, usually the Platoon Leader or Commander, was responsible for conducting an inventory of personal effects. There was a separate inventory for all military equipment, including the weapon, helmet, combat gear, grenades, ammunition, and boots. The Supply Sergeant would reissue those items if they were in good condition. A detail would burn the soldier's military clothing.

Others assisted in an inventory. Help and support were crucial. Additional eyes might prevent something from slipping past. That is why Butler's Platoon Leader and Platoon Sergeant were there to assist Captain Thompson.

In an inventory, the team recorded every item with an explicit identification.

Every item.

When evacuated by helicopter from the battlefield, the soldier's wallet remained with the body. If a wallet was among the soldier's personal effects, the team removed cards, photographs, and money in it. Every member of the inventory team counted money twice, recording amounts by denomination. All jewelry, including rings, a bracelet, and a watch, were specifically identified and recorded.

Every member of the inventory team would read every personal, private letter twice. Reading private letters could be painful because many soldiers in Vietnam left unpleasant family situations and the unpleasantness followed.

Not only was it sad because of the death, but the sadness deepened when another life the soldier had been dealing with was exposed. Sometimes, also sad to say, there was deep embarrassment.

A family would write about trials, tribulations, and disasters. As if a soldier didn't have enough to worry about every day in Vietnam, a battle-tested young man, a combat veteran, might receive letters about how bad things were back home.

An inventory could expose family, money, or other private personal problems.

There were lawsuits, extortion, bank robberies. Stolen cars, property, or money.

Car wrecks, repossessions, forged check charges, and banks or loan sharks demanding the weekly juice and payment in full.

There were legal or addiction issues. And pregnancies. Happy pregnancies, unhappy pregnancies, unwanted pregnancies, pregnancy by another man, abortions, divorce, child custody, and child support. Even child abandonment.

Things never imagined, never even thought about, were things a young soldier had to hear about and deal with while trying to survive and stay alive in Vietnam.

Mom and dad letters fell on both sides. There

were reassuring letters of mom and dad's love, and their warm and comforting thoughts for their son. Then there were needy letters where mom and dad begged or demanded money.

Single mothers depended on her soldier son's income.

There were horror stories about a soldier's brothers or sisters.

There were problems from, or about, his wife or his girlfriend, or both. Wife and girlfriend letters fell on both sides. There were reassuring letters of faithfulness and love. There were "Dear John" letters, some downright mean and vindictive.

Letters from a wife about her pregnancy by another man were heart-shattering, crushing, and cruel.

There also were letters about the soldier's child with another woman. These letters came from the child's mother, as well as the solder's irate, furious wife.

In an Army unit, in any military unit, an inventory revealed a lot about real people. And real people do great, and not so great, things.

Unsavory, unauthorized, and illegal items, including pornography, drugs, drug paraphernalia, and the like, would never be returned to the next of kin. The inventory team destroyed these types of items.

Captain Thompson looked at the small, rectangular, cardboard carton measuring six inches long, six inches wide, and five inches deep. The top line printed on the lid indicated the box was for a ***MEAL, COMBAT, INDIVIDUAL***. The next line below this heading described the despised contents of ***Ham and Lima Beans***, and below this cautionary announcement of a canned food was the type of ration – a ***B-3 Unit***, used as a meal for breakfast, lunch, or dinner. Ninety percent of soldiers hated Ham and Lima Beans, but most ate it in spite of an unlucky draw. C-Ration Ham and Lima Beans would win out over hunger.

The fourth line, written in pencil, stated *Property of.*

The fifth line, in pencil, read *PFC William A. Butler, Jr. Esq*.

The commander opened this chest of Butler's personal treasures and fingered the contents. Only seven items lay in the bottom of this small carton.

Sergeant Holt came through the doorway. "Here are the forms, Sir. And I brought some extra pencils and a pad of paper."

Thompson held the box up. "Is this all there is? Did you search his fighting bunker and the infantry truck?"

"I personally searched the bunker and the truck, Captain," Boss said.

Versailles nodded. "We searched everywhere, Sir."

"Butler had only been in the platoon forty days, Captain. I asked all his bunker buddies, Hawk, Fowler, Jenkins, and Johnson. Jenkins was the one person who knew Butler well. Jenkins told me that Butler said if anything happened to send this box home to his folks. Said it was all his personal stuff."

"You mean all his stuff is in this little C-Ration meal box? Seven items?"

"Yessir, reckon so," Sergeant Tweed acknowledged.

"Yesterday was his birthday, Captain," Versailles said. "He just turned nineteen."

"Jesus." Thompson drew in a deep breath and released a slow exhale through protruding lips. "Forty days in Vietnam, now he's dead. Nineteen years old. Jesus, my heart aches for him and his family."

"I know, Sir," Versailles said. "Even in the short time he was with us, he was well liked and respected."

"Billy used to wash the infantry truck in the creek while naked, Captain," Tweed said. "Everybody teased him about that."

"He always wanted me to give him the Ham and Lima Beans soldiers would bring to my supply room, too," Holt said. "That boy could eat Ham and Lima Beans for every meal."

"Okay, let's do the inventory. Alex, you write it down. Sergeant Tweed, you're our third person, the witness, you're another pair of eyes, Boss. Sergeant Holt, go find Jenkins, maybe he can be of help."

As Henry Holt walked away, Thompson removed the seven items from the C-Ration carton.

A black and white photograph of Butler dressed in Army khakis with his arm around an older woman who wore a black dress with white embroidery on the collar. The woman was grinning. Her hand and fingers cupped his narrow chin, forcing Butler's lips to protrude like a blowfish. The woman's lips also jutted out. His mother, Thompson thought.

A black and white photograph of Butler in jeans and a leather motorcycle jacket sitting on a Cushman scooter. A girl in white shorts, flip-flops, and a black, short-sleeved shirt sat behind him, leaning into his back, her arms around his waist. They grinned at the camera. Friend, cousin, sister, girlfriend, or wife, Thompson wondered.

Two letters addressed to PFC William A. Butler, Jr. One had a return address for Susie Moffett, the other listed Mr. and Mrs. William A. Butler, Sr.

There was a folded, tattered copy of orders assigning Butler to Delta Troop.

There was a folded, tattered copy of orders awarding Butler's Combat Infantry Badge.

And, there was a folded page ripped from a *Playboy* magazine of an inviting, smiling, voluptuous, beautiful brunette, posing in full frontal nudity for the camera, her legs fully spread in complete, unabashed exhibition.

Captain Thompson removed Mr. and Mrs. Butler's one page letter from the envelope and unfolded it. He looked at the Lieutenant and Platoon Sergeant and told them he would read it aloud first, and then both of them could read it silently.

Our Dearest Billy,

Your Dad and I worry about you every day, son. We were heartbroken when you left in anger. You knew we did not have $1,000 to give. At the time, we did not understand why you wanted that much money.

After you left for Vietnam, Arlene told us about the baby. She said you wanted her to have an abortion and she guessed that was what the money was for. Arlene said she will have your baby, she was against an abortion. She will raise your child even if you won't marry her.

Write to us as often as you can. Your little sister was thirteen yesterday, she sends her love. Maggie wished you could have been at her party.

Love,

Mom

Captain Thompson folded the letter, returned it to its envelope, and handed the envelope to Versailles.

"I don't feel right about this, Captain," Sergeant Boswell Tweed said.

"I don't think any of us feel comfortable going through somebody's private business, Boss."

"It's got to be done, though, Boss," the Lieutenant said.

Thompson withdrew Susie Moffett's letter. It was more a note than letter. Actually, it was an announcement. He began reading aloud.

My Darling Billy

We are going to have a baby in November. I hope it will be a boy. I will name our son William A. Butler the third. He will have III behind his name. I've told my parents and they accept our love, and hope we can be married when you come home.

Write to me, my love. Tell me you love me and will love our son.

Love and Kisses, S.

Captain Thompson folded the letter, returned it to its envelope, and handed the envelope to Boss Tweed.

All three remained quiet, solemn, and pensive.

"We're here, Captain," Sergeant Holt announced, interrupting their thoughts. "Jenkins says Butler was married."

"How do you know that, Jenkins?"

"He told me, Sir."

"Look at this picture of the girl on the motor scooter, Jenkins. Is that his wife?"

"No, Sir. That's Maggie, his little sister."

"Look at this envelope return address. Is Susie Moffett his wife?"

"I don't think so, Captain Thompson."

"Is his wife's name, Arlene?"

"No, Sir. He called his wife Emma. His wife was a model, for magazines, Sir."

"Look at this *Playboy* magazine page, Boss."

"Holy shit! Oh, Jesus. Ah, excuse me, Sir. Geez, I'm sorry, Captain."

Lieutenant Versailles and Sergeant Holt looked over Sergeant Tweed's shoulder, at the magazine sheet.

"Show it to Jenkins, Boss."

"Yeah, that's Billy's Emma, Sir. Ain't she something?"

CHECKPOINT

Staff Sergeant Darby Dutchman's return to Linebacker from R & R coincided with Red and Mickey's *Stand-Before-The-Man* and the Third Platoon's mission to provide security for a National Police checkpoint east of Sông Bé on Road 3-10 at the Sông Bé River Bridge.

Lieutenant Versailles and Platoon Sergeant Tweed discussed who would remain on the firebase to secure the platoon's part of Delta Troop's sizable area of responsibility. They decided Boss would stay back with the platoon's two 1-0-6mm recoilless rifles and eight crewmembers. Since each recoilless rifle was mounted on a jeep, that gave flexibility to put a gun on each flank of their sector of the perimeter. A reduced force, with recoilless rifle anti-personnel rounds and enfilading fire, could defeat any attempted assault through the concertina wire because when a 1-0-6mm flechette shell burst, the little arrows pierced flesh with exquisite ease.

It fell to Boss to tell the platoon's 81mm mortar squad leader, and they knew the decision to keep the five-man squad back to staff fighting bunkers would bring the wrath of Staff Sergeant Alonzo Medina.

"Why does my squad always have to remain on guard duty? We're part of the cavalry platoon, and we should go where the platoon goes when the platoon goes."

"Lonzo, you know as well as I do that you're not as mobile as the scouts or infantry. If we were going to set up in position for a day or two or three, then your squad could provide fire support. But you know the police might stay in one place for a few minutes before they move their checkpoint to a different location. When they go, we gotta go. And we never know when they're gonna move – or where they're going."

"Well, Boss, my squad could go, too. We never get to go out on missions with the platoon."

"We give you fire missions here. Your squad fires interdiction on days and nights, you shoot more than a hundred rounds a week. Your boys shoot a half dozen illumination rounds almost every night, sometimes more. You get to keep your precision up, your skills sharp, here on the firebase. You get to play soldier."

"But it ain't the same. We want to be in the action, Boss. We want to be in a fight, if there is one."

"Look, Lonzo, listen to me. The scouts and infantry got the heavy machine gun firepower in case we need it out there in the wilderness. Your squad has five rifles and five pistols. We keep you safe, outta harm's way."

"It ain't right to treat us this way, like we was security guards in a motor pool. We're combat soldiers just like the rest of the troop."

Platoon Sergeant Tweed's patience with Sergeant

Medina was real; he remained cordial while he searched for a reasonable rationalization. While Platoon Sergeant Tweed understood Sergeant Medina's desire, he also was realistic where the squad leader was not.

"Sit down. Sit there on the sandbags, Lonzo. I know we treat your squad differently. We have to. I'm gonna give you reasons why we decide for your squad to remain on the firebase when we go out on police checkpoints. You've heard the expression about not being able to see the forest for the trees? What I'm going to say ain't anything new for you, but I think you'll see why when I go through it step-by-step for you."

Sergeant Medina drew in a deep breath. His exasperation was evident when he exhaled. "This is frustrating, Boss, but I'm listening."

"Let's say we are in a tactical march on Road 3-10, moving toward a checkpoint, hadn't got where the police are gonna set up."

"Okay."

"We receive fire from an ambush."

"Okay."

"Well, what's your squad gonna do?"

"Set up the mortar, Boss. You know that. To return fire."

"Right. Besides the five rifles and pistols, the mortar is your squad's weapon."

"That's right. That's why we'd unass the truck and drop rounds on the bad guys."

"Well, Lonzo, it ain't that easy, is it." Boss meant it as a statement, not as a question for Sergeant Medina to answer. "I mean the platoon, maybe even the troop, is under fire, maybe pinned down, in the middle of the road with no cover. Bullets and rockets flying all around."

"So?"

"So, here's what your squad's got to do in a hail of gunfire. First, get outta your truck. Then, find a place to position the mortar. Lift the heavy base plate out of the back of the truck. Lift the mortar barrel out of the back of the truck. Lay the base plate in position. Attach the mortar tube. Unload the mortar ammunition out of the back of the truck."

Tweed paused looking into Lonzo's eyes.

"Are you with me so far, Lonzo?"

"Yes, Boss, I'm with you." Lonzo nodded his reluctant agreement.

Boss continued. "Now you have to unpack the mortar ammunition from the crates and remove the packing material. Remove the safety rings and adjust the mortar ammunition for firing. Attach the mortar sight. Place out the aiming stakes, you know a lone rifle bullet could take out the exposed mortar crew member holding the aiming stake for sighting and alignment. Uncase the mortar plotting board. Mark the grid coordinates on the plotting board. Give the azimuth. Adjust the sight and level the bubbles. Call for a round. The loader brings the correct mortar round that's been called for from the back of the truck. The gunner drops the first round in the mortar barrel. Wait for the round to impact on target. Shift the azimuth, adjust the tube, and level the bubbles for the next round. Plot the second round. Drop the second round down the tube. Wait for an impact, make adjustments."

Boss Tweed stopped talking; they sat in silence.

"What do you think the enemy is gonna do, Lonzo, when they see four guys running and hustling and jumping around on the road, out in the open? And the fifth guy, like he was out on a prairie, holding a tall red and white painted stick waving his arm?"

Sergeant Medina nodded again. "Okay, Boss, you made your point. But it still ain't fair."

"It may not be, Lonzo, but I keep you and your boys outta harm's way when I can. Now, will you do this for me? Take up bunker positions on the perimeter with Sergeant Haggard's 1-0-6 section?"

"You leaving Odell back here, too?"

"His guns will be on the flanks, you will be in the center. His eight and your five spread thin will barely cover our sector."

"What about Red and Mickey. Why can't they take one of the bunkers when the Colonel and the Old Man finishes with them?"

"Well, they can, Lonzo. But that's gonna be a decision for the Lieutenant and Darby. I don't know how all that's gonna turn out. I expect both will be busted to buck-ass-private."

Captain DeSoto, the Brigade Adjutant, looked up from the military orders and personnel folders sprawled on top his small field table. He wiped sweat from his upper lip with his right index finger.

The soldier before him was dressed in clean jungle

fatigues, with the shirtsleeves evenly measured in a neat fold across muscular biceps. The sergeant stood erect in front of DeSoto's work area. A steel pot, tucked tight under the left arm, pressed against the rib cage. Pronounced on the left elbow were a large scrape and brown scab.

"I'm Sergeant Raleigh Hawk, Sir. I'm here to report to Colonel Carson, Sir."

"Ah, yes, Sergeant Hawk. The Brigade Commander is expecting you. Stand easy, wait a moment. I'll tell Colonel Carson you're here."

Captain DeSoto rose from his stool, lifted a folder off the pile, opened it, and scanned the documents inside, before turning and walking through an opening between walls of filled sandbags. He closed a wooden panel that fit slightly canted in the two-by-four frame of the doorway.

Sergeant Hawk evaluated the artistry of a soldier's hand-drawn Brigade crest on the door. He decided it was a pretty damn good piece of work. Painted in white blocked letters above the emblem was the Brigade Commander's name, COLONEL ELI CARSON, and below it was COMMANDING OFFICER.

"Sergeant Hawk is here, Sir," the Adjutant said. He handed the military folder to the Brigade Commander. "This is his service record and the Article 15."

"Thanks, Danny." Colonel Carson took the file and laid it on his desk. "Have Sergeant Hawk come in."

As instructed, Hawk went through the opening, closed the flimsy door, turned, snapped to attention, and saluted.

"Sergeant Hawk reporting to the Brigade

Commander, as ordered, Sir."

The soldier's bearing and appearance impressed Colonel Carson.

Before speaking, he returned the smart military salute. "Have a seat, Sergeant Hawk."

Hawk had never been in officer country. The accouterments he saw in Colonel Carson's office impressed him.

The Colonel sat in a huge, high back, leather chair, a cigarette holder clamped between his lips. The desk was a dark mahogany. A brass nameplate perched on the forward edge of the workspace and two .50 caliber shells flanked it. A .45 caliber pistol lay on its side on top of the desk as if it were resting after a hard day's work. The American colors and the Brigade flag hung in folds from staffs behind the Commanding Officer. Between the ensigns, attached to the sandbag wall, was a wood craved Brigade emblem. There were no windows, but, as if fitted in a window opening, an air conditioner stuck between a wall of sandbags hummed and pushed cool air.

A green melon, the size of a volleyball standing in the middle of the executive's work area also impressed Sergeant Hawk. Red could see yellow rind exposed by a circular cut line as if a lid was on top. Among all the stuff on the Brigade Commander's desk, Sergeant Hawk thought the melon was most unusual and couldn't take his eyes off it.

Colonel Carson opened the folders, covered the preliminaries from the official typewritten documents, and read the charges.

"You're here because you gave a false report about

a combat action in which Private William Butler was killed in action. During an inquiry conducted on my order Jenkins, Fowler, and Johnson told their side of the story. Now, I want to hear your side of the story, Sergeant Hawk. I want to know why you thought it okay for a non-commissioned officer to render a false report."

"I understand, Sir."

Colonel Carson nodded. "Before we go any further, I want you to acknowledge you understand you do not have the right to counsel, Sergeant Hawk, since my Article 15 is non-judicial. But if you wish I will grant your request and permit anyone, officer, non-commissioned officer, or soldier to be with you here while we resolve the matter."

Hawk shook his head. "I understand, Sir. And, no, Sir, it's not necessary for anyone to be here."

"Sergeant Hawk, you have the right to refuse this Article 15 and request a Court-Martial."

"No, Sir. I accept the responsibility."

The Colonel paused and peered at the soldier. He leaned forward and placed forearms and elbows on the desk before clasping his fingers together. This maneuver, Red noted, encircled the melon and captured it in a pincer movement.

What the fuck was a goddamned melon doing like a canary perched in the middle of the Brigade Commander's desk, Red wondered. Why the fuck don't he put the fucking thing on the floor?

"That's good, Sergeant Hawk, because I didn't want Westmoreland's lawyers down here meddling in our business. The reason for the Article 15 is to avoid judicial punishment."

This admission interested Hawk.

Lieutenant Versailles, Platoon Sergeant Tweed, even First Sergeant Morris, had offered counsel and advice. To a man, all said to keep ears open, mouth shut, and take what the Brigade Commander would dish out. Red knew punishments for a Field Grade Article 15 and a Summary Court-Martial were about the same, but if convicted by a court-martial his military record would have a permanent stain.

With the Colonel's Article 15, Hawk knew the worst punishment would be a bust to Private (a demotion of two pay grades) and forfeiture of two-thirds pay and allowances for two months.

"I understand, Sir. I'm prepared for your decision."

The Brigade Commander opened Sergeant Hawk's personnel folder.

In silence, Hawk watched while Carson read.

"You have two Silver Stars, Son?"

"Yes, Sir."

"A Bronze Star for Valor?"

"Yes, Sir."

"Two Purple Hearts?"

"Yes, Sir."

"You were top of your class in Basic Training, Advanced Infantry Training, and graduated top of your class at Fort Benning NCO School?"

"Yes, Sir."

Carson leaned back in his chair. "Then why, Son? Why the false report?"

Now it was time for Sergeant Hawk to come clean, to tell his side of the story. There would be no embellishment, no asides, no excuses, no squirming. His heart ached as he spoke.

"Because of Billy, Sir. I did not want his family hurt. If they knew a comrade killed their son, by friendly fire, it would break their hearts even worse. This was in my mind, in that moment, in the rain, in the dark, on that bridge. Billy is a hero in my mind, Sir. He received two Bronze Stars for bravery and a Purple Heart for a bullet wound. He deserves to be remembered by his friends and family as a brave soldier who died in the heat of battle over here in this forsaken place, far from home. It was dark, Sir, wee hours of a morning. That's when VC move, not farmers. When Mickey opened up and killed the three, we all suspected they were VC, not vegetable farmers. And when I yelled, that's when Jinks, Jenkins, killed the one running back. We were in combat, Colonel. It was for real. I also told about the AK-47s to support my false report about our combat action."

Hawk paused and met Carson's gaze.

"And I think I'd do the same thing, again, Sir, to protect Billy's honor and his family."

The hum of the air conditioner was the only sound for twenty-three seconds. Colonel Carson released the captured melon. When he leaned back, his chair creaked.

"You see that melon, Son?"

"I see it, Sir. It's been difficult not to look at it sitting high in the middle of your desk, Sir."

"The Phuoc Long Province Chief, Colonel Phan, brought this melon to my office this morning."

Sergeant Raleigh Hawk held his tongue.

"Have you seen it before, Sergeant Hawk?"

"I've seen melons like it, Sir, but I don't think I've seen that melon." Red wondered what trap the Colonel was setting. This cat and mouse shit made him nervous. Why didn't the bird-colonel go ahead and bust him to private and get it over with?

"Do you know Colonel Phan?"

"No, Sir."

"Have you ever seen Colonel Phan?"

"I have, Sir. Sometimes when we are on police checkpoints, the Province Chief comes out to inspect his policemen."

"Well, one of his boys found this melon."

Hawk didn't know what to say. "Yes, Sir."

"On the bank, under the Dak Toll Creek footbridge."

Sergeant Hawk steeled himself for an expected blast of criticism and chastisement.

"Yes, Sir. At the creek, Sir."

"Want to look at it, Sergeant Hawk?"

Now what? Red wondered what the hell he was supposed to say, how to respond? The fire team leader grew tired of the Brigade Commander's game.

"Not really, Sir. If you don't mind, Sir, I'd rather not."

"Well, I know you're probably tired of the game I'm playing," Colonel Carson said, "so let's get on with it."

The Commander leaned forward and grasped the body of the melon in his left hand. He lifted the top off with his right and tilted the fruit toward Hawk.

Two round balls of C-4, wrapped in detonating cord with a blasting cap stuck in the white plastic explosive, snuggled inside the hollowed out innards.

"They were not farmers, Son. Colonel Phan said one of his policemen found this rigged charge this morning. He hurried to bring it to me. Your team killed the enemy, Sergeant Hawk. They were part of a VC cadre bringing explosives to town to support an attack."

"Holy Shit," Red blurted. "They *were* bad guys. Mickey said he thought he saw them holding rifles on their shoulders. That's why he opened fire. But there were no rifles, just the end of the bamboo sticks they use to tote baskets."

The confession was a thunderclap to Red's ears. He knew he had the right, he had been warned, to keep his mouth shut. But he didn't have the ability. When the Colonel said they were VC, he felt vindicated.

"DANNY!"

The door burst open. "Yes, Sir?"

"Send a runner right away. Interrupt whatever he's doing, wherever he is, even in the latrine, and bring Captain Thompson here right away. And, PFC Fowler, too."

"Yes, Sir. I'll take care of it."

Mickey Fowler faced a Company Grade Article 15 for lying to his platoon leader about a combat action.

Unlike Hawk's environment in Colonel Carson's office, Mickey sat on a water can facing his Troop Commander. Space was sparse; there were no frills in the command post/office/sleeping quarters. There was no air conditioner, no desk, no chairs. The Troop guidon staff was stuck in the dirt at the bunker's entrance, the red and white pennant limp in the hot afternoon sun. Thompson's driver and radiotelephone operator had vacated the premises so the Troop Commander could conduct this piece of business with a sense of dignity.

Thompson had proceeded through the official introduction, covered the purpose, and read the charge. He now paused to listen to Fowler's offer of explanation leading to mitigation.

"It was dark, Sir. There was some light, reflection off the low clouds. It had been raining. I don't remember, but it may have still been raining when we saw, when I saw them, coming along the footbridge toward us. All I could think of was they was bad guys, Captain. I didn't want nobody in our team to get hurt. I squinted to make sure I could make out the weapons they were carrying across their shoulders. They was like a hunter walking home with his rifle resting along the top of his shoulder, holding the front end of the barrel, like this. Later, of course, we saw, I saw, it was bamboo sticks instead of rifles. The flat sticks they use to carry baskets. And of course, Sir, their hands was holding the front end of the sticks. But at the time, in my mind, in the dark, it was rifles in their hands. I knew it was. So, I opened fire and took care of business, before they could shoot at us. Sir. I got three, and the fourth turned and run back toward Jinks and Johnson."

"Why did you render a false report? Why did you lie to Lieutenant Versailles?"

"Billy, Sir. When we calmed down, when Sergeant Hawk decided what we were to do I knew what he was doing was to protect Billy, Sir. His family would have some solace if they knew Billy was killed in battle with the enemy. If it was reported that we killed farmers and Billy was shot by one of us, his family . . . well, Sir, that's why. Me and Red decided, Sir. Because of Billy, Captain Thompson. It was because of Billy and his family, Sir."

Captain DeSoto entered the CP and saluted.

"Beg pardon, Captain Thompson. My apologies. Colonel Carson sent me to fetch you and Fowler. Both of you are to come with me now and report to the Brigade Commander."

The discussion was short, Colonel Carson did all of the talking. Thompson, Red, and Mickey kept quiet. They were pleased, relieved actually, the Province Chief had presented the melon stuffed with C-4.

"Whatever we do, whatever we say, is not going to bring Private Butler back," Colonel Carson said. "It is understandable but regrettable that grave misfortune occurs in tense military situations.

"I promise you, if I had a magic wand to wave to bring that boy back I would do it. In a heartbeat. But I don't. Private Jenkins did not intend harm. He used poor judgment, but who among us is perfect in all that we do in life.

"Even though your action was against a hostile force, I cannot accept a false combat report. Leaders and commanders make decisions on accurate information and reports. You both lied – to yourselves and to your superior officer. That is why both of you are being punished."

The punishment meted out, on the spot, in the group of four, with further formalities and privacy waived, was severe.

Carson busted Red two grades, from Sergeant to Private and fined him two-thirds pay for two months, the maximum punishment.

Thompson busted Mickey from PFC to Private, and fined him a months pay, the maximum punishment.

Carson and Thompson suspended the punishments for six months. This meant Sergeant Hawk and PFC Fowler could keep their rank and pay, if they kept out of trouble for six months. If they screwed up, though, within the six-month suspension, then their punishment would be reinstated on top of whatever punishment was served for the new infraction.

What remained now was the letter of consolation Captain Thompson would write to Mr. and Mrs. Willaim Butler to tell them about the death of their son, who, while on a mission with members of his unit, was killed in action in a firefight on a rainy night at a footbridge across Dak Toll Creek in Phuoc Long Province, 100 miles north of the capital of the Republic of Vietnam.

KIM

The small shadow was fleeting, a flash in the corner of his eye. J J paused. He waited a couple of seconds before continuing to arrange his clothing.

His half-full laundry bag sat next to his cot when he returned from morning chow. The laundry lady had made rounds and delivered the infantry team's wash.

The mess hall had served the usual – powdered eggs, powdered milk, World War Two-era heavily salted and dried pork some dared call bacon, a slice of roofing shingle nominally termed bread, and fifty-weight, scalding hot coffee a spoon could stand straight up in. Even though the crew had no choice what foodstuffs the quartermaster issued, he'd stopped complaining how meals were prepared because they had no clue how to make it tasty and no interest in making it palatable. C-Rations often were his preferred meal over firebase mess hall fare.

So, J J had returned and opened a B-1 unit of Ham and Scrambled Eggs. The contents of the meal box lay spread out on the PSP flooring beside his rifle, ammo pouches, and four grenades – two fragmentation, one concussion, and one incendiary.

The shadow flashed again. Something had darted past the opening of the bunker. The interruption of sunlight was only for a couple of seconds as if a child was playing peek-a-boo. J J shrugged it off. Maybe a soldier on the troop street had run past.

J J put down, opened his backpack, and removed the set of underwear and pair of socks in it. He opened the laundry bag and removed clean underwear and socks, rolled them, and placed them inside the pack.

The definition of clean clothes was a matter of heated, divided debate between the washers and wearers.

Soldiers placed dirty clothes in a laundry bag and set the bag at the entrance of their sleeping bunker for morning rounds. Laundry crews picked up the bags, tossed them on a cart, and brought them to the laundry point on Dak Toll Creek. There they washed the soiled belongings in creek water, hung the items on communications wire strung as clotheslines to dry in the hot sun, folded and stuffed the clothes in the bag, and delivered the wash. Soldiers paid one dollar a month – a month – for this valet laundry service.

Clean clothes was a euphuism for a soldier's jungle fatigues, underwear, socks, washcloths, and towels because they came back reeking like dead fish. Sweat, sun, and dirt masked the fishy stench, but it was always there. It was no wonder. Dak Toll Creek also was the sewage line for Phuoc Long and Sông Bé as well as the trash dump. The only time fresh water, actual fresh water, was in Dak Toll Creek was when it rained for an entire day, and that liquid flowed off Nui

Ba Ra.

The shadow flashed again. This time J J reached up to his gear hanging on a support pole and withdrew the bayonet from its scabbard. He waited for the shadow, and when it flashed again, he rolled over to his left, sprang to his feet, whirled, and crouched with the steel blade poised for combat action.

The little person standing in the bunker's opening giggled and squealed with playful delight.

J J dropped to his knees and lowered his bayonet.

"Hello, young lady." J J gestured with his hand. "Come in. What's your name?"

She responded to his invitation by stepping through the doorway. Her left index finger and thumb pressed together and against her lips hid shyness.

From her height, J J guessed she was five, maybe six years old. She wore the traditional black pajamas – a black cotton shirt and black cotton pants. The pink flip-flops were tiny and distinctive. As she came inside, she turned more to face him, and the sunlight accented her features. Her banged, black hair and dark eyes reminded him of Nancy on the bus and his little sister, Jodie.

"My name is J J. Can you say J J?"

J J met her gaze. She tilted her head forward with her chin tucked down. She was cautious but fearless.

J J patted his chest. "J J," he repeated. "My name is J J. Can you talk?"

"Yes, she can speak English," a voice said from the doorway.

J J turned, but the figure standing there was in silhouette.

"My name is Mai Li. I bring your laundry. This is my daughter, Kim."

J J stayed in place, on his knees. "Hello, Mai Li. My name is J J."

Mai Li laughed and stepped inside. "Yes, I heard. How do you do, J J. Kim, say hello to J J."

Now that she had entered and turned, and was standing in sunlight beaming through the bunker's entrance, J J was surprised at Mai Li's beauty and youth.

Kim giggled again. "J J. Chao ban."

"Chao ban means hello," Mai Li said.

J J bowed toward Kim. "Chao ban, Kim. I'm very glad to meet you."

He rose and extended his hand toward Mai Li. "And I am happy to meet you too, Mai Li."

She took his hand and matched his warm smile.

Both turned to look at Kim. They froze in fear.

"Oh, shit," J J said.

Kim held one of J J's fragmentation grenades in her right hand. Her little, left index finger was hooked through the ring attached to the safety pin.

"Bum, bum," Kim said.

J J acted casual while his heart skipped with anxiety. He did not want to make a sudden lunge to take the grenade from Kim's hands for fear he would frighten her and cause a sufficient tug with her finger to pull the pin. He smiled and held out his hand. "Kim, give me the bum, bum, please."

He could see the ends, bent and flared in their position to prevent the safety pin from slipping out. He didn't think Kim had the strength to draw the ring to straighten the tips as the pin was pulled through, as a soldier would do to prepare it for action. But, at Sugar Babe's, J J had heard Mr. Dickerson speak often about Murphy's Law: *if something can go wrong, J J,* Mr. Dickerson was fond of saying, *it will, Boy*. J J knew shit happens and he didn't want it to happen in the enclosed bunker where the thunderous, powerful blast would kill them if shrapnel didn't.

Neither Mai Li nor J J stepped toward Kim. They did not want to frighten or alarm her with a sudden move. Both kept an eye on Kim.

J J also kept his focus on the grenade. He was ready to pounce if Kim made the slightest tug on the safety pin ring.

Mai Li's voice was calm, conversational, as she spoke.

"I pick those up all the time. Grenades, flares, ammunition, I've picked up Claymore mines with the trigger attached. Bayonets, even loaded rifles and pistols."

J J kept his eyes on Kim's hands. "Clacker. It's a clacker, not a trigger. We call it a clacker. It sends the electrical current to the detonator."

"Yes, clacker. All of you are like my two brothers. They never did any house cleaning. Never organized. They left clothes and belongings lying around. I had to pick up after them. Here, *my boys* leave grenades on the floor or their cot like they were a ball. Very dangerous. Even a child can get to one so easily." Mai Li pointed. "You see?"

"You have two brothers?" J J did not look away from Kim's hands and fingers.

"They were killed by VC who came into the hamlet looking for food. The VC called my brothers spies. The VC executed them in front of me and our mother."

Kim's squeal and piercing scream scared the shit out of J J. He was stunned, frozen in place with his arm still stuck out and hand open for the bum, bum. He thought the fucking grenade had exploded. He felt his heart jump and flutter.

As Mai Li stepped forward and grasped her daughter, Kim dropped the grenade. The little girl hid behind her mommy, wrapped her arms around Mai Li's leg, and held it tight.

"What the fuck is going on in here?" Sergeant Holt asked from the doorway. "That kid scared the shit outta me with her screaming and squealing and carrying on. Thought I was gonna have a heart attack. What's going on, J J?"

"I'm getting ready to go on a checkpoint mission, Holt."

Holt stepped into the bunker and inched toward Mai Li and Kim.

"I been looking for you, Mai Li. You don't keep promises and show up for appointments. Customers are *very* disappointed."

"You stay away from me and my Kim. I do my job for laundry. That is all I do."

Holt moved closer.

Kim squeaked with fright, and Mai Li reached behind and pulled her closer, tighter against the back of her leg. There was nowhere to run, no escape. Holt stood between them and the opening.

J J stepped in front of Mai Li and Kim and braced

Holt. He put a hand up to halt Holt's advance.

"Hold on," J J said. "I don't know what's going on here but you've scared Mai Li and Kim, and I don't like that, Holt. They haven't done anything to you."

Holt stopped in place, six feet in front of J J.

J J shook his outward facing palm at Holt. "I think you better vacate the premises, Sergeant Holt."

Holt snorted. "What the fuck is going on here between you two? Did I interrupt a little hanky-panky? You gittin a little pussy on the side during laundry hours, Cookie?"

J J was startled, surprised. Anger rose, the top of his ears felt as if touched by a searing branding iron. "You're a asshole, Holt."

"This woman is one of my whores, J J. I had a paid customer lined up to enjoy Mai Li's services and she didn't show up at our scheduled appointment. I may have to give a refund, and I don't like giving refunds."

"I know, you son-of-a-bitch. You owe me ten dollars."

"I am not your whore." Mai Li's voice was flat and cold, filled with contempt.

J J looked over his right shoulder and saw that Mai Li's face was flushed with hot anger. Her small nostrils flared, her skin tone had turned red-black with fury. J J saw murder in Mai Li's squinted eyes. This woman can kill, J J thought.

Holt leaned forward to step closer but halted when J J stepped toward Holt.

"Leave, Holt. Get out of my bunker. And leave these two alone or I'll kick your ass, you son-of-a-bitch."

"Why you fuckin punk, I'll have your stripes, Boy, for threatening a NCO."

"You ain't gonna have nobody's stripes, Holt. What's going on, here?" Boss Tweed demanded. "I heard a scream. Like somebody's been hurt."

"It was Kim, Sergeant," Mai Li answered. "She was frightened, but she's alright. May we leave, Sergeant? I have my laundry rounds to do."

"Yes, you can go. I don't remember your name."

"It is Mai Li. This is my daughter, Kim."

"Okay, Mai Li, you and Kim can go."

Mai Li lowered her head and avoided eye contact with the soldiers.

"You take care, Mai Li. Bye, bye, Kim," J J called after them.

"Now, ain't that just the sweetest thing," Holt mocked. "*Bye, bye.*"

"Fuck you, Holt."

"Now hold on, you two. I want to know why you think you gonna get J J's stripes, Holt."

"He threatened me, Boss. Said he would kick my ass if I didn't leave Mai Li and Kim alone."

"So?"

"Well, it just so happens me and Mai Li have a business agreement, Boss. And she failed to follow through with her side of the deal."

"He's a fucking liar, Sergeant Tweed. He said Mai Li was one of his whores. She said she wasn't."

Platoon Sergeant Tweed did not look at J J. Instead, he focused on the supply sergeant. "What do you mean, *one of your whores*, Holt? You a pimp?

You run a whorehouse here on Linebacker?"

"Not here. Not on the firebase. Down at the laundry point. A couple of women came to me as a go-between. They wanted to offer services down at the laundry point, they just wanted my help."

"What kind of help?"

"Word of mouth, so to speak, Boss."

"You worthless bastard. You are a pimp. You will cease operations immediately, you hear me, Holt? If I get word that this is still going on I will go right to Top and the Old Man and they'll bust you so quick it'll make your head swim. And when they're done with you, I'll beat your ass till you wished you was dead. You hear me?"

Silence. J J looked at Holt and back to Sergeant Tweed.

"Answer me, Holt. Do you understand me?"

"Yes, Boss," Holt said. "I hear you."

"Now, get the fuck outta here and get back to doing your job to support the troop."

J J grinned. As Holt exited the bunker, J J wanted to hug Boss Tweed.

"What are you grinnin at?" Boss Tweed grinned too. "Get your shit together. Red and Mickey were released for duty, they're at the truck. Dutchman is waiting on you. I came to find out what was taking so long. Now, get movin. The squad is ready to move out to link up with the police and escort them to the checkpoint."

"You are something else, Platoon Sergeant. I wanted to hug you. Holt deserved a ass whippin and you gave him a good one – without layin a hand on his worthless ass. He's a sorry son-of-a-bitch."

"Listen to me, J J. Holt's kind is ruthless. He can be a vengeful bastard, so you watch your back. You hear me?"

". . . hear me? Can you hear me?"

J J could hear, but didn't know how to answer. The words were not there. He could not nod his head either. He was in a fog. It felt like he was almost asleep. It was dark where he was, or his eyes were closed. He couldn't figure it out. Something happened, but he couldn't remember what. I'm dreaming, he thought, I'm in a dream and it's dark.

Beside that voice, he heard others too.

Is he dead?

Naw. He's breathing. Chopper's inbound. What will we do with the other two? Dimples and Red?

Wrap them in ponchos. The bird will bring them out, too. To Long Bien.

We ain't got no ponchos.

Well, they'll have to go as they are, then.

What about the policemen? Two are wounded and two are dead.

J J wanted to look, but he didn't know where to look. Anyway, he didn't know what he wanted to look at. Maybe at the wounded policemen and the dead policemen. But where were they? Why were they wounded and dead?

And Dimples and Red?

"I dunno," a voice answered his dream. "Put em in the truck. We'll haul em back with us. I don't think we should put em on the Dustoff."

"We can't use the truck. It's blowed up and still burnin."

"Okay, put em on the gun jeeps."

"What about the kids?"

"What about em?"

"We gonna leave em here, in the road."

"Throw em over there, over there on the shoulder where everybody who passes by can see em. Are all of em dead?"

"Naw, two are, the third one is shot through the neck. He's still alive."

"Well, throw all of em over there on the shoulder. I'll put a bullet in the head of the live one."

"He's the one that had the incendiary. The other two just had frags."

"Well, then, it'll be a pleasure to pop a cap in his brain while he's watchin me do it."

J J tried but had no voice. At least he thought he spoke the words *gas tank*. He was sure he said *gas tank*. But for the moment he couldn't think why, or remember why, he said *gas tank*. He didn't say the words, he yelled them. Yeah, he yelled *gas tank*. Why the fuck would he yell *gas tank*?

He heard a chopper, then felt the downdraft of its blades.

Okay, they're all in, he heard a voice shout above him, *lift off is clear*.

Echo Five-Five Dustoff, forty minutes out, he heard another voice shout.

He felt a cool breeze sweeping across his body.

Even though he was in a fog, in darkness, J J knew

there were fingers around his dick – warm, soft fingers. He didn't think they were his fingers – although he couldn't be sure. He did need to pee, but he couldn't remember if he was holding himself to pee. Anyway, he couldn't quite grasp, so to speak, how he could hold himself in the way the fingers were positioned. He had no answer to Ole Ham's query that Miss Broadstreet, his English teacher, posed during her recitation of Shakespeare. Whether to pee or not to pee was the question. She loved Shakespeare, and he loved Miss Broadstreet. He imagined – oh, yeah – he imagined Miss Broadstreet and him. He had to admit, though, what Miss Shakespeare was doing to him, at the moment, felt pretty damn good. In fact, it was pleasurable. Was it Olivier, for whom the bell rang?

"He's waking up, Katie," a voice said. "He's stirring."

"Do you think he felt me bump into him?" another voice asked.

"I don't think the bump mattered, Katie. I think the way you reached out to steady yourself will be a topic of conversation for the duration."

"Sally, don't you tell anybody I grabbed him. You know I didn't mean to do that, in that way, for Chrissakes."

"Well, I saw what I saw, Katie. You didn't turn loose quite as fast as one would expect in that unusual predicament."

"I was not holding it more than a second – or two, or three. I mean, I didn't – I mean I didn't mean to hold it. I was – I stumbled and reached out to catch it – myself."

"Hey, girl, what can I say? You caught what you caught, and it appeared to me held onto it for dear life. It ain't the first time, by no means. I'd seen it done before, but under different circumstances, if you know what I mean. Uh-huh. Sure have. I've even done it myself a time or two."

"My goodness, Sally, shame on you."

"Well, Katie, you know I've got to tell Captain Dormand. As Charge Nurse, she'll have to make an incident report for the chief of patient services. I'm certain, too, she'll post a carbon copy on the bulletin board, as an advisory of how not to grab and hold a wounded warrior. There will be a need for training aids, practical demonstrations."

J J could hear these voices now, but these voices were female, American female voices. They were strange, soft but high-pitched, sweet and soothing. He couldn't see Miss Broadstreet though, then he realized his eyes were still closed.

The chopper. He had been in a chopper.

When J J's eyes opened, his head ached as it had after Wayne's Lucchese hit him in the temple. They had been playing football in the front yard, and J J's attempt to block Wayne's punt failed.

"I need to pee," J J groaned.

"I'll get the bed urinal, Katie. You can hold him while he does his business."

"Oh, Sally, what am I going to do?"

"Well, girl, you already had a little practice, so the pointing and aiming part ought to come natural."

J J finally became aware he was on a bed, a mattress, and naked. He tried to turn. Pain shot across his shoulders, up his neck, and throbbed in his head. He closed his eyes and lay still, hoping he wouldn't puke or pass out.

A cool breeze swept across his body, a fan was oscillating near him. He felt a chill.

"Jesus, my head hurts. I can't move," J J moaned. "I really need to pee."

He felt fingers again. Yeah, the head pain faded as warm, soft fingers held him.

"Okay, the urinal is in place," a female voice said, "you can go ahead. I've got you."

J J opened his eyes. He stared at the most beautiful girl he'd ever seen while she held him in her grasp as he peed in the plastic, hospital container.

"Jesus, that feels good. Who said Coke is the pause that refreshes?"

"Well, it's about time for your body to return to normal. Urination is a good sign, Soldier," another female voice said. "You've been out for more than two days."

The angel released him and removed the pee pot.

He turned his eyes to peer at the face where the voice came from.

"I'm Lieutenant Sally Norman, ward nurse. This is Lieutenant Katie Patton, shift nurse. You're in the Sixty-Second Field Hospital. A Dustoff brought you in to us a couple days ago. You've been in a coma."

"I was on a checkpoint with my squad. We were on a checkpoint, providing security for the police."

"There was detonation," Lieutenant Norman said.

"Why am I naked?"

"Fever. We've bathed you in ice and put the fan

on you to bring your temperature down," Lieutenant Patton said. "Seems like we were successful."

"Why am I in pain? Why does my head hurt so bad?"

"Your truck exploded," Sally said.

"From what we know, you were thrown up and out," Katie said. "You landed on your head. You've been in another world for the past sixty hours."

"Gas tank," J J said. "The kid dropped a grenade in the gas tank of my truck."

"I'll get a sheet to cover you," Sally said. "I'll be right back."

Katie smiled at the soldier who lay naked before her.

She felt something strange sweep through her abdomen, like butterflies. It was a warm, deep, sensual, tingling sensation she had never experienced. With anyone, any man. Her heart beat faster. She wanted to kiss him but instead posed a question.

"Are you hungry?"

"I think I love you, Lieutenant," J J said. He looked through her brown eyes into her soul and saw the woman he wanted to spend the rest of his life loving and pleasing.

SECURITY

Staff Sergeant Darby "Dimples" Dutchman, the third platoon infantry squad leader, was old school. He was a soldier's soldier who had been there, done that.

At 0140 hours, June 6, 1944, when he was a Private in the 505th Infantry Regiment, Dimples jumped into the French village named Sainte-Mere-Eglise. With mouth open, sucking wind, while climbing a ladder to help his comrade, Private John Steele, who was still in parachute harness hanging from the town's church steeple, a bullet pierced Dimples' right cheek and exited through his left cheek without touching jaw, gums, or teeth.

Dimples fell to ground bleeding from his wounds. Assisted by another 505th warrior, Dimples scampered away before attacking German soldiers captured or killed him and his savior, Sergeant Early Benson.

Rifleman Steele, who witnessed the churchyard skirmish from his prime position above the fray, survived the fight, and the war, and became famous when Cornelius Ryan published his book and the film, "The Longest Day", hit the screen. He had seen

Dutchman climb the ladder, heard the gunshots, watched the fall, and witnessed Benson's intervention.

At 82nd Airborne Division reunions, Steele always made it a point to hug Dimples and thank him for the rescue attempt. Early Benson never received a hug, recognition for his bravery, or a decoration for saving Dimples' life. But Sergeant Dutchman never forgot Benson's daring heroics and told everyone interested about Early's feats.

In a hole, in the dark, in haste, and under intense enemy fire, the medic's nervous stitching to close the bullet holes in Dutchman's cheeks created scars that appeared to be deep dimples, thus . . .

Now, he sat in the passenger seat of the three-quarter ton truck.

"Where have you been, Johnson?"

"I got tied up, Sergeant Dutchman. Sorry."

"Sorry? I'm glad you could join us for this very important mission, Corporal."

Sergeant Dutchman's public chastisement was sharp.

The platoon, minus the mortar squad, recoilless rifle section, and Boss Tweed, stood idle, lined up in tactical formation for its march to the police checkpoint. Two scout jeeps would lead followed by Lieutenant Versailles' jeep, then the infantry truck, with two scout jeeps pulling up the rear.

Red sat behind the steering wheel.

Mickey, Jinks, Remo Vance, Lucky Jerrigan, and Tex Pollard sat in the back of the truck. Sergeant Mosley, Leader of Bravo Fire Team, was sick with a bout of malaria and Kellen Averyman was in Thailand on R and R. No replacement for Billy Butler had arrived.

"We've been waiting on you."

"I know, Sergeant Dutchman."

"I want you to sit up front between Hawk and me. Mount up, Johnson."

"Okay."

Red started the engine as soon as J J and Dutchman got in. When Dutchman closed the door, the truck's wheels were in motion. Lieutenant Versailles wasted no time moving out. They were late for their rendezvous with the police at the western end of the bridge across the Sông Bé River. The platoon column sped east along Road 3-10 at 40MPH.

"After he brought Red and Mickey to me, I had to explain to Platoon Sergeant Tweed why we were sitting here with our finger up our ass instead of moving out to link up with the police. He went looking for you. We have a mission to do, Son," Sergeant Dutchman said.

Even though he was surprised, the instant J J met his squad leader he liked him. Surprised because Sergeant Dutchman did not match the image J J had created in his mind. Dutchman did not look, talk, walk, or act like the John Wayne J J had seen at the picture show. Where Wayne was a measured, gruff, and blunt character with other soldiers in the movie outfit, Dutchman was friendly, helpful, and unassuming. Where Wayne never smiled, Dutchman often did. In fact, Wayne was overall larger than Dutchman. Where Wayne stood six feet with a full head of hair, Dutchman was bald and five-nine.

But J J accepted other's assessment that the infantry squad leader would jerk a knot in a soldier's ass if slackness, dereliction, or inattention to detail were shortcomings. Word was Dutchman did his duty and expected everyone else to follow his lead, he led by example.

"I know, Sergeant Dutchman. I got involved with a situation with Sergeant Holt."

"*Holt.* What a asshole. What was the situation?"

"I thought he was going to attack a laundry lady in my bunker. I stepped in to prevent it."

"Holt was going to beat up on one of his whores?"

J J objected. "Mai Li's no whore, Dutchman. She was bringing in our laundry. She was there with her little girl, Kim. Holt claimed she was his whore. But she isn't."

Darby Dutchman eyed his young Corporal. "Touched a nerve, did I, Kid?"

"Well, you said it with disrespect. Mai Li handles our laundry to earn a living. I've not been over here long, but I see common folk trying to get by without getting killed by their own soldiers, or by the VC, or by us. Mai Li just does her laundry job to get a little money to support her family and Kim. She sure as hell ain't no whore."

"Well, I been here longer than you and I know Mai Li and her baby, Kim. Her old man is in a division down south, if he ain't dead. Before I left for R and R, she told me she hadn't heard from him in six weeks. She thinks he might of been wounded or been killed, or maybe even captured, and won't nobody tell her anything. All she gets from the chain of command is *he's on a mission in the Delta*. I know she's not a whore, J J. You got feelings for her?"

"What do you mean?"

"Like an attraction. Like you might have an interest, a boy meets girl interest?"

"No. Anyway, she's married. I respect that."

"Uh huh. She may be a widow. Would that make a difference?"

"Look, I don't know what you're getting at. I just met Mai Li and we had a ten-minute conversation. That's all." J J looked at Darby. "That's all."

"Uh huh. Well, by the tone of your voice it don't sound like *that's all*. It sounds like you might be smitten."

"Well, I'm not."

"Well, you may not think you are but sometimes what we don't see is lookin us right in the face."

"What do you mean?"

"The way you reacted to what I said told me there might be a spark between you and Mai Li. Take care, Red, watch them folks walking there."

"There ain't no spark."

Red eased on the brakes and steered the truck around pedestrians shuffling along the shoulder of the road. Barefoot kids grinned and waved.

Two little boys stood at attention and rendered a salute. As the truck passed them, one shot his middle finger in the air and shouted, "Fuck you, number ten."

"The more you deny it, J J, the more likely there might be an attraction."

"She's older than me."

"There. You see."

"See what?"

"You calculated the age difference. That only happened cause you measured your age with hers. How old are you?"

"I'll be twenty-two in seven days."

"Did you know Mai Li is only twenty-two?"

"No. Kim is five or six."

"So?"

"So, that means Mai Li had to be sixteen, seventeen, when Kim was born."

"So?"

"When I see the right one, I'll know it. I'll know when I'm smitten." Cookie paused. "I'll know it when the right one comes along. I'll see it in her eyes."

"I didn't. I sure as hell didn't," the squad leader admitted. "When I was being patched up in England, every morning and every evening my wife came to clean my wounds and put fresh bandages on. Of course, she wasn't my wife, she was a nurse, actually a nurse's aide. I didn't know I was smitten until she didn't come on the ward one morning."

"Red told me the story how you got shot through the cheeks. And the patch job they did caused the scars that look like dimples."

"Shot clean through both damn cheeks by the same bullet," Red laughed.

Sergeant Dutchman laughed, too. "All through high school and early on in the Army I was always Dutch, instead of Dutchman. Then, with the scars, I was no longer Dutch. I was Dimples."

"Do you mind that nickname? Dimples? It sounds sort of sissy."

"Naw, Dimples is kinda neat when you think about it. Anyway, the point I'm trying to make is, you never know when love is gonna grab you and turn your world upside down. It happened to me while I was in a hospital bed with my face wrapped in gauze, in jolly ole England. Been married going on nineteen years."

"Do you have any kids?"

"Nine. Five boys and four girls. Two of my boys are twins, two of my girls are identical twins. The girls look just like Molly, their mom."

"Nine? My God, Sergeant Dutchman, you got a infantry squad with nine kids."

Red slowed the truck as the column arrived where twelve policemen stood on the shoulder of the road.

"Everybody stay put till I get instructions from the Lieutenant," Dutchman said. The squad leader dismounted.

J J watched his squad leader walk away, marching toward Lieutenant Versailles' command jeep. He doesn't even walk like John Wayne, J J thought.

"Holt is gonna get hisself killed foolin around with civilians," Red said. "He's got a couple of whores workin down at the laundry point."

"Jesus. Mai Li ain't no whore, Red. She's just trying to make a living, taking care of her little girl, Kim."

"I know that, J J, I know. But unless somebody stops him, Holt is gonna hurt her, and maybe Kim, too."

"I'll kill him if he does, Red."

They faced each other. "I swear I'll kill the son-of-a-bitch if he even makes out like he's going to harm them."

"Because of the ten dollars he owes you?"

"No. No, Red. Because Mai Li and Kim didn't do nothing to deserve his shit. And, because he's a son-of-a-bitch. That in itself is enough, don't you think?"

"Yeah, I guess."

"What went on with your court martial?"

"It wasn't a court martial. It was a field grade Article 15. A policeman found a hollowed out melon by the creek. Inside it was two C-4 wads wired with a detonator."

"No shit? A melon."

"Yeah, a half pound of C-4 wired up in a melon."

"I'll be damned."

"The four of them were VC, J J. They was bringing the explosives to town, to support the attack on Sông Bé. We killed bad guys, J J."

"And Billy."

"Yeah, and Billy. We killed Billy, too."

"So, you got off scot free?"

"No, the Colonel busted me and fined me two months pay. But he suspended all of it for six months and released me back to duty. So if I stay out of trouble the Article 15'll be removed from my record."

"Why? If they were bad guys why did the Colonel bust you?"

"Cause I lied. I made a false report about a combat action, and the AK-47s."

"Oh, yeah. The automatic rifles."

"So, I'll keep my nose clean. I only got twenty-eight days and a wake-up before I'm back in the country of the big PX, round-eyed girls, and Dairy

Queens."

"You only got a month left in Vietnam?"

"Yeah, a month, less than a month. I can do that standing on my head. It'll be a piece of cake."

"You ever thought about an extension? For another six months? Jinks told me we get a thirty-day leave and a good bonus if we take a six-month extension."

"Nah, I got a wife and two little girls with big blue round eyes waiting for me in Tulsa. I'll go back to driving a truck for T-O-K Express. I like the Army, but my family wants me to get out. They want me to get out of Vietnam, to get out of this war alive. And I do too. Here comes Dutchman."

"Okay, boys," Sergeant Dutchman said, as he approached his infantry squad sitting in the truck. "Here's the deal. The White Mice are going to split up. Six are going across the bridge to the east end and six will stay on this side.

"The Lieutenant and Sergeant Wolcynski, with two of his scout gun jeeps, will go to the other side.

"The Lieutenant put two on this side. I want Mickey, Jinks, and Remo to go to the east side with the Lieutenant and Reggie. Lucky and Tex will stay with the six policemen and the two gun jeeps on this side of the bridge. Red will stay behind the wheel of the truck and Johnson will stay in the back of the truck for security. Johnson, you man the radio as well. I'll float hither and yon. Any questions?"

There were none. The five guards moved to their appointed stations.

The police officers' mission was to intercept

movement along Road 3-10, to check papers and conduct inspections of bicycles, motorcycles, wagons, cars, trucks, buses, and pedestrians. They also monitored riverboat traffic sailing under the bridge.

The 90-meter long vehicular and pedestrian bridge over the Sông Bé River east of the village of Sông Bé was a convenient chokepoint and permitted easy control of traffic for inspections.

"Here come the kids." Dutchman looked up at Johnson. "You've got an elevated perch, J J, so you be on a swivel, keep a three-hundred-sixty-degree lookout. Be on your toes."

J J looked at a dozen or more kids approaching. Most wore raggedy clothes. The children were unkempt, unwashed. A few appeared to be older teenagers. The moment J J recalled the words Deakins told him – *never take chances, even when it looks innocent enough. Kids with their hand out for a cigarette, chewing gum, money, or a C-ration meal might have a grenade in the other* – the group split up.

Gunfire from the direction of the bridge jolted the trio and drew their attention away from the approaching children. All three looked to see why shooting was going on.

Standing in the back of the truck, J J could see two policemen in the middle of the long bridge with their arms stretched out and pointing down toward the river. In hands were their .38 caliber revolvers. They had fired on two fishermen in a Sampan. The policemen and the fishermen were shouting, the fishermen waving their arms with clenched fists. It was a dispute. The policemen held the edge with their weapons, and the fishermen objected to whatever the policemen had ordered.

"Gum?" a voice asked.

In quick succession another asked, "Cigarettes?"

"You give me dollar?" a third begged.

"J J, get them kids outta here. Get them away from the truck," Sergeant Dutchman shouted.

One of the fishermen in the sampan on the river opened up with his AK-47 and dropped the fussing policemen on the bridge. The other fisherman sprayed the contingent on the east side of the bridge. Several were wounded by this gunfire.

Mickey, Jinks, and Remo dashed to the bridge and opened fire on the two on the river. Their hail of concentrated bullets was enough to kill the fishermen as well as blow out the bottom of the boat. The trio of infantrymen continued firing until the sampan with its sailors sank.

"*GRENADE*," Red shouted. "Oh, fuck. A grenade."

J J pulled the trigger of his rifle and shot a boy opening the gas cap of the truck. "Gas tank," J J shouted. "He dropped a grenade down the gas tank. Get out, Red, get out."

Sergeant Dutchman reached toward the driver's door, as Red opened it.

"OUT," Dimples shouted. "Out of the truck."

The explosions were thunderous. Shrapnel, from the grenade dropped in on the floor of the truck, escaped through the open door and ripped into Red and Dimples. When the grenade in the gas tank detonated, ignited fuel spewed like a flamethrower.

The disintegrating truck tossed J J up and forward as a catapult might sling a baseball. The flames were searing.

J J couldn't hear anything. He imagined his clothes were on fire, he smelled burnt toast and popcorn. He felt weightless, sailing and floating through silent air. His helmet tumbled off his head, and he lost his grip on his rifle. Then he felt the impact, followed by a numbing, teeth jarring pain before a sense of calmness and darkness engulfed him.

His body was hot and ached. His head throbbed; it hurt like no sensation he'd experienced. He could hear voices, but it wasn't children asking for chewing gum or money. J J imagined what it was like to be dead. His dreams were serene.

Elmer kept talking about killing people in *Nom* who never did J J or anybody else no harm. Vernon went on and on about defending somebody else's money. It's all about France's money Vernon kept repeating. Imogene caressed him. She put her red lips on his ringing ear and whispered how much she wanted J J to come to her bed. Mr. Dickerson appeared and shook his head, the sad smile of a clown painted on his face. The cafe proprietor patted J J's shoulder and said he was sorry but he would have made him Manager of Sugar Babe's when he returned from the war, if only he had lived.

J J grinned at them all and turned to kiss Imogene, but she disappeared. In her place stood fat ass Lillie Mae, who blew smoke from her stinking French cigarette in his face.

J J looked at his cracked-open head and watched

two farmers stuff C-4 in it. He winced when they grasped his head with dirty fingers and placed it with other green melons on a basket hanging from the rusted barrel of a rifle.

He relaxed, though, as warm fingers grasped his dick.

KATIE

Kathleen Tatum Patton was twenty-two, going on thirty. She had found and lost serious love twice in her short adult life.

Her first love died in a motorcycle crash. Her teenage beau tried to run up a makeshift ramp and vault five forty-five-gallon iron trash cans laid horizontally together. He made it over four. The emergency room doctors and nurses worked for seven hours, shaking their heads every twenty seconds at the futility, to save a young life. Her friends said Katie deserved more than a showoff responding to a dare. Kathleen returned the engagement ring to his mother.

Her second intimate love died of stab wounds received in a corner convenience store when drawn into a robbery-in-progress. He attempted to mediate and interpret the ensuing argument between perp and proprietor, neither of who spoke the other's language nor American. In the wrong place at the wrong time, her Good Samaritan was there to buy a condom Katie had insisted on. Kathleen waited three weeks after the funeral to give the engagement ring to his mother.

A month later, she graduated University of

Washington nursing school with a BS degree. At the recruiting office, she completed and submitted her application for a United States Army Commission in the Nurse Corps. Since there was a big war going on in a little nation called Vietnam, there was a desperate need for doctors and nurses. She was immediately accepted and appointed as a First Lieutenant.

As shift nurse in the Sixty-Second Field Hospital, Katie hugged and kissed a thousand wounded or dying soldiers while struggling to avoid emotional involvement. It was her job to be nurse and confidant to the young boys in her care, but she knew these combat veterans would never be the same, nor would she, afterwards. A few who could or would talk told of their love for her, but this one was different.

She smiled at his profession of affection.

"It's the uniform, Corporal Johnson. Soldier's can't resist a woman in uniform."

J J grinned. "Nope, it's the girl with the beautiful smile, a ponytail, and gorgeous brown eyes that captured my heart."

Katie blushed.

"Okay, Soldier, here's a sheet, shorts, and tee-shirt," Lieutenant Norman said. "I've sent a runner to supply for P J bottoms. How's our patient?"

"I think he's recovering quite nicely, Sally," Katie said.

Sally looked at Katie's face. "Uh hum. What went on between you two in my absence? Did you grab him again?"

"My goodness, Sally. Shame on you."

"I told Lieutenant Patton I love her, Mam," J J said.

"You did, did you?"

"Yes." Katie laughed. "Yes, he did, Sally."

"And I'm going to marry her," J J said.

"I see," Lieutenant Norman said. Then, "Ah, Lieutenant Patton, would you please check if the runner has returned with Corporal Johnson's pajama pants and slippers?"

Lieutenant Patton walked away.

"I'll help you with the shorts and tee, because I don't want you to try to sit or stand before Doctor Schoessler sees you," Sally said to J J.

Lieutenant Norman laid the sheet across his abdomen; she did not spread it over his body. She shook the underwear, lifted each leg, inserted each foot, and wiggled the shorts up into place for J J. Sally rolled the tee, slipped it over J J's head, and drew it down to his shoulders. With skillful agility, Sally lifted each of J J's arms and slid the white tee onto his upper body. Lastly, Sally shook out the sheet, spread it over J J's legs, and folded the top across his waist with military precision. Throughout this perfected performance neither spoke.

Sally Norman placed her hand on J J's shoulder. Her tone was official. "I want to tell you something, Corporal. Two things, in fact. One's professional, the other is personal."

J J looked at Lieutenant Norman but said nothing. He was afraid to nod his head because of the pain. By the flat tone of her voice, he recognized this was now a Lieutenant talking *to*, not *with*, a Corporal.

"The professional part, Corporal Johnson, is about fraternization. It is against Army regulations for an enlisted man to fraternize with an officer, or the other way round. Do you know the meaning of fraternize, fraternization?"

"No, but I think you're going to tell me, Lieutenant."

"That I am, Soldier. To fraternize, fraternization, means to socialize, mix, hang out, or hobnob with. Under the UCMJ, it is a punishable offense for you, an enlisted man, to fool around with Lieutenant Patton, an officer. Do you understand?"

J J continued to look into Sally's eyes. He did not speak.

"I need you to acknowledge what I just said, Corporal," Lieutenant Norman said. "This is an official discussion, a counseling that I will record in your medical file."

J J answered. "Yes Mam, Lieutenant, I understand."

"Good, now for the personal part of our little tea party." Sally Norman patted J J's shoulder tenderly. She stood next to his bed.

"Why did you tell Katie you love her?"

J J frowned at her puzzling question. "Because I do, Lieutenant."

"Do you have any idea how many wounded, crippled soldiers who are far from home, worried about surviving this war, and thankful they're here out of harm's way, still alive, tell all the women nurses that? Tell us they love us?"

"Probably a lot."

"You're right, a lot. She's had her heart broke twice in her short adult life, Soldier. Now I want you to leave Lieutenant Patton alone. You hear me?"

He met Sally's piercing stare. J J did not blink. "When I looked through her beautiful brown eyes into her soul I knew right away that she was the woman I wanted to spend the rest of my life loving and pleasing. I could not catch my breath. I thought my heart would fly outta my chest. I do love Lieutenant Patton, Katie, and I will ask her to marry me. Flaternized or not."

Lieutenant Sally Norman smiled, leaned over, and placed her lips next to J J's ear.

"Can you hear me, Corporal?" she whispered.

"Yes, Mam," J J whispered.

Her warm hand rested against J J's opposite cheek. Her position was normal for a nurse attending a patient. To an observer on the ward, it might even appear as a nurse kissing the cheek of a patient.

"Don't you fuck around with her, Soldier," she whispered. "If you hurt Katie, I'll cut your dick and balls off and stuff them up your ass. You hear me, Johnson?"

She stood erect, brushed hair off his forehead, and patted his shoulder again, but this time it was not tender pats; it felt to J J more like jabs, punches.

"Do we understand each other, Corporal?"

J J grinned. He understood the language and implication. Sally Norman was Katie's protector, a hell of a bodyguard. He was impressed.

"Yes, Mam. I hear you loud and clear. I know you will and can take care of *bidness*. I will ask Katie to marry me, I will love and please her for the rest of our lives, and I will not hurt her. I say what I mean and mean what I say. I am a man of my word, Lieutenant."

A voice behind Lieutenant Norman interrupted their chat.

"Nurse, I'm looking for Corporal James Jerome Johnson."

J J tried to rise to look toward the voice. Pain shot up his neck and electrified his temples and forehead.

"Jesus, son-of-a-bitch, that hurts." J J groaned. "Thought I was going to puke and pass out."

Without turning or looking over her shoulder, Lieutenant Norman responded. "He's right here, Doctor Schoessler."

"So, how's our patient doing?"

"He's awake and alert." Lieutenant Norman pinned J J with her black eyes. "We had a good chat, Doctor. The Corporal understands my words and their meaning."

J J looked at a teenager who appeared at the nurse's side.

"Corporal Johnson, I'm Doctor Schoessler. How are we doing?"

"We, Sir?"

Doctor Schoessler smiled and let it pass. "I'm glad to see you're alert and pert."

"Excuse me, Doctor Schoessler. I have other chores and patients to look after. I'll be near if you need me. Lieutenant Patton is seeing about pajamas and slippers for Corporal Johnson."

"Thank you, Nurse Norman. I'll only be a few minutes here, then I'll finish rounds."

"Lieutenant Norman and Lieutenant Patton are

taking good care of me, Doc."

"I see. That's good. Now, we do permit some level of informality on the wards in the Sixty-Second but, when others are present, I prefer Doctor or Captain. Okay?"

"Yes, Sir. I'm sorry. We call Doc Swanson, Doc. He's senior medic in my Troop. A habit, Sir. Won't happen again."

"That's good. Let me have a look in your eyes and ears and listen to your heart."

Captain Schoessler held his little flashlight and shined the beam into J J's eyes, switching back and forth to determine degree of clarity, dilation, and sensitivity. The Doctor brought the light around and peered into the right ear and then the left.

"Well, that's good. No sign of bleeding."

"Jesus, Doc, you look like a teenager. How old are you?"

Immediately J J regretted his informality.

Doctor Schoessler laughed. "I'm thirty-three. Yesterday, as a matter of time." He leaned forward and placed his stethoscope against J J's chest.

"Happy Birthday."

"Thank you."

"I'm sorry I said, Doc again."

"Ah, that's good, your heart beat and its rhythm sound normal." Doctor Schoessler's smile faded. He pulled the stethoscope from his ears. He patted J J's shoulder. His face acquired its professional facade. His voice was flat, authoritative, matter of fact.

"Corporal Johnson, you've had a bad knock on your head. X-rays show two features I believe are cranial hairline cracks just above and forward of your left temple. Along with the normal and expected external swelling, there also may be some internal inflammation. We don't think your brain suffered severe injury, although it must have been roughly jostled and shaken when you banged it. We did not detect any enlargement of the brain. But the impact on your head when you hit the ground may have caused fluid to accumulate and press on your brain. And that's not good. That's why you were out for over two days. So, we're going to keep you with us, for a week to ten days. For observation."

"It was a grenade, Doctor Slosher."

"Grenade? I don't understand."

"A kid dropped a grenade in the cab of our truck and another kid dropped a grenade down the gas tank. I was standing in the back of the truck. There was shooting going on, on the bridge. The police were shooting at some fishermen. We were distracted. The kids came up quick."

"Yes. I see. There were two grenades. And the explosions . . ."

"The explosions blew me out of the truck. I was on fire, my clothes were on fire, I remember that."

"Well, you weren't severely burned, thank God for that. Singed a little but you have no burns or blisters. We've x-rayed your back and spine and there are no broken bones. You're bruised and that causes your body pain. But my main concern is your head trauma. That's why you're going to stay with us for a bit."

"I killed the kid, Doc. My rifle was on automatic. I blew him away, cut him to pieces."

"Yes, I see." Doctor Schoessler paused. "While you're with us, I've asked a psychologist to visit with you because of your concussion. The other reason I'm referring the specialist is because you were calling out names."

J J stared at the doctor, thinking, remembering.

"Red? Dimples?" Doctor Schoessler waited.

"Red and Dimples."

"Yes, that was two of the names. The others were Holt, Kim, and Made Lee?"

"Red is my fire team leader, Sergeant Raleigh Hawk. He was in the cab of the truck. Dimples is my squad leader, Sergeant Darby Dutchman. He was standin by the driver's door, hollering about the kids. Sergeant Dutchman was shot through his cheeks in World War Two. He's got nine kids."

"And the others?"

"Holt is the Troop supply sergeant. It's Mai Li, not Made Lee. She is our laundry lady in the Troop. Kim is her daughter, a little girl about five, six years old."

"Good. I'm pleased your memory function is active, seems normal. That you can recall people with their name is encouraging."

"What about Sergeant Hawk and Sergeant Dutchman? Are they here with me?"

"Not that I know of. I'll have someone check to see if they're here.

"Now, I want to make sure your brain continues to function properly. After the psychologist's visit with you, we'll determine when it's suitable for you to be released. I've prescribed medication to help with the pain now, but it will return. I did not want to over sedate you, I wanted you to stay awake and alert.

"So there still will be pain. In fact, it may get worse. When you feel like you need a little relief, just tell the nurses on the ward. A ward physician will take over from here."

"My head, neck, and shoulder hurts. I have a flaming headache, feels like a volcano erupting. My body aches all over, like I was run over by a tank."

"Yeah. I have no doubt about that, Corporal. While no bones broke, there are deep bruises. You're lucky to be alive. When you came in, we immediately administered ice packs to reduce the swelling. At first examination, I thought we might have to bore a hole in your skull to insert a tube to drain fluid away from your brain.

"Do you have any questions of me?"

"No questions, Doc. I'm thirsty. I could use some water."

"I'll let Lieutenant Norman know."

"Could I get something to eat?"

"I'll let Nurse Norman know that, too."

"Would you also tell Lieutenant Patton? She was going to check on some clothes for me."

"I think Lieutenant Patton's shift ended thirty, forty minutes ago. She's left the ward. I'll have the clothes brought to you."

"Thank you, Doctor Slosher."

"It's Doctor Schoessler. Well, with our conversation and your ability to recall, I feel confident you don't have internal brain hemorrhage or damage. Being able to remember the names is encouraging. I'll have some water brought and see if we can get a meal from our mess hall. After two and a half days without eating, I've no doubt you could use some food. I've not made any food restrictions on your chart. You take care, now, Corporal Johnson. Nurse Norman will be with you in a few minutes."

"Sergeant Burl Deakins. He's a squad leader in Hotel Company, Sir."

"Yes, I know him, Jerry. I'm surprised you've come to me requesting Deakins. I've had dealings with Sergeant Deakins. It seems a weird coincidence you've come to me asking he be assigned to your troop as an infantry squad leader."

"I've come for your help, Colonel Tolon. Both my sergeants were killed in action. I need replacements. I need experienced infantrymen."

Colonel Tolon nodded. "I understand your need to replace both your men, Captain Thompson. What I don't understand Is why you specifically asked for Deakins?"

"He was suggested by a young man who's judgment I trust. I've talked this over with Lieutenant Versaille, Platoon Sergeant Tweed, and First Sergeant Morris. My first sergeant made inquires. They're aware of the shortcomings, but all are in agreement."

"Shortcomings? Jerry, two recommendations are on my desk concerning Sergeant Deakins. Did First Sergeant Morris tell you about Deakins?"

"Yes, Sir, I'm aware there've been problems. Top said there had been issues."

"Issues? It's not just issues, Jerry. Deakins has a

reputation as a merciless killer, he may even be a murderer. Of course, he's killed bad guys, he's got the decorations to prove it. But he's not only killed bad guys, he's killed innocent people, too. Old men, women, and children. He's accused of burning people to death."

"First Sergeant Morris said there had been some instances where Sergeant Deakins set fire to peoples' houses without confirmed evidence of enemy affiliation. But, I need a battle-hardened squad leader to replace Sergeant Dutchman. I mentioned Sergeant Deakins as a potential replacement for Sergeant Dutchman because I don't have anybody else. I need the leadership."

"What about your other casualty? Sergeant Hawk? Who do you have to take over the fire team?"

"I'm going to promote Corporal Johnson to Sergeant and make him fire team leader. The remaining soldiers in the squad respect him. He's a natural leader and warrior."

"Listen, Jerry. I'm not certain you know what you're getting into if I give you Deakins. One of the recommendations for Sergeant Deakins is a Special Courts-Martial for manslaugther, or the military equivalent of such crime. The other recommendation is for a Distinguished Service Cross. This boy is a two-sided saber. He's deemed a criminal as well as a brave warrior."

"But he hasn't been convicted, Sir."

"No, that's true, Jerry I've not accepted the recommendation for the court-martial. There doesn't seem to be sufficient evidence available to convict him.

There are no Vietnamese eyewitnesses who could or would point the finger, and his colleagues can't or won't be sure they saw him burn the houses. But I know Mike Baker, his CO, probably would be happy to get rid of him."

"I'll take him, Sir. Warts and all."

"Okay. I'll grant your request, Jerry, I'll have Deakins transferred to you. But you keep an eye on him. You have to watch out for the warts. I don't want Cronkite telling everybody in America we knew Deakins would flame houses and cremate innocent men, women, and children, and that we continued to let him do it."

On the second morning after awakening, J J was able to sit up. He did not rush it because he discovered sudden movement created a throbbing headache. On the third morning, he walked around the ward.

Katie was on middle shifts and was there by his side, holding his arm day after day, as he moved about as often as he could for a little exercise. Katie often came after evening chow when she was off-duty. They would walk outside and sit on the rear step of an ambulance that was parked in backwards, its rear end faced the storage Quonset hut. There, hid behind the vehicle, they talked.

They discovered each other. Katie told J J about returning the engagement rings, and J J told about Sugar Babe's and Holt, about handing over ten dollars to join the Army to be a cook.

Katie said he was gullible. They laughed about it; she laughed with J J, not at him.

Even though J J continued to profess his love, he had not tried to kiss Katie. When they sat on the rear step, when they were in private, she held the hand he offered. When she placed her hand in his, she slipped her fingers through his and folded them over. J J felt a thrill pass through his soul when she did that, the warmth of her palm against his made his heart race. Her perfume was magic to him, but he resisted taking her in his arms.

"Your perfume drives me crazy, Katie. I hold back from taking you in my arms and smothering you with hot passionate kisses. It's all I can do to hold back. I love you, Katie."

She looked at him. "It's Chanel. Number Five."

He laughed, looking into her brown eyes. "The Vietnamese sometime call us Number Ten. *You number ten, G I,* they say. They give us the finger, too. It's like a schoolyard taunt. Then they scamper away. I didn't know what number ten meant until Red told me."

J J paused. He nodded his head at Katie. "I really like you, number five."

She giggled. "I've never met anyone like you, J J. You make me laugh."

"I'm one of a kind, Katie."

"No, I mean . . . Well, I mean . . ."

"I mean to marry you, Katie Patton. Come hell or high water."

They talked and laughed until veils hid the crescent moon. The snap of thunder opened the gates in the dark navy clouds for a downpour. The night monsoon arrived and drenched them before they could rise off the step.

J J, still holding Katie's hand, turned toward the pathway to run into the hospital ward to escape the drenching.

He felt the jerk to his hand as Katie resisted. She tugged and pulled him back.

"In the ambulance," Katie said.

The rain soaked them as Katie fiddled with the back door handle.

J J saw her struggle to lift the latch and stepped in to force it. With his arms around her, his hands on the door, she turned into him and kissed him.

He let go of the door and wrapped her in his embrace. They stood in the rain holding their sweet kiss for the longest moment.

"Open the door," Katie whispered.

Once inside, she unlaced her boots and tugged them off, slid away the rubber band holding her saturated ponytail, pulled her clinging olive-drab tee shirt over her head, and removed her bra.

J J moved in to take her in his arms again, but she put a hand out to stop him.

"You must get out of those wet clothes, Soldier," Katie said, "or you'll catch cold."

She unfastened her brass belt buckle, shimmied her jungle fatigue trousers down her legs, and stepped out of them. Then she removed her panties and dropped them on the floor of the ambulance.

J J did not hesitate shucking his wet PJs, shorts, and tee. He stepped out of his soggy, tan hospital slippers. He stood ready for her.

Katie never hesitated. This time, a condom was the farthest thing from her mind. Katie wanted him, all of him. She moved into his arms, there in the back of the Army ambulance.

She made passionate love to him in the dim light, on a mattress dragged to the floor off the top of a medical gurney, as thunder cracked and rain pounded the metal roof.

She had found the love of her life and clung to him, his warm body pressed to hers. She caressed him and kissed him and whispered her love in his ear.

"I love you, J J. You fill my heart with happiness and peace, Sweetheart. I do love you so."

She kissed and held him, and ran her fingers along his bare back with strokes of tenderness. Katie was fulfilled, happy, and content. She felt this third time would be the charm.

She had found the man she wanted to spend the rest of her life loving and pleasing.

PROPOSAL

On the morning of the seventh day of hospitalization, J J received two letters, one from Miss Imogene Sandlin, the other from his mother.

He read Imogene's short note first.

Dear J J

I pray God protects you. Elmer got put in jail for demonstration against the war. He was bad beat up and come out with a broke hand. He got kicked out of his place and is staying with me. We been talking about staying together. Vernon says hi, he bought a new LaSaber last Saturday and it got stole at church on Sunday. Mr Dickerson talks about selling Sugar Babe's but no buyer yet. Your Momma showed us the pictures you sent when you got decorated and promoted. You are a good boy, J J. Bless you.

Your friend,

Love Imogene

He folded the page and slipped it back into its blue, *Airmail* franked envelope.

He opened the letter from his mother.

My Dearest Son

I pray you are well and safe. Kip and Jodie say hello. We all miss you. We are well, so don't worry. I showed your pictures to everybody at the cafe. They are proud of you, as I am. The money you send each month is a godsend and I thank you so much for helping. I got a little promotion at the VA and a few dollars more each month. Your Papa called last week. He was in jail and wanted me to come with money to get him out. I told him he could rot there for all we care. Write when you can, Son.

Love,

Momma

As he folded the letter and put it away, he reflected on his hasty decision to leave Sugar Babe's. It was a brief reflection, interrupted by the appearance of Lieutenant Versailles and Platoon Sergeant Tweed. His thoughts about remaining as a cook in the cafe faded when he saw his platoon leader and platoon sergeant. J J was pleased to see them and felt special they came from Linebacker to visit him in hospital.

After handshakes and congratulatory exchanges, Lieutenant Versailles spoke first about the business of their errand to deliver a message from their Troop Commander.

"Boss and me bring a proposal from Captain Thompson."

"Wait, Sir. Tell me about Red and Sergeant Dutchman. Nobody here can find out about where they are?"

Lieutenant Versailles looked at Boss.

"They didn't make it, J J," Tweed said. "Both were

killed when the truck exploded."

"It was kids. One tossed a grenade in the cab with Red," J J said. "I saw the other drop a grenade down the gas tank."

"Yeah. We think it was planned," Lieutenant Versailles said.

"Mickey said he thought the kids knew the checkpoint was gonna be at the bridge because there were so many of them," Tweed said. "Mickey said they were bigger kids than usual, fighting-aged kids, not youngsters."

"Lucky and Tex ran to Dutchman and Red," Lieutenant Versailles said. "Red's legs were ripped to pieces from the blast. He bled to death lying on the road. There wasn't anything we could do to save him. Shrapnel hit Sergeant Dutchman in the face and neck. He died before Dustoff got to us."

"He has nine kids."

"Who does?" Lieutenant Versailles asked.

"Dimples," Boss said.

"Sergeant Dutchman has nine kids," J J said. "What is his family gonna do without him?"

"He's got Army insurance," the lieutenant said.

"It ain't much money, Sir," J J said. "Twenty-five thousand dollars won't last long for a family of ten."

"Well, Mrs. Dutchman will receive half his pay each month, I think," the lieutenant said.

"That's right, Sir," Boss said. "She'll get that for the rest of her life, unless she remarries."

J J looked at his platoon leader. "It ain't about money, Sir. Their daddy is gone."

"I know, Johnson. I know. It is what it is and we

can't change it."

"You were lucky, J J. Jinks and Remo told me they watched you sail outta the truck and hit the road with your noggin. They said you looked like one of them clowns who gets shot out of a cannon at a circus. They ran all the way across the bridge and snuffed the fire offa your clothes," Tweed said.

"Jinks said he thought the fishermen in the river were decoys for the kids' sabotage move," Versailles said. "It was all planned. When the shooting started, I moved to the policemen on the bridge to see what it was all about. The firing and my movement distracted everybody. That was the plan all along, I think, to draw attention away from the truck."

"I killed the kid who dropped the grenade in the gas tank. My rifle was on automatic. Blew him away."

"Well, Remo killed two others who ran," the platoon leader said. "We searched them but found no grenades or weapons. Remo may have killed kids who came only to beg for money or food."

"The lieutenant has come here with a proposal for you, Johnson," Platoon Sergeant Tweed said.

J J looked at his platoon leader and waited.

"Captain Thompson's promoted you to Sergeant, Johnson. He proposes to appoint you as Alpha fire team leader when you get back to Linebacker."

"I'll replace Red," J J said.

"That's right," the platoon leader said. "And the Capn asked Colonel Tolon to give us Sergeant Deakins to take over as squad leader."

"Burl?" J J grinned. "I'll be damned. Cuz is gonna be squad leader."

"He's your cousin? Deakins is your cousin?" Versailles asked.

"No, Sir. Not really. He told em at the replacement station in Long Bien we were cousins so we could get assigned together."

Lieutenant Norman approached.

"Excuse me for interrupting," Sally said. "I've come for you, Corporal Johnson."

"Lieutenant Norman, Mam," J J said, "this is Lieutenant Versailles, my platoon leader, and Platoon Sergeant Tweed."

They shook hands, but there was no exchange of pleasantries. Nurse Norman was there on official business.

"Corporal Johnson, you are to report to the hospital commander right away. I'll escort you to his office."

"Okay, J J," Tweed said. "We'll head back to camp. We'll see you in a few days. Take care."

They all shook hands in farewell. Versailles and Tweed marched off in one direction toward the exit while Sally and J J marched down the hallway to the CO's office.

"Why does the commander want to see me, Lieutenant?"

"The Colonel read my notes."

"Corporal Johnson reporting as ordered, Sir."

Colonel Dermott Dickerson, commanding officer of the Sixty-Second, returned the salute. "Have a seat, Corporal."

J J sat in the burgundy leather chair placed

squarely in front of the Colonel's massive mahogany desk. There was a wooden in-box on the forward left edge of the desk, an out-box sat on the right front. Both had stacks of paper in them. Medical records folders were stacked behind each wooden box. A single medical record lay in the center of the desk, which the Colonel tapped with tips of his right-hand fingers.

"I've had a look at your file, Corporal Johnson. I've talked with Doctor Schoessler, Lieutenant Norman, and the psychologist, Doctor Marker. They all agree you are ready to return to duty. What do you think?"

"I'm ready, Sir. I feel pretty good. The Doc and Lieutenant Norman and Lieutenant Patton have taken good care of me. Well, all the doctors and nurses on the ward have taken good care of me, but especially Doctor Slosher, Lieutenant Norman, and Lieutenant Patton."

"There is a memorandum for record in your file about fraternization. It's about you and Lieutenant Patton."

"Yes, Sir. Lieutenant Norman counseled with me about that."

"It's a court-martial offense."

J J did not hesitate in the face of the authority sitting across the desk.

"I love Katie, Sir. I'm going to propose to her, Sir. I love her and I'm going to ask her to marry me."

The Colonel leaned back in his over-sized leather chair.

"Have you thought about the future, Son?"

J J had to admit he hadn't. "No, Sir. I'm living in

the present. I'm in love with the woman I want to marry now. The future will happen, one way or the other."

"Well, in the present both of you stand to be disciplined for fraternization. It could be the end of Lieutenant Patton's career. I am in a position to ask her, to make her resign her commission."

"Would you do that, Sir?"

"No, Son, I wouldn't. Lieutenant Patton is a fine young woman, an outstanding nurse. She has a great future in the Army. She'll be promoted quickly and advance faster than her peers. She may even become a general officer, that's how smart and talented she is. You've come close to screwing that up, Johnson."

The Colonel's chastisement stung J J. He understood the implications, the possibility of destroying Katie's career. He felt helpless, weak. He didn't know what to say.

Colonel Dickerson continued. "Army regulations are words on paper. Sometimes commanders use those words as a guide rather than as the letter of the law. As a commander, I have some leeway to act on transgressions of good order and discipline. There aren't any words in the UCMJ written to cover love between a woman and her man, or the other way round. Love is blind to chevrons on sleeves and bars on shoulders. Where are you from, Son?"

"Oregon. Lake Oswego. It's a few miles southeast of Portland, Sir."

"About ten miles southeast. As the crow flies. What did you do there before your enlistment?"

"I was a fry cook at Sugar Babe's."

"Which one?"

J J paused. How did the Colonel know about Sugar Babe's and Lake Oswego?

"The one on Ferdinand Avenue, Sir."

"A couple of blocks over from the bus station."

"Yes, Sir. Have you been there?"

"I've eaten at your cafe many times. In fact, I've eaten at all three of Albert's places. Bird Parkway, Broadway, and Ferdinand."

"You know about my town? You know Mr. Dickerson?"

"My relatives live in Portland. My wife and children are in Portland while I'm here. Your former boss is my brother. I think I remember seeing you in the cafe."

With those words from the hospital commander, the recognition was immediate for J J. "I'll be damn, Sir. You're Colonel Dickerson, Mr. Dickerson's brother. Sugar Babe's Dickerson's brother? You're Doctor Dickerson, the baby doctor."

"Pediatrician."

"I remember. I remember you, Sir. You told a joke one time about two men from Texas pissin off the Broadway Bridge."

Doctor Dickerson kept a straight face. "The one from Lubbock said 'the water in the Willamette sure is cold'."

"Yeah," J J nodded, "and the other one, the one from Odessa, said, 'yeah, and it's deep, too'."

Both roared with laughter.

"It is a small world, isn't it Corporal Johnson."

"Yes, Sir. It is."

"Now, Son, back to this business at hand, this

fraternization business. You've been honest and forthright with me about your love for Lieutenant Patton. I'm sympathetic to your situation. I have been married to my sweetheart for nineteen years, four daughters. I'm assuming Lieutenant Patton has the same feelings for you as you have for her?"

J J did not hesitate. "I believe she does, Sir. I sure hope so."

"I will assume it is so. So, I'm going to be up front with you, one Oregonian to another, so to speak. I need a Mess Sergeant in my hospital mess hall. Sergeant Wurtz' tour is up in six weeks and I need a good man to take his place.

"I cannot condone your relationship with an officer in my command. I can, however, make it happen, so you're not in the same unit but will be close at hand. I'm not playing Cupid, mind you, Soldier," Colonel Dickerson said with a huge grin, "but I propose you be the replacement for Sergeant Wurtz, to be my new mess sergeant. I'll promote you to Sergeant at the time you assume your new post. What do you say?"

"You know, Sir, I paid a recruiter ten dollars to join the Army to be a cook."

"You did what?"

"Yes, Sir. Gullible as hell, Sir. It's my weakness. I'm a trusting man. I trust a person when they give me their word. When they go back on their word, or I find out they lied to me, I lose all respect. I did that with Holt, the recruiter. Instead of going to cook school to be a 92-Golf, I went through infantry training so he could draw a bonus. But I like the infantry. I am a soldier, Sir. I'm an 11-Bravo, infantry."

"Well, I just offered you the chance to fulfill your aspiration of being a cook in the Army."

"No, Sir, you didn't. You offered me the mess sergeant's job, not the job of a cook."

"You'll be in a mess hall. You'll be in charge. You can cook when you want to."

"I guess I could, Sir. But you know what? I learned this morning that my leaders in the cavalry troop think a lot of me. They want me and need me. Before I reported to you, my platoon leader brought a message from my troop commander. Captain Thompson promoted me to sergeant and said when I get back to Linebacker he'll make me a fire team leader. I will be responsible for soldiers in combat. I've traveled a long journey, from being a nobody cook on Ferdinand Avenue to being somebody who has responsibility. I will be responsible for others and I think that will be fulfilling. I am an infantryman, Sir, and I find combat exciting. And that's what I am going to do, Sir, be a combat infantryman."

"Fair enough, Son. I like your cut of the cloth. You are a credit to the uniform. Consider yourself verbally reprimanded for fraternizing with an officer.

"Now, here's my personal opinion, Son. I don't think your sweetheart is going to be happy you passed up this opportunity to be near her. I don't think Katie will be happy about your decision."

Lieutenant Katie Patton led the way to J J's bed. She held a small cake with two candles and sang in perfect pitch. Captain Schoessler and Sally harmonized. Nearby soldiers joined in and murdered *Happy Birthday*.

Katie held out the cake. "Make a wish and extinguish the flames, Soldier."

J J sat up, grinned, swung his legs off the bed, and nodded. He blew out the candles. He looked at Katie and his heart raced. J J was flattered she had feelings for him. In his eyes, she was beautiful, perfect in every way.

Katie placed the birthday cake on the wheeled hospital over-bed tray table Doctor Schoessler pulled bedside.

"Happy Birthday," each of them said.

"HAPPY BIRTHDAY, JOHNSON" voices shouted.

"Thank you. THANK YOU, EVERYBODY."

Sally took his shoulders and kissed J J on each cheek. "I hope all of your wishes come true, Corporal Johnson. Happy birthday."

"Thank you, Lieutenant. We're gonna find out in about a minute."

Doctor Schoessler shoved a hand and J J grasped and shook it.

"Happy birthday, Corporal Johnson. I wish you the best."

"Thank you, Doc. I appreciate how well you've looked after me."

Katie stepped forward.

J J met her broad smile. His heart fluttered. He wanted to take her in his arms and kiss her. He was so in love with the Army nurse who stood before him.

She shoved her hand out to him for a handshake.

J J took her hand with both of his, slipped off the

bed, and knelt. He didn't drop to one knee, twinges of pain sometime reoccurred, but he managed to get into the proper position for his proposal.

Katie gasped.

Only the swishing sound of twirling overhead fans filled the ward. Time and motion had stopped for three seconds before normal life returned to the ward floor.

"Lieutenant Kathleen Tatum Patton, will you marry me?"

"Oh, shit," Sally Norman whispered.

"Atta boy, Johnson," a voice said.

"Say yes, Lieutenant. Make him happy," another voice said.

"I serve as an official witness to this proposal of marriage," Captain Schoessler declared.

"I'm deeply moved," Katie said. "Surprised. I don't know what to say, I . . ."

"Choppers inbound! Dustoff! Wounded inbound!" a voice blared over the ward intercom. "All staff on the pads, NOW!"

"Let's move. Now," Doctor Schoessler said.

The Doctor and Lieutenant Norman turned and hustled away.

The wop-wop-wop sound of Huey choppers grew louder as the Med-Evac birds settled on the pad to discharge their precious cargo of broken, pierced, mutilated, and shattered bodies of battle.

Katie withdrew her hand from his grasp. Her smile was forced. "We'll talk about this. Later." She turned away from J J and double-timed toward the sound of turbine engines.

J J clung to the edge of the mattress for support and struggled to his feet. He sat on the edge of the bed and shook his head, bewildered.

He wondered what just happened. He expected Katie to scream *YES*, rush into his arms, and smother him with kisses. He looked at the untouched birthday cake. He wanted to mash and bash it with his fist. He was certain, sure, of Katie's love. He recalled Katie's word, gullible. A gullible idiot, he thought. Now, her rejection created doubt. Well, he argued, she didn't reject the proposal. She didn't out-and-out say no, he thought, or get lost, or screw you. He needed to talk with Katie, to find out what was the matter. His heart sank. He had been certain she would say yes.

Four hours and forty minutes later Katie returned.

"I'm off shift in an hour, at twenty-two hundred, at lights out. Meet me at the ambulance a few minutes after lights out." She walked away without waiting for J J's response.

He was early. He sat on the rear step of the ambulance they had used two more times for a passionate rendezvous after lights out. There was no bed check so he could walk off the ward whenever he wished, like others did to go outside to smoke. He was always early, Katie would arrive a half-hour later. Waiting for her was agonizing. They would sneak inside and close the door. After hot love, they would lay in each other's arms and whisper and talk until before dawn and then slip back to their own beds.

This time, though, he imagined he had somehow

screwed things up by his public proposal of marriage. He had detected Katie was not herself as he knelt before her.

His decision to return to Linebacker instead of taking the job Colonel Dickerson offered to stay close to her would not set well, he suspected.

He stood when Katie came around the ambulance.

J J put his arms out and stepped forward to embrace her.

Katie placed the palms of both her hands on his chest and held him away, at arm's length.

In the dim light J J could see tears sparking in her eyes, he could not mistake the sadness on her face.

She moved around him and sat on the ambulance step.

He kept his mouth shut and sat beside her, his bare arm touching hers. J J wanted to put his arm around her, hold her close, caress, and kiss her.

They sat for the longest time in silence.

Katie's head was down, J J looked at her face.

In his heart, he knew then he had hurt his sweetheart.

He wouldn't blame Sally for cutting his dick and balls off and stuffing them up his ass.

He would loan her his bayonet.

AMBIVALENCE

Except for four armed soldiers on guard duty patrolling their quadrant, the hospital grounds were silent. After lights-out on the wards, a quiet peace settled in. Only nurses and attendants stirred. They moved about in a hushed, noiseless, attentive, and urgent vigil checking on patients who needed constant care and tender touches.

And so that was the way it was as they sat together, on the rear step of the Army ambulance, in that stillness, their shoulders and bare arms touching. A slight breeze moved the humid late-night air across them.

Katie's perfume aroused him. His heart thumped, his pulse hastened.

J J looked again at Katie's face. The seconds he had waited before he whispered seemed like dozens of minutes. "I've hurt you, my love. I see tears in your eyes and sadness on your beautiful face, but I don't know what I've done wrong, Kathleen."

It was the first time J J spoke her name, her personal name, her first name, her real name.

Katie did not speak, but she nodded once.

He was encouraged by her small movement.

J J looked at her hands in her lap, her fingers intertwined as if in prayer. He drew in a loud deep gulp of air and shook his head with such vigor the ambulance shook. This time, J J did not bother to whisper.

"I'll need to get a bayonet from the supply room," he said. "They're probably closed now, so I'll go get it in the morning. First thing. I'll be there at the supply room door when the supply sergeant opens for business. I'm sure he has a bayonet, somewhere on some back shelf. I'm sure Sally will be waiting for me, I'll bring it to her right away, even before I've had my coffee and grits and tea and crumpets."

That was also the first time J J spoke Lieutenant Norman's first name.

"She told me," Katie whispered.

J J's heart skipped, he felt lightheaded. He knew this breakthrough required patience and restraint of mind and body. Any sudden energy or expression he made might be rejected with a complete shutdown of conversation. He felt hopeful as long as they were talking.

"I figured she would. She's your protector, your bodyguard. She told me, *in no uncertain terms*, what she would do if I hurt you. I understood the exact meaning of her words and the dire implications of her actions."

"What are you talking about?"

Katie's question surprised J J. Now, panic set in. Fear gripped his chest. Oxygen seemed to disappear from the air. He felt a shortness of breath.

"I'm talking about what Sally told me," J J said. "I thought that's what you meant when you said Sally told you. Didn't Sally tell you what she'd do to me if I hurt you?"

"What did she tell you?"

"That if I hurt you she'd cut my dick and balls off and shove em up my ass." J J watched Katie's face.

Katie giggled; a snort found its way through her nostrils.

"That's why I need to go to the supply room in the morning, to bring her a bayonet."

She did not whisper, but neither did she look at J J. "Sally doesn't need a bayonet. She's pretty handy with a scalpel."

Was the frozen tundra broken? J J wondered. Did the ice crack? He felt like maybe Katie's giggle and snort was a good sign.

"Well, that'd probably give a faster, cleaner, neater slice with a little less agony and pain rather than sawing with a dull bayonet."

After a pause, Katie spoke again. "Sally told me what you told Colonel Dickerson."

Oh, shit, J J thought, deep-ass do-do.

"Is that why you feel hurt?"

"No." Katie paused. "Yes."

Another pause before she spoke again.

"Why did you have to make such a scene on the ward? I was so embarrassed. Everybody watching, listening, cheering you on like it was a game, a conquest, for Chrissakes. You have no idea how many of those guys on the ward have told me they love me and want me. I lost count after a thousand. Some died in my arms while telling me of their love."

J J listened to the hurt in Katie's voice. He kept his mouth shut. He wanted to put his arm around her but knew it best to wait. He kept his arm pressed against her softness. He knew, he felt, she was not ready and would not accept his embrace.

"I'm sorry, Kathleen," J J whispered. "I'm am so sorry I hurt you. If I had suspected, if I had had the slightest notion you would be hurt by my public display of love for you and my proposal of marriage, I would have kept my mouth shut. It hurts my heart to know that I hurt you."

"I was in shock when you got on your knee. I thought I would have a heart attack. I thought I would scream. You're lucky the chopper call came."

"You know I love you. You knew I was going to ask you to be my wife. Why were you surprised?"

"I expected it to be private, between the two of us. Maybe even here on the step of the ambulance, in our private spot. Not in front of everyone."

"But you said you love me too. What difference does it make whether it's here in the moonlight or in front of your friends?"

"You don't understand, do you?"

"I guess not. I guess it's a guy thing."

"To a girl, a proposal of marriage is special, it is supposed to be her moment with the man she loves. She is the center of attention for him, for no one else, not for the world to watch. Your demonstration on the ward *is* a guy thing. It announced you made a conquest. I was embarrassed, I felt like you were showing off to the other guys. And some of them cheered, as if their teammate had made a score."

They sat for the longest time in silence.

Katie's head was down, J J looked at her face.

In his heart, now he knew why he had hurt his sweetheart.

"I'm sorry, Kathleen. I understand now why you feel hurt. I am truly sorry. Please forgive me."

"Colonel Dickerson offered you a job here, in the hospital. He told Sally about talking with you, because of her entry in your record about fraternization. She said you would be in charge of the hospital mess, you would be promoted to sergeant, be the mess sergeant."

Katie raised her head and looked at J J. "You'd be in the rear area. You'd be safe, near me."

J J looked into Katie's eyes. "Before the Army I was a fry cook at one of Colonel Dickerson's brother's cafes. Sugar Babe's, on Ferdinand Avenue, in my hometown of Lake Oswego. I told you about it."

Katie nodded, holding her gaze. "I remember. You paid a recruiter to be a cook in the Army."

"That's right. Holt. I wanted to be a cook. Red called me Cookie."

"Red, your fire team leader? The one who was killed?"

"Yeah. I kinda liked the nickname. Cookie."

"I like it, too. Cookie."

"Yeah, well, instead, I went through infantry training and was assigned to an infantry squad in a cavalry troop. I was in combat, as an infantryman. My journey has been along paths I never imagined. I like being a soldier, Kathleen. I like the structure, the discipline, and friendship. Everybody has a job to do, they know what to do, and we look out for each other. I never experienced that. Freeman and Oradondo never pulled their weight, and fat-ass Lillie Mae . . . well. Well, she was worthless. It's different with my Lieutenant and Boss Tweed and Jinks and Deak and the other guys. They think a lot about me. Sergeant Dutchman and Red, and Billy did too. And my First Sergeant and Captain, too. I don't think I'll ever want to be a fry cook again."

"You don't want to cook anymore?"

"Not in the Army. Listen, Sweetheart. You love the Army. You love your job as a nurse. You've told me a career in the Army was something you've thought about. Well, I have, too. If we both stay in, make it a career, we could be assigned to places together. You would be at the installation's hospital or a clinic, and I would be in one of the unit's or in a headquarter's job."

"I'm an officer, and you're an enlisted man. That would never work for us to be together on the same post. I think it's against Army regulations for an enlisted soldier and an officer to be married to each other."

"Well, Colonel Dickerson said flaternizing was against the regulations. He reprimanded me for flaternizing with you. Said you'd be in trouble too, it could affect your career. But he said the regs didn't say anything about the love between a woman and her man."

"He said that? To you? About me, my career?"

"Well, wait a minute. Don't get mad about it. He

said you had a lot of talent, you were special. He even said you might be a general one day."

"He said that, too?" That revelation softened Katie's tone.

"He did. Did he reprimand you too, for fooling around with me?"

"No."

"So, you see. He thinks you're special. Otherwise, he'd been on you about flaternizing with me, an enlisted man."

"It's fraternizing, Cookie, not flaternizing."

"Frat? Fratern? Fraternizing."

"Have you thought about becoming an officer?"

"No."

"Maybe you could go to OCS?"

"That's what Holt mentioned. But I didn't finish high school. He said I couldn't go to OCS without high school and some college, an Associate Degree."

"You could get your GED."

"What's GED?"

"The official name is General Education Development. There are other names, too. Some call it General Education Diploma, or General Equivalency Diploma, or Good Enough Diploma. It's for people who didn't finish high school, they can take a test to receive their high school equivalency certificate or diploma."

"You don't have to go to school?"

"It's a written test. The study material is provided before the test."

"Maybe I'll look into it when I get back on the firebase. Vannoy'll know what I need to do."

"I'm afraid for you to go back up-country. I'm afraid, J J. Before the Army, both the boys I was engaged to, had promised to marry, died. I don't want that to happen to you. It's like . . . well, it's like a jinx. I'm afraid if you go back to your unit you could be hurt bad or killed."

"That won't happen to me, Kathleen. I promise you I will not be hurt or killed."

J J slid off the ambulance step and knelt in front of Katie at her knees. He took both of her hands in his.

"Oh, Cookie."

She did not resist and looked at her man with affection. Her faint smile grew into a grin.

"Kathleen Tatum Patton, I love you with all my heart and soul. I want to be with you for the rest of my life. I want to love you and please you for the rest of our lives together. You are my sweetheart. I am asking for your hand in marriage. Will you be my wife? Will you marry me?"

J J remained on his knee, holding Katie's hands in his.

"HEY! What's going on here? Identify yourself."

The guard held his rifle at the ready.

J J released Katie's hand and struggled to raise himself to face the sentry and screen Katie's escape.

Katie dashed around the side of the ambulance and fled.

"I was trying to ask my girl to marry me," J J said. "You scared the shit out of both of us. Now, she's run away."

"You ain't supposed to be out here. This area is off limits after lights-out."

"Who says?"

"Lieutenant Bacon, Officer of the Day, that's who, asshole. What's your name and rank? Identify yourself. Advanced to be recognized."

"I'm right here, Soldier," J J said. "If I advance, I'll be on top of you. I'm Major Bennett, the hospital shrink. What's your name and rank soldier?"

"Oh. Sorry, Sir. Private Mason, Sir. I was just following my guard duty orders. Excuse me, Major, but you don't look like no doctor."

"It's the dim light, Mason. I'm much older than I look. It's the genes. Do you mind lowering your rifle? It makes me nervous when a soldier points a rifle at me."

Private Mason lowered the muzzle but continued to hold it with both hands, at the ready. "How come you ain't in hospital garb if you're a doctor?"

"My patients relate to me if I dress like them. I deal with all the crazy ones, Private Mason. Maybe I could help you, Son?"

"I don't need no shrink, Sir. Excuse me, Major, I'm on duty so I need to get back to my rounds."

"Very well, Private Mason," J J said. He came to attention and raised his hand in a slow-motion salute.

Private Mason snapped to attention and smartly brought his rifle into the position of Present Arms for a return salute. "By your leave, Doctor Bennett, Sir."

"Carry on, Private Mason. If you ever need somebody to talk to, look me up. I'm in the hospital directory. I work behind the locked, meshed screen doors, Ward Four Charlie."

The following morning Lieutenant Patton did not

appear on the ward. Lieutenant Norman did.

"Here's your release orders, Soldier. After chow report to the supply room. You'll be issued clothing for your trip to your firebase. The chopper will lift off the pad at 1000 hours. Be there."

"Where's Lieutenant Patton, Mam?"

Sally paused. She took a deep breath. "Usually I don't share information about a hospital staff member with a patient or provide information about the status of an officer to an enlisted man. But this morning you'll be an exception to my rule, Johnson. Lieutenant Patton called in sick. If I find out that she is sick because of what you've said or done to her, I will hunt you down and cut your dick and balls off. You hear me, Corporal?"

"Yes, Mam. And if you find out that's the case, I'll help you with the scalpel."

There was no humor on Lieutenant Sally Norman's face. She meant business.

"Don't you fuck around with me, Johnson." Nurse Norman folded her arms across her chest. She spread her feet in a combative stance. Her glare was serious.

J J perked up. He wondered who would win, but concluded he didn't want a confrontation with this woman who would look after and protect his sweetheart. And who might just be able to kick his ass. J J decided he should stop shoveling shit to Sally.

"I know where you are, Johnson, I've been to Linebacker. I can get a pilot with a Slick, Loach, or Snake to bring me to your firebase, to any firebase, at any hour of a day or night. Any of us here can call for a chopper anytime. Now get your ass to chow, then to the supply room, get dressed, and report to the chopper pad. I don't want to see you on the ward again. Is that clear?"

"Yes, Mam. Wilco."

As Corporal Johnson marched down one hallway toward the hospital mess, Lieutenant Kathleen Patton entered the ward from the opposite corridor. She went to the counter of the nurse's station where Lieutenant Sally Norman stood.

"I've sent him to chow and to supply to change clothes. You've been crying, girl. Your face is a mess."

Fresh tears formed in Katie's eyes, she tried to smile for Sally. "I don't know what to do?" She shook her head. "I've never been this confused in my life."

Lieutenant Norman came around the counter and put an arm around Katie.

"Let's go into the doctor's office. We can close the door and have a few minutes of privacy."

Katie sat in the patient chair, Sally sat in the doctor's chair at the small desk. Their knees almost touched, Sally held Katie's hands – and waited. She was prepared to listen, would listen, before speaking.

"I met him last night, at the ambulance."

"Uh hum."

"I was angry, hurt, confused."

"Uh hum."

"I told him his display in front of everybody embarrassed me. I don't know what I would have done or said if the call for choppers had not happened."

"Uh hum."

Katie pulled her hand from Sally's grasp and used the back of a thumb to sweep rivulets of hurt streaming down her cheeks.

Sally turned in the chair, jerked several tissues from the box on the desk, and handed them to Katie.

Kathleen wiped her eyes, blew her nose, and laughed. "He said you'd cut his dick and balls off."

Sally grinned. "Uh hum. You have no idea, Honey. I can do it too. All through Hardin County high school, I helped daddy castrate bulls. I've used them all, a knife, emasculator, bander, BelZac, or the Burdizzo. I know what to do to make it happen."

"He asked me again to marry him, out there at the ambulance."

Sally waited. She had done this with a thousand patients – held their hand, looked them in the eye, and let the hurt and disappointment spill out, at their pace. But now, with Katie, the anticipation and pause were murder, but she held her tongue.

Katie looked at Sally.

Sally reached up and with the tip of a thumb wiped away Katie's tears.

"I'm here for you, Honey, you take your time. You can tell me about it if you want. There is no pressure. If you don't want to tell me, that's okay too."

Sally said those words but didn't mean them. She was dying to know what Katie's answer was. She closed her mouth and waited, caressing Katie's hands.

"I didn't give an answer, I didn't have a chance. A guard came up on us. I ran away. I was afraid for him to be caught with me outside in the dark. You've already reported him to the Colonel. I didn't want him to get into trouble, to be punished."

"I'm sorry, but you know I had to do what I had to do. So, we still don't know your answer?"

Katie shook her head again, despair filled her brown eyes. "I don't know what I want to do."

"Do you love him, Honey, or is just lust?"

Katie didn't answer.

"Listen, getting your sail trimmed in the back of an ambulance is one thing, I mean, I know, I've been out there a time or two, or three, myself. But this love business means something else altogether. It changes lives, forever sometimes. A life with him will be different. What about your work as a nurse? You've told me you've thought about staying in the Army, making this your career. You're an officer, he's an enlisted man. How is that going to work if you stay in the Army? What's he going to do? Stay home with the kids?"

After chow and changing clothes, J J returned to the ward in spite of Lieutenant Norman's order. There was no one at the nurse station, the staff was tending to patients. He thought about knocking on the closed door of the doctor's office, at least to say thank you and goodbye, but didn't. He knew a closed door meant privacy, patient-doctor business, so he walked past without a second thought. Certainly, if he had known Katie was in there, he would have entered without knocking. If he had known she was in there crying her heart out, he would have busted the door down.

On the chopper pad, the crew chief added J J to the flight manifest and motioned him to mount the bird.

The door gunner nodded as J J scampered aboard and sat on the bench. He was the only passenger.

The crew chief gave a thumbs-up, trotted around the front of the chopper for a last minute clearance check, and took his position as the right door gunner.

J J scooted along the bench to the edge. He peered out, looking at the hospital ward doorway, mentally issuing a summons for Katie to appear.

The Huey's turbines whined and its blades began a slow rotation. Within seconds the engines had reached lift-off RPM, and J J felt the chopper rise off the pad.

"The chopper?" Katie stood.

Sally stood too but continued holding Katie's hands.

"He's aboard, going back to Linebacker," Sally said. "Let him go, Katie."

"No. NO." Katie pulled her hands away and opened the door.

"Katie?"

Sally stepped into the doorway and watched Katie rush down the corridor. She folded her arms across her chest and smiled as Katie ran through the ward's exit to the chopper pad.

"Yep," Sally whispered. "That girl is full of love alright, smack-dab, neck deep in love. Bless her heart."

As the chopper hovered above the pad, J J saw Katie come out just as the bird nosed over to gain speed and altitude.

J J raised his hand. "Katie," he whispered. "Katie, I love you."

She did not wave. He wasn't sure she saw him. His heart ached. He kept her in sight until she became a speck in the vast landscape of the Sixty-Second Field Hospital and buildings of Saigon. Tears burned his eyes, he did not try to hide his sadness.

Katie stood in place, arms folded across her chest, steadying herself against the push of propeller blast.

She remained in place until the slick disappeared from her sight.

SEPARATION

As J J's chopper lifted off the pad, gained altitude, and disappeared from view, Sally stood at the ward's exit waiting for Katie. Sally felt pangs of concern and sadness for her colleague and friend standing alone, with her head bowed, near the white painted H. She pushed open the screen door and called.

"Katie? Katie, Sweetheart? Katie, come inside."

Katie raised her head and looked in the direction of the chopper's flight path. She searched skyward for what seemed like a dozen minutes before turning to walk to Sally.

Fresh tears sparkled in Katie's eyes. "I'm so afraid for him, Sally. I've lost two already. I don't want him to be hurt."

"I know, Honey. I know. You sure are neck-deep in love with this boy and I can see you're in pain."

"I do love him." Katie looked at Sally. Her plea was evident. "But, I don't know what to do."

"We'll figure it out, Honey."

Sally reached out and pulled Katie into her arms, held her tight, and embraced her. "I'm here for you. It'll be alright."

Katie buried her face into Sally's shoulder and wept.

Sally tenderly stroked the length of Katie's ponytail and whispered soft, soothing words of comfort.

"You're gonna be alright, Girl. I give you my word. We'll figure it out, you and me. I know you love the boy, and God knows he is dead in love with you, in spite of what I said I'd do if he hurt you."

Katie's muffled voice was clear. "He said you would cut his dick and balls off if you found out he hurt me."

Sally laughed and snorted. "That I did, Honey. I sure as hell told him that. And I might have to follow through on that promise I made to him."

Katie pulled back and looked into Sally's eyes.

Both grinned and hugged each other.

"Don't do that, Sally. I like what I found there."

Their loud, boisterous laughter rumbled throughout the grounds and corridors of the eight wards of the Sixty-Second Field Hospital. Their unbridled mirth may have pierced the animated war stories told by the sock-folders and straphangers who were sipping Dubonnet in the officer's club in downtown Saigon.

"Okay, now. That's good. Laughter is the best medicine. Let's go inside and get a cup of coffee."

As Sally poured the liquid, the nurse station phone rang. She handed a cup to Katie, then answered the call.

"Two B, Lieutenant Norman." She paused. "Yes, Sir." She listened. "She's not on duty, Sir, but I'll send a runner to tell her you want to see her." She listened. "Yes, Sir. Thirty minutes. I'll have her come to your office, Sir." She listened and nodded. "Yes, Sir. I understand, Sir. I'll take care of it. Goodbye, Sir."

Sally looked at Katie.

"You need to go freshen up and get in uniform. Colonel Dickerson wants to see you in a half hour."

"What does he want?"

"It's about my report, Sweetheart. About Corporal Johnson and fraternizing, with you."

"J J told me Colonel Dickerson reprimanded him, for flaternizing."

"You mean frat. Fraternizing."

"No." Katie grinned. "I mean flat, flaternizing."

"Well, whatever. Now, listen to me. The Colonel thinks the world of you, Honey. We all do. He will not punish you for, well, flatnerizing, but he will caution you about fooling around with an enlisted man, even one who proposed marriage in a public military station."

"Once in public and once in private. Both times interrupted."

Sally paused and smiled. "You see. You're feeling better. You're a soldier, Kathleen. You're an outstanding nurse and a great friend. You'll be okay. And after this chat with our hospital commander, you and me will talk about how to handle this soldier boy you told me wanted to be a cook."

For thirty minutes, the flight to Linebacker was uneventful. J J sat at the edge of the bench and peered at the passing terrain. Jungle canopy, patches of rice paddies, and a hamlet enclosed by bamboo trees lazily sauntered beneath the slick. J J imagined being on a patrol and tactically paralleling the thin creeks and streams where the sun's reflection created natural, brilliant sparkles.

He saw peasants walking behind water buffalo, pushing or pulling carts along trails in the wilderness. Pedestrians, bicyclists, and pedicabs moved freely along the shoulders of the asphalt highway the chopper's flight path followed. Merchants or family members toted baskets of goods and vegetables to market to sell or to their homes for nourishment.

As J J took in the men and women scurrying along with the baskets bobbing at the ends of the bamboo stick across their shoulder, he wondered about Billy and Billy's mom and dad, and Billy's wife, Emma, and Billy's children. What a mess, J J thought, two kids, three women, and a wife. How could anyone sustain a sane life with all that?

Well, J J shook his head; Billy didn't have to worry about it anymore did he? All those lives messed up, screwed up, broken hearts, dealing with the loss of Billy.

The clouds below the chopper skids came into view like the edge of a thick gray carpet. One second the ground was visible in bright sunlight and hidden in the next second. As the blanket appeared, cool air whipped into the helicopter. It seemed to J J the temperature dropped from ninety to sixty degrees. J J shivered from the immediate chill.

In five seconds, they were in the soup. The sharp scent of rain preceded water blowing in on J J. He scooted to the center of the bench to get out of the spray.

J J looked at the back of the helmets of the pilot and co-pilot. From their movements, he suspected they were trying to figure out what the fuck to do. What in the hell is wrong with a pilot who flies straight into such bad weather? J J wondered. If the visibility is so poor from the side of the chopper, J J reasoned, the aircraft commander and pilot can't see shit in front of them. That's when J J looked forward, through the front Plexiglas. There was nothing but dark grayness. The son-of-a-bitch is going to fly into the side of Nui Ba Ra, J J's brain screamed. We gonna fucking die in a fucking helicopter crash. J J resisted the temptation to yell and restrained himself from jumping forward to grab the stick and fly the bird. He realized he was holding his breath.

The pilot cut power, the chopper nosed over, and somebody shouted, "OH, SHIT."

The aircraft commander turned and looked at J J. That's when J J realized he was the one who shouted.

The bird came out of the clouds and cool air into clear and humid space. J J inhaled a deep gulp of oxygen when he saw chopper pads and the small airstrip on the southern edge of Linebacker's perimeter.

The pilot landed the craft and reduced throttle. When the crew chief gave a thumbs up, J J pushed out of the Huey and trotted, bent at the waist, a safe distance away from the still whirling blades. As three soldiers boarded the taxi for its return flight, the turbines increased blade spin to lift off speed and the chopper rose into the humid air.

Since this trio had no combat gear, J J suspected they were on their way to Long Bien where they would change into khakis to begin an R and R, or meet with Sandra and Sergeant Kane to process out for home, the land of the big PX, and final separation.

Little moisture had reached ground here; the red dirt was not even damp. The rain moving north had bumped the southern side of the mountain and skirted around the edges of the firebase.

J J stood in place and watched the bird lift off the pad. He felt like giving the pilot the finger. The chopper sailed low over the concertina wire on the western perimeter, Delta Troop's sector, and began to gain enough altitude to skirt the canopy of rubber trees eight hundred meters beyond the minefield, but stayed under the clouds covering the hamlets near Phuoc Binh. The wop-wop-wop faded as the helicopter banked left to take up a flight path due south toward where he had been an hour earlier.

In the momentary quietness, he thought about how it would be great if he were aboard returning to Katie. On the other hand, maybe the separation would give Katie time to decide her answer. He had proposed twice on the same day, but interruptions took control.

The first, Katie had admitted, freed her from having to answer in front of the staff and patients on Ward Two Bravo – the second, Private Mason, freed her from a commitment as well.

Maybe he should have accepted Colonel Dickerson's offer, Cookie thought, and taken the job of hospital mess sergeant. Katie wanted that; he knew she did. He remembered the disappointment in her beautiful brown eyes when he told her he had decided to return to Linebacker and take up the job and responsibility of Alpha fire team leader.

While standing there, on the edge of the firebase chopper pad, the sound of a busy military camp returned. He surveyed his surroundings. The camp proper appeared unchanged since his arrival with Deak five months ago or his eleven days in hospital. The number of sandbagged bunkers had not increased or decreased. Two soldiers manned each of the sixteen guard towers; one stood alert behind the machine gun. Soldiers played volleyball on the only court on Linebacker, other soldiers carried materiel, a saw buzzed, and two hammers pounded nails somewhere off to his left.

The rain, if there had been some, had not affected life and activity on this Army camp. On the contrary, most often a good soaking refreshed the will and cooled things down. Soldiers would stand in the rain, just to do something different, unusual. Like Billy, who would stand naked in the rain while washing the vehicle in Dak Toll Creek.

Nothing seemed different to J J. Vietnamese civilians swept out bunkers, dumped trash barrels, and scurried about. He saw laundry ladies pulling carts, some loaded with clothes going to the sleeping bunkers to deliver jungle fatigues and underwear that smelled fishy, and some taking clothes that smelled ripe to the laundry point. He saw tykes tagging along. He thought about Mai Li and Kim. And Holt.

The six 1-5-5mm cannons were still there, each gun in its pit as before. But three pits for the 1-0-5mm howitzers were vacant; only three guns were in position. Those three pieces, with muzzles elevated and pointed north, and as if synchronized and on cue, fired in unison. The muffled thumps shook J J from his reverie.

Smoke from these guns floated toward Phuoc Binh with a westerly breeze. J J inhaled the smell of burnt powder and cordite. He smiled, savoring the pleasing odor.

He turned and walked toward Delta Troop's Command Post. He saw the detail of five soldiers behind one of the outhouses. They were shuffling around three latrine barrels – cut-down, fifty-five-gallon drums – where black smoke spiraled up from the burning excrement. The aroma drifted his way; a pungent and memorable stench of burning shit.

Once more, James Jerome Johnson had arrived home.

Vannoy was pecking at his manual typewriter as J J entered the orderly room. First Sergeant Morris stood with papers in hand in front of a tall, gray metal, three-drawer file cabinet. Morris was fingering full folders filed in the pulled out middle drawer. Both looked up when J J spoke.

"Hello, Darlings. I'm home."

"I'll be damned. Hey, Johnson. Welcome home," Vannoy said. "We been expecting you. How you doing?"

"Well, it is good to see you, Johnson. I'm glad you've recovered enough to return to duty. We need you."

"Thanks, Vannoy. Thank you, First Sergeant. I have to admit I missed being here with you."

"Captain Thompson'll want to talk to you, but he won't be back for an hour or so."

"I need to draw some clothes, gear, and my weapon. All I got is what I got on. My jungle fatigue shirt don't have my nametag or US Army sewed on, or my chevrons."

"Well, go see Holt, get outfitted with the stuff you need. He's got your rifle, too. Take your stuff to your bunker and put it away. Once you put your gear away, come back here for the Captain."

"Okay, Top. Lieutenant Versailles and Sergeant Tweed came to see me in the hospital. They told me about Sergeant Dutchman and Red."

"Yeah," Morris said. "That was a big loss."

"He's got nine kids," J J said.

"Yeah, I know," Morris said. "And Sergeant Hawk has two little girls. He was due to go home in a month. It's a goddamn shame."

"I don't understand why the fuck Johnson don't cut our losses and bring us all home," Vannoy said.

"That's President Johnson, to you, Mr. Vannoy," Top admonished.

"Anyway, these fuckin people over here don't appreciate what we do, the lives we give up," Vannoy persisted.

While looking at Vannoy sitting behind the typewriter, J J thought he heard Elmer's voice.

"You sound like Elmer," J J heard his own voice say.

"Who's Elmer?" Vannoy asked.

J J blinked and shook his head. "Never mind. Look, before I go to supply I have a couple of questions."

First Sergeant Morris nodded. "Go ahead."

"In the hospital somebody mentioned something about a high school diploma. They called it a GED."

"Yeah, it's a test you can take to get a certificate, the equivalent of a diploma, as good as one anyway. Most all business accepts it, and the Army certainly does."

"Well, First Sergeant, I don't have a high school diploma and I was wondering if . . ."

"Vannoy, give Johnson an application."

Vannoy opened his field desk drawer, rifled through folders, withdrew a form, and handed it to J J.

"Sign this form. Vannoy will send it to Division. Personnel will send it to USARV, and they will send the study material and tests up here to you. It's all pretty simple and straight forward. You can probably have your certificate by the end of next month."

J J signed the form and handed it to Vannoy.

"Okay, what?"

"There is something else, First Sergeant. I want to get married and I want to go to OCS."

"No, shit, J J. You wanna be an officer?"

"At ease, Vannoy. Okay, Johnson, I heard what you said, but the first one set me back a bit. You took a knock on your noggin. You been in the hospital, out cold for a couple of days, we hear, and you come back with all these ideas. And the one about marrying. Who you want to marry? I hope the hell it ain't one of these Vietnamese girls."

"It's Lieutenant Patton, First Sergeant. Kathleen Tatum Patton. She was my nurse at the hospital."

"You can't marry a Lieutenant, Johnson. You're an enlisted man. It's against Army regulations, I think."

"That's why he wants to go to OCS, Top. To be an officer so he can marry an officer."

"Vannoy, if you don't stop interruptin, I'll send you over to the mess hall to pull KP for a week. Is that why you want to go to OCS, so you can marry an officer?"

"Yes, Sir. Mostly. I never thought about being an officer until it was mentioned at the hospital."

"So, all this ties together. The GED and OCS and marriage?"

"Yes, Sir, Top. It's one ball of wax. I been thinking about this for a couple of days."

"You sure you want to be an officer?"

"Well, I've thought about it, First Sergeant. I've seen what they do. It looks pretty easy to me."

"Reeel-leeee." Top let the word roll off his tongue. "It looks easy, you say."

"Yes, Sir."

"Does your Platoon Leader and Platoon Sergeant know about this?"

"No, First Sergeant. I came straight from the chopper pad, right away to the orderly room."

"Okay, go see Holt. Then come on back to see the Troop Commander. In the meantime, when he gets here, I'll tell Captain Thompson what you have in mind, what you want to do. He's gonna be interested to hear about this marriage business and officer business. Particularly how easy you think bein an officer is. Yeah, he's gonna like that."

J J grinned. "Okay, Top, I'm going to Supply and draw my gear. I'll come back when I get it put away."

"Don't fool around, now, get on back. Don't make the Capn wait on you."

Standing behind the supply room counter when J J entered, was a PFC.

"Hey, my name's Johnson. I'm coming back from hospital. I need some clothes and gear and my rifle."

"Okay, we heard you were coming in today. I took your duffle bag down to your bunker. I put a towel and wash cloth in it for you. Sergeant Holt put other stuff in."

"Thanks. You're new."

"Yeah, I got here a week ago. Me and two other guys. First Sergeant assigned me to Holt."

"Yeah, good luck. What's your name?"

"Lindseed, Oliver Obadiah Lindseed. I go by Cotton."

"Okay, Cotton, welcome to Delta Troop. Where's your boss?"

Cotton pointed at the doorway.

"Well, well, look what the cat drug in," Holt greeted. "How was your vacation, Cookie?"

"Fuck you, Holt. I'm talking to Cotton. I need to draw some clothes and gear, and pick up my rifle."

"Okay, Linseed, go ahead. Get Cookie's stuff together and stack it on the counter. There's been some changes since you been away on vacation."

Lindseed turned and went through the doorway behind the office desk.

"You're an asshole, Holt. You know damn well I was in the hospital. Sergeant Dutchman and Red were killed when our truck blew up."

"I know. Damn shame, too. I liked Dimples and Red. They were good people. Unlike some of the new boys we got as replacements."

"I know about Sergeant Deakins being appointed as squad leader. He's a good man."

"Well, Cookie, I don't know about that. His reputation got here before he did, and it ain't so good."

"What are you talking about?"

"Murder. Women and children. Scuttlebutt is he burned up a lot of women and children. Set fire to their houses. Then stood at the doorway and shot them if they tried to escape the flames."

"Who told you that?"

"I got connections, Cookie. People talk to me, tell me what's going on around town. Word gets around quick where murder happens."

"You mean the people down at the laundry and shower point. Some people say you have whores down there. Up here, too."

"Now that's not a nice thing to say about people trying to survive and make a living, Cookie."

"Well, I ain't gonna knock that. People do have to survive, anyway they can. But you're a son-of-a-bitch, Holt. And you know it. I'm surprised somebody ain't cut your throat."

"He was gonna be court-martialed, but Thompson

got him off the hook. The Capn ask for him, asked Colonel Tolon to transfer him to us, here in the troop. If you ask me, Thompson just got a handful of trouble. And the other two newbies, as well. The Mafia brothers. They come in with Linseed last week."

"That's Captain Thompson to you, Holt."

Holt was unfazed by the correction. "Yeah, The Old Man."

J J remembered his conversation with Deakins on the bus, about burning houses. Burning houses because of receiving fire from the hamlet, or because the hamlet inhabitants were VC, or VC sympathizers. It didn't matter, J J remembered Deak saying. *You'd do it too, if your buddy was killed,* Deakins had told J J.

"Well, I like Sergeant Deakins. He stood up for me at Long Bien."

Lindseed returned with a bundle in his arms and in fluid succession, Holt pulled them off the top and laid two sets of jungle fatigues, two sets of underwear, two pairs of wool socks, a web belt and harness, two ammo pouches, three loaded M16 magazines, a first-aid bandage pouch, a canteen cover, canteen cup, and canteen on the counter.

Cotton went out again. Within seconds, he returned with J J's rifle and laid it next to the stack of clothing. J J printed his name, signed, and dated the appropriate typewritten lines on the sheet of paper Cotton placed on the countertop. On the next lines of the sign-out form, he put his initials next to Cotton's by the serial number of the weapon.

"I had one of my people bring your duffel bag,

blanket, and air mattress down to your bunker this morning. When you get down there open your bag, you'll find towels and wash cloths inside. I put in a backpack, mess kit, razor, shaving cream, and soap, too. If there's anything missing, come back and Lindseed'll take care of it. I take care of my boys," Holt said.

"I need tags sewn on my shirts."

"We don't do that no more, enlisted are exempt because we spend money on new tags and when the clothes get ripped up or wore out we got to do new tags all over again. Soldiers can't afford it. We issue metal chevrons now."

"What did you mean by Mafia Brothers?"

"Bonino, now ain't that a mafia name if I ever heard one. Bonino Vitali and Francesco Cheek . . . Cheekin . . . Cheechin . . . Cicchinello. They even look like mafia hitmen."

"How the fuck would you know what a mafia hitman looks like. You seen too many picture shows. Anyway, you wouldn't know a hitman until he popped a cap in your ass, Holt. Just because a person is Italian don't mean they're in the mafia."

"When we were at Long Bien," PFC Lindseed said, "they told me they were from New Jersey, or New York. I forget."

"These two boys are grease-balls if I ever seen one. I've had my time with the Mafia," Holt said. "I was almost an associate, never a made guy, mind you, but I was among them. Then I joined the Army."

"You are so full of shit, Holt. Made guy, my ass. You were made perfect to be a recruiter. By the way, where is my ten dollars? You said you'd give it to me four paydays ago."

Henry Holt did not shake his head as one would expect in a rejection, but waved it from side-to-side, as a Bombay merchant might in refusing an unreasonable offer for a trinket.

"I don't have it on me, Cookie. I promise I'll look you up payday and give it to you."

"You know what, Sergeant Holt? Forget it. I forgive the ten dollars. There. I said it. You don't have to pay me the money you ripped off. It's done, don't worry about it."

"No, no, I ain't gonna do that. You wanted your money, and I'm gonna give it to you. I don't want you to keep going around telling everybody I ripped you off, that you paid me to join the Army."

"Well, I didn't pay you to join the Army. I gave you the money because you said you could fix it so I could be a cook. So giving me the money ain't gonna change any of that. I was gullible, Holt. But I ain't no more. Now I see you're trying to bribe me to keep my mouth shut. You don't ever stop with your schemes. Like you were doing with Mai Li."

Holt said nothing.

J J looked at Holt's blank stare.

"Mai Li, Holt. Where is she? What have you done? What did you do to Mai Li and Kim?"

"You are hot for her, ain't you Cookie? I figured as much when I caught you in a bunker all by yourselves. If I hadn't come in, you two woulda been . . ."

"What did you do to Mai Li and Kim, Holt?"

"I didn't do nothing. She's been away for about a

week. She left after you went on vacation, as a matter of fact. The group boss told me her old man got killed south of Saigon, down around Vung Tau."

"KIA?"

"Naw, a Army truck run over him."

"Son-of-a-bitch."

"Yeah, and you know she'll get a pile of money from Uncle Sam because of that."

"Is that all you think about, Holt, money?"

"It's what makes the world go round, Cookie."

"She lost her husband. Kim has lost her Daddy."

"Yeah, and now she's separated. Free. You can go on and have your way with her. Maybe even marry her and be little Kim's papa."

"You are a piece of work, Holt."

"Okay, Lindseed, help Cookie here bring all this stuff to his bunker. Then, on your way back, stop at the mess hall and bring me a cup of hot coffee."

As PFC Lindseed and Sergeant Johnson went to the door, Lindseed's arms laden with clothing and J J laden with gear and his rifle, Holt waved.

"Have a nice day, now. Welcome home from your vacation, Cookie. You take care, you hear?"

Out on the path to J J's sleeping bunker, Lindseed could not resist asking his question.

"J J, why does Sergeant Holt call you Cookie?"

"It's a long story, Cotton. I'm tired of telling it."

TRAPPED

"Lieutenant Patton reporting as ordered, Sir."

The hospital commander sat behind the massive desk. This time there were no papers, folders, or medical records on its polished, shiny top.

Dickerson returned her salute and with his other, opened hand invited her to sit in the leather chair now alongside his desk. "Have a seat, Lieutenant Patton. I have someone else coming by in a few minutes. Before they arrive, we need to talk about a situation brought to my attention."

Kathleen steeled herself. She fought building anxiety and panic. Her heart rate quickened. She decided the best defense was an aggressive offense. She drew in a deep gulp of fresh oxygen that filled her lungs and gave energy for the spearheaded attack.

"I know, Sir. I'm prepared for your decision, Sir, whatever it may be."

The hospital commander smiled.

"I've been in and out of the Army for a couple of decades. During that time, my wife and I met and worked with many good people. We have daughters, Margaret and me, and you remind me of all four of them. You are a special person, Kathleen."

She relaxed when he said her first name.

"You graduated top of your class in high school and maintained a four-point-oh throughout your pursuit of a BS degree in nursing. You have consistently received outstanding compliments from your colleagues, superiors, and patients. You are greatly admired in this command."

Katie smiled but said nothing. She was pleased and flattered to hear her commanding officer's praise. She had never suggested to anyone that she viewed him as a role model; she would have been too embarrassed to say such a thing.

She knew he had been an infantry private and had come ashore on the Normandy coast at Utah Beach as a rifleman. Within an hour of arriving in France, he had dashed across open ground under intense fire, stormed and destroyed three enemy machine gun positions, and killed the crews.

Among other prominent tales was one about the time his platoon sergeant directed him to report to the aid station in the rear area for treatment of a gunshot wound. When he arrived, there were no combat medics. All his battalion medics had died on the beach. Dozens of wounded soldiers lying about at the aid station needed attention, so he just chose to be their doctor.

After the war, he remained in the Army Reserves and graduated Magna Cum Laude from Yale medical school. After twelve years as a pediatrician in Portland, Oregon, he volunteered to leave his successful practice to return to active duty to serve in

Vietnam as Commander, Sixty-Second Field Hospital.

Katie was impressed by and grateful for his skills with staff and patients. She knew from first-hand experience he was an outstanding medical professional and leader. With his background, he related to soldiers and their plight.

One of Sally's compliments for him was entertaining. *This ain't the first rodeo that boy's been in.*

Most of all, Katie knew Doctor Dickerson never refused to treat a Vietnamese mother and child in his military hospital and encouraged all doctors, nurses, and technicians to take an interest in the well-being of children.

Lieutenant Patton felt comfortable sitting before her Commanding Officer. Whatever he was going to say and do, she was prepared.

"I know why you summoned me, Sir."

"I suppose you do, Kathleen." Colonel Dickerson nodded. "There are no secrets on the wards. And, that's a good thing."

"I do love him. I can't get around that. He's proposed. Twice. Both times, we were interrupted. I've not given him my answer. Now, he's gone. He left this morning on a helicopter, going back to Linebacker."

Colonel Dickerson raised his hand, and Lieutenant Patton stopped talking.

The colonel wanted to ask what Katie's answer would be to the proposal but knew better than to pose such an abrupt, forthright question. If they knew he asked a young lady such a pointed question, his wife and daughters would have scalded him. He knew better and let the thought simmer.

"My apologies for interrupting, but we need to get the official business out of the way before Doctor Schoessler arrives. As hospital commander, I have the responsibility and duty to maintain good order and discipline in the Sixty-Second. Accordingly, it has come to my attention that you may have violated certain Army regulations and protocol by your close association with an enlisted soldier.

"Fraternization is a serious issue that might result, could result, in the breakdown of military order and discipline. When warranted, certain punishments, including involuntary resignation from the service, are available to commanders in this regard. I have received information that identified a certain patient, an enlisted man, Corporal James Jerome Johnson, who seems to be interested in developing an affectionate relationship with you. Further, it appears you have not avoided the involvement but encouraged its progression."

The commander paused.

"Yes, Sir." Kathleen smiled. "I know the soldier you're talking about."

"Okay. What do you have to say about this information passed to me?"

"It is accurate and correct, Sir. I do love Corporal Johnson. It is a true and rewarding attachment. I have encouraged it."

"I see. You say that in spite of the issue of fraternizing?"

"It's flaternizing, Sir." Her brown eyes shined with

gleeful mischief. Kathleen could not restrain the huge smile sweeping along her face. "J J, Corporal Johnson, called it flaternizing. Sir."

Colonel Dickerson grinned. "I see. Flappernizing."

"No, Sir. Not flappernizing. He said flaternizing. I helped him pronounce it correctly."

"I know the boy. He was a fry cook in my brother's cafe a few miles south of Portland, in Lake Oswego."

"He told me about that. And, a joke you told there, in the cafe on Ferdinand Avenue."

The hospital commander's laughter boomed and bounced off his office walls.

"He told you that?"

"The whole joke, Sir, deep water and all."

Colonel Dickerson shook his head. "Okay, Katie. Let's get this flaternizing business out of the way. You are hereby reprimanded for an unauthorized association with an enlisted man. That is my decision. Further, I caution you about developing close relationships with *current* patients on your ward or within the hospital proper.

"Any questions?"

"No, Sir."

"My decision and action will not be recorded in your military record. When you leave my office, it shall never be a point of discussion between us or anyone else hereafter. Understood?"

"Yes, Sir."

"Now, I'm sure you were probably made aware I stated that you are an outstanding nurse. I even suggested you have the potential to be a general officer."

"I was told about your statements, Sir. I was taken aback that you revealed your thoughts to another person before you told me."

"I'm sorry that displeased you, Lieutenant Patton. I must admit to you that I made those statements in a relaxed situation with someone I knew from the past. It was an unfortunate transgression of proper military ethics and protocol. I apologize."

"Thank you, Sir. At first I was angry you told him, and then pleased you said it."

"A point I was making to this individual was the potential injury he would make to your career. I told him he could jeopardize it. You see, I do think you have great potential in the Army. I have written a special OER for you. It's in the typing pool now. A special officer efficiency report in a war zone has significant implications for your advancement ahead of your contemporaries. My OER will place you well ahead of your peers for selection for schooling and promotions. Each special assignment will prepare you for higher levels of responsibility. You will achieve great success, Kathleen, and yes, I mentioned specifically in your OER that you should be groomed for promotion to general officer and high office. Nevertheless, you must be aware of the trap. Frank Sinatra sang his famous song about it, about this trap."

Lieutenant Patton nodded, waiting.

"Love," the colonel said. "Love is the tender trap."

Dickerson leaned forward, placed his arms on his desktop, and clasped his hands. "I've always been a romantic."

Katie nodded her agreement. "I feel trapped, Sir. I do love Cookie. I love the Army, too. I want to make the Army my career. I love my job as a nurse. I think about him. I think about the possibility of a life with him, too. I know that an officer married to an enlisted man would be difficult."

The pause was his way to let his nurse regain her composure.

"I'm not certain that's possible, Kathleen. Our Army doesn't seem ready for that. One of you may have to leave the Army."

Dickerson's assumption stunned Katie. She had not considered resigning her commission and leaving active duty. In the Army, she had found her calling and profession.

"I want to remain in the Army, on active duty."

Colonel Dickerson repeated his doubt. "That might not be possible."

Lieutenant Patton did not surrender and stayed positive.

"Yes, Sir. I know. We might be able to serve at the same post most of the time because there are hospitals or clinics to support the installation's troops and dependents. As an enlisted man, he could have an assignment to a unit or be in a headquarters staff position. Of course, there would be no problems if he were an officer."

"Is he interested in a commission? Corporal Johnson?"

"I don't know. Until I mentioned it to him, he had never thought about it."

"Probably he never thought about it because he had not met and fallen in love with you."

The conversation between the hospital commander and shift nurse was at ease. Katie felt like she was talking with a close friend, maybe even an uncle whom she trusted with her innermost personal, intimate feelings. Her anxiousness and panicky sensations had waned, she felt secure.

"He didn't finish high school. I mentioned GED to him."

"You know, Kathleen, there is a new program for young combat soldiers to have a shot at becoming an officer. It began three months ago. Under this program, applications to attend OCS receive special consideration if a soldier has the Combat Infantry Badge, a battle decoration for bravery, and a Purple Heart. The request by a soldier with those credentials goes to the top of the list.

"There are two catches, though. He must have a high school diploma or GED certificate. The other catch is he must be in a university program and *enrolled* in at least one college course. *Enrolled* in the course is the key word. The University of Maryland has an office in Saigon that handles all of it for service members serving in-country. If Corporal Johnson has those three prerequisites, acceptance into the program will be easy for him. Fortunately, the Army has determined there is going to be a need in this war for seasoned leaders who are combat officers. Westmoreland has requested another quarter million men, and the President will surely approve. So far, nine out of ten who applied are now in OCS."

"I had not heard about that program."

"It's called Boot Strap."

"Boot Strap."

"My adjutant has the forms, but I'm sure all forward area commanders, first sergeants, and orderly room clerks have applications, too. They have the regulations and know what to do."

"I'll write a note to him about it. Thank you, Sir."

"You have a bright future. I know you love the Army, but other opportunities may come your way. You never know what might develop for you."

Before Katie could ask what her CO meant, there was a knock on the door.

"I'll explain the possibilities later," the Colonel said. "COME IN."

Lieutenant Patton turned to look at who opened the door.

"We're all gathered together on the ward, Sir," Dr. Schoessler said.

"Right." As Colonel Dickerson stood, Katie rose from her chair. "Lieutenant Patton, please come with us to the ward. This concerns you."

The three of them walked onto the ward. Smiling staff members greeted and applauded them. Sally Norman was grinning like a possum.

Colonel Dickerson pointed at a spot on the floor. "Lieutenant Patton, please stand here. Lieutenant Norman, here, please, next to Lieutenant Patton. Okay, Doctor, please read the order."

"By order of the President of the United States of America, the following First Lieutenants are promoted to the grade of Captain, United States Army. Kathleen

Tatum Patton, Sallsetta Malmarie Norman. Signed by the Secretary of the Army."

Colonel Dickerson held out a hand to Doctor Schoessler. "The railroad tracks, please."

Doctor Schoessler handed over a set of silver double bars, and Colonel Dickerson pinned them over the first lieutenant silver bar on each nurse's jungle fatigue shirt collar.

The hospital commander stepped back and saluted.

"Congratulations, Captain Norman."

Captain Sallsetta Malmarie Norman, smartly saluted and grasped Dickerson's hand for the congratulatory handshake. Her grin grew wider.

He turned to Katie and saluted.

"Congratulations, Captain Patton. I hope your dreams come true and wish you the best."

After things settled down, they returned to duty on the ward.

"A small box arrived this morning for Sergeant Farmer, Leon Farmer, bed 18-B," Captain Norman said. "Do you want to handle it or you want me to do it?"

"I will," Captain Patton answered. "Why did you ask it that way?"

"Well, others hesitate because of his condition. I just thought maybe you'd prefer not to, is all."

"I've talked with him before. Read letters for him. He sometimes responds. He can talk, you know."

"I know, I know. It's just that, ah, well . . . He's in pretty bad shape, with the trauma and all. Like Corporal Johnson was."

Captain Patton looked at her colleague, friend, and

soul mate. She nodded and smiled.

"I'm alright, Sally. J J is a soldier. He's an infantryman. He had to return to his unit. I knew he had to go back."

"He didn't *have* to."

"I've thought about it. You're a nurse, a Ward Nurse, wouldn't you want to return to your job if you'd been away?"

Captain Norman nodded. "Okay, I see what you mean."

"I could've thrown a hissy fit and huffed and puffed and demanded he accept Colonel Dickerson's offer and take the mess sergeant job, and stay here with me, where it's safe."

"*Yeah*. Why didn't you?"

"Where would that put us, if he had stayed only because of my tantrum?"

"Well, he'd of been out of harm's way, that's for sure."

"I know, but I wouldn't do that to him."

"Okay, hold on, let me get the box for Sergeant Farmer."

Sally walked away to fetch their patient's mail.

Katie looked down the pathway between the thirty-six occupied beds on Ward Two Bravo. Her eyes scanned the wounded and injured soldiers who lay silent, in deep thought. Katie's gaze paused on the gauze and bandages that covered Sergeant Farmer's head, eyes, and right hand.

"Here's his mail," Sally said. "It looks like a watch box, or maybe for a bracelet or necklace. I'm surprised a slim, little box like this made it all the way from Virginia."

Katie took it, looked at the addresses and post date. The Hampton, Virginia post office date stamp indicated acceptance thirty-two days ago. The return address was for a Miss Shirley Simpson who sent the box to Sergeant Farmer at his unit. The 101st Airborne Division mail clerk had forwarded the package here. Whatever news, wrapped in brown paper and tied with string, was old.

She walked to the foot of his bed and grasped the folded canvas stool that leaned against the cot's leg.

"It's Nurse Patton. Are you awake, Sergeant Farmer?"

In acknowledgment, he lifted his left fingers off the bed. He did not speak.

Katie unfolded the stool and sat on it.

"In the morning mail, a package arrived for you from Miss Shirley Simpson. Shall I open it?"

He lifted his fingers.

Katie slid the string off and put it on Sergeant Farmer's bed sheet. She inserted a finger, pulled scotch tape off the folded paper end, and shook the box out into her hand. She pulled the lid off. Inside, folded stationary lay and taped on top of the note was a ring, an engagement ring with a small marquis diamond.

As she looked at the folded paper and ring, her heart raced. She feared the worst. In the months she had been on the ward, this was the third time she had seen it. For an engagement ring to be in a box with a letter, sent to a soldier in Vietnam, she knew there could only be one reason. Katie sucked wind to fight the building panic attack.

She tried to put a happy smile in her voice. "There's a letter and a ring in the box. Shall I read the letter for you?"

The fingers did not move. Katie waited fifteen seconds. "Maybe later?"

Sergeant Farmer sighed. "No, that's okay. Congratulations, Captain Patton. I heard the promotion."

"Thank you."

"What you bring, the letter and the ring, won't smell any better later. Let's get it over with."

"Okay." Katie pulled the tape off. "Here's the ring."

She held his left hand and placed the ring in his palm. He closed his fingers around it. She unfolded the paper and began to read.

Leon

I am sorry. I'm returning your ring. I know Mike is your best friend.

Katie paused. She was afraid a cry out would escape her lips for what she was about to read to the wounded warrior. The pause helped to calm her jitters. She took a deep breath and continued.

When you introduced us and asked him to look after me while you were over there I had no thought of falling in love with him. He helped me cope all these months you've been away. I felt trapped between your absence and his presence until I finally gave in. I know this is terrible for you because of where you are. I am going to have Mike's baby and will marry him next Saturday. I'm sorry but I hope you understand this is for the best.

Shirley.

Tears welled in Katie's eyes. She clasped and bit her bottom lip to keep from wailing. She folded the letter and put it in the box.

She cleared her throat before speaking. "I'll throw the wrapping away. I've put your letter in the box and I'll leave the box in the drawer of your bedside stand."

"Here," Sergeant Farmer said. He raised his hand. "Hold your open hand out, under mine."

Katie did so, touching the heel of his hand so he knew her hand was in under his.

Sergeant Leon Farmer, jilted groom-to-be, dropped the engagement ring into her palm.

"I heard the proposal. I know Johnson had no ring to give you. So, when you see your boy again, give him this ring to use before he can buy one that you like. It can be a temporary engagement ring, a stand-in, until you have your own."

"I can't do that."

"Why not, Nurse Patton? It will only lie in the drawer. Anyway somebody might slip it away."

"But it was meant for someone else."

"I understand. You don't feel right wearing it because someone else wore it first?"

Katie shrugged. "Yeah. Kinda."

"Okay. Think of it this way. A girl brings her boy to the store and points at a ring. He buys it. She wears it for a week, changes her mind, gives it back to the boy. Boy takes it back to the store for a refund. Store sticks it back in the case. You come along next day with your boy, point at the ring, and your boy buys it. The store don't tell you somebody already wore it, cause it don't matter. Here, it only matters cause you know somebody wore it. Right?"

"But I didn't give an answer. We're not engaged."

Sergeant Farmer wrapped his fingers around Katie's hand and closed her fingers over the engagement ring.

"Well, put it in your pocket, Captain Patton, keep it handy. You can never tell what happens next."

At the nurses' station, Katie held her hand low so observers could not see. She slipped on the ring, stretched her fingers out full length, admired the diamond, and smiled.

"I'm engaged to be married to Cookie Johnson, the man of my dreams," she whispered. Her heart fluttered with delight and pleasure, her ears warmed.

"My, my, that is a pretty ring, Girl," Sally said. "I knew it was gonna happen in here sooner or later with all these handsome, naked boys around."

Embarrassed, Katie pulled her hand into her abdomen and slid the ring off her finger. She held it in her hand and closed fingers around it.

"I feel trapped, Sally. How can I marry an enlisted soldier *and* stay in the Army? I feel like I'm selfish because I want both, but I don't know how to have both. I don't want to give up my career. I'm a Captain now. That makes a big difference for me, and for schools, promotion, and assignments."

"Well, Sweetheart, even though we are Captains, in the bigger scheme of things we're minnows in a deep ocean, you and me. Let me give some free advice.

When you know it, you know it, and when you don't know it, it will end up biting the cheek of your butt."

"That's no advice. What does that mean?"

"It means to fish or cut bait. Tell the boy you'll marry him, or cut him off now. Get him out of your system. Out of sight, out of mind. Plain and simple. Don't drag it out. That's not fair for either of you. Send him a note or call him."

"I could do that? He has a phone?"

Sally laughed. "No. It's not likely he has a phone in his foxhole. But the orderly room will get him if you say the doctor's nurse is following up on his medical condition and recovery and needs to talk with him."

"I'll do that. I'll call him. I'll ask him when and where he can meet me."

"Do this, Sugar. He's probably eligible for an R and R, or soon will be. Plan your seven-day, in-country R and R with him. Go into Saigon, stay in one of the luxury hotels, live a normal life for a week and enjoy the Paris of the Orient. Or, get a ride out to the coast, spend time on the beach, swim in the sea, relax at one of the resort hotels in Vung Tau, Qui Nhon, or Cam Ranh Bay. Spend a week somewhere with him away from all of this. That way, you'll have privacy to talk it over. I know that boy loves you, Sweetheart, so you have to know how he feels about what you want. And what he's willing to do."

Katie nodded.

"Then, make your decision, Sweetheart."

DEAK

"Corporal Johnson reporting as ordered, Sir."

In the cramped space of Delta Troop's command post, Lieutenant Versailles, Boss Tweed, First Sergeant Morris, and Vannoy stood shoulder to shoulder.

"Stand easy for a moment, Corporal Johnson," Captain Thompson said. "You look well. How are you doing?"

"I'm doing okay, Sir, feeling pretty good. Not quite there yet, still some pain ever now and then."

"Good. That's good to hear. I'm pleased you've mostly recovered from your injury and are able to return to full duty."

"It's good to be back, Sir. I missed it. I truly did."

"Let's have the chevrons, Vannoy."

Vannoy handed two sergeant chevrons to the troop commander. Captain Thompson passed one of them to Lieutenant Versailles. They moved into position to pin the newly issued metal rank on J J's shirt collar.

"First Sergeant Morris, please read the order," Thompson said.

"By order of Major General D. D. Smith, the following Corporal is promoted to Sergeant. James

Jerome Johnson, Infantry."

"These are new, Johnson," the Troop Commander said. "Instead of chevrons on sleeves, the military services are issuing black, metal emblems of rank and branch of service." They pinned the rank.

Thompson stepped back and saluted. "Congratulations, Sergeant Johnson."

"Thank you, Sir." J J returned the salute and shook his troop commander's hand.

After all the congratulatory handshakes, the CO addressed the other business.

"Your platoon leader and platoon sergeant came to me with the recommendation of appointing you as Alpha Fire Team Leader in Sergeant Deakins' infantry squad. I supported their selection and approved their recommendation. What do you say? Want the job?"

"Thank you, Capn, I sure do. I accept the responsibility. I am honored to be chosen as the replacement for Sergeant Raleigh Hawk."

"Good, now First Sergeant Morris said you had other things on your mind."

"Yes, Sir, I do."

"Okay. Here in front of your Platoon Leader and Platoon Sergeant or in private?"

"I'm okay with it either way, Sir."

The CO nodded at Lieutenant Versailles and Platoon Sergeant Tweed. "Alex, Boss, let us have a little time. Sergeant Johnson will be along in a bit."

Versailles and Tweed saluted and left.

First Sergeant Morris pointed at the doorway and gave instructions. "Vannoy, take a break. Go outside, give us some privacy."

"Okay, Top, I'll go to the mess hall for coffee."

Thompson pointed at a stool. "Sit there, J J. Relax. Tell First Sergeant and me how we can help."

"There are three things, Sir."

"I understand. Go ahead."

"I don't quite know where to start."

"Okay, start with the one most important."

"I want to marry an officer, Sir. Lieutenant Kathleen Patton. She's a shift nurse in the Sixty-Second Field Hospital, Sir."

Thompson looked at Morris and grinned. He looked at J J, the grin still in place. "Yes, that sounds like it would be most important. First Sergeant told me that was one of the things on your mind. I've never faced this, but I think Army regulations prevent it or at least frown on it. Fraternization."

"Yes, Sir. The hospital commander talked with me about flaternization, er, sorry, Sir, frat-ter-ni-zation. He said it was against Army regulations. But, Sir, I don't want to frat-ter-nize with Lieutenant Patton, I want to marry her."

"Yes, J J, I understand. I do, believe me. But I've never . . . I . . . Look, here's what I'll do. I'll run it up the flagpole. I'll put the issue before the proper authorities in our chain of command and get some guidance from Brigade or Division. That's about the best I can do at this point. Okay?"

"Yes, Sir."

"It'll take a few days, but I'll get back to you as soon as I get word from Headquarters."

"Yes, Sir, I understand. Thank you, Captain."

"What does Lieutenant Patton say about this

marriage business?"

"Well, Sir, she hasn't said. One way or the other. Twice I proposed to her, once in public and once in private. She was not happy about the public one. Anyway, both times there were interruptions before she gave me her answer. But, I'm pretty sure she will say yes, Sir."

"What are the other things?"

"I want to get my GED and go to OCS."

"Well, the GED is easy to take care of. First Sergeant said Vannoy already put your request for the test in the mail pouch. That'll go out to Division tomorrow."

"The study material and test should be here within four or five days, Capn," Morris said. "They've streamlined the process for soldiers in Vietnam. Johnson can get it done pretty quick, send it back, and have his certificate in less than a month."

"That's good. Now, J J, in the past, OCS for you would have been out of the question. That's because you don't have a high school diploma and don't have at least two years of college credits."

"That's what my recruiter said. Sergeant Holt."

"Sergeant Holt? Our Sergeant Holt. Our Supply Sergeant?"

"Yes, Sir. He told me all of that, about high school and college courses. Said without a diploma and college, I didn't have a chance."

"In fact, there is, Sergeant Johnson. Yesterday, in a commander's meeting at Brigade, I learned the Army introduced a high-priority, fast-track program three months ago called Boot Strap for deserving enlisted soldiers."

Sergeant Johnson and First Sergeant Morris focused open-mouthed attention on their Commander. Neither spoke, their interest peaked. The terms high-priority and fast track, along with the catchy title of Boot Strap, aroused their curiosity.

"With this war, we're going to need leaders, combat leaders with experience, and that's why Boot Strap was created," the CO continued. "If an outstanding combat soldier has a decoration for valor, which you do, has a Purple Heart, which you do, has the Combat Infantry Badge, which you do, is enrolled in a university course, and has favorable recommendations and endorsements from his chain of command, is eligible to apply for Boot Strap. You have three out of four, and I'm confident you will have the favorable support. So, as soon as you secure your GED you can enroll in a university course. Enrolled is the key, not completed. The University of Maryland has offices in Saigon and at all the major bases like Qui Nhon, Cam Ranh, Da Nang, and Vung Tau. With that availability, it will be easy to enroll, as long as you have a high school diploma or equivalency."

First Sergeant Morris closed his mouth and looked at J J.

Sergeant Johnson closed his mouth too and swallowed. "I think I can do all that, Sir."

Thompson nodded. "I think you can, too, Sergeant Johnson. I'm confident you can do all of it."

"Well, first things first. The GED, that's first. Once that's done, the ball can start to roll, Johnson," Top said.

"First Sergeant mentioned something you said about being an officer."

"Yes, Sir. I said I'd seen what officers do and it seemed pretty easy. I think I'd make a good officer, Sir."

"Well, you probably will, Sergeant Johnson. The reason what we do looks easy is because we work with great solders and non-commissioned officers such as you." Captain Thompson grinned. "That's why being an officer in this troop looks easy. Is there anything else?"

"No, Sir. Thank you, Sir, for listening and for your help."

"Okay. Let's get the GED done. I'll get the scoop about marriage and come back to you as soon as I hear something, a day or two or three, probably. Now, Sergeant Deakins is waiting to introduce you to two new members of your fire team," Thompson said. He stood.

Top and Johnson stood too, and Johnson saluted. "Thank you, Sir. By your leave, Captain."

"As you were, Sergeant Johnson. Carry on."

J J found Sergeant Deakins, Jinks, and Mickey, along with the two new squad members, in the fire team's sleeping bunker.

"Hey, Cuz, welcome home," the infantry squad leader shouted. He rose from the field stool and hugged Johnson.

J J embraced Deak and patted him on the back. "It is good to see you, Deak. I'm glad you're our squad leader."

Jinks and Mickey stood and grasped J J's hand in a warm, brotherly, greeting and congratulated him on his promotion and appointment as their new leader.

Vitali and Cicchinello stood too but said nothing.

Deak made the formal introductions.

"They call me Bo," Private Bonino Vitali said.

"I'm called Nelly," Private Francesco Cicchinello said.

"I'm J J."

"Sometimes, he also answers to Cookie," Deak said.

"Cookie?" Nelly asked.

"Yeah, don't get me started on that." Cookie laughed and shook his head.

"Why Cookie?" Bo asked.

"See what you did, Deak? Look, guys, it's a long, boring story. I'll tell it to you later, okay?"

Both nodded.

"When I came over they told me about Sergeant Dutchman and Sergeant Hawk. And about you, in the hospital. You doing okay now?"

"Yeah, Deak. Ever now and then I get a catch in my giddy-up, but I'm on the mend."

"Well, I was just makin the rounds to tell everybody we're on stand-down for a bit. Gives us time to clean our weapons and gear, get a shower, some clean clothes, a little rest, and some hots in the mess hall. We been told bad weather is movin in, so we might be down for longer than a day."

"Okay, that's good, Deak. That'll give me some time to get acquainted with my team."

"Right. Okay, I'm going over to see Sergeant Mosley and tell his team about the stand down and weather. Oh, for you newbies, Sergeant Jordon Mosley is the Bravo Fire Team Leader. Jordy and his boys were on an ambush at the footbridge last night, but nobody came along the path. They heard a lot of firing on the south side of the mountain. In fact, there's been sporadic firing going on all day. Scuttlebutt is it's probably sappers trying to penetrate the perimeter to get at the communication complex on top of the mountain. Anyway, something is going on, but the leadership just haven't figured it out yet or what to do about it.

"Okay, see you guys later. Welcome home, Cookie." Sergeant Deakins saluted and left.

J J sat on the stool Burl vacated.

"Sit down, guys. Let's talk a minute," the fire team leader said. He waited until the four settled comfortably on the red dirt, then continued.

"First off, I will tell you I will do my best to earn your trust and respect. You and I know I've just been promoted, and I've never been a leader of a fire team. I do have some combat experience, but I need your help to make our team a good one. I want you to know my two main goals is to accomplish the mission of closing with and destroying the enemy and to keep you as safe as I can so you can go home standing up instead of lying in a box."

J J paused. He looked at each face and held his gaze.

"I like your honesty, J J," Jinks said. "I will do my best to support you and our missions."

The other three nodded and grinned.

"Okay, now, this is confession time. Let's keep it short and sweet, and then we'll go to the mess hall for supper. I'll go first, then Mickey, Jinks, Nelly, and Bo. Alright? I come from Lake Oswego, Oregon. I left school in the twelfth grade to go to work to help my mom support my brother, Kip, and my little sister, Jodie. I finally got a job at Sugar Babe's, a cafe on Ferdinand Avenue, as a fry cook. After more than a year there, I got tired of the filth of my co-workers and bullshit of my boss and quit. I walked down the street to join the Army and paid the recruiter ten dollars because he said he could fix the papers so I could be a cook. That's how the name Cookie developed, guys. I went through infantry training and rode the bus with Deak to Fort Lewis. We shipped over together and at Long Bien he said we were cousins so we could be together at Linebacker. I was hurt when a kid dropped a grenade in our truck's gas tank and it exploded. At the hospital, I met a nurse who I asked to marry me. I asked her twice."

"Son-of-a-bitch," Jinks said. "You asked a nurse to marry you?"

"I did. Twice."

"Twice. So, she said no, then?" Mickey asked.

"Nope, not yet. She didn't get a chance to give me her answer. We were interrupted both times."

"Well, the third time'll be the charm. Always is," Mickey said.

"What's her name?" Bo asked.

"Kathleen Tatum Patton. Katie. She's a First Lieutenant."

"Holy shit, you asked an officer to marry you?"

"That I did, Nelly. Okay, that's enough about me for the time being. Now, I know you guys have already met and talked while I was away, but I'd like for everybody to tell a little about yourself. You go first, Jinks."

"Okay, I'm Holly Jenkins. Everybody calls me Jinks. I been in the Army four years. I come from Millvale, a Pittsburgh neighborhood. I'm a Steelers fan, of course. My old man is a iron worker and my mom is a school teacher. I have an older sister, Erica. I been in the Troop seven months. Came over with Rosey. He was killed by a sniper in the rubber plantation, over there. Died in my arms." Jenkins voiced softened. "I killed Billy, too."

All were quiet, no one stirred. Jinks's remembrance of Rosey and Billy brought home reality, that they were vulnerable was unmistakable.

Responding to J J's nod, Mickey broke the silence.

"I'm Michael Fowler. I go by Mickey. I'm big enough and strong enough that Red picked me to be the team machine gunner. My hometown is Appleton, south of Green Bay." He looked at Jinks and smiled. "My dad is a butcher for Piggly Wiggly and my mom is a hairdresser. After I was born, my mom said no more. I played fullback in high school and two years of college. Tried out for the Packers, but got drafted when my grades went south. I been in-country seven months. I'm due for a two-week R and R in a month. Thinking about going to Australia to check out some round-eyed girls."

All the boys laughed and nodded. They knew what

Mickey's 'check out' meant.

J J nodded.

"Private Francesco Cicchinello, I go by Nelly. I been in Vietnam eighteen days. I live on Jewel Avenue in Queens. My dad is a dock worker for a truck company and my mom is a nurse. I got three older sisters and four nephews. Bo and me joined the Army together on the buddy system."

Nelly looked at his friend.

"Private Bonino Vitali, Bo. My folks live in Jackson Heights, Queens. My pop is a baggage handler for TWA at LaGuardia. I don't know where my mom is. She left us about five years ago. I sang for a local band before Nelly talked me into enlisting. I was gonna be drafted anyway, so I tagged along with him."

"This boy can sing," Nelly whispered. "If you close your eyes when he's singing he sounds just like Walden Cassotto from the Bronx."

Bewildered at the strange name, Mickey shook his head. "Who the hell is Walden . . ."

"Bobby Darin."

All looked at Bo and waited.

"What? Here? Now?"

J J grinned. "Go ahead."

Bo did and sang *Dream Lover*.

The boys sat with mouths agape, starring, disbelieving but astounded, astonished. It was magical, there in the sandbagged sleeping bunker on a firebase in Phuoc Long Province in the Republic of Vietnam, to hear 'Bobby's' suave voice. They felt privileged, honored, to be Bo's audience.

Their enthuisatic applauding was met by Private Vitali's broad grin and shinning black eyes. He nodded, shook his head, and nodded again in a polite bow.

"You guys warm my heart," he said. "I've performed on a stage for two, three thousand people in a concert hall, but this set, sittin here on red dirt, in front of the four of you, is the best feeling of love I've ever known. Thank you."

For a few seconds, they settled into their thoughts of home, or at least of a place more comfortable and safe.

"Okay. I'd like for us to work together in the team. I'll be the Sergeant, but I want your opinions, suggestions, comments, and help. I don't know it all. I don't give nobody orders. I say what's gotta be done, and it's up to us to do it. Jinks and Mickey's got more experience than I do. I know Deak has a lot more experience than all of us put together. So, let's say our motto is cooperate and graduate, okay?"

"Okay," they responded in unison.

"Now, let's go to the mess hall for supper."

The storm did not bother to adhere to the Army meteorologists' timetable. It arrived in a rumbling, windswept rage with gushes of rain covering Phuoc Long Province. The nighttime temperature dropped to 60. Sergeant Medina's mortar squad and the recoilless rifle section were manning the fighting bunkers on the perimeter. The chill soaked through every man to bone. The rain did not tarry, it pushed west. Low clouds remained.

Sergeant Deakins came into their bunker with his

flashlight beam searching soundly sleeping soldiers wrapped warmly in their green, camouflaged, nylon blankets.

"Up, guys, you gotta get up. We got an urgent mission, a rescue mission."

He shined his beam onto the light switch and turned on the single 40-watt bulb in the bunker.

They came awake, responding to his insistent, commanding voice, and rose from slumber. Without speaking, they pulled on their jungle fatigues, wool socks, and jungle boots.

Deakins bumped the bulb with his helmet and its electrical cord swung side to side. The cast of dim light caused eerie shadows on the sandbag walls as soldiers gathered harnessed gear and slipped it on.

"I need volunteers to make a jump into the small base on top of the mountain. The boys up there are surrounded, taking fire all around. We're the quick reaction force until the rifle battalion can get a couple of companies organized to march up the slope to relieve the post," Burl said. "Who is parachute qualified?"

"Why don't we use the truck and just drive up?" Nelly asked.

"There's no road, Nelly," Jinks said.

"If there *was* a road we'd be cut to pieces trying to charge up the side of a mountain," Mickey said.

"Who's jump qualified?" Burl repeated.

All five raised their hand.

"Good, get your weapon and follow me to the chopper pad."

"Wait a minute, Sarge," Mickey said. "You asked

two questions. I raised my hand in answer about who was a paratrooper."

"So?" Deakins asked.

"Well, first, you said you needed volunteers."

"So?" Deakins asked. "You want to volunteer to jump on top of the mountain? It'll be a Hollywood jump."

"Helicopter?" Jinks asked.

Deakins shook his head. "Too many of us for a chopper. We'll jump off the back ramp of a Chinook."

"Do we get jump pay for doing the jump?" Mickey asked.

Deakins nodded. "Yes, we'll draw fifty-five dollars each month for three months."

"I volunteer," Mickey said.

The others chimed in, extra money was an easy persuader.

Had they been told beforehand the top of the mountain was only one hundred square meters and the LZ was hot they may have hesitated. As it was, though, just to be able to make a parachute jump again was enough enticement for young warriors.

"Okay, everybody got their stuff? Bo, you bring the radio. Now, everybody follow me to the chopper pad."

They trotted through puddles toward flashlights.

Captain Thompson, First Sergeant Morris, Lieutenant Versailles, and Platoon Sergeant Tweed stood at the base of the ramp and greeted the small contingent.

They all exchanged handshakes.

Captain Thompson patted each soldier on the back

and wished them good luck.

"You men be safe," the CO said. "We'll relieve you as soon as we can."

The helicopter crew chief intervened and directed Burl's squad up the back ramp of the CH-47.

Inside, they picked up a parachute and reserve. They chose a partner to help slip into the rigging. Once suited up, they stood in single file formation in the Chinook's aisle for the jumpmaster's check.

Sergeant Deakins was their jumpmaster and conducted his safety inspection one by one. His tap on their buttock was the signal they passed his check and for them to sit. J J's fire team of five sat together. They sat on the canvas bench on the right side of the fuselage.

The Bravo Fire Team, Sergeant Jordy Mosley, team leader, PFC Leroy 'Lucky' Jerrigan, machine gunner, and PFC Glenn 'Tex' Pollard, rifleman, sat on the canvas bench opposite the Alpha Fire Team.

Sergeant Deakins stood in the cargo walkway, between the fire teams.

"Okay, there are nine of us. On the mountain, there are twenty-eight in the scout platoon providing perimeter security and seventeen specialists manning the signal equipment. The commo complex is under siege. They have one KIA and two WIA. The Chinook will hover at about eight hundred feet. First, the crew chief will kick out the chuted boxes of ammo, C-rats, water, and medical stuff. Then, you'll take my commands for the jump. We'll attach our static lines and walk off the ramp. The LZ is hot. They're taking small arms, automatic weapons, and machine gun fire.

We'll be jumping in the dark so our chances of not being seen as we come down are good. As soon as a doctor, chaplain, and Doc get on board we'll lift off."

The big bird shuddered as turbines whined, the fore and aft drive shafts gained RPM, rotors spun, and its six heavy blades whirled.

J J kept focused on the lowered ramp, waiting for the three additional passengers. As if a magic act, they appeared from the darkness and hurried up the ramp. J J recognized all three. Doctor Archie Box held his little black medical bag, Doc Swanson, the troop medic, held his medic's backpack, and Captain Carlos Delvecchio, the Chaplain, held nothing.

Sergeant Deakins, J J, and Jordy rose off the bench and helped the arrivals don their parachute.

While J J knew Sergeant Merlin Swanson was jump qualified, he didn't know if Box and Delvecchio were. It didn't matter. If they were on board, he concluded, they're going to jump too because the big ass chopper had no chance setting down on a small patch of space amidst gunfire.

The crew chief flipped switches; the Chinook's ramp hummed as it closed.

With roaring engines, the CH-47 lifted off Linebacker.

The pilot nosed her over to gain speed and lift.

As it climbed, low clouds and darkness swallowed the *Hook*.

ASSAULT

From Linebacker, the Chinook climbed to fifteen hundred feet on a vector passing over Sông Bé and the river. After coming out of the clouds, the helicopter turned south.

The pilot would steer the workhorse in a southerly direction for eight miles, turn west for twenty miles, turn north for eight miles, and finally turn east and approach at eight hundred feet. Estimated flight time was twenty-eight minutes to the drop zone atop Nui Ba Ra.

With the noise of the dual engines, it was impossible to hear a voice in normal volume so arm and hand signals supplemented communication.

J J was deep in thought about the peril he and the other members of the squad were about to face, and his courage to meet it.

The Hook's first lean pressed J J's parachute against the back of the canvas bench. The lift of weight off his shoulders and back was a brief relief. He twisted to peer through the Plexiglas portal. The half moon lighted the top of Nui Ba Ra that poked through clouds lying like a rumpled blanket below the helicopter. They would be jumping in clear skies. He turned away and scanned the Bravo fire team, Doc Swanson, Doctor Box, and Chaplain Delvecchio.

He watched Tex and Lucky in animated conversation. Tex would turn, talk into Lucky's ear then look straight ahead while Lucky would talk into Tex' ear. J J wondered what they were so excited about that their dialogue could go on for so long. It was like watching a ping-pong match.

Tex and Lucky were poker players. Captain Thompson frowned upon gambling among soldiers and officially forbade it. Unofficially, he turned a blind eye to its occurrence. J J had stood in wonderment as they played and bet enormous amounts of money.

J J asked Lucky about it, about the amount of money he won and lost. They were in the latrine – a four holer – each sitting on a hole expelling the crappy breakfast after the infamous Monday morning malaria pill.

During his first four weeks in-country, J J discovered that until the body acclimated to it, the Monday pill was renowned as a great laxative. He learned to stay within trotting distance to a latrine when on Linebacker. Otherwise, he, and others from time to time, commanded whoever was driving to conduct an emergency stop of their truck. On dismounted patrol, soldiers dropped drawers and presented a gift for the VC to step in, or on.

"It's just money, J J," Lucky answered. "I look at it as paying for entertainment. I'm gonna die over here anyway, so money ain't important to me. If I die with winnings, it'll be divvied up among my friends cause I ain't got no kin to give it to. If I die broke, it ain't no big deal, is it."

There, in the Linebacker outhouse, idle, to a degree, when he questioned Lucky's explanation, J J found the answer bothersome.

"It's preordained. I had a dream about it. I'm gonna die on top of that volcano over there. It's weird, even scary sometimes, but all my dreams come true, J J. They always have."

That was a month ago. Now they were in flight, rushing forward to fulfill Lucky's fate.

He shifted his gaze to Jordy, who was looking at him. Jordy smiled and nodded.

J J liked Jordy, a fellow Pacific Northwesterner. Jordy was from Tacoma; his wife and their twin boys lived in Lakewood just outside the northern fence of Fort Lewis.

Jordy was husky and squat, a champion wrestler and bench presser in high school. He was as strong as the proverbial ox. J J had watched Jordy lift the rear end of a gun jeep and push it forward to get it out of the muck of a drained rice paddy.

J J grinned and returned the agreeable gesture when Jordy gave a thumbs-up.

The helicopter leaned again, now headed west on the longer leg. He was aware of the path. Deak covered it in pre-flight, after performing his jumpmaster duties. J J's heart rate increased, his pulse quickened, he drew in a deep gulp of oxygen.

"When we make the turn east," Deak said during the briefing, "we'll be about ten minutes out. The pilot will turn on the red light and the crew chief will lower the ramp. That's when I want everybody to close one eye and keep it closed. When we're out of this bird, open the closed eye. That way we'll have night vision as we drop to the mountain top."

J J looked at Tex. Why people called Glen Pollard Tex baffled J J. He knew Tex was from New York City, was a ballroom dancer, and a gigolo. Tex, Glenn, bragged about providing services to widows and single women over sixty years of age. He was handsome and suave, spoke with a trained stage or broadcasting voice and never ever cursed. Instead of fuck, Tex said fig. After awhile, J J got a kick out of hearing Tex exclaim *Fig it.* Lucky and Tex were close, always together. In an odd way, the two reminded J J of the comedy team, movie characters, Stan Laurel and Oliver Hardy.

Doctor Box' loud sneeze drew J J's attention. Twice more, in rapid succession, the Doctor sneezed.

Red always volunteered Alpha fire team to accompany Doctor Box on visits to hamlets. An interpreter from Brigade came along to help with communication. J J watched the doctor conduct triage and treatment of Vietnamese men, women, and children in an efficient and caring manner. J J thought the doctor was young; he guessed no more than twenty-five, but Archie Box was forty-two, blessed with youthful genes.

Doc Swanson drew J J's attention when the senior medic stood to adjust the parachute straps under his crouch. Sergeant Swanson treated clap and headaches the same way. He took care of business and never asked questions or gave advice. If told about an ache or hurt, Doc Swanson fixed it. The one thing Doc Swanson loved to tell, and everybody loved to hear over and over, was how Holt reacted to the bullet stuck on his butt and whined about the touch of alcohol and prick of a needle. J J laughed each time; finally, it occurred that Doc might have a second career as a comedian.

The chopper turned and picked up its short leg north.

J J looked at the Chaplain and wondered if the preacher could, would, marry a Sergeant to a Lieutenant. He would ask about it once they were on the ground. He remembered the touching words Chaplain Delvecchio spoke at Billy's memorial service on Linebacker. J J was impressed when the Chaplain came with them on patrols and security missions. J J learned Delvecchio saved lives by picking up a weapon and killing enemy soldiers. His boss, the Division Chief of Chaplains, came down hard on him for taking up arms in battle and killing a human being. J J liked Delvecchio and hoped he would perform the marriage ceremony.

The Hook leaned right; the crew chief stood and flipped switches. The ramp lowered, and the red light came on.

The crew chief held out both hands with thumbs and all fingers extended – *ten minutes.*

Sergeant Deakins nodded and gave his thumbs-up signal. He stood in the aisle and stomped his right foot three times. All looked at the jumpmaster and closed one eye.

Deak extended his arms, palms facing the

paratroopers.

"GET READY," he shouted.

They leaned forward and stomped their right boot on the helicopter's floor. They positioned their feet to stabilize their lurch forward and up, and for support and balance to lift body and weight off the bench.

Deak continued to shout jumpmaster commands coupled with his exaggerated arm and hand signals.

"STAND UP."

With palms up, he waved his extended arms up and down twice.

Everyone stood and faced Sergeant Deakins.

"HOOK UP," he shouted.

Deak raised his arms, elbows bent. He formed a hook with curled index and middle fingers and thumb on each hand. He moved his arms down and up in a pumping motion three times, his fingers signaling hooking.

Each parachutist detached the static line snap hook from the top carrying handle of the reserve parachute and hooked up to the overhead anchor line cable. They ensured the snap hook locked, then inserted the safety wire in the hole of the snap hook and folded it down. They formed a bight in the static line and held it at eye level. They would release the bight on the ramp when exiting.

"CHECK STATIC LINES."

At eye level, with thumb and index finger of each hand, Deak formed an 'O'. He pushed the 'O' forward toward the two sticks of paratroopers and back three times.

Visually and by feeling with the free hand, they

checked their static line and the jumper's in front. They did not release their bight. They verified the static line snap hook was attached to the anchor line cable and was not misrouted around their neck.

Doc Swanson and Doctor Box faced about and the next to last jumpers, Tex and Lucky, inspected the last jumper's static line. Tex and Lucky gave a sharp slap on Swanson and Box' parachute pack to indicate their static line was checked and safe for jumping.

Up the line, the parachutist to the front got a sharp slap on the parachute pack; their static line was checked and safe for jumping.

"CHECK EQUIPMENT."

Deak extended his arms to the sides at shoulder level, fingers and thumbs extended and joined, and palms facing the two sticks. In rapid motions, he bent his arms at the elbows, brought fingertips to the center of his chest, and returned his arms to the extended position three times. Deak checked his own equipment.

Like the others, J J checked his equipment, starting at the helmet and chin strap. He physically seated the activating lever of the chest strap ejector snap and his leg strap ejector snaps. He completed these actions with his free hand while maintaining a firm grip on the static line bight with the other hand. He checked the equipment on Jinks' back.

"SOUND OFF FOR EQUIPMENT CHECK."

The jumpmaster cupped his hands and placed thumbs behind his ears.

Sergeant Swanson and Doctor Box sounded off, both shouting 'OK', stomped their jungle boot on the floor, and gave Tex and Lucky a sharp tap on the thigh. Shouting and tapping continued to Jinks, who pointed at Deak and shouted, "ALL OK."

With the ramp open, the noise was deafening.

J J's heart raced, his skin tingled. This was only his sixth parachute jump; it was a combat jump. He was excited and anxious but not fearful. A flash crossed his mind. Jumping into combat, at night, was very different from what Holt had projected. J J grinned; it also was way off the chart from his job as a fry cook at Sugar Babe's. He liked being a soldier, an infantryman, what he was doing, and about to do – to make an aerial assault by parachute into battle. It was something he never dreamed, expected, or predicted.

The moment Deak looked at the red light the jumpers felt the Hook slow and hover. The pilot was a master aviator and held the big bird steady. In that second, they knew it was show time; they were at the drop zone.

The green light came on.

The jumpmaster shouted his last command.

"GO."

Jinks and Jordy were first and walked off the ramp into the darkness. The rest followed. After all had exited the helicopter, the crew chief closed the ramp and the pilot drove the taxi home.

When J J walked off the ramp, he tucked his chin in, opened his closed eye, held a rigid body position, and counted four seconds as the static line pulled his parachute out of the pack. He looked up to check canopy. Suspension lines trapped and folded one side. The silk caught no air and did not fully deploy. He had a streamer. He was dropping fast.

J J grunted, pulled, struggled, kicked, and jerked on his risers until the suspension lines untwisted. He breathed again when his chute billowed and opened. He checked again to ensure his canopy filled with air. Above his head the nylon was transparent, filtered by moonlight, and through it, in a manufactured sort of way, lines of intricate stitching were artistic.

He looked down. He was on target to land on the row of lights soldiers on the drop zone rigged to direct the pilot and aid the parachutists.

In the moonlight, it was evident the top of the mountain was scraped clean. The layer of clouds surrounding the peak appeared to J J like the tip of a bald head poking through gray foam.

A blanket of green tracers rose from the west and south side of the mountain before J J heard the gunfire. At eight hundred feet above Nui Ba Ra, the Chinook was a clear target in the light.

The enemy cadre above the clouds could see the Chinook, but looking up into the moonlight distorted their depth perception. They fired AK-47s in the direction of the shape. Those below the clouds fired in the direction of the noise.

J J could make out other jumpers and saw tracers sweep across one of them. That jumper returned fire, his red tracers sailing toward where green tracers came from. Red and green created a flaming, two-lane highway before the red ceased.

J J suspected the worst. He and the others held their fire. They were vulnerable, hanging below a canopy that controlled descent at twenty-two feet per second. He was surprised and thankful firing from below ceased too.

Eleven paratroopers landed, and their arrival on the ground quieted enemy weapons. While soldiers from the signal detachment and scout platoon unpacked ammunition, rations, water, and medical supplies, Alpha and Bravo fire team leaders counted noses.

"He's missing. My boy is missing." Bo spoke with a calm voice. "We've got to get him."

J J's team was short a man. Private Cicchinello was missing.

All the other soldiers in the squad knelt at the ready or lay in a prone position with weapons poised, awaiting instructions.

Deakins took the fire team leaders' reports.

"Nelly is missing, Deak. I saw green tracers sweeping up, he may have been hit," J J reported.

"Yeah," Deak said. "We all saw the gun fire and his return fire. He must have dropped in a hornet's nest."

"We gotta go look for him."

"We can't do that, Cookie. Our mission is to hold the complex until relieved."

"But, Deak, we . . ."

"Cookie, listen, we can't stumble around among jungle growth and underbrush on the side of the mountain in the dark looking for somebody. All that, besides the bad guys. We don't even know where to start the search."

"He ain't just somebody, Sergeant Deakins." J J's official tone and tart response drew silence. "He is a member of my team, his name is Private Cicchinello."

Two men approached.

"I'm Lieutenant Myers, Signal Corps. I'm the OIC of the complex. This is Lieutenant Arnold, scout platoon leader."

Deak saluted. "Sergeant Deakins, Sir. I'm the infantry squad leader."

Both officers returned the salute and shook Deakins' hand.

"I've got a man missing, Sir. He exchanged fire on the descent. He may be wounded or killed, or captured."

"I understand, Sergeant Deakins. I'm sorry about your man. We can't search for him now. We'll look for him when relief arrives and it's daylight. We appreciate you bringing reinforcements and coming to our aid and rescue."

"Yes, Sir. This is Doctor Box, Chaplain Delvecchio, and Sergeant Swanson, our senior medic."

"You can't leave my man out there. We have to go look for him." It was not a request; it was a demand from J J.

"And you are?" Lieutenant Myers asked.

"Sergeant Johnson. Alpha Fire Team Leader. His name is Private Cicchinello, Sir."

"Yes, I understand how you feel, Sergeant Johnson. But it's impossible. We must hold and secure this communications complex. At all costs. Do you follow me, Sergeant Johnson?"

J J surrendered. In his heart he knew he had no choice. He also knew it was the right thing to sacrifice one man for the safety of the radio relay stations and spy equipment on the mountain. He was a soldier, he knew the mission came first.

"Yes, Sir, I follow you."

Lieutenant Myers took charge of the support contingent, and Lieutenant Arnold took charge of the fresh combat force now numbering eight.

"Doctor Box, please come with me," Myers said. "My two wounded are in the command bunker. One took a bullet in a leg, the other has shrapnel from a grenade. Corporal Patterson is over there, in the supply shed, Chaplain."

"Right," Chaplain Delvecchio said. "I'll go to the supply shed first for rites and blessings. Then I'll join Doctor Box and Sergeant Swanson in the bunker."

"Okay, Chaplain, wait here. I'll take the medical team to the bunker, then I'll come back to bring you to the shed."

Lieutenant Arnold directed Sergeant Deakins to place fire teams on the north and east perimeters.

"We expect an attack at any time but so far they've stayed at a distance. The heaviest concentration of automatic weapons fire comes from the west. Over there, I have four fighting positions, two men in each hole. That's where the chopper pad is. On the north, I have four spots, two men in each hole. North and east are my quiet sides. If you'll put your squad there to cover those points, I'll bring my seven guys off to reinforce the south and west. Nelson is in the shed with Patterson.

"At first light, my battalion commander will lift two rifle companies out of the jungle and set them down at the base of the mountain. One company will sweep up the south slope, the other up the west. When that begins, the bad guys will stand and fight or they'll slip around to the east and north sides and fade away. They always do. I'll call now to report your missing man so the rifle company coming up the west slope can search for him as they ascend."

Sergeant Deakins nodded. "Okay, Sir. My Alpha team has four and my Bravo team has three. I'll put Alpha on the north and I'll stay with Bravo on the east. That balances the force I have to support you."

Initially, the lieutenants acted as escorts. Once orientation was complete, and the newbies knew where everyone and everything were located, the fighting force took up defensive positions.

On the north side, Mickey and Jinks got in one spot; J J occupied a hole with Bo. It was 0430 hours.

Deak and Jordy settled in – waiting for an assault or daylight. The assault came first, from the east.

Where Tex and Lucky were.

ILLUMINATION

Absentmindedly, Chaplain Delvecchio waited alone in the moonlight in the center of the mountaintop after Doctor Box and Doc Swanson followed Lieutenant Myers, and Lieutenant Arnold walked away with Sergeant Deakins' reduced infantry squad.

He lost focus that enemy soldiers were within rifle, pistol, and grenade range from where he stood. If his mind had been on Army business, he would have at least crouched, knelt, or lain flat on the ground. Instead of Army business, however, his thoughts were about death and of the soldier Lieutenant Myers said was in the shed. In his heart, too, he knew he needed to be with the casualty.

In the silence, Delvecchio looked around. He took in shapes and shadows that dotted the landscape. He could make out the fighting positions and detect slight movement there. The command bunker was obvious because he had watched Myers and the small medical group move toward it. He saw the latrine to the right of the bunker and a small structure to the left. He was sure the small structure was the shed because it was in the direction Lieutenant Myers had motioned. He wanted to go right away to the shed and not wait for Lieutenant Myers but hesitated. Strolling around without escort among tense soldiers with loaded weapons in an anxious atmosphere was dangerous. He looked at the shed again and marched the twenty-eight meters to it. He lifted the latch, pulled on the handle, and opened the wooden door.

"Who goes there?"

The voice startled him.

"Chaplain Delvecchio."

"Oh, sorry, Chaplain."

"I've come to pray and say blessings for Corporal Patterson."

"Yes, Sir. I'm sorry there's no light in here. I mean there's light, I just can't turn it on. Moonlight through the cracks in the boards is all we got."

"That's okay. Would you tell me your name?"

"Nelson, Chaplain. Private Nelson. Bobby Nelson."

"Okay, Bobby. We don't . . . God doesn't need light, Bobby, to save souls. He sees *all*, in light and darkness."

"You sound like a preacher I knew at home. Preacher Andrew. He was high on spreading the Gospel, talking about God, and busy trying to save souls. He was pretty good at it too. Talked me into getting dunked in the creek, that's for sure."

"Where is Corporal Patterson, Bobby?"

"He's over in the corner, to the left of the door, to your left, Chaplain. He's wrapped in a poncho, we didn't have nothing else. The Lieutenant didn't want him to stay alone in here, in the shed, so I volunteered to stay with him. I get a few minutes relief every couple of hours when the VC leave us alone."

Delvecchio turned to his left. Slivers of gray slicing through spaces between boards gave some illumination. He could make out the bundle on the ground against the wall. The Chaplain inched closer and knelt beside Corporal Patterson's shrouded body. He turned his head to the right and looked at Private Nelson's shape.

"Will you pray with me, Bobby?"

"I will, Chaplain."

"*Our Father who art in heaven, Hallowed be thy Name. Thy kingdom come. Thy will be done, on earth as it is in heaven. Give us this day our daily bread. And forgive us our trespasses, As we forgive those who trespass against us. And lead us not into temptation, but deliver us from evil. For thine is the kingdom, and the power, and the glory, forever and ever. Amen.*"

"That's the Lord's Prayer, Chaplain. I like that. Can I say a prayer?"

"Of course, Bobby. You go right ahead."

"*The Lord is my shepherd. I shall not want. He makes me lie down in a green pasture, and He leads me beside still water. He restored my soul. He leads me on the path of righteous. Yea, I walk through the valley of the shadow of death, and I fear no evil, for Thou are with me. The rod and staff comfort me. Thou prepared a table for me in the presence of mine enemies and anointed my head with oil, and my cup runs over. Surely goodness and mercy shall follow me all the days of my life, and I will dwell in the house of the Lord forever and ever. Amen.*"

"Amen, Bobby, bless you. I've never heard that prayer said quite that way, but you did a good job."

"Yes, Sir. That was the twenty-third Psalm, Chaplain. I learned that in Sunday school a long time ago. I may not have said all the words right, but I got close."

"Yes, Bobby, you did. I recognized it and He heard you."

Delvecchio said another prayer. "*Dear Lord, bless this fallen warrior and bring him home to your kingdom for his everlasting rest. And bless and give comfort to his family and loved ones. In the name of Jesus Christ, I pray. Amen.*"

For a few moments, it was quiet. Then Private Nelson spoke.

"Will you say a prayer for me, Chaplain?"

"Yes, my Son, I will." And the Chaplain did.

"Thank you, Sir. I've never been religious, I never prayed like I did in here with you and Drake. I *talk* sometimes. I think He listens, I hope He does. What we did opened my eyes, Chaplain. It felt good."

The shed door opened.

"Here you are, Chaplain. I was scared for a minute when I came back for you. I thought you probably had come here. Everything alright?"

"Yes, yes it is, Lieutenant Myers. I will pray for you, Bobby. You take care."

"I will, Chaplain. You do the same."

"Come with me, Chaplain, I'll bring you to the bunker to talk with my wounded soldiers."

He was an experienced fighter, he could feel, smell, danger. He was more cautious than nervous. It was too quiet and idle for Sergeant Deakins. He scampered to J J and Bo's hole to use the radio to call in a fire mission. He wanted a more distinctive light above the side of the mountain.

Sergeant Medina's mortar squad fired two 81mm mortar rounds, twenty seconds apart, from Linebacker. When the fuze in the nose of the first shell popped, soldiers knew to close one eye.

The detonation of the fuze expelled and ignited the illuminant canister assembly. Because they hung by suspension lines from a small, white, silk canopy, this parachute slowed the descent of the burning candle that provided sixty seconds of 600,000 candlepower illumination.

With his open eye, Tex saw movement before the figure rose and lobbed a grenade at him.

"GRENADE," Tex shouted.

It dropped in the hole by Lucky's boot. He grabbed it and tossed it back toward the perimeter wire. It exploded mid-flight and shrapnel cut through the duo's jungle fatigue shirts and pierced their skin. When squad members later expressed wonderment the scratches even qualified for the award of their Purple Hearts, Tex and Lucky would only grin and shrug.

The blast seemed to be a signal. Enemy weapons opened fire on all sides of the perimeter. It was 0537 hours, and the desperate fight was on to defend the complex and repel the assault.

Lucky saw them rise up and charge. He shouted a

warning.

"IN THE WIRE. IN THE WIRE."

With bunches of young, long stalks of bamboo limbs held vertically in their arms, four VC cadre rushed the perimeter. They threw the leafy strips across the concertina wire and flung their bodies on top. Running at full speed right behind them, four other cadres with AK-47s spewing green tracers trod over the backs of the prostrate soldiers and stormed the hole.

With his M-60 machine gun blasting raking fire, Lucky's tracers chewed the four lying on the wire and cut down three of the runners.

Tex stuck the fourth with his bayonet and pulled the trigger of his rifle. His gun blast ripped the back of the black pajama shirt off and blew the cadre's skin and bones away with it.

"Cease fire. Cease fire. Cease fire." The non-coms began the shout for all weapons to go silent, somewhat to save ammunition but mostly to break the killing trance a soldier enters into during a deadly fight. Once the spell was broken, all soldiers yelled cease fire. This relieved their fear and anger and helped them breathe again.

The charge, fight, defense, and repel lasted less than a minute. The first illumination round continued to burn for nine seconds as candle and parachute lay on the northeast slope of Nui Ba Ra. Its glow eerily penetrated the cloud cover. The second candle fizzled out before reaching the layering.

Only mild moonlight remained. A nervous calmness prevailed.

Soldiers stayed in their holes, one snoozed as the other remained awake and alert.

As the warm sun rose, clouds below them dissipated and choppers with infantry platoons arrived. Foul weather and enemy soldiers, who had skulked away in defeat, were gone as daylight dawned. Sergeants formed details to gather enemy weapons. The bodies of enemy dead were tossed down the mountain, peace reigned.

Since all four sides of the mountain felt the attack, the size of the enemy unit was estimated to be a regiment of five hundred. It was a futile endeavor for a unit to split its forces and climb a thousand feet through dense jungle to conduct an attack uphill where defenders could pour heavy firepower down on them. The climb itself exhausted the fighters and there was no way reinforcements or supplies – water, food, ammunition, and any medical aid – could be brought up without incurring the wrath of gunships and F-4 Phantoms. It was a waste. But more than that, it alerted the infantry commander on Linebacker where a large enemy unit was and caused him to commit a sizeable force to find and destroy the remnants as they descended to escape.

Bo dozed.

From the top of Nui Ba Ra, J J imagined he could see into next week; that's how clear it was. He could see all of Linebacker, the airstrip, and the towns. As he searched the vastness, his eyes paused on the little parachute snagged on top of a wild Rhododendron half way up the northern slope. An approaching shadow drew his attention.

"Hello, I'm Chaplain Delvecchio. How are you doing, soldier?"

"Sergeant Johnson, Chaplain. J J. We're doing fine. It's a beautiful day."

"Yes, Sergeant Johnson, it is a great day. I thought I'd make the rounds and say hello to everyone. Who's your foxhole buddy?"

"Bo. Private Bonino Vitali. He's exhausted. I thought he would just doze a bit but he's out like a light. I don't think he can hear us."

"Where is home, J J?"

"Lake Oswego. Oregon. A few mile south of Portland."

"Beautiful country up that way, the Pacific Northwest. I was at Fort Lewis for awhile."

"Yes, Sir. I was there too, before coming over here."

"Well, J J, when he wakes, tell Bo I came by to say hello. Is there anything I can do for you, J J?"

"Okay, Chaplain, I'll tell Bo you said hi. I saw you on the chopper with us. I wanted to ask a question, but I'm not sure if it's proper for me to ask. How to ask, I mean, the words."

Carlos laughed. "I've heard it all, Sergeant Johnson, heard all the words. Regretfully, I've used most of them. Go ahead, fire away."

J J paused, unsure. Then, he fired away. "Will you marry me, Chaplain?"

Carlos Delvecchio's laugh bellowed up from his abdomen. He bent over and coughed and choked. Snot slipped and dripped from his nose.

"Sweet Jesus, I don't think I've ever laughed so

hard. Your question gives me great relief, J J. You give me fresh air. It is a wonderful question, an exhilarating query, it's tremendous to be asked to wed."

Chaplain Delvecchio knelt and reached for J J's hand and grinned when he took it.

"Thank you, J J. But I'm already married."

J J grinned, too. "I didn't mean it that way, Chaplain. I mean will you marry me, ah, marry me and my sweetheart."

"That I can do, my good man. Where does she live? You're hometown, Lake Oswego?"

"No, Sir, she lives here. In Vietnam."

Chaplain Delvecchio released J J's hand and stood.

"I'm sorry, Son. I thought your girl was back in Oregon."

J J stood, his eyes were level with Delvecchio's belt buckle. He looked up at the towering Chaplain.

"No, Sir. My girl is at the Sixty-Second Field Hospital."

"Oh, does she clean the toilets, empty bedpans, do the laundry?"

J J's ears flamed, his face flushed with reactive anger.

"You mean is she Vietnamese?"

"Yes, I thought you . . ."

"My girl is a Lieutenant, Army Nurse Corps, Chaplain. And even if she was a Vietnamese, she would still be my girl."

"You're right, J J. I am so sorry." Chaplain Delvecchio squatted. "The pressures have been a bit much these last few days. I am truly sorry. We are all

God's children. I don't know what came over me to be so misguided with such misjudgment. I feel ashamed."

J J watched in amazement as Chaplain Delvecchio's transformation blossomed. From biased bigot to human being, Carlos' true attrition and remorse for his transgression softened J J's heart.

"I can see you feel bad, Chaplain. We all have been under a strain. It's alright. It's alright, Sir."

Carlos Delvecchio drew in a deep breath and shook his head. "God forgives us, my Son. In due course, He will see I mean to do better. Now, about this marriage business?"

"Lieutenant Kathleen Patton is an Army nurse at the hospital. I was there for several days after I was wounded. I told her I loved her and I asked her to marry me. Twice. She never gave an answer."

Bo stirred, came awake, and smacked his lips. He looked up at the Chaplain.

"Hello, Bo, I'm Chaplain Delvecchio. How're you doing?"

"Okay, Sir. I'm hungry and thirsty."

"Up here, there's no eggs, bacon, and toast," the Chaplain said.

"The chopper dropped a lot of C-rations, Bo. I'm sure you can find some Ham and Lima Beans," J J said.

Bo withdrew his canteen from its pouch, unscrewed the black plastic top, and gulped liquid from its mouth.

"Mr. Vitali, why don't you go hustle up breakfast? Sergeant Johnson and I were mapping out a strategy, and we need a little privacy."

"You mean about his marrying Lieutenant Patton."

"Yes, Bo. That's what I mean. Take a hike."

The three grinned at each other. "Okay, Chaplain. I can take a hint."

"Delta Troop, the real cavalry, Specialist Vannoy speaking, Sir."

"Specialist Vannoy, I'm Lieu . . . Captain Patton, Sixty-Second Field Hospital. May I speak with Corporal Johnson?"

"He's not here, Captain."

"What do you mean he's not there?"

"Not here, Captain. He's not in the Troop and not on Linebacker."

"Where is he?"

"Sorry, Captain, I can't tell you that."

"Corporal Johnson was a patient in the hospital. I'm calling on behalf of Doctor Schoessler, to follow up, to see how Corporal Johnson's recovery is coming along. How can I contact Corporal Johnson and speak with him? It's urgent."

"Afraid you can't, Captain."

"Why not? Is something wrong? Has something happened to Corporal Johnson?"

"I'm not authorized to divulge that information."

Katie's anxiety flared, she felt panicky. She inhaled slowly for calm before speaking.

"I understand, Specialist. May I speak with your Commanding Officer?"

"Not here, Captain."

"Look, Specialist, I'm calling on official business. I want to know if Corporal Johnson is alright."

Vannoy heard the unease in her voice. He hesitated and then gave a partial assurance. "Captain Patton, I follow my commander's orders, instructions, and directives. As an officer, I know you can understand my position. If, and I say this with great emphasis, *IF* I happen to maybe see Corporal Johnson, I will tell him you called. Okay?"

Relieved, Katie acknowledged the clue. "Thank you, Specialist Vannoy. *IF* you see him, ask him to call Captain Patton, Ward Two Bravo."

Katie replaced the handset and looked at Sally.

"I heard," Captain Norman said.

"I think he's probably okay," Captain Patton said. "He's probably on a mission and will return to Linebacker."

"You know his squad sometimes provides security for police checkpoints," Sally said. "He came to us off one of those missions."

"You're right. He'll probably call later today."

But he didn't.

Sergeant Deakins later passed the word that the squad might stay on the mountain longer than planned.

"Why?" Sergeant Mosley asked.

"Lieutenant said air resources were committed to a Brigade operation out toward Cambodia," Deak answered. "Word is the bad guys disappeared and the infantry companies turned around and are going off the mountain. They'll be picked up and shuttled off to god-knows-where. Just one slick is coming up here to pick up the scout platoon's two WIAs and the KIA."

"How long you think, Deak?" Jordy asked.

"I think we're gonna be here a while, so let's make the best of it."

CROSSROADS

Bonino looked at the approaching helicopter. He tossed the empty C-ration cans and meal carton in the trash barrel, ripped the lid off the Chiclets box, and popped the two small squares of chewing gum into his mouth. Bo tore open the pack of four Chesterfield cigarettes, pulled one out, and stuck it between his lips. He lit it, drew in a deep drag, and moved toward J J.

Windblast from the chopper's whirling blades forced him to stop at the edge of their hole and lean into the turbulence. He cupped his cigarette and watched. The pilot maneuvered the slick within ten inches above the rectangular shaped PSP landing spot, slowed the turbines, and let the bird's skids touch, bounce, and settle onto the pad.

"I guess the chopper has come for the wounded," he said.

"Yeah, and the dead guy," J J said. "Okay, you hold the fort, Bo, I'm going to pee and get a C."

They swapped places and J J looked down at Bonino.

"Even though everything is quiet now, Bo, you stay

alert, you hear."

"HEY YOU."

J J heard it, didn't realize the shout was for him.

"HEY YOU."

J J turned; a soldier was waving, beckoning him.

"COME HELP ME."

J J hurried.

"My name is Bobby Nelson. Come inside, I need help to bring this body to the chopper. What's your name?"

"Sergeant Johnson, Bobby. J J."

"Oh, sorry, Sarge, I didn't see your rank. He's heavy, so take holt with both hands. We need to shuffle through the door, you walk backwards, and when we're outside you can turn and walk straight as we carry him to the chopper."

They gripped and squeezed the ends of the poncho that held Corporal Patterson's body. Once outside, J J was on the left with Bobby on the right. Because of the weight, they could not move fast. Two four-man teams rushed past them carrying the two wounded soldiers in poncho litters.

Doctor Box, Doc Swanson, and Chaplain Delvecchio followed the two teams but stopped in the center of the complex.

"Wait a minute, Sarge. Set him down. I got to get a better holt or I'll drop him. My fingers were killing me."

"Did you know him? Know his name?" J J asked.

"Yeah, sort of. He was a nice guy. Okay, let's go again."

"What's his name?"

"Corporal Patterson. Drake."

"Where's he from?"

"Texas," Bobby answered. "Around Dallas, I think. Or maybe Fort Worth. Somewhere around there. Goddamn, this boy weighs a ton."

"How long has he been over here?"

"I don't know for sure. About two weeks in-country, I guess. He'd been in our scout platoon four days before we came up here. He liked the Dallas Cowboys. He tried out as a linebacker, I think."

"I like the Oakland Raiders," J J said. "Was he your friend?"

"Yeah, sort of. We called him Coach. He was a high school football coach, Oak Leaf, or Red Leaf, or Cliff, or something like that."

"Is he married?"

"Drake planned on marrying his girl when he got home. He talked about her all the time. Gloria. He said her name was Gloria. They was going to honeymoon at Disneyland, in California. He said she loved Mickey and Minnie Mouse."

"Hold on, Bobby. I'm losing my grip. Set him down a minute."

They stopped again. They were breathing hard from the exertion and half-shuffling steps.

J J wrung his hands to refresh the flow of blood through his fingers.

"That ain't gonna happen now."

J J first looked at the bundle lying between them, then at the teams and crew chief loading the wounded.

"What ain't gonna happen, Bobby?"

"Goin to Disneyland. Okay, Sarge, let's pick him up and go again. The crew chief is lookin attus."

"Yeah, that's a shame. His girl, Gloria, she'll be heartbroken." When he said those words, J J's immediate thought was of Katie and about someone carrying his body in a poncho. He imagined the Chaplain and Colonel Dickerson and Lieutenant Norman bringing the news of his death to her and how she would react. His heart sagged, he felt saddened. It was painful for him to think about it.

"She'll get over it, Sarge. Gloria'll find somebody else. They always do."

"That sounds callous, Bobby."

"It's just the way it is, ain't it, Sergeant Johnson? Drake ain't here no more. There ain't nothing we can do that's gonna change things, change what happened, is it? He's dead now. Forever."

"What about his folks? If he's got a mom and dad, they're going to be heartbroken, too."

"Yeah, I guess they will be. But they're no different than a lot of other mommas and daddies, though. They sittin home thinkin everything is okay."

"What do you mean, Bobby?"

"The time difference."

"What about it?"

"What time is it now, here?"

"I dunno, six, six-fifteen."

"Okay. It's morning here, we're twelve hours ahead. So, it's six last night there, in Texas, in Dallas."

"Yeah, Bobby. So?"

"What do people do back there at six in the evening, Sarge?"

"Well, most people come home from work. They eat supper. They spend time with the kids, with the family. They watch TV."

"Yeah, they watch *Uncle* on the evening news on TV. Watch him go on and on about what we doin, tellin about the hundreds ever week that's dyin over here."

"Who is *Uncle*?"

"Crocklight."

"Oh, yeah, Cronkite. Walter Cronkite. I watched him on TV. I thought he did a pretty good job."

"Drake's folks are sittin home watchin the evenin news with Cronlight, thinkin everything is okay."

"Oh, I see what you mean, Bobby. About them being no different than a lot of other mommas and daddies who's son is over here. About everything being okay."

"Exactly. They don't know what happened to Drake. Everybody is gonna be heartbroken. Gloria *and* his mommy and daddy."

"Yes, I see, Bobby."

"In another twelve or twenty-four hours an Army sedan is goin to pull up to their front door and a officer is gonna knock," Bobby Nelson said. "And then they'll learn their boy is comin home, in a box."

They followed the crew chief's instructions, laid Corporal Drake Patterson's body on the floor of the Huey, turned, and moved away. Both rendered a smart military salute. The crew chief came to attention and gave his salute for theirs to Corporal

Drake Patterson. The pilot increased throttle and the turbines revved. The crew chief gave his thumbs up and climbed aboard the chopper.

After the UH-1 lifted off and turned south, an eerie silence settled over the mountaintop.

For twenty seconds.

"Two wounded and one dead hero who died fighting for our country. We honor those brave warriors," the infantry squad leader said.

Bobby Nelson turned around and faced Deakins.

"You're full of shit. This fucking war is a farce, it's a crime. He didn't die fightin for our country. He died cause he got shot on top of this fucking volcano. He'd be alive if he'd of run off to Mexico or Canada. What we're doing over here is protecting a corrupt government and somebody's money interests. LBJ don't know how to fold the fucking tent and bring all of us home, alive. We ain't fightin and dyin for our country. That is bullshit propaganda."

With that, Private Bobby Nelson marched away.

They gawked at him as Nelson walked toward the wooden shed.

J J's mind wandered, as he stared, thinking he was looking at Elmer's back. Months ago, in Sugar Babe's, Vernon and Elmer had spoken as vehemently as Bobby had done. Were they right? J J shook his head. Did he stand alone thinking what he was doing in Vietnam was defending his country?

He looked at Deakins, but before he could say anything, they heard a yell.

"HAAAAAY."

The shout came from below, beyond the western

perimeter wire.

"HAAAAAY, ON THE MOUNTAIN."

It was an American voice.

Every soldier in a hole stood up to look in the direction of the hail.

Deakins and J J, open-mouthed, waited.

Someone inside the wire answered.

"HEY, WE HEAR YOU. ADVANCE TO BE RECOGNIZED."

First, they saw two raised hands; one held an M-16 rifle.

Next, they saw two heads with black hair.

Then, they saw a Vietnamese in black pajamas and Nelly with his rifle.

The Vietnamese's hands were behind his back, bound together by a strip of parachute suspension line. The traditional cadre uniform hung loose on his small, thin frame.

"Private Cicchinello, Delta Troop, Linebacker."

"NELLY," J J screamed and double-timed forward. "He's one of us, he's one of us."

"MINEFIELD. DO NOT ADVANCE," a soldier shouted. "We'll come out and lead you in. Stay where you are."

The Chaplain, Box, and Swanson approached and stood with Sergeant Deakins.

The rescue took less than three minutes.

Nelly's explanation took longer.

The prisoner looked to be a young, frail teenager. Ripped black cotton pajama trousers exposed a bullet hole in his right thigh. Scratches and dried blood covered his dirty feet. His toenails were cracked and snags of rubber were missing from his worn flip-flops. He had a knife or bayonet scar along his jaw line. Two teeth were missing.

J J sensed the soldier did not feel threatened. He stood among them, patiently waiting, while Private Francesco Cicchinello told his war story of landing softly on top of jungle canopy, hiding, and, at daybreak, finding his wounded prisoner fast asleep.

"Okay, everybody step back. Step away," Sergeant Deakins said. He withdrew his .45 caliber pistol from his shoulder holster. He waved the business end of the pistol, his signal for onlookers to step aside, to move away out of the line of fire.

"Wait a minute, Sergeant. I need to take care of this boy's nasty wound," Doctor Box said. "What are you going to do?"

Sergeant Deakins moved to the prisoner's left side. "I'm going to take care of infantry business, Sir. I'm gonna close with and destroy the enemy."

Deakins placed the muzzle of his pistol against the prisoner's left temple.

When their eyes met, J J could see fear flood the Viet Cong cadre's face.

"*Tôi đầu hàng. Tôi đầu hàng.*" The youngster's eyes bore into J J's soul.

Even though none of the Americans spoke Vietnamese, the fright in the prisoner's eyes and plea in the voice was plain and unmistakable to all of them.

"Hold on, Deak, wait a minute," J J pleaded. He raised both hands, palms out. "Don't do this. It ain't right."

"Wait, Sergeant," Chaplain Delvecchio said.

"Sergeant, please lower your weapon."

Deakins squeezed the trigger.

The report reverberated.

The pistol recoiled.

The bullet penetrated, the prisoner grimaced, and flopped to the ground, limp as a puppet released by its puppeteer.

A geyser of dark red blood erupted, spurting from the bullet hole, and rivulets streaked his forehead and flowed across the enemy soldier's open eyes.

"Jesus fucking Christ," J J shouted. "What the fuck have you done, Deak? Good God!"

Doctor Box and Doc Swanson reacted as medical professionals would. By the time they could kneel, the enemy soldier's heart had stopped pumping, no more blood poured onto the ground. Chaplain Box shook his head and murmured his prayer.

"None of you have seen what these bastards do to our boys taken prisoner. I have. I know what these sons of bitches do. None of them deserve to live."

"He was a prisoner," Doctor Box said. "You murdered a prisoner."

"That's your opinion, Doctor. I killed an enemy soldier." Deakins raised his pistol to his hip but kept the muzzle pointed toward the ground. "Now, why don't we all return to our duty? Nelly, you and J J help me with this gook's body. We'll take the path they brought you in on, Nelly, and toss this bastard down the side of the mountain. If his comrades don't come get him, the ants, monkeys or tigers can have a meal of skin and bones."

"I will report this to the Brigade Commander,

Sergeant," Doctor Box said. "I will prefer charges against you. Murder charges, among others."

"You go ahead, Doc. Do your thing. In the meantime, you two help me with this piece of shit."

J J could see Deakins' face, his black eyes, and the pencil mustache, but heard Red's voice.

Doctor Box reported the incident to Brigade Headquarters by radio. Until relieved, the passing hours were somber. No one spoke about what happened. They smoked, ate C-rations, and dozed.

It was another two days before a Chinook arrived with an infantry platoon and fresh communication specialists, as relief. The heavy bird airlifted all the weary occupants off Nui Ba Ra.

From the chopper pad on Linebacker, Doctor Box went straight to the command bunker. He reported to Colonel Carson, who was waiting in his office with Colonel Tolon. The Doctor gave names of those present that saw what happened and demanded the senior Commander convene a general court-martial to try Sergeant Deakins for insubordination, conduct unbecoming a non-commissioned officer, and murder.

Later, when the Brigade and Battalion Commanders were alone, they reflected on it.

"I was afraid this would happen," Colonel Tolon said. "His mother died from breast cancer, and I sent him home on emergency leave for her funeral. Deakins was not the same when he came back. He'd changed, he was mean. I don't know, maybe it's stress. He's been through a lot. He lost a lot of his boys, KIAs. This is not the first time he's been accused of murder. I had reports he set houses on fire and shot the people as they ran out trying to escape the flames. But there's never been enough evidence to proceed with a court-martial because it was a combat action. Now it's a bigger mess with this killing of a prisoner with hands tied behind his back. We should have nipped it in the bud earlier and sent him home with a medical discharge. I think the boy is dangerous."

"Well, I'll have to order an Article 32 investigation," Colonel Carson said. "I don't have a choice now. There're too many witnesses for me to ignore Archie's charges against Deakins."

"When you run it up the chain of command, Westmoreland will send a team down, for sure," Colonel Tolon said. "He won't want this to turn into a public affairs nightmare. He'll try to keep the reporters off it, try to keep it in Vietnam, out of the TV evening news at home."

The Brigade Commander sighed. "Well, we know that won't happen. With all the cameras, reporters, and freelancers over here, somebody will get a whiff and the frenzy will start, like a pride of lions feeding on a carcass."

At the same time Archie Box was with the senior commanders, J J and Doc Swanson, in a private meeting, told their accounts to Captain Thompson, Lieutenant Versailles, First Sergeant Morris, and Platoon Sergeant Tweed.

"It's been days since we've had a bath or clean clothes," Sergeant Johnson said. "We'd like to go down to the shower point."

"Permission granted," Captain Thompson said.

On their way out, Vannoy pulled J J aside.

"Here's your GED stuff." Vannoy held out the official manila envelope. "As soon as you can finish the sooner I can send it special delivery to Saigon. It'll be a quick turnaround because I got friends in high places down there."

"Thanks, Vannoy."

"No problem. There's one more thing, Cookie. You're supposed to call a Captain Patton. She's a nurse. She called a few days ago. Said she was following up on doctor's orders to see how your recovery is coming along. I said you were not available."

"Captain? Captain Patton? She's a Captain?"

"That's what she said. She sounded pretty anxious, concerned that she couldn't talk to you. She wants you to call her at the hospital, Ward Two-B."

"Captain Patton. I'll be damn. Katie's a Captain."

MERCHANTS

"Staff Sergeant Deakins, Sir."

Colonel Carson returned the salute. He ignored the lack of official protocol but did not permit Deakins to stand at ease or sit.

With military discipline, Deakins remained at attention. He had never been in officer country. Oh, he had been in the Lieutenant's hooch. He also had stood at attention in the Hotel Company Commander's bunker, getting his ass chewed out. But he never set foot in the big boy's playpen, nor did he wish to. He tried to maintain a professional posture but let his eyes drift from the American colors and the Brigade flag hanging in folds from staffs and dart to the wood-craved brigade emblem attached and centered to the sandbag wall, between the ensigns, behind the Bird Colonel.

He looked down at Colonel Carson, had never been this close to the Commanding Officer. He never realized the Brigade Commander was gaunt, with a full head of trimmed, groomed, prematurely white hair, and white eyebrows that accented dark, sunken eyes. With wire-framed, rimless glasses the CO resembled pictures of President Roosevelt Deakins remembered seeing in civic and history books at school.

The Colonel sat in a huge, high back, leather chair. The desk was fancifully etched, dark mahogany. It was an unusual piece of furniture to be in a sandbagged, fortified bunker in the middle of the Republic of Vietnam. A brass nameplate perched on the forward edge of the workspace and two .50 caliber shells flanked it. Deakins noted the .45 caliber pistol lying on its left side on top of the desk. Its position such the Colonel only had to place his right hand over it to raise it for action. Its muzzle pointed at Deakins' groin.

Carson leaned back, opened a Zippo lighter with its familiar creak and clack, flamed the tip of the cigarette stuck in the holder clamped between his yellow teeth, inhaled, and closed the lighter with its recognizable clank. He placed the silver cigarette lighter on top of a pack of Chesterfields. Deak noted the pack of twenty butts was not from an accessory packet of the C-Ration box of four.

There were no windows in the command bunker, but, as if fitted in a window opening, the air conditioner that was stuck between walls of sandbags hummed. Its flow of cool air pushed the gray cloud aside as Carson exhaled. Deakins enjoyed the smell of cigarette tobacco smoke. He wished the Colonel had offered a Chesterfield.

"Sergeant Deakins, charges of insubordination, conduct unbecoming a non-commissioned officer, and murder have been preferred against you. As Brigade Commander, it is my duty and responsibility to take these charges seriously, look into the allegations, and take appropriate action, including where warranted, a recommendation to the Commanding General that he convene a general court-martial.

"Accordingly, I appointed Captain Ballesteros, Brigade Assistant S-4, as the Article 32 investigating officer. He will be conducting interviews of witnesses and will talk with you. He will read you your rights before questioning. Ordinarily, I would order you to remain on the firebase while the investigation is underway, but considering the S-2's estimate of the enemy situation, I will permit you to continue your duty as squad leader. However, when on combat operations in the field, you will work under the supervision of your troop commander, platoon leader, or platoon sergeant. You will not operate independently. Do you understand?"

"Yes, Sir."

"The enemy faded away since the action against the communications complex on the mountain, but our intelligence gathering effort reveals while the larger force dispersed there are still smaller units, probably squads, holed up in hamlets west of Linebacker. The S-2 reports indicate there were at least two companies of VC on the mountain. Today, a scout and his observer in a Loach conducting a BDA counted a hundred and eleven dead on the slopes of Nui Ba Ra."

"Yes, Sir."

"Sergeant Deakins, if this current situation wasn't before us, instead of a potential court-martial, I'd probably be decorating you and your men for saving the detachment and equipment up there."

"Yes, Sir."

"Your record reflects you are a fearless warrior and an out-front leader. I need, I want, both in my Brigade."

"Yes, Sir."

"Nevertheless, another part of your record is filled with reprimands for your indiscretions in battle. It was reported to me you demonstrate aggressive violence before an enemy is confirmed."

"Beg pardon, Sir?"

"You shoot first before determining if a person before you is an enemy soldier."

"I see. I know you fly around in a helicopter, Colonel, above the fight. You sit comfortable out of the line of fire looking down on us while we search for the enemy on the ground. Have you ever got your boots bloody? Have you ever been down there with us? Watching these sons-of-bitches kill your buddies? I doubt you've ever looked at the face of a dying chopper pilot captured and tortured by these bastards. You don't know what aggressive violence is, Colonel."

"At ease, Sergeant. Hold your tongue. Watch yourself. I'll rip your goddamn balls off and stuff them down you smart-ass mouth. You understand me?"

Deakins felt the sting of chastisement. He swallowed, kept his eyes straight ahead, and, for a moment, felt apologetic. He could not imagine why he spoke disrespectfully to the Brigade Commander. This Colonel had never done anything to him. But, he did not apologize.

"Yes, Sir."

"I want to know what happened on the mountain,

why a prisoner – hands tied behind his back – was shot. A prisoner who may have given information that would have saved your buddies' lives. But it is inappropriate for me to ask. I must make my decision based on findings presented by the appointed investigating officer. Only then can I decide whether to refer your case to the court-martial convening authority. Do you understand?"

"Yes, Sir."

"Do you have any questions?"

Burl did, but he didn't know how to ask them.

He knew he needed help, medical help, mental help, but he would never complain. He had not felt the same upon returning to Vietnam. He was angry. Angry his mom had cancer. Angry his mom had died from the disease. Angry he had to leave his grieving dad, who was sick with diabetes, suffered from angina, and had no money for medications. Angry he lost so many men, his ten-man infantry squad had the highest replacement rate in Hotel Company. Sergeant Burl Deakins was angry he could not kill all of the Vietnamese people and bring all Americans home safe. He was mad as hell. And now the Brigade Commander was going to court martial him for doing what he was trained to do, for doing his duty. As an infantry leader, he wanted to close with and destroy the enemy, ever man, woman, *and* child, and burn down every fucking house in the country.

Sergeant Jordan Mosley was senior, in rank and age, among the group, so he had dibs on sitting on the passenger side of the three-quarter ton truck.

"Lucky, you drive. The rest of you mount up. We all need a shower and clean clothes so everybody is gonna go without question."

"Why you look at me when you say that, Jordy?"

"Cause, Mickey, I know you'd wear the same damn jungle fatigues and underwear for the duration, if I didn't say anything."

"That ain't true, Sergeant Mosley, and you know it. I take showers and change into fresh fatigues."

"Yeah, once a month. For payday. Now, come on, everybody hop on."

Jinks, Bo, Nelly, Tex, Mickey, and J J climbed into the back. Jinks Jenkins, Mickey Fowler, and J J Johnson sat on the right side bench. Bonino Vitali, Francesco Cicchinello, and Glenn Pollard sat on the left.

"I hope you still have your camera after the shower, Bo," Pollard said.

"I will, Tex, I've brought it with me before."

"It could come up missing," Tex said.

"I don't think so. Never has. Those people want to keep their job more than they want a Pentax," Bo said.

Once out through the Linebacker gate, Lucky Jerrigan turned left on Road 3-10 and drove east toward Sông Bé and the laundry and shower point on Dak Toll Creek. It was a leisurely drive along a bustling, well-traveled thoroughfare. They did not wear combat gear, nor did they bring their rifles. Jordy and J J were armed with pistols. Soldiers going into the three villages near Linebacker did not carry weapons. In a way, these villages were like towns back home, and the environment was relatively safe. Only non-coms and officers wore a .45 caliber pistol into Phuoc Long, Sông Bé, and Phuoc Binh.

The going was slow. Jeeps, military trucks, civilian trucks, buses, pedicabs, Lambrettas, motor scooters, bicycles, pedestrians, and carts drawn by weary water buffalo filled the roadway.

"Damn, there's a lot of traffic on this road but there ain't no cars," Lucky said.

"Yeah, only rich folk, senior government people, and Michelin employees have cars," Sergeant Mosley said, "all Mercedes-Benz."

"You'd figure there'd be some French cars," Lucky said. "Even old ones."

"Yeah, I've seen some," Mosley answered. "They're all in Saigon. The most popular is the catch-a volt."

"Catch-a volt?"

"Yeah, it's a little four cylinder job. That's what catch-a volt means in French. I saw a thousand of them down there, mostly taxis. I saw some douche-a volts, too. I heard guys call the douche-a volt the cigarette roller."

"Why they call it that?"

"I guess because it looks like the old-timey cigarette roller. My Kentucky grandpa had one of those."

The Renault Quatre Chevaux and Citroën Deux Chevaux were indeed popular in Vietnam and France because they were efficient and inexpensive.

Along both sides of the road, merchants going to

and civilians coming from market trotted along balancing evenly distributed loads in straw baskets suspended from each end of a bamboo pole. In some cases, pails of milk, water, gasoline, kerosene, or other liquids hung from poles and because of their skilled movement no liquid spilled. Vietnamese shouldered the pole perpendicular to their body to navigate crowded areas more easily.

For vendors, baskets were a means of transportation of goods as well as platforms at the point of sale. They set their baskets filled with merchandise, normally fruits and vegetables, on a small stool in a place with plenty of foot traffic, including paths to and from markets. Here, along 3-10, anything was sold and bought – animals, fowl, and fauna.

On the eastbound shoulder, everyone headed in the direction of Sông Bé. The westbound shoulder handled traffic walking to Phuoc Binh. No one in an eastbound direction walked on the westbound side, or the other way round. It was a common courtesy to go in the direction of motorized traffic.

It was just another normal day in the lives of normal people who endured killing and maiming while trying to survive, go shopping, or pay bills and taxes to the provincial government.

Along the way, the truckload of soldiers gaped at and commented on the contents of merchant's baskets or wares displayed at a vendor's stand.

"Those are big ass canaries in those two cages," Bo said.

"That ain't canaries, they're too big," Nelly said.

"They're parrots. I wonder if they talk."

"If they did, you couldn't understand what they say, Nelly," Jinks said.

"Why not?"

"Cause, if they did talk they'd talk in Vietnamese, asshole." Tex' laughter was good-natured, pleasing, friendly. "You number ten, GI. You speak Vietnamese?"

J J was amused. Tex poked fun at Bo and Nelly who acted as if they were on a tour bus taking in the sights.

"Look." Nelly pointed. "There's a woman with a cart full of Army clothes and a little girl wearing a straw hat."

J J leaned forward to look, thinking it might be Mai Li and Kim. It wasn't, but he wondered if perhaps Mai Li had returned to duty and he had not seen her on the firebase.

The game, *I Spy*, came to J J's mind as the passengers in the back of the infantry truck identified various items merchants were bringing to market, or customers were bringing home.

They were entertained by squealing piglets that four farmers, marching in single file, toted. There were two little piggies, feet tied, on each straw platter that hung from the end of the bamboo stick.

"Goddamn, look at that," Lucky yelled. He slowed the truck so they all could have a look at a six-foot tall square box. On three sides, mesh screen covered the top quarter part of the box. On the front, mesh screen covered half with an opening between wood and screen. Outside this opening was a segment of board, the serving platform. The bottom part of the box was white. The words neatly printed by an American hand, properly apportioned, and painted in red announced:

HAMBURGERS

FRENCH FRIES

STEAK.

"McDonalds on wheels," Bo yelled.

All of them gawked at the hamburger joint.

A short male, the server, stood inside the hamburger stand. Three soldiers in jungle fatigues stood in line to buy a hamburger from this merchant.

"No telling what the meat is," J J said.

"Probably water buffalo," Mickey said.

"Would you buy a hamburger and French fries there?" Jinks asked.

"Fuck, no," Tex screamed. "I wouldn't buy em and I wouldn't eat em. Only a fool would buy food from a Vietnamese set up on the side of a road."

"Well, look around, Tex," J J said. "There's a lot of people buyin and eatin what's on the menu."

"Look," Bo said. "Look there, a dog and her pups. Three pups. Momma's tired of feedin those growin kids and she's headed to the store to pick up some Dog Chow."

They were black with tan muzzles and bellies. They ignored the traffic and weaved through and around pedestrians. Momma-dog led, marching at a quick pace. Her puppies trailed in tandem with heads down, panting, their little pink tongues hanging out. It was obvious this pack was on a mission.

"I'm surprised that little family is still alive," Mickey said. "Vietnamese eat dogs."

"No shit?" Nelly asked.

Lucky steered the truck off the road and parked at the shower point. Everybody jumped off the back. They stood in a group at the tent's entry and stretched.

The shower point was a huge general-purpose canvas tent that measured twelve feet tall, eighteen feet wide, and fifty-two feet long. The flooring of the shower point was reused wooden pallets, which had held 1-0-5mm and 1-5-5mm artillery shells.

Inside the entrance were stools in the dressing area, only jungle boots remained by the stool. Laundresses picked up the dirty fatigues, underwear, and socks while the soldier was in the shower. These soiled items were inspected, serviceable fabrics were transferred to the laundry, unserviceable were carried off to the trash dump and burned.

There were ten, three-foot by three-foot open-ended stalls. Inside each stall was a bar of soap, washcloth, and fresh towel. Gravity fed water poured through showerheads out of fifty-five-gallon drums that perched on stanchions outside the tent wall. Engineers pumped water out of Dak Toll Creek into tanker trucks with filters and transferred it into the drums. Used water flowed through a filtering and drainage system back into Dak Toll.

After showering, soldiers found clean clothes, socks, and underwear on their stool. NCOs removed their pinned chevrons and left those emblems on the stool. Soldiers left their jewelry and wallets on Linebacker. In a recent change, enlisted members had nothing sewn on uniform shirts because of wear and tear. Somebody finally decided it was too expensive for soldiers to sew stuff on a new shirt when the old one wore out or ripped apart. Only officers paid for the sewing of accouterments.

The laundry tent was next door to the shower point. Laborers and laundresses washed soldiers' clothing in the creek. Once clean, jungle fatigues smelled as if washed in water with dead fish. Within a couple of days, though, sweat, dirt, and grit absorbed the fishy odor.

"Some of you may want to buy fruit, a slice of melon, or souvenirs from the vendors. I'm gonna buy some VC flip-flops and a cross-bow to send to my kids back home," Sergeant Mosley said. "Meet back here at the truck in an hour."

A three-quarter ton truck pulled in and parked next to theirs. They recognized the driver but not the soldier in the passenger seat. Cotton stood up in the back and called out.

"Hey, guys. We got here just in time with some nice clean clothes, socks, and underwear."

Holt slid out from the driver's seat. "Well, ain't this a rag-tag looking outfit. I ain't seen you boys since you come off the mountain."

"Hey, Cotton, how you holdin up workin with this asshole?" Mosley asked.

J J was pleased to hear Jordy tag Holt. He felt better that someone else thought Holt was an asshole.

"I'm okay." Cotton demurred, not knowing whether the comment was serious or joking. After all, Holt was his boss.

"Lindseed, hand me the AK," Holt said.

The infantry squad perked up at the mention of an AK-47 and watched Private Lindseed hand the weapon down.

"Now, you go ahead and bring the clothing and supplies inside. Me and Horton are gonna walk down the creek to the trash dump so I can show him this thing shoots like it's supposed to," the supply sergeant said.

"Where'd you get the AK, Holt?" Sergeant Mosley asked.

"It's a war trophy I captured when I was on a patrol," Holt answered.

"Bullshit," J J said. "I bet that's one of the seven AKs me and Boss captured months ago."

Horton looked at J J. "He's got seven. He's offered a good price, and my investors are interested in buying all of them."

"Well, it ain't, Cookie. I'm a combat soljer, just like you. I go on patrols, I set up ambushes, I fight the gooks. I been wounded in action and received my Purple Heart. I say I captured this enemy weapon, it's my war trophy. And Mr. Horton, here, is the purchasing agent for some interested investors. He just wants to make sure it works."

"Combat soldier? Wounded?" J J laughed. "You got a nick in the butt, Holt, from a ricochet."

To everyone's surprise, most of all J J, Mai Li and Kim came out of the laundry tent.

"Mai Li. Kim, hello," J J said.

"Hello, Corporal Johnson, I mean Sergeant Johnson," Mai Li said. She smiled and nodded.

"Hello, little Kim," J J said.

Kim looked at J J for three seconds before she recognized him and spoke. "Bum, bum."

As Holt lowered the muzzle at her, Mai Li glanced at the AK-47 but ignored his scowl.

Holt said nothing.

"Hey, Bo, take our picture." J J moved to stand beside Mai Li.

Mai Li nodded again and pulled Kim in front. She placed her hands and fingers on little Kim's shoulders.

"Take our picture, Bo."

"Okay, say Betel nut," Vitali said and snapped two photos.

"Okay, now, Bo, take some pictures of all of us," J J said.

MAI LI

Momma-dog and pups walked up to Kim as if they were returning home to a warm welcome after a long trek. There's something about dogs, especially puppies, and kids. It is a natural attraction, from both sides of life.

Kim giggled and stuck out both hands to pet two puppies at the same time. The other one moved in to enjoy the caresses. Then all reared on back paws, little tails happily wagging. Their front paws fell on Kim's chest and shoulders, tongues lapping sweetness from the child's face as she hugged the trio.

In a continuous, happy motion, her tail whished approval as Momma-dog woofed twice at the small human, a show of appreciation and acceptance for Kim's love and affection for her brood.

Kim looked up at her mother. "Chúng ta có thể đưa họ về nhà không, Momma?"

"No, Kim."

Mai Li looked at J J and smiled. "Kim wants to take all of them home."

"Okay, the little reunion is over. Get back to work, Mai Li," Holt ordered.

"Yes, Sergeant Holt," Mai Li said.

"Wait a minute, Holt," J J said. "Just wait a minute."

He turned to Mai Li. "I heard about your husband, Mai Li. I'm sorry."

"Thank you, Sergeant Johnson. My family is heartbroken. Kim cried for her papa many days. We all cried, but we must go on."

"If there's anything I can do, let me know how I can help."

It was a courteous gesture, intended as a social manner. J J had nothing in mind that he could help with. He had no money in his pocket to give to Mai Li, the few dollars he owned were in his bunker. He thought he would give Mai Li some money later when they were at the firebase.

Mai Li did not interpret it in the off-handed way J J spoke it. For her, no one spoke of help if it were not sincere. Her nation was in a crisis. Everybody needed help one way or another, big or small, to survive. As a little girl, she had seen, experienced, the aftermath of defeat and the brutal murders that followed. What Mai Li and her mother lived through was not pleasant, and she wanted a better life for Kim. Mai Li knew killing in Vietnam would not end when the war concluded, when the Americans left. It would not be safe. People of the North hated people in the South. It would be decades of torture, bondage, and slavery. She knew America would be a safe place for her daughter, and J J was the ticket.

"Thank you, Sergeant Johnson. The war in my country will be more terrible when the full Army comes from Hanoi. Trapped between our corrupt government, the Viet Cong, the North, and the Americans, there will be more deaths. I am afraid for Kim. If anything happens to me, maybe you will bring Kim to America. S'il vous plait."

Without hesitation, or consideration of consequences, J J agreed. "Yes, of course, Mai Li. But nothing will happen to you. You'll be safe."

He responded as many would with a friend or an acquaintance. At that moment, J J gave no thought of the seriousness of his promise to Mai Li.

It was a grave assurance that Mai Li and Kim would trust.

All of the others stood silent and listened to this exchange, and to a man, they knew they had witnessed an impossible contract J J could never fulfill.

"That's it, Cookie. Mai Li, get back to work. Lindseed, you know what to do. After you bring all the supplies to the quartermaster, find Anh. It's collection time from my three fillies," Holt said.

Before walking toward the laundry tent Mai Li and Kim hesitated, they watched Momma-dog and her troop trot toward the flowing stream for cool water. Kim tarried after Mai Li went inside. The infantry squad moved to the shower point entrance.

Bo paused and watched Holt and Horton walk toward the creek, the dogs ahead of them.

"That boy, Holt. Does he always act like a piece of shit, bragging and carrying on?" Bo asked.

"Always. He's an asshole, Bo," J J said.

"One time I heard Holt say he was almost a made guy in one of the families in New York," Jinks said.

"Yeah, he said that to me too," J J said.

"Oh, yeah? Which one?" Bo asked.

"He never mentioned a name, just that he was among them," Jinks said.

"Well, I have family in New York," Bo said and smiled. "One is in Queens, the other is in Brooklyn."

"Holt is bragging all the time about something," J J said. "He's full of shit. One of these days somebody's gonna take exception. His chubby ass'll end up snagged on the sharp end of a stick."

"If Holt is bragging about being a made guy, his mouth is writing a check he won't be able to cash," Bo whispered. "I might just serve as bill collector."

Jenkins and Johnson looked at Bonino Vitali.

"You in the Mafia, Bo?" Jinks asked.

"I know not of which you speak. What is this Mafia, anyway?" Bo asked. A huge grin filled his face. His black eyes sparkled with mischief. "J Edgar and his college kids spread a lot of lies about nice Italian families who live and work in New York."

J J and Jinks matched Bo's grin.

J J was impressed. He felt special in the presence of a real live gangster, just like the picture show.

Inside, they chose a stool and sat. After removing jungle boots, they rolled the damp, woolen socks off wrinkled toes and feet. Since coming off the mountain, this was the first time their feet felt fresh air.

Mickey held the top and heel of a sock, stretched, and dragged it through the space between his big and middle toes. He did this in quick succession for both feet. On the second go-round, the vigorous sawing with the sock lasted longer.

"What the hell are you doing to your feet, Mickey?" J J asked.

"Athlete's foot. Itches like hell, J J. I can't get rid of it. Itching drives me crazy. Tried everything. Powder, soap, alcohol. I have to be careful with scratching and rubbing because I'll cut the skin and it'll get infected. Using my sock feels good and gives relief."

The crack of the first gunshot jolted the squad members.

The blood-curdling screams and unintelligible chatter of the Vietnamese women startled the infantrymen.

J J did not have to understand the words to realize something terrible was taking place. Frightening screams, crying, and wailing were a universal language.

Before he could dash outside, the second, third, and fourth pop created mass hysteria. The bone-chilling, continuous squeal that pierced J J's ears and tore at his heart came from little Kim.

When he heard Kim, J J's fear mounted. As he swept through the tent doorway, barefoot, J J pulled his pistol from his shoulder holster. He imagined Holt had shot Mai Li. He was frightened but prepared to kill Holt and face the court-martial and conviction.

J J glanced right and saw little Kim standing at the entrance of the laundry tent.

Frozen in place, her high-pitched, horrible screams spilled across her small hands and fingers balled into tiny fists that she held to her lips. Rivers of tears flowed down her round cheeks. "Chó con. Chó con." Kim kept screaming. " Chó con. Chó con."

Mai Li came out, knelt, grabbed her baby, and held her tightly in a secure embrace.

"Kim sees the little puppies," Mai Li screamed.

J J looked left and saw Holt with the AK-47 walking toward the Momma-dog and her three pups lying on the bank of Dak Toll.

"He's shot the dogs," J J murmured. J J realized Holt shot the pack marching along the road, the family that showered Kim with adoration. "The son-of-a-bitch has shot four poor animals."

Kim could not stop crying and screaming.

"Holt," J J shouted. "Holt, you son-of-a-bitch."

Holt stopped at Momma-dog.

"Holt," Horton pleaded. "That's enough, Holt."

Now, J J could hear the mournful whimpering. One of the pups was whining, crying, its little front legs trying to gain traction, its rear legs pushing to run, to escape the carnage Holt dealt.

"HOLT," J J yelled. He held his pistol at the ready and took three steps toward the supply sergeant. He paid no attention to the pebbles stinging his bare feet. "HOLT!"

Holt held the barrel with both hands and raised the automatic rifle to chest high. He slammed the butt with full force and grunts onto the head of Momma-dog. Her legs churned, she yelped, and her cry was heart wrenching. Wounded by the gunshot, she was unable to rise and run away.

J J could now see Momma-dog's eyes. She looked sideways at the killer standing over her.

Holt slammed the butt down on Momma-dog's head in rapid, pumping motions. With each thunderous blow, the animal cried out in death throes of pain until there was only the sound of thumping of the rifle butt against skull.

Holt turned to the nearest pup and slammed the butt of the AK-47 against its head. Their duet reached the outskirts of Sông Bé as little Kim's matched the puppy's screams.

The rifle wasn't enough for the sadistic slaughter. Holt raised his foot and stomped on the puppy's head three times.

J J rushed, lowered his shoulder, and knocked Holt backwards into the creek.

"Stop, Holt. You worthless son-of-a-bitch," J J shouted.

Holt stood up in the water and raised the AK-47 to shoot J J.

J J froze, unsure whether Holt would pull the trigger, and unsure if he should kill Holt here and now and claim self-defense.

"Lower the weapon, Holt, or I'll blow you away." Jordy's quiet voice was an instant restraint.

J J turned and looked.

Jordy held his automatic pistol level, pointed at Holt, with the hammer cocked. Sergeant Mosley and his pistol were ready for action – and death.

Holt lowered the AK and sloshed ashore.

"I won't forget. I'll get you for this, Johnson," Holt said. "Come on, Horton. Let's go back to Linebacker and finalize our transaction. LINDSEED! LINDSEED! Come on, let's go."

When everyone was back on the firebase, some were refreshed; others were determined.

"Okay, Holt. I'm going to my money handler and tell him the weapons function as they should. I'll pick up the cash, and a vehicle, and be back in an hour or so. In the meantime, make sure all the weapons are cleaned and individually wrapped, and all the accessories are in a box."

"Okay, Horton. A couple of months ago, you left me hanging. I didn't think you were coming back. Don't do that again. I will be very disappointed. You understand?"

"Well, like I told you, there was some dickering going on about who would get first pick and all that. But that's been resolved. The moneyman has the cash and a storage place I can put the stuff until we can get the weapons distributed to the new owners or shipped to the states for them. Officers don't want to get their hands dirty, if you know what I mean."

"LINDSEED. Okay, Horton, I expect to see you in an hour, with cash in hand. Don't fuck around. That'll make me very angry, you hear? LINDSEED."

Horton turned and strolled toward the artillery gun pits. He was in no hurry. He waved and spoke to the gun crews as he weaved around the sandbagged cannon emplacements. He didn't appreciate threats from Holt. Horton thought Holt was an asshole and figured he would really piss somebody off one of these days.

"Yes, Sergeant Holt?"

"How much money did you collect from Anh?"

"One hundred eighty-three dollars."

"Okay, put it with the rest of the cash, in the Folgers coffee can on my desk."

"I already did, Sergeant Holt."

"Oliver, my boy, we just made a killing on these AK-47s. I thought that asshole was gonna renege on the deal. I'm going in the conex and get all the weapons ready for Horton. I want you to find a box big enough to hold all the magazines, ammo, and harnesses. The undergarments box ought to be big enough. When you have all of that together, bring the box to me. When this deal is done, I'll give you a percentage."

"I don't want a percentage, Sergeant Holt. What you're doing is against Army regulations. I don't like it. You can go to the stockade for what you're doing with the women and what you're going to do with the weapons."

"Well, Lindseed, I don't give a shit whether you like it or not. And if I go, you'll go too because you're part of this outfit. You're just as neck deep as you can get."

"No, I'm not, Sergeant Holt. I'm not a part of this."

"Oh, yes, you are, Sonny Boy. Anh didn't give me the money, she handed it over to you. So, shut up and do what I tell you to do. Go on, get with it, get it done."

J J had hung his shoulder holster and pistol on the nail for his trip to the orderly room to call Kathleen. He left his rifle next to his sleeping area. There was no need to bring a weapon to the command post to make a phone call.

Once J J was out of the bunker, Bo slipped J J's .45 caliber pistol out of its holster and shoved it into his fatigue trouser pocket. For Bo, family sentiment ran deep, old scores never faded away. It wasn't personal, just business. Bo made a stop at the mess hall for a relaxing cup of Army coffee on his way to the Troop supply bunker to have a family conversation with a made guy.

Depending on the answers to questions and affiliation, Bo was prepared to make an unsanctioned hit on Linebacker. Well, Bo surmised, it *was* personal because Holt was an asshole and braggart. He thought it would be a pleasure to pop a cap on the chubby piece of shit whose claim to fame was puppy-killer.

Neither Bo nor J J noticed the combat harness hanging from the same nail was missing a grenade.

In the supply bunker, Cotton laid out the accessories. He picked up one of the bayonets, fondled it, and slid his thumb along the sharpened blade. He imagined how it would pierce and sink to its hilt with a shove and twist, or slice soft skin. He looked at the doorway and listened before walking to the counter. He formulated a plan, went through his interrogation, and rehearsed his testimony of self-defense. He had not wanted to be involved; the threatened blackmail was enough. He saw no other way but to take matters into his hands and end the circus.

Mai Li, working on soldiers' clothing in a nearby

sleeping bunker, pulled the straight razor from her pocket and snipped loose threads hanging from cleaned fatigue shirts and trousers. She paused, staring at the gleaming sliver of sharp steel. With the blade open, Mai Li stood and walked from the bunker, her mind on a mission of ending tyranny. In a trance, she lost focus, lost a sense of time and place, lost the absence of Kim.

The phone connection to the Sixty-Second was no different from a long distance call in the states.

A technician answered. J J remembered to ask for *Captain* Patton and to say he was returning her call for the follow-up on his recovery.

Within a few seconds, Katie answered.

"Officially, this is a follow-up call on your recovery, doctor's orders. How are you doing, Soldier?"

"I'm fine, Sweetheart. I love you."

J J looked at Vannoy and winked. The troop clerk sat with his mouth open enjoying his official position as eavesdropper.

"Me, too," Katie said. "Captain Norman is standing here with me. She says hi."

J J's heart raced at the sound of Katie's voice. He longed to hold her, kiss her, love her.

"*Captain* Norman. Damn, I'm in the wrong branch of service, everybody's getting promoted to Captain. Tell Sally hello, I think of her often."

"Yeah, I bet. I'll tell her. Let's go on an in-country R and R to Vung Tau. I'll make reservations at the Imperial Hotel. As an officer, we'll have a better room with a view. I have news I want to tell you in private."

J J's heart thumped. He hoped Katie's news was to say yes to his proposal of marriage.

"R and R in Vung Tau? The Imperial Hotel. That sounds great, Kathleen. I'm in the orderly room. Let me check if I'm eligible for an in-country R and R."

Vannoy shot a thumbs-up at J J's raised eyebrows.

"Yes, I'm eligible."

"Two weeks, beginning the 22nd?" Katie proposed.

"In two weeks, the 22nd. Okay, but I'll have to see my Platoon Leader and Platoon Sergeant and get their permission."

The detonation was horrendous, the ground vibrated, the command post shuddered, Vannoy's desk and typewriter shook, the shock numbed their senses.

"HOLY SHIT!" Vannoy yelled.

It felt like a two-thousand-pound bomb dropped from a B-52 had exploded.

J J held onto the handset and hit the dirt.

"A bomb just hit Linebacker," he shouted into the phone. "A bomb just hit the firebase, Katie."

"Cookie? Are you alright, Darling? Cookie?"

"I . . . I gotta go. I'll call again when I get permission to go on R and R. I love you."

"Cookie? J J? Oh, my God. J J?"

R and R

When the conex container exploded, Bo rushed to the mess hall door. Flames erupted in a broiling, churning, orange and black mushroom, the heat so intense he stepped back from the doorway.

The moment the blast slammed the left door of the container into the side of the sandbagged supply bunker, Lindseed dropped to the ground. He covered his head, bayonet still in his grasp.

The violent detonation pushed a shockwave across Linebacker, its force so powerful Mai Li fell face down. The open razor flew out of her hand and landed in the dirt near her head. The impact knocked her breath out, and she laid gasping and gulping for air. Snot dripped from her nose, and sagging saliva strings slid from her mouth as she struggled to get a breath. Feeling faint and sick to her stomach at the same time, she rolled onto her side and puked. The vomit flowed across her cheek and down her neck.

Vannoy and J J jumped up and ran out of the command post. The soaring temperature gave them pause. Instant death waited, if they chose to charge into the fire.

"I think Holt's in there." Cotton had gained footing and now stood safely away. He pointed at licking flames. His nonchalant gesture and voice projected no emergency.

"We can't get in there," Vannoy yelled.

J J thought about it, about how he could save the asshole. But he didn't know where Holt was inside the container – front, back, which side, how deep. Even if he were able to get through the inferno, he knew it was useless because nothing could survive the devastation.

"That fire is too damn hot for just a bunch of clothes, boxes, and wooden crates burning," J J said.

"That's gotta be a Mogas fire," Vannoy yelled.

"Holt had six five-gallon cans of gasoline stored in there," Cotton said.

"Jesus Christ. Where's the fire truck?"

"We got no fire brigade or fire truck on Linebacker, J J. Anyway, it's too late."

Even there on the ground, several yards from the burn, Mai Li felt the heat. She strained to look up, as a shadow approached.

"Kim? Baby?"

"Momma. Momma."

Mai Li got a breath and rose to her knees. She stretched her arms out, and Kim walked into the embrace.

"Kim. My Baby."

"Qui, Momma. Bum bum." The reflection of the burning heap danced in little Kim's black eyes.

Once the fire died out and steel of the huge metal box cooled, their search found the black, charred, crisp chunk of corpse. Holt's body lay on its back. The skin from his elbows covered the seared floor like melted Velveeta cheese. His upper arms stood tall, exposed finger bones curled as if clawing at fleeting freedom. Even in that death posture and the position of the skewed head, what was clear was Holt's slashed throat.

Lieutenant Versailles and Boss Tweed were agreeable to J J's request for an in-country R and R to Vung Tau. Both had been there and enjoyed the luxury, water, and beach.

"But, we can't let you go for a whole week," Platoon Sergeant Tweed said. "Just for three days."

"Intelligence reports keep coming in that North Vietnam Army forces are moving down the Ho Chi Minh Trail through Cambodia. Because of the NVA activity, Brigade issued a directive. Until further notice, only three from a unit can be on R and R out-of-country and only three can go in-country at the same time. In-country is further restricted to just seventy-hours," Versailles said. "And more than that, everybody on in-country R and R are subject to immediate recall."

"There's been a lot of V C activity near Phuoc Binh, around the hamlets of Dau Tron and Ap Trong, the rubber plantation hamlet," Boss said. "So, three days is best we can do, Johnson. And you better take it now because Brigade might freeze all leaves and passes without notice."

"I'll take it, Boss. But I can't start until the 22nd,

Lieutenant. I'm going to meet somebody on the 22nd."

"I see," the Lieutenant said. "I'll put you in for the pass, but you risk not being able to go at all if you're going to wait two weeks."

"I understand, Sir."

"The other thing is, you don't go straight from here to R and R, Johnson. You have to go to Long Bien, draw your clothes from storage, change, process out on a three-day pass, and then get a chopper ride out to Vung Tau. There's sort of a chopper taxi shuttle to R and R sites, Cam Ranh Bay, Saigon, Vung Ro Bay, Vung Tau."

"I didn't know you had to go through all that, Sir. Does my seventy-two hours begin when I sign out on pass at Long Bien or when I leave Linebacker?"

"When you leave the firebase, Cookie," Tweed answered. "The clock starts ticking when you sign out here."

"Then could I leave on the first chopper out of Linebacker going to Long Bien?"

"Sure. I'll ask Vannoy to arrange it for you. When you're in Vung Tau you gotta eat at Vittorio's," Versailles said. "Great spaghetti."

"Spaghetti? In Vietnam?" J J asked. "Was the meat from water buffalo, Sir?"

Alex laughed. "Probably. But it was spaghetti, Johnson, off a real menu, a little round table, red-and-white checkered tablecloth, candles, and red wine. Just like the movies."

"Where you stayin, J J?" Boss Tweed asked.

"Imperial Hotel."

The Platoon Leader and Platoon Sergeant looked at each other and raised their eyebrows.

"What?" J J asked.

"That's officer country, Johnson," the lieutenant said. "Officers and civilians stay at the Imperial. NCOs stay at the Vung Tau Plaza or Seaside Resort and enlisted stay at other places. All of the hotels are on the beach, but there's no mingling."

"You mean like flapper – flater-ni-zation."

"Yes," the lieutenant nodded and grinned. Alex did not offer to correct J J's mispronunciation.

"How'd you get a reservation at the Imperial?" Boss asked.

J J had not revealed Katie to Lieutenant Versailles or Sergeant Tweed and hesitated to do it now.

"The girl I'm going to marry made the reservation, Boss. She's got connections."

"Oh, okay."

That answer was simply accepted, and J J decided to stay quiet about details.

In the days that followed, J J and his fire team pulled shifts in fighting bunkers on the perimeter. Each day they either listened to lectures by PsyOps experts on winning the hearts and minds of the populace, set up security for police checkpoints, received three thirty-minute lessons on and practiced intonations of Vietnamese words, or enjoyed the relative respite. During those days, not a shot was fired in anger.

The NVA ordered a stand-down while infantry and

sapper regiments infiltrated and scurried toward Saigon, their main objective for the coming attack.

After one of the map reading classes, J J showed Mai Li his piece of military map sheet and asked her to point out her hamlet.

She stuck a finger to the map. "There, *Đầu tròn*."

"Dau tron," J J repeated.

Mai Li grinned. "*Đầu tròn*. *Đầu tròn*." She emphasized the intonations.

J J tried again. "Dau tron."

Mai Li laughed. "*Đầu tròn*. In English, a close translation means round top. My hamlet sits on a rise in the ground."

"Round top," J J said.

She pointed north of Linebacker. "Yes, over there, about two kilometers up Road 3-11 on the right side. Several families live in *Đầu tròn*."

J J looked in the direction she pointed. "Dau tron. Round top," J J said. "Your house is on the road to the Cambodia border. It's less than a half mile from here."

"Yes," Mai Li said. "We are between the rock and the hard place. Like your Sergeant Deakins."

J J was not surprised Mai Li knew about Deakins. Word of mouth was powerful communication. The Viet Cong also used it as a controlling tool to engender fear. Adept VC cadre promoted unfavorable events as strong, effective propaganda against Americans.

No one in the squad, even in the troop, had doubt about whether Deakins would face a general court-martial for murdering the prisoner. They knew Colonel Carson's Article 32 investigation was a formality, to protect the rights of the accused. J J was impressed how thorough Captain Ballesteros conducted his business; there was no bullshit, no trickery about it. In a straightforward manner, the Captain questioned witnesses twice, mainly to determine if what each said the second time matched their first account.

Deakins did his duty, leading his infantry squad, without incident or discussion. J J tried twice to talk with Deak about what happened and why, but Deak shrugged it off each time.

"I can't change things," Deak responded once to one of J J's questions. "There isn't any reason to dwell on it, Cuz. It's done."

"I wish it hadn't happened," J J had said softly. "You're a good man, Deak. You were there for me when I called on you. I wish I could be there for you, but too many saw what you did."

Deak had looked at J J and smiled. "Even if you were the only one there, Cuz, you couldn't lie about it. That's not you, and that's why I like you. You're a straight arrow, a stand-up guy. Anyway, you couldn't have saved him, Cookie. It was his fate and my destiny, that's how I see it."

They had not talked about it again since that brief exchange. They did not avoid the subject, it just wasn't a focus of their daily lives and activities. They went about Army business twenty-four hours every day.

The evening after the explosion, J J wrote three letters.

He sent a light, carefree note to Imogene who loved to hear about the combat exploits of his infantry fire team. He asked her how the cafe business was going and to pass his thoughts and regards to Vernon and Elmer. He said he thought about them often, about working at the cafe.

The warm letter to his mom told about Katie, his love, and intention to marry her. He also told his mother about the impending R and R to the fancy Imperial Hotel. He wrote about Mai Li and Kim. In closing, he sent his love to her, Kip, and Jodie. As a P.S., he remarked how closely Kim resembled and reminded him of his little sister.

J J's third letter was to Mr. Dickerson at Sugar Babe's. He told of meeting Colonel Dickerson and Katie at the hospital. As professional as J J could write it, he wrote of his thoughts and interest when he learned from Imogene that all three cafes were on the market. He loved the Army, J J expressed, but still in his heart wanted to be a cook. Finally, he penned, he didn't quite know how to phrase the question but hoped for an understanding consideration.

At 0600 hours, with J J aboard, the mail chopper lifted off Linebacker for the forty-minute zip to Long Bien. J J looked at the bulging, gray canvas bags marked U. S. MAIL and thought that maybe he would receive answers on this mail carrier's evening shuttle back to the firebase. It had been two weeks since his letters flew to America.

From the pad at Long Bien, he thumbed a ride on an Air Force blue bus hauling new arrivals from Tan Son Nhut. There was no seat available, so J J stood on the step and looked at all the fresh faces.

The ride was quiet and short. The driver stopped in front of J J's building and opened the door.

"See you later, alligator," the chauffeur laughed.

"After while, crocodile," J J retorted as he stepped off the bus. He jogged up the Processing Center steps two at a time.

"Well, hello, Cookie," Sandra shouted.

J J grinned and shook his head. "I am impressed. How in the world can you remember the name of a soldier who passed in front of your desk months ago, Sandra?"

She laughed. "Hey, Cookie, you're the only one who came through here that paid a recruiter ten bucks to be a cook in the Army and wound up in Vietnam as an infantryman."

"And, you remember all that too?"

"I'll never forget that, or you. Hey. Sergeant Kane. Look who's come home from the hills."

"COOKIE!" Kane shouted. "Son-of-a-bitch."

Sergeant Kane, a thick bundle of military orders under one arm and manila file folders in the other hand, approached. He shifted folders.

J J shook his head, grasped and shook Sergeant Kane's extended hand.

"What about your Cuz, Sergeant Bleachers? Bleakins?"

"Deakins. Jesus, you guys have great memories."

"Yes, Deakins. How's he doing?"

J J told them about the incident. They shot the breeze for three minutes before returning to the business at hand.

"Your belongings are three buildings down on the right," Sandra said. "You can change into khakis, leave your jungle uniform and boots in storage and change again when you return from your three-day pass."

"I wear my khakis on pass?"

"Yep, unless you brought civilian clothes or buy them from a shop." She held out the card. "Here's your pass. Keep it on your person at all times." She grinned. "At least when you have your pants on."

J J nodded and matched her roguishness. "Okay, I know how to follow instructions."

"Because there are restrictions now on night flights up to your firebase, you must return here by 0700 Saturday to be able to get a return flight back to Linebacker by 0600 hours, Sunday."

"So, my seventy-two-hour pass ends up a forty-eight pass."

"Fraid so. That's the Army way."

"Don't I know it, Sandra. Okay, after I change clothes, what then? I need a ride out to Vung Tau."

"Wow, Vung Tau. That's a ritzy place. Catch an Army shuttle bus out front of this building. One runs every fifteen minutes. It'll pass by the chopper operations center. Bus driver'll tell you when to get off and what door to go to. There, a crew chief will put you on a waitlist manifest. When a ride is available, you'll be on your way."

"How long you think I'll have to wait?"

"Less than an hour wait, twenty-minute flight, fifteen-minute bus ride to the hotel, and you're in high cotton. What hotel are you staying in, Cookie? Plaza or Seaside?"

"You're going to like this, Sandra. I'm staying in officer country. The Imperial."

"It'll be another half-hour before the hotel shuttle bus comes by here again," the Army operations center clerk said. "You missed it by ten minutes. What hotel you going to, Private?"

"It's Sergeant. Sergeant Johnson. When I arrived here months ago, I was a private. Khakis been in storage, never had a chance to sew on chevrons. Probably won't need to anyway, Specialist Thornton."

"Why not, Sergeant Johnson?"

"I'll probably be a Colonel when it's time to go home."

Both roared with friendly laughter.

"Damn. A half-hour wasted waiting on a bus."

"Well, go out to the street, turn left, walk a couple hundred meters down to the gate. There you can hire a pedicab. You ever rode in a pedicab, Sarge?"

"Nope. This will be the first time. Thanks. See you in a few hours."

The pedicab peddler was an old man. Gray hair and beard, watery, gray eyes, yellow teeth, and raggedy flip-flops. He wore a conical hat, black cotton pajama trousers, and an American tee-shirt advertising Walt Disney's Magic Kingdom with images of Mickey and Minnie in a huge red heart. By sign language, they quickly agreed on three dollars, American, and the old man nodded as J J pronounced *Imperial* three times.

"Number one," the old man said.

J J was surprised. The ride was a pleasant, entertaining experience. The septuagenarian set a quick pace to make the breeze refreshing, his thin legs pumped and churned, wheels hissed on asphalt. They weaved in and out of halted cars and buses, and through and around pedestrians, bicyclists, motor scooters, and other pedicabs.

J J noted people on the street were different from those around Phuoc Binh and Sông Bé. Here, there were few suits, it was too hot, most men wore a white, cotton or silk, long sleeve shirt, light colored slacks, black belt, and loafers. Women wore western or traditional styles; J J saw several adorned in colorful silk Ao Dais. He could count on one hand those wearing black pajamas and straw hats.

Vung Tau was modern, French. Its people appeared European or Eurasian compared to the local populace J J was familiar with.

The instant the driver stopped at the front steps of the Imperial Hotel, shouting and frantic shooing away by the two doormen, two porters, and three bellhops started. It was apparent to J J, pedicabs, particularly pedicab drivers, were not welcome. The poor man trying to catch his breath bowed at the discouraging remarks.

J J made it a point to pause and gave another dollar to the driver for the service. He smiled and patted the old man's shoulder. "You Number One."

"Cảm ơn ngài. Cảm ơn ngài. You Number One." The old man bowed, grinned, and looked up at the assholes looking down on him.

"Welcome to the Imperial Hotel, Sir." One of the doormen opened one of the glass doors for J J.

"Thank you, my man," J J said and strode into opulence. At least it was a big ass difference from his customary surroundings on Linebacker.

The front desk check-in clerk looked up but did not greet J J as a guest.

"Yes?" It came out with a French accent.

"I'm checking in."

Just like a stereotype in the movie, the Frog looked J J up and down before speaking.

"The Imperial Hotel is for military officers only, it is not for Privates."

The rebuff reminded J J again his khaki shirt bore no sergeant chevrons. To the clerk, J J was a slick sleeve private.

He nodded and moved away, stopping at the gift shop window. He stood there peering in at the expensive tokens and watched the reflection. A soldier dressed in Army khakis relieved the Frog and the Frenchman disappeared through a doorway behind the counter.

J J made his move, a quickstep, urgent dash.

At the counter, he discovered the soldier was a well-groomed, shiny, polished brass, Second Lieutenant. The lieutenant wore Quartermaster insignia on his left collar.

"Excuse me, Lieutenant, Sir."

"Yes, Soldier. What is it?"

J J looked at the black, plastic nameplate.

"Lieutenant Burr, Sir, I'm Private Johnson. I'm a runner for the Sixty-Second Field Hospital Commander,

Colonel Dickerson. I bring an important message from the Colonel for Captain Patton, his chief nurse at the hospital, who is a guest in your care, Sir."

"Okay. Give me the message, Private Johnson. I'll see that Captain Patton receives it right away."

"Oh, no, no way, Sir. Colonel Dickerson would have my ass, Lieutenant, if I gave his message to anyone cept Captain Patton. You, of all people, Sir, know how all that stuff works. I have my orders, Sir."

J J did not mistake the disdain Lieutenant Burr displayed, although J J would not have thought of it as condescension but more like the butter bar was a snob.

"Okay, Johnson, stand over there." The Lieutenant jabbed a finger toward the end of the counter. "Over there, Private, out of the way. I'll ring the Captain's room."

J J waited at the position designated and watched the one-minute phone exchange.

Lieutenant Burr looked at J J, raised his hand, and snapped his fingers.

J J stared at Lieutenant Burr but did not respond. The Lieutenant snapped his fingers again three times in rapid succession and then beckoned J J with upended fingers in a come-hither motion.

J J played innocent, pointed to his chest, and mouthed *Me – you want me, Lieutenant?*

Lieutenant Burr nodded vigorously and snapped his fingers three times again, beckoning with his fingers.

J J snapped his fingers three times, balled a fist, pointed at Burr with an index and middle finger as a gun barrel, and saluted.

"Captain Patton expects you to bring the Colonel's message to her right away. Room 711. She said tell you she will give you her most urgent attention and response. Off you go, Johnson."

J J could not resist. "Right, Sir. Eleven-seven."

"No, you idiot, 711, 7-1-1. Now hurry up, don't keep the Captain waiting."

J J tapped on the door with a knuckle, and caught his breath when Katie opened it. She wore a white cotton dress with string shoulder straps and no bra. She had unbound her ponytail; her hair lay loose on her shoulders. Her eyes sparkled, her smile warm and enticing.

"Where have you been, Soldier Boy? I've been counting the minutes for this moment. Come in and give me your message."

J J entered. She closed the door and took him into her arms. They kissed and held each other in a sweet, tight embrace.

He pulled away, looked into her brown eyes, into her soul, and grinned.

"I've missed you so, Kathleen. I love you so, Sweetheart. God, you look great. You take my breath away."

They kissed again, enjoying the pleasure that swept through their hearts.

J J wanted to make love with his sweetheart right away, but restrained from making advances.

Katie took his hand and led him out onto the lanai. There their conversation was light, chatty, mostly about nothing.

Their love nest on the seventh floor offered an uninterrupted view of the white sandy beach beyond the exquisite, sophisticated patio dining area sprawled below them. It was a peaceful setting.

From the elevated perch, they watched joyful play in the shallow water. There were officers, male and female, Vietnamese girls, servants, and waiters in white uniforms stomping through the sand to serve refreshments from round silver trays.

Out past the sandbar, fishermen in Sampans watched the frolicking of foreigners. Standing there, J J saw a different life from soldiering. He saw a breed of officers whose boots and brass were polished by others. J J could not stomach those types and thought about his own officers in Delta Troop. He reflected on and dreaded what he knew Katie would ask about.

"I've brought some clothes from the hospital for you. Hawaiian shirt, khaki trousers, belt, underwear, socks, and canvas sneakers. All the tuxedoes were taken."

"How did you know what sizes to bring?"

"Experience. I'm a nurse, remember? I'm a pretty good judge of height and weight, all sizes and shapes. Now, go freshen up. I'll wait for you."

The warm water from the modern shower was soothing and relaxing. He came out recharged, with the towel wrapped around to ask about the clothes.

Katie lay nude on the bed, tips of her brown hair touching her breasts. A cool breeze swayed the curtains at the patio doorway. South China Sea's waves did not interfere.

J J walked to the bed. He stood there admiring her loveliness. He could smell her freshness, her sweetness, her humanness, and his heart pounded with passion.

Katie smiled, raised her eyebrows, half closed her eyes, and opened her arms toward him. Invitingly, she wiggled her fingers for him.

"Come to me, lover. I waited too long for this moment. I've got what you need and you can have as much as you want."

J J dropped the towel on the floor.

CRASH

Uninhibited movement down the Ho Chi Minh Trail permitted thousands of heavily armed NVA units to pour across the Cambodian border into the Republic of Vietnam every month. These groups ranged from five-hundred-man infantry regiments to small, highly trained sapper cells consisting of no more than five individuals. Combat organizations moved into positions across southern Vietnam, from the frontier barrier to the coastal cities, to charge firebases and headquarters base camps while smaller sections would carry out diversionary attacks as a cover for the larger scale actions. There were plans to strike highly visible targets such as city centers, shopping areas, fancy restaurants, and luxury hotels.

Other plans included violent assaults against small villages and hamlets near large military complexes to draw combat forces into a fray, away from the protection of direct lines of communication and defense of high-speed avenues of approach into Saigon, the capital city. The storming, destruction, and annihilation of the meager forces on Fire Support Base Linebacker were part of this strategy.

After evening chow, the alert duty changed over from first to third platoon and Lieutenant Versailles designated the infantry squad as his QRF. A Quick Reaction Force was to move out in urgent response to enemy action in under fifteen minutes.

Sergeant Deakins and his squad sat in or around their truck, no one wandered away. There was no trip to the latrine. If a soldier needed to pee, he irrigated the truck's tires. There was no authorization for bowel movements. They used idle time to sharpen bayonets, wipe down weapons, and insure their ammunition was clean and set in the magazines. Some wore their combat gear; others laid it next to their leg or hip, within reach. There was no grab-ass, what little chatter existed was in hushed tones.

The Scout Section was the RRF, under the overall supervision of Platoon Sergeant Boswell Tweed. The Ready Reaction Force's mission was to support Sergeant Deakins' QRF and move out in under thirty minutes when called.

Deakins sat on the passenger seat of the three-quarter-ton truck in deep thought. He continuously opened his Zippo cigarette lighter, rolled the flint wheel with his thumb, focused on the ignition spark, stared into the tall flame, and closed the lid. Each time, in methodical rhythm, the hinge creaked as the lid opened and clanked when he shut it. Creak, clank. Creak, clank. Creak, clank. He had intentionally pulled up the wick so that it extended through the eyelet.

The lighter's motion continued even as Deakins looked toward the sound of a revving engine and propeller. He turned his head to watch the OV-10 scoot down the asphalt airstrip on Linebacker. He followed the single engine plane as it lifted off the tarmac and began its climb toward the setting sun. As it banked north, his mouth dropped open in astonishment when he saw four streams of green tracers sail into the belly and cowling of the small aircraft. The ripping chatter of automatic rifles and the crump of the aluminum plane crashing reached him in less than six seconds. He sat up and called out to his squad at the same time his radio came alive.

"STAND BY! STAND BY!" Deakins yelled. "PLANE DOWN! PLANE DOWN!"

* * *

The Troop Commander had gathered this group to hear their individual and collective stories and to get answers so he could report to Colonel Carson, the Brigade Commander.

Even though he purposefully made it a relaxed meeting by having Sergeant Hale serve coffee in the dining facility, Thompson knew he was under the gun. The Troop CO was fully aware the Brigade CO was not a happy camper. His soldiers' accounts would prepare him to respond to Carson's summons to explain how and why such a tragedy could have happened.

The third platoon leader, Platoon Sergeant Tweed, Lieutenant Webb, the XO, First Sergeant Morris, and Sergeant Mosley, Jenkins, Vitali, Cicchinello, Mickey Fowler, and Tex Pollard sat at mess hall tables across from Captain Thompson who faced them.

"Who's missing, Sergeant Mosley?" the

commanding officer asked.

"Sergeant Johnson, Remo Vance, and Kellen Averyman, Sir."

"Where are they?" Captain Thompson asked.

"Vance and Averyman are manning a fighting bunker on our perimeter with Sergeant Medina's boys, Capn," Boss Tweed answered.

"Were they on scene at the hamlet?"

"No, Sir," Lieutenant Versailles said. "I've talked with them. Remo and Kellen were on the other side of the road, on the north side of 3-11, in an OP providing security."

"Johnson?"

"He wasn't there either, Capn. J J is on an in-country R and R at Vung Tau," Alex said.

"Oh, that's right, Alex, you told me. The Imperial Hotel," the Troop Commander smiled. "That boy's got connections to be able to get a room at the Imperial."

Alex smiled. "I think he does, Sir. He said he was meeting someone there."

Gossip was rampant, so they all knew Colonel Carson had his hands full with a bevy of recent disasters, and they all guessed this new development might explode into a public relations nightmare if not handled properly. The Commanding General, they believed, could just let the hammer down and relieve Colonel Carson.

Captain Thompson nodded at his platoon leader. "Okay, Alex, go ahead."

"Yes, Sir," Lieutenant Alex Versailles continued. "Deakins' squad was the QRF, and Sergeant Reggie Wolcynski's scout section was RRF. When I got the call that the Bronco had drawn enemy ground fire and crashed north of the firebase, near the Dau Tron hamlet, at grid coordinates 085125, I ordered Deakins to respond. I alerted Sergeant Tweed and Wolcynski's scouts to mount up and follow us to the hamlet because I knew there would be a bunch of bad guys. I suspected we'd find the body of the pilot, who I figured died in the crash. And if he wasn't in the aircraft then I knew they captured him. I didn't expect to drive into a hornet's nest."

"Yes, Sir," Sergeant Tweed affirmed. "By the time we got organized almost fifteen minutes lapsed. We followed as quick as we could. It was still light so we made good time up 3-11 to the hamlet. Dau Tron sits on a little rise, fairly prominent."

"We found the plane right away, alongside the highway. It did not crash into the hamlet," Versailles said. "There was no fire. I later discovered the pilot was dead. He'd taken a round through the bottom of his chin that exited out the top of his head. It was gruesome, Captain, but I don't think he suffered. With that kind of wound I'm sure he died instantly. Deakins' squad fanned out to secure the perimeter around the crash."

"When we pulled up with the scouts, Captain, all hell broke loose," Boss Tweed said.

Alex shook his head. "The enemy fire was so intense it had to be a company of NVA soldiers. Almost like a damn ambush, Sir. Like they knew, like they were waiting for the scouts to come in."

"We were lucky the scouts were there," Boss Tweed said. "We returned fire. Those four scout machine guns and the two with Lucky and Mickey suppressed the enemy's weapons. Once the firing ceased, the NVA pulled the VC tactic, they just faded away."

They paused. It was a brief silence.

Captain Thompson nodded. "Okay, go on."

"This is when it all gets kinda fuzzy, Captain," Alex said.

"Did you see Deakins light the house on fire, Alex?" Captain Thompson asked.

Boss Tweed jumped in to rescue his Lieutenant.

"I saw it, Capn, and Jinks did too," Boss Tweed said. "You had told us Deakins was to be under our visual control. I saw him do it."

Captain Thompson nodded at Tweed, looked at Private Jenkins, and peered at the Platoon Leader, waiting for his explanation.

"He was under your supervision, Alex," Thompson prodded.

"Yes, Sir, he was."

"And you didn't see it?"

"No, Sir. When the NVA evaporated, I focused on pulling the pilot out to bring him back to Linebacker. After the firefight, I was in rescue mode. At that time, though, I didn't know he was dead. That was my concern, Sir, rescuing the pilot and bringing him out."

"It's because Lucky was killed, Captain," Tweed said. "There was one NVA who remained behind, a rear guard of sorts, I guess, with an AK. He's the one who shot Lucky, and Nelly killed the NVA soldier."

"We couldn't believe Lucky was shot, Sir," Alex said. "We thought all the bad guys had run away."

"We put the pilot's and Lucky's bodies in the infantry truck and I told Tex to bring them here to the firebase when everything settled down," Tweed said. "There was no rush because both of them were dead. But we had them. Their bodies were safe with us, Capn."

"Colonel Carson expects me to give him all the details. He believes this latest episode will bring Westmoreland's investigators. After Billy Butler, Deakins' killing the prisoner on Nui Ba Ra, and Holt's death the Colonel needs to prepare for the heat from MACV. So," the Troop Commander said, "I need to hear it all, good and bad."

"After the initial exchange of fire with the enemy and they fled, Deakins yelled to burn the houses," Boss said. "I told him, no, to stand down. I told him no, twice, Capn. I yelled no twice. But he lit the straw with his cigarette lighter, anyway. That straw and stuff just burst into an inferno. When you think about it, a little cigarette lighter . . . It was an immediate curling, roaring blaze."

Platoon Sergeant Tweed looked at his hands, clasped them, and rubbed them together, as he shook his head.

"Then the last NVA soldier opened up with his automatic rifle and cut Lucky down. Lucky was five or six meters from the house, he was distracted by the woman and child in the doorway. The enemy soldier used them as a shield, standing behind them, firing at Lucky."

"Lucky had a premonition he was gonna be killed over here," Fowler whispered.

They all looked at Mickey.

"He was going to burn the houses anyway," Jinks said. "Sergeant Johnson told me how Deakins believed if we were ever fired on from a hamlet, the hamlet should be destroyed and the occupants killed because the people were either VC or VC sympathizers. Because weapons fire from the hamlet shot down the pilot, Deakins intended to burn it even before Lucky was killed. And when Lucky got it, Deakins went off the deep end."

"I looked in his eyes, Sir," Bo said. "He wasn't with us, Capn. He was someplace else, in his own world."

"Screams of the little girl were agonizing. Her and the woman were going to burn to death. I think the screams spooked the gook and that's when Nelly had a shot."

"Put one between his eyes, Capn," Cicchinello said with a grin and nod. "Easy shot, Sir."

"That's when Jinks yelled," Boss Tweed said.

Captain Thompson looked at Jenkins.

"It was Mai Li and Kim, Sergeant Johnson's friends. We talked with them one time at the shower point. She was our laundry lady, for the squad. She and her little girl were always around. We spoke, played with the little girl, gave her candy and gum and peanut butter and crackers. She loved lima beans. But we never really talked much. J J had talked with her a lot, though. Bo took a lot of pictures of us down there that day at the shower point," Sergeant Mosley said. "Bo made a lot of pictures of the squad."

"What did you yell, Jenkins?" Captain Thompson asked.

"That's J J's friends, Deakins. That's Mai Li and Kim, Deakins. They belong to us. That's J J's friends, Deakins. They belong to us. Sir. Then I heard Deakins say, 'Cuz' friends?'"

"And that's when he rushed in," Boss Tweed said softly. "Deakins rushed the house. When he did, I think the woman and kid thought he was coming in there to kill them. So they shrank back, took a couple of steps back deeper into the house."

"And all the time the straw is burning, the flames were licking and curling, Capn," Mickey Fowler said. "It was hottern a firecracker. I saw them step back into the house. That meant Sergeant Deakins had to go in farther to get to them. I could hear them both screaming bloody murder. I'm sure they thought he was intending to kill them."

"But he wasn't. He intended to save them. He went into that firestorm without regard to his safety, Sir," the platoon leader's voice was quiet, soft.

"The woman kept screaming *Papa, Papa,* so I guess Deakins was looking for him too," Jinks said.

"Sergeant Deakins went in, knowing the burning roof could cave in," the lieutenant said.

"And it did, Capn," Boss said. "There wasn't anything we could do until the fire died out. We brought all of them back to the firebase, the FAC pilot, Lucky, and Deakins."

"When we were down at the shower point, J J made a promise to Mai Li. We couldn't believe what she asked him to do," Bo shrugged, "but he didn't hesitate. Cookie said he'd do it."

"Have a seat, Jerry," Colonel Carson said. "I've asked Danny and Benny to sit in, to listen to your report. Maybe the four of us can sort through this mess and figure out a way to handle it."

"Well, Sir, the mess, as you call it, started when Colonel Wilson's Bronco was shot down near the hamlet we call Round Top, on the map it's shown as Dau Tron, about two kilometers north of the firebase." Thompson proceeded to outline, in depth, exactly what his men had told about the action.

"Sergeant Deakins set the fire," he concluded. "Deakins intended to burn all of the houses in the hamlet."

Jerry Thompson knew to pause on the name of Deakins.

Colonel Carson shook his head. "That's our mess, Jerry. One of our NCOs who brutally murdered a bound prisoner has now created an international incident by setting the houses of innocent people ablaze. It's a goddamn mess. Go on."

"In one of the burning houses were people we know, a laundry lady, Mai Li, and her little girl, Kim. When they came to the door to escape, the NVA stood behind them, used them as a shield. That's when Jerrigan was killed. Private Cicchinello took out the shooter, and I guess his shot frightened Mai Li and Kim. When Deakins found out we recognized the woman and child, that they belonged to us, he moved toward them to bring them out of the fire.

"Mai Li and Kim withdrew from the doorway, probably fearful of Deakins, maybe thought he would kill them. Mai Li screamed for her father, or her husband's father.

"Anyway Deakins went in. He went in twice, and he perished in the blaze."

The Brigade Commander looked at Captain Ballesteros. "Well, Benny, I'm relieved. That closes your investigation. Now we don't have to worry about his courts-martial for murder."

Thompson's pulse quickened, his face grew hot, and he realized Carson's concern was more about covering his Brigade's ass than the sacrifice and death of a soldier.

"What we can do, Colonel, is give Deakins a posthumous promotion to Sergeant First Class and decorate him for bravery," Captain Danny DeSoto, the Brigade Adjutant said.

Colonel Carson picked up the lead offered by his Adjutant. "Yes, Danny, that's a wonderful idea. We can say he was already on the promotion list to Platoon Sergeant and decorate him with a Bronze Star for heroism."

"Yes, Sir. One of our brave Sergeants rushing into a burning house to save a Vietnamese mother and her young child will go a long way to win the hearts and minds of the locals," Danny said.

"And, our folks back home too," Benny added. "Cronkite will pump this on his evening news show for all it's worth."

"Yes. Yes, of course. I like that. Take care of it, Danny, will you?"

"I will, Sir, and the posthumous promotion will add a little money for his family when the Army pays out the insurance policy."

"What about the woman, her little girl, and the father?" Benny Ballesteros asked. "Mai Li and Kim?"

The three looked at Captain Thompson.

Thompson shook his head. "The father didn't make it. Once the fire cooled, we found him in a back room. The only body remaining in the house was the NVA soldier. Lieutenant Versailles left him there, in the embers."

"And Mai Li and Kim?" Colonel Carson asked.

The Troop Commander nodded. "Lieutenant Versailles called a Dustoff. They were taken to the Sixty-Second Field Hospital."

"He used a medical evacuation helicopter for civilian non-combatants?" Ballesteros questioned.

"Yes, of course," Carson nodded. "I've heard the hospital commander, Colonel Dickerson, accepts Vietnamese mothers and their children for treatment."

"But it's doubtful either one will make it, Sir," Thompson added.

"Why not, Jerry?" the Brigade Commander asked.

"Both suffered serious smoke inhalation and painful burns, Sir."

SUPPOSE

They lay together, spent, wrapped in their loving embrace.

"Oh, that was nice," Katie said. "You make me feel so special, Cookie."

She kissed J J's neck, slid her hand down his back to a cheek and squeezed.

"You can't even imagine how great it was for me, Sweetheart. You were something else."

"I was, wasn't I? Amazing."

"I always had the idea it was only the guy who needed and enjoyed sex. You have changed my mind, Kathleen. I have seen the light of a new day. You are *the wonder* of all wonders."

"Why do you say that?"

"Say what?"

"That you had the idea it was only a guy who enjoyed, or needed, sex."

"Because, you know. Just because."

"No, I don't know. Tell me."

"I can't tell you that, Kathleen."

She rose on an elbow and smiled. "Are you bashful? Look at you. Oh, my goodness. *Look at you.* You are bashful."

"Well, it's a guy thing."

"What does *that* mean?"

"It's what happens to a guy when he's anticipating . . . when he's ready . . . you know what I mean. You saw it."

"Oh, yes. I did."

"So, you see what I'm talking about, about a guy thing."

"Oh, really? For your information Sergeant Johnson, girls like it, need it, enjoy it, too. Maybe not in the same way as guys, but if God hadn't fixed it that way, guys would be left hanging."

Kathleen shook J J playfully.

"If you know what *I* mean."

"Yeah, I think I know what you mean. Come just a little bit closer, Captain Patton, let me see if I can get that fixed like you like it."

They laughed, and kissed, and kissed, and made passionate love again.

While Katie and J J were indulging in their pleasing pleasures, Captain Ballesteros was in Colonel Carson's office to report the findings of his other investigation.

"It's as complete as I can make it, Sir. I've also received word from the Sixty-Second Field Hospital that Sergeant Holt's body is soon to be examined by one of their pathologists before release to Graves Registration for processing and shipment to his next of kin."

"Good, Benny. Thank you for handling this. I

know it seems I ask you to do all the shitty little jobs, but I do it because you take care of Brigade and Army business. I trust you, trust your judgment. You do a good job, and I appreciate it. When I prepare your officer efficiency report, I guarantee you'll be pleased."

"Thank you, Sir. I know how you want things to be handled. I do my best."

"What else did you want to tell me?"

"I believe Sergeant Holt's throat was cut. He was murdered, there's no doubt about it."

"Murdered. Are you sure?"

"I have no doubt, Sir."

"How do you know his throat was cut, Benny?"

"It was an easy deduction, Colonel. Three people who saw the charred body swore Sergeant Holt's head was askew, not in its normal position attached to the neck.

"Even though his burnt body was beyond recognition, Private Lindseed said it was Sergeant Holt. The body had Sergeant Holt's dog tags. Nevertheless, medical forensics at the hospital will still need to confirm it."

"How will they do that? Fingerprints? Dental? Blood?"

"Yes, Sir, most likely one or all of those, plus his dog tags."

"My God. Murdered. Who killed him?"

"I've only been able to determine PFC Oliver Lindseed and a laundry lady were closest. Lindseed, he goes by Cotton, is the troop supply clerk. Sergeant Holt was his supervisor. The laundry lady was working in one of the sleeping bunkers and her little girl, a six-year-old child, was with her. I was not able to determine why she was only a few feet away when the conex exploded."

"Could Lindseed or the laundry woman have cut his throat?"

"Either one is possible, Sir. During questioning, Lindseed produced an unsecured, sharpened, AK-47 bayonet and the laundry lady revealed a straight razor she used to trim clothing. Lindseed did not hold back about his boss. He had nothing favorable to say about Sergeant Holt. The Private said Holt intended to sell seven captured AK-47s and was in the conex preparing them for the buyer. Lindseed said Holt was a bully, a real asshole to the people who worked for him. The laundry lady, her name is Mai Li, said about the same thing Lindseed did. She also accused Holt of blackmailing Vietnamese women, making them work at the laundry and shower points as prostitutes."

"My God. He was one of those. How do those types get in the Army?"

"Sometimes county judges offer military service rather than jail, less expensive for the county and they rid themselves of that problem."

"So, his throat was slashed by Lindseed or the laundry woman for revenge?"

"Maybe. But there's something else, Sir. I believe an incendiary grenade exploded inside the conex and that set the enclosure ablaze."

"Clothing, boxes, wood crates, that sort of thing?"

"No, Sir. Gasoline."

"What? What do you mean?"

"Lindseed disclosed there were six five-gallon cans

of Mogas stored in the conex. He said he warned Holt of the danger, of the regulations prohibiting the storage of fuel in an enclosed space with flammables, but Holt ignored him."

"Good grief, that's a terrible safety hazard."

"Not just terrible, Sir, but deadly, obviously."

"Why you say that, Captain?"

"Well, I'm fairly certain Sergeant Holt's throat was slit because of statements about the head's position. I talked to a Sergeant Johnson and a Specialist Vannoy, the troop clerk. Both saw the aftermath and mentioned how the head appeared separated from the neck. But I also suspect he may have still been alive when the grenade was tossed in."

"Good God. A fragging. I've heard about it happening at other firebases, even in Saigon for Chrissakes, but it's never been a problem here."

"Lindseed produced an inventory sheet that indicated there were all types of crated and uncrated grenades in the conex – practice, fragmentation, concussion, smoke, white phosphorous, and incendiary – but I'm afraid it was an intentional fragging, Colonel."

"Why, Benny?"

"I found a grenade safety pin on the ground at the front of the conex. Whoever pulled the pin did not think about keeping it to hide it from discovery. I'm thinking a soldier would have held the ring on a finger and walked away with it, knowing if it were found it could be connected to the blast."

"So, there appears to be two suspects, one for the throat laceration and another for the grenade. Could have been Lindseed? The laundry woman? Both? I doubt the child would have pulled the pin and tossed the grenade into the conex. You think?"

"I don't think we'll ever know, Colonel. But I don't think the cut or the grenade explosion killed him. It is very possible Sergeant Holt lay on the floor of the conex bleeding and incapacitated from the cut, but he probably burned to death. If he was conscious, he had to know he was going to die, that the flames were going to consume him. And he probably died in great anguish and pain. The pathologist will determine the exact cause of death, of course. We should receive that report in a week or so."

"Okay, Benny, since we may never find out the truth, I want to know what your thoughts are?"

"Suppose, Sir, you make your own assessment of the situation and reach your official conclusion."

"Okay, I'm listening. Go ahead."

"Suppose, Sir, your determination was the fact that unbeknownst to security forces, enemy cadre penetrated the perimeter, attacked, overwhelmed Staff Sergeant Henry Holt's fighting position, and killed him while he fought to the death in defense of Fire Support Base Linebacker. Suppose his bravery in the face of a superior enemy saved the lives of his fellow soldiers at the sacrifice of his own and, accordingly, for his meritorious achievement in ground operations against a hostile force, you decorated Sergeant Holt with a Bronze Star."

"Posthumously."

"Yes, Sir, and this decoration is in gratitude for his devotion to duty and is in keeping with the highest traditions of military service and reflects great credit upon himself, his unit, and the United States Army."

"I like that, Benny. That sounds like a good citation. Take care of it, will you?"

"I have, Sir. I passed this to the Adjutant, Captain Desoto is working on the citation for the decoration now."

"Right, Benny, and tell Danny to fix up an award of the Purple Heart too."

"I think this is the right decision, Colonel Carson. I'll prepare my final report to reflect your assessment and conclusion, Sir. His family will be pleased Sergeant Holt died defending his country."

"Yes, you're right, Benny. It's the patriotic thing to do."

"I suppose too, Sir, it'll also keep Westmoreland's investigators away."

"Right, by God. I got a war to fight here, Benny. I don't have time for his bevy of ass-kissing Colonels. I hate it when he sends those sock-folding, dick-holding, sons-of-bitches up here to snoop around."

By the time Colonel Carson, Benny Ballesteros, and Danny DeSoto got all the paperwork typed up, arranged, stamped, and signed, it was chow time on Linebacker.

At the Imperial, resident chefs and bakers were preparing their specialties for the dinner-time crowd.

"Cookie?" Katie nudged J J. "Cookie? Are you asleep?"

"No, Sweetheart. I was just thinking about going

another round?"

"You've got to be kidding. You've used up all my energy."

He laughed. "I do know the feeling, but it was fun running out of vigor."

"I'm hungry. I'll shower and get ready. You get dressed, and we'll go down to the patio restaurant."

"We going to eat here?"

"The patio restaurant downstairs has a wonderful reputation. What did you have in mind?"

"A place called Vittorio. They make great spaghetti."

"How do you know that? You've been there before? You ate there?"

"No, my platoon leader and platoon sergeant ate there and recommended it."

"That would be fine with me, but I have to stay close at hand in case the hospital calls. I'm sort of restricted to the hotel, so I can easily be summoned."

"Oh, yeah. My Lieutenant said I was subject to urgent recall. There's a lot of movement down the Ho Chi Minh Trail, west and north of the firebase. How would you get back to the hospital?"

"They would send a chopper for me, a fifteen-minute or so flight. There's a chopper pad out back of the hotel. VIPs come and go. The Vice President stayed here once."

"What Vice President?"

"Our Vice President. Of the United States."

"Wow, that's kinda neat. That's power to have a helicopter taxi at your beck and call."

"Yeah, sort of. You know what I do at the hospital,

J J. I have important responsibilities."

"Of course, I didn't mean to be offhanded about it. I know you are an important person, Kathleen."

Katie looked at him, judging, analyzing.

"So, is it okay if we eat here? Sally ate here. She told me they have great seafood."

"I'm with you, Kathleen. Whatever you want, I want. It'll always be that way."

While Katie was prepping, J J donned the clothes she brought from the hospital supply room for him. The underwear, khaki trousers, and socks fit, but the sneakers were tight. The Hawaiian shirt was a large where he usually wore a medium. After he checked his appearance in the mirror, he walked out on the lanai to wait for her.

Below, he could see waiters escorting diners to restaurant tables covered with white tablecloths. In the center of every table was a small jar with a burning candle inside it. A little farther out he watched the last few people on the beach gather belongings and towels and move toward the hotel, reluctant to give up their day of fun. Three individuals in white shirts and dark trousers were off to the side. Oddly, they stood out, seemed out of place. They were not swimmers nor were they dressed for an outing at the beach. J J watched, focused on them, his instinct wary.

He smelled her perfume before he turned. It was just right, tantalizing, agonizingly inviting. When J J looked at Katie, his heart skipped; he took in a deep breath. His smile telegraphed adoration and bliss.

She wore a black dress the same style as the white

one, with string shoulder straps. But where she had been radiant, glowing in the white, she was now heart-jumping, heart-thumping gorgeous. Katie had put her hair back into its signature ponytail, added eyeliner with a touch of makeup, painted her kissable lips a shade of pink, and wore a small link gold chain necklace with a pendant. She held a black leather clutch.

"My, God, you *are* beautiful. I thought my heart was going to stop when I looked at you."

"Do you like what you see, Soldier Boy?"

"I am a lucky guy."

As they came off the elevator in the lobby, J J glanced at the counter to see if the Frog or Lieutenant Burr detected him. Only the lieutenant was there, but he was busy and did not look up as they walked to the restaurant.

The maitre d' pulled out a chair for Katie, the place J J planned to sit. But he said nothing and sat opposite her with his back to the hotel's entrance.

"Minh is your waiter. I send him over with water and menus right away. My name is Xuan, if there is something to do for you please tell. Thank you. Enjoy your evening with us."

Xuan hustled away, gave orders, and took care of other patrons who stood at his stand.

"Why did you hesitate when Xuan pulled the chair for me?"

"I just wanted to watch the stairs and front doors, but it's no big deal."

Minh appeared with bottled water and menus. "I come back quick to take care, okay?" He disappeared as quickly as he had arrived.

"Kathleen, I'm not sure I have enough money to pay the bill here. This looks and feels like a ritzy place."

She smiled. "My goodness. You take me out on our first date to a fancy hotel restaurant and expect me to pay for my own dinner?"

"What can I say, Captain. Surely you're aware sergeants just don't rake in the big bucks like officers do."

She laughed. "Okay, I'll treat."

The Imperial had plenty of Kansas beef and Idaho potatoes to satisfy the longing, but Katie suggested they let Minh guide them on Vietnamese fare.

For an appetizer, Minh brought Gỏi cuốn, spring rolls with greens and shrimp. For their main dish, he served Bún chả – rice, grilled pork sausage patties, herbs, bean sprouts, and pickled veggies along with Nước Chấm, a dipping bowl made with fish sauce, lime juice, sugar, garlic, chili peppers, and shredded lemongrass. Finally, he brought Banh Cam for dessert, golden-fried glutinous balls speckled with sesame seeds and filled with a sweet mung bean paste.

Minh kept their wine glass full of the Sauvignon Blanc from Bordeaux. After opening and pouring from the second bottle, he left the corkscrew.

Service was fast, Minh was attentive, the white wine superb, and they enjoyed a delicious meal. Katie was pleased J J had tried strange food and seemed to enjoy it. Afterwards, a comfortable calm claimed their surroundings.

J J leaned forward placing both arms on the table.

"You are lovely, Kathleen. I love you, Sweetheart."

Katie opened her clutch and withdrew Sergeant Farmer's engagement ring. She held in between her fingers, sides of the small diamond glinted from candle light.

J J's eyes followed the ring as Katie laid it on the tablecloth. She clasped her hands, fingers entwined.

"Does that mean what I think you intend it to mean, Kathleen?"

"One of my patients, Sergeant Farmer, Sergeant Leon Farmer, loaned this ring. His girl, Shirley, wrote to tell him she was going to have his best friend's baby and was returning the engagement ring."

"His best friend made a move on his girl while he was over here. That's cruel."

"Well, it was more than a move, Cookie."

"Yes, a baby."

"Leon heard your proposal on the ward. He can't see right now. Hopefully, it's a temporary blindness, but he heard you. He said he knew you had no ring to give me. So, he said when I saw my boy again, to give you this ring to use before you could buy one that I like. Sergeant Farmer said it could be a temporary engagement ring, a stand-in until I had my own. I told him I couldn't do that, but when he insisted I accepted it."

J J reached across the table and picked up the diamond. He held it at eye level, looked at Katie, and half closed his eyes. "This is the third time," he said softly. "The third time's gotta be the charm. Kathleen Tatum . . ."

"Cookie, wait." Katie shook her head. "There's

something we need to talk about first."

J J paused. He suspected what was coming next and, as an experienced infantryman, decided that rather than defense, his best course was offense. He cleared his throat and swallowed with difficulty. He lowered his hand and let the ring slip from his fingers. Unsettled, it rocked twice on the cloth.

"I know. Two weeks ago you said on the phone you wanted to talk with me in private about something. I think I know what you want to talk about. So let me begin by saying I've watched a lot of picture shows and TV programs. A lot of times characters talk fast, none of them stutter, they say their lines, say the right things to move the story, and then shut up. I don't have a script, Kathleen, but I'll do the best I can for you."

He paused, just like the movies, and looked into Katie's eyes.

She waited, her mouth closed, just like the movies. Her hands did not move.

"I know you love the Army, Kathleen. I know you want to stay in the Army. Make it your career."

He waited; there was no response.

"You know Colonel Dickerson told me he thought you were special, so talented that you had the potential to be a General. I believe that too, Sweetheart. And I would not want to shatter your dream. I love you so much I would walk away from you so you could be what you hope to be in the Army."

He paused.

Katie did not blink.

J J reflected on an axiom he heard – to get out of a hole, stop digging, or something like that. At the moment, he didn't know how to stop digging. He gestured with both hands as if to shrug.

"So, suppose I leave the Army. That way, we could be married, and there'd be no issue with fraternization, protocol, regulations, or the issue of you having to explain you married a sergeant."

J J smiled. He expected Katie to smile when he pronounced fraternization correctly.

She remained impassive, showing no emotion.

He continued.

"And there'd be no issue about when and whether I would have to say *Yes, Mam,* and *No, Mam,* and whether to salute in public."

He raised his eyebrows to emphasize his attempt at humor, inviting her response or reaction.

Katie's eyes did not stray from his face or blink.

"Our children wouldn't be embarrassed to be seen with me in the NCO club because they would be privileged to go with you, with us, to the officer's club."

He closed his mouth and waited. Katie stared.

"You didn't do your GED, did you," she stated.

He felt relief that she spoke. He was finally able to swallow the cotton ball that formed in his mouth.

"I did, Kathleen, as you asked me to. I sent it in. I'm sure I'll get a certificate."

"You didn't apply for OCS, did you." Again a statement, not a question.

He nodded. There it was. He knew it was inevitable.

J J didn't know how to tap dance around a sticky circumstance, but he tried. "Kathleen, suppose I didn't apply for OCS."

"How could that happen if you met the criteria and qualifications?"

He advanced his attack, somewhat. "Well, suppose I don't want to be an officer."

"Okay, I'll play suppose with you. Suppose you get out of the Army, what will you do?"

"I will own a cafe to start, maybe three, and in time more."

"Suppose I can't have children."

J J felt like a sledgehammer slammed his chest. He realized he was holding his breath. He cocked his head, nodded, smiled, inhaled deeply, and slowly exhaled.

"I . . . you can't or won't?"

"Can't."

"How do you know?"

"Jesus, J J. I'm a nurse. I work in a hospital. I work with doctors. I take tests. I can't have children."

J J saw tears sparkle in Katie's eyes, but she did not cry. He could see she pressed her lips together so they would not tremble. He wanted to rise and go to her, take her in his arms, and comfort her. Instead, he reached across the table and took her hands in his.

"That's one of the things I wanted to tell you in private."

J J felt eaten up with the dumbass, thinking he was smart to preempt something he imagined she would force. He regretted his thought of superiority, of thinking he knew how to handle her consternation about his not applying for OCS to become an officer. He grasped the reason now that she was ready to marry him but wanted him to know this fact first. He felt like a damn fool.

"Do you like children, Kathleen?"

A tear from each eye spilled over and slid down a cheek. Her nod was feeble.

"I've always thought of children in my life."

He leaned forward, reached up with a thumb and swiped away her anguish.

"I like kids, too, Sweetheart. We can still have them, as many as we want."

She blinked and shook her head with the slightest doubtful motion.

"We can adopt."

For the first time after dinner, J J saw Katie smile. His own torment eased.

"Suppose I leave active duty in three months when my tour is finished here?"

Now it was J J's turn to be silent. He squeezed his lips tight so as not to open his mouth and stick his foot in it. Be quiet, his brain shouted, keep your damn mouth shut.

But, he couldn't help it. He needed a script to say the right words. "That's weird. I thought you were dead set on being a General."

She raised her napkin and blew her nose into it loudly. She dabbed at her eyes.

"Colonel Dickerson asked Sally and me to join him in a partnership. He and several of his doctor friends are building a medical center in Portland, and they asked him to run it. He will be the President and Chief

Medical Officer. He proposed Sally be Vice President Medical Staff and he asked me to be Vice President Nursing Staff."

"What about your Army career?"

"I will leave active duty but join the Army Reserve and progress through the ranks there. Every summer I will return to active Army status for two weeks and sometimes go on short temporary assignments. So, I will still be with the Army."

"Suppose I told you I wrote a letter to Colonel Dickerson's brother, Albert, and asked him to sell me Sugar Babe's. All three of the cafes in Lake Oswego, about a grenade throw from Portland."

Her beautiful smile warmed his heart. "You've always wanted to be a cook. There's no better place to start than your own cafe."

J J grinned.

"This is the other thing you wanted to tell me, isn't it. That you signed on with Colonel Dickerson."

"No, Cookie. That's not it at all."

"What then?"

Katie lifted Sergeant Farmer's ring from the table and held it to him.

J J took her hand and kissed it before taking the ring from her fingers.

"I wanted to tell you the third time *is* the charm, Cookie. Please continue."

J J shook his head, stood, walked to her, and knelt.

He extended his arm and held the ring toward his bride-to-be.

"I love you with all my heart. I will keep you safe and never hurt you. I am asking for your hand in marriage. Will you honor me by accepting my proposal? Kathleen Tatum Patton, will you marry me?"

"Yes, James Jerome Johnson, in front of all these people, I will be your wife."

Cookie slipped the temporary engagement ring onto Katie's finger, leaned in, and kissed her.

Applause on the patio was deafening, even Minh and Xuan joined in. The maitre d' snapped his fingers and a bottle of champagne and two glasses appeared.

As Minh poured, two men in white shirts and black trousers rushed up the steps, shoved the doormen aside, dashed through the entrance into the lobby.

Gunfire preceded an explosion inside that shattered glass and blew both front doors into the street.

Blood splashed onto the white tablecloth as shards of glass struck them.

"Oh," was all J J said.

Katie watched his limp body lean off the chair and tumble to the floor.

"COOKIE!" Kathleen screamed. "COOKIE!"

She shoved her chair aside, knelt by J J, and lifted his head.

"Cookie, Sweetheart, you've been hit by pieces of glass. I'll go get help. I'll get you to the hospital."

Blood dripped from her wounds and mingled with his in the gash along his cheek and nose. As she attended to J J, a shadow moved over them.

"He's hurt," she said. "We need to get a Med-Evac chopper."

"You're hurt, too. Pieces of glass are stuck in your neck and face," Lieutenant Burr said. "Let me help you. We'll bring him to the chopper pad."

The lieutenant knelt beside Katie.

"There were two," Katie said.

"I know, Mam. The blast killed one, and I shot the other. Pierre called for a Dustoff. Several people are injured. You have a bad cut along your chin. We need to get you to the hospital."

The third attacker ran up the steps, paused at the open space where the double doors had been, and swept the lobby with blasts from his AK-47.

Lieutenant Burr stood, whirled, raised his revolver, and squeezed the trigger twice. The hammer clicked, falling on spent caps.

The VC cadre turned to Burr and Kathleen and tried to fire his weapon. Nothing happened. It was jammed or out of ammo. He jerked on the automatic rifle's charging handle.

Katie grabbed the wine opener and went for the sapper. She body slammed and pinned him on the top step of the hotel entrance. She looked into his black eyes as she plunged the corkscrew into his jugular and violently twisted it. Drenched by his blood, she stood, kicked the dead man, and cursed him. "You Number Ten, you son-of-a-bitch."

"Come, let's get you both to the hospital." Burr knelt to lift J J. "Captain Patton, this man was Private Johnson, the runner for Colonel Dickerson."

"Yes, Private Johnson is my husband."

FEATS

"My God, look at you. It's been six, eight years and you're even more gorgeous. Give me a hug, Sweetheart."

Her face blossomed with glee as she moved into his embrace.

"You certainly know how to flatter a woman, Senator Vitali." She kissed his cheeks. "If I lived in Nevada, every election you would have my vote. And it's been ten years."

The Senator laughed. Holding both her shoulders, he stepped back at arm's length and admired her. "Ten years? Time flies, don't we all know. Well, my sweet little Kim, you're going to have the chance to cast your vote for me. I've decided to run for President."

"Oh, my goodness, Lord Jesus," she whispered. "I'm going to kiss a President."

She hugged him tightly and kissed both of his cheeks twice.

"Hey, what's going on here? Who is this old man kissing and having his way with my wife?"

Bonino turned, howled with boisterous laughter,

and opened his arms in welcome. "Cray, my God, you look great. Are you still twenty?"

Cray wrapped his arms around the Senator and patted his back affectionately. "It is so good to see you, Bo. They will be happy you came for their special celebration."

"Well, Cray, it is unusual these days for a man and a woman to be together for a quarter century."

Three quick flashes from a nearby cell phone recorded the moment.

The politician stood between them, put his arms around their shoulders, turned in a practiced maneuver, and grinned.

The photographer took three more quick snaps.

"Our next president is holding you in his grasp, Cray," Kim said.

"No, shit. Holy smokes," Cray blurted. "You're going to run for president, Bo?"

"That's the plan. I'll win too. This idiot in office now is going to face charges of impeachment before he can serve out his term. And the Vice President is just as incompetent and corrupt. Adkinsen himself may be impeached. I'll win by a landslide. It'll be a slam dunk."

"There are dozens here at this occasion who will vote for you," Kim said. "Come, they will be thrilled you've arrived."

They walked toward the closed double doors.

"I talked with General Jenkins a month or so ago. He told me he wouldn't miss this event for the world. Said if he had to, he'd low crawl on his belly like a reptile to come to this party," Bonino said.

"Jinks is already here, Bo," Cray said. "The General came in about thirty minutes ago. Sally's here, too, and Kip and Jodie. They're all in the ballroom having drinks before the show starts. Come in, they're excited you could make it, Mr. President."

"I like that sound, Cray," Bonino said. "You keep saying it, broadcast it to the hills. It fits nicely."

"I like the sound of it too, Mr. President," Cray said.

Before Cray could open the doors, the Senator paused and put a hand on Kim's elbow to stop her.

She faced him, a warm smile on her face.

"Your mother would be so proud of you, Sweetheart. I know you remember how much she loved you. You were her life."

Kim's smile remained, as she nodded. "Thank you, Bo. Yes, I remember. And I remember what you've done for me and my family."

"Just so you know, Kim, I have you in mind to serve in my cabinet when the time comes. Are you interested?"

"Yes, and flattered, too, Mr. President."

Cray opened the doors to a noisy room and steered his wife and the Senator to the group standing together and talking.

"Oh, my, God, look here. Welcome, Senator. I am so honored you made the time in your busy schedule to come."

She opened her arms and hugged him, and held the embrace as a lover would.

He barely touched his lips to each of her cheeks to avoid messing up her makeup. He stepped back and admired the soul mate of his closest friend.

"I would not have missed your Silver Anniversary, Kathleen. Twenty-five years with him is a hell of a long time."

Katie laughed. "Thirty-one, in fact, Bo. It was like dragging a stubborn mule to water to get his agreement to do this, even six years late."

"Hello, Sally, you are more beautiful than the last time we were together. Maybe you and I could run off to Las Vegas and let what happens there stay there."

"My convertible is outside, Bo. We don't even have to drive that far, a Motel Six is down the street."

They all roared with delight as Sally kissed and hugged the Senator.

"Hello, Kip." Senator Vitali hugged him and smiled. "The grapevine tells me you're going to run for a congressional seat next year."

"I am, Bo. I want to represent Oregon's First District."

"I will campaign for you, Kip, but I want a favor in return."

"Thank you, Bo. Your support means a lot to me and it probably will help get me elected. What can I do for you?"

"Campaign for me. I want to serve as our country's next President."

Kip smiled and slowly nodded. "I will do all you ask or need, Mr. President."

"I thought you'd say that, so please prod your brother to stand with me."

"He loves you, Bo. I'll do what I can. You'll win by a landslide."

"And, I'll be there, too, for you, Mr. President."

Bo looked at her and grinned. He took her in his arms, hugged her and swayed her. "I know you will, Jodie, so please help Kip prod your brother."

"I know Cookie will join Kip and me to do what it takes."

"And one other thing, please."

"Anything for you Senator."

"I want you to leave your job as the university president, Jodie, and serve as my Secretary of Education."

"You can count on it, Mr. President. I will be there for you."

"It is so good to be . . . my, my, here they are, a tough pair to bet against." Senator Vitali held open his arms for an embrace.

"Bo, you never age."

Bonino hugged his friend. "General Jenkins, flattery will get you promoted to four stars."

They stepped apart and admired each other.

"Did Kathleen tell you, Bo?"

"Tell me what?" The Senator looked at Katie.

"I was promoted last month, Bo. The Governor jumped me two grades to Major General and appointed me as his Adjutant General."

"That's outstanding, Katie. Congratulations."

"And now, even in our bedroom, the General insists I address her as *Yes, Mam* and *No, Mam*."

They all laughed.

He caressed the scar on her cheek, took Kathleen in his arms, and kissed her tenderly on her lips.

Then, Cookie took a step forward. Bo opened his

arms. They hugged warmly and stroked each other's back, as brothers would after years of separation.

"How have you been, my friend?" Bo asked.

"Well, Bo, I'm doing well. It is so good to see you. Thank you for coming. I know you are busy taking care of business. It is a special treat for Katie and me for you and Jinks and Sally to come. You three are our closest friends."

"We will come to your fiftieth anniversary, too, Cookie. I read in the Journal you sold the Sugar Babe's franchise for two-point-eight billion."

"I did, that was the public figure. There was loose change involved, too, Bo."

"A hell of a lot of loose change," Jinks said.

"I brought a beat up picture for you, Cookie, I thought you might want to keep it," Bo said.

They gathered around and peered at the black and white he held in both hands.

"I remember this. You took it at the shower point. Kim was six," Cookie said.

Bo pointed at each face and spoke their names, including Holt.

"Bum bum," Kim said.

Katie and Cookie looked at her. He half closed his eyes and cast his head in a questioning cant.

Kim smiled at her adopted mother and father and nodded slightly, twice.

Available at TankGunnerSix.blogspot.com.

Available at TankGunnerSix.blogspot.com.